Remember This
A Novel of Love and Hope

By Susan J. Eck

NFB Publishing
Buffalo, New York

To Kathleen
My Happily Ever After

NFB Publishing
119 Dorchester Road
Buffalo, New York 14213
For more information visit Nfbpublishing.com

Remember This

CHAPTER 1

O h, Eva!" Lily muttered as she leaned over the porch railing and peered along Humboldt Parkway. She no longer noticed the perfection of the September Sunday weather, a windless sunny day with an almost-hot temperature. It was the ideal Labor Day weekend and this day each year was always the date for the Kepler's Fine Home Furnishings company picnic at Lein's Park in Ebenezer near West Seneca. And that was where Lily's family was by now while she stayed behind to wait for her childhood friend who always accompanied Lily to this event.

Lily paced the porch in long, slow steps absent-mindedly, thinking about how different things were going to be in two weeks when she left for college. She did not know how different, but understood that some great change was happening in her life, just as she had understood in June during the Class of 1903 graduation at Central High that a door was closing. And now, for her, a door was opening.

She heard heels hurrying on the sandstone sidewalk and spied Eva Bond, her best friend since they were eight years old, hustling toward her, one hand holding up her white lawn skirt and the other holding her hat on her head.

"I'm here!" she cried, out of breath, from three houses away. On Humboldt Parkway, with its large homes on generous lots, that was quite a distance.

Lily leaned on the railing and watched her approach. She wanted to be angry with Eva, had every right to be. Lily's mother cared less and less for Eva each year and just half an hour ago gave Lily a reproachful look when she determined to leave for the picnic without Lily to avoid being too late in her role as the hostess.

But it was difficult for Lily to be genuinely angry with Eva Bond, a motherless girl sent as an infant by her father from Canandaigua to Buffalo to be raised by an aunt and uncle who once had hopes of being parents but had accepted a childless life by the time Eva came along. They thought her a treasure, something little Eva had discovered early, making her wants known in age-appropriate ways. Her mystified guardians were happy to fulfill them, too much so. They failed to appreciate that, under her vivacious personality, Eva was almost desperately needy.

Barely five feet tall with dark, wavy hair and deep brown eyes, Eva had seized upon the quieter Lily when they were schoolchildren. Lily was her reliable peer and Eva kept the friendship alive long after it was clear to Lily that their interests had diverged.

"I know I'm late, and I am so *abjectly* sorry, dear Lily!" Eva said, speaking hastily to head off any criticism that might be coming.

Lily sighed and shook her head. "What's to be done with you?"

Eva smiled up at Lily from the sidewalk. "You could take me to a picnic," she offered coyly.

Lily was putting on her hat. "I hope you realize that you have one more blot on Mama's ledger now. She left a half hour ago, having already delayed so that we might all go together."

Eva hung her head. "I know," she admitted. "But I was held up by the cars. They're so full today that I had to wait for several to come by before I could find one where I could wedge a foot on the step."

Lily came down the steps pulling on her gloves. They headed back to the sidewalk and toward a trolley stop that would begin their journey to rural West Seneca.

Eva slipped her arm through Lily's and squeezed it happily.

"But your mother has one consolation," she said tartly. "In two weeks, she won't have to see me for a long time."

Lily nodded.

"And I have moments of pride when I think that I am responsible for your getting to go to college."

Lily smirked.

"It's a true fact!" Eva pronounced. "You said that your mother finally agreed that you could go to Vassar College so that she could get you away from me. Though I can't understand why," she added.

"Well, we spend a lot of time together, and I think she might wish I spent more time receiving calls from *eligible young men*," Lily commented.

"And she hopes you'll spend time with *eligible young men* at an all-girls school?" Eva asked incredulously.

They both laughed at that.

"I expect to become very educated and somewhat sophisticated," Lily offered, "and she may think that I will become attractive to a higher class of eligible young men when I return!"

"Here comes our car," Eva noted, looking down the street. "So long as you don't become too educated and sophisticated for me," she added after a pause in what tried to be an offhand remark.

Lein's Park was a sprawling entertainment venue divided in half by a long fence. When you stepped from the trolley at the station inside the grounds called "Noah's Ark," you were on the side of the park with a ball diamond and picnic area. If you went to the right and under the giant horseshoe, you entered the amusement park side with all manner of entertainments. A big canvas banner was suspended at the station announcing "Kepler's Fine Home Furnishings Company Picnic" in bold red letters with gold embellishments.

Lily and Eva strolled around the picnic grounds, two stylish young girls in cool white summer shirtwaists and matching skirts of lawn fabric. Eva's shirtwaist had a broad lace collar and lace cuffs, an expensive look that her aunt enjoyed buying as much as Eva enjoyed wearing. Lily's was more tailored but she never minded the attention Eva received in school or parties because of her attire. She thought of Eva as her lightning rod, something to draw attention away from her and let her observe, something she always found educational and entertaining, fodder for the little stories that no one except Eva knew about. A baseball game was under way in the dusty diamond in the center of the grounds. The players were mostly young men, stock clerks and deliverymen, but a few were middle-aged, perspiring as much as the younger ones but with redder faces and necks. A few classmates who had gone to work for Kepler's after graduation waved at the girls as they went by.

Near a long wooden shelter were two tents. The one for beer was easy to identify because a loaded beer wagon was backed up to one side of the tent. Three great wooden kegs had apparently already been emptied and rolled carelessly alongside the wagon. The Keplers and nearly all of the employees were from the East Side of Buffalo, the German side. Beer was their mother's milk, the beverage most men drank during their workday. They were certainly enjoying the boss's beer on Labor Day weekend.

Another tent was for the caterers, men in long white aprons already smudged around the middle with roast beef juices. They were slicing roast beef from enormous roasts onto large platters. Others were slicing ham, and a smoky haze behind the tent indicated that chicken was being cooked over a wood fire.

Lily and Eva entered the shelter, where buffets were set up with potato salads, slaws, bread, pickled condiments, and platters of meat. Children were eating or dashing about with their peers. Lily observed some of the older men she remembered from the early days of the store when there was only the one location on Genesee Street. They were her father's most trusted people, the ones he put in charge of opening the second location on William Street. Here they sat, some retired on a small pension, their gray heads nodding over their picnic lunch, their wives beside them. Lily went over and greeted them by name, respectfully, as she had been taught from the time she was small. Her father had explained that good people are hard to find and, when you do find them, a good boss works hard to keep them. She thought her father a good boss.

They saw Lily's mother positioned at a table near the center of the shelter, easy for employees to see and pay their respects. Elda Kepler was a sturdy matron, exuding a formality that always put others on their best behavior when speaking with her. Where her husband, Heinrich, was a talented salesman who warmly extended his hand to all in greeting and asked just enough questions of a customer to gauge his or her taste and means, his wife had a discriminating eye that divided people into those who mattered and those who didn't. Elda's tongue was as sharp as her nose, and her husband had found responsibilities for her that kept her away from the customers in the early days when Kepler's rented a small storefront in the Fruit Belt neighborhood. After the children started coming, she began her full-time career at home, a task that grew incrementally with the Keplers' success in business, culminating eight years ago with the construction of a big Foursquare house on Humboldt Parkway, the best address the East Side could offer at the time. No one had to tell Elda Kepler that Buffalo's best society lived on the west side, the other side, of Main Street on Delaware and Linwood and The Circle, but she could sit at the top of the social ladder in her own milieu.

She was enjoying herself today, bowing slightly and smiling broadly as she offered her hand to the employees and their wives when they stopped by. It was a regal gesture and her watered silk dress with beaded patterns across the breast was surpassed in grandeur only by her hat, a broad-brimmed imported Italian leghorn straw with two enormous pink silk roses nestled amid dark green silk leaves. Elda did not live amongst Buffalo's elite, but she could afford to dress like them when she chose.

Even the approach of her only daughter, at least an hour later than requested and with the ever-present Eva in tow, could not dampen her pleasure.

"Well, here you are at last, dear!" she beamed at Lily, opening her arms to embrace her lightly. "People have been asking where my pretty graduate with the chestnut hair is keeping herself."

"And here we are," Lily repeated, smiling in company as she had been taught. "Eva had a terrible time getting a car that was not packed with holiday goers. But, she persevered, didn't you, Eva?"

Eva stepped forward. "I did, because I knew how important this day is to your family. I would even have walked the whole way."

Mama Kepler waved her aside to make room for an employee and wife who were approaching her. "Then you would have been even later, dear. Circulate, girls," she instructed as she put on her welcoming face to receive the couple.

Lily retreated from her mother's radiance, giving Eva a look that said, *Whew! Dodged that one!* and they laughed.

Outside, they ran into her brother, Will, dusty and out of breath, collarless with his sleeves rolled up. Christened Wilhelm at his mother's insistence, he had always been known as Will, a nickname that perfectly suited him. Two years older than Lily, he had his father's warmth although he lacked a seriousness of purpose about anything except sports and having fun. Easy-going, he was a loyal friend and very popular with girls. Unlike their oldest brother, Alfred, who never had a nickname and seemed to have inherited nothing but seriousness of purpose, Will was content to work for his father and follow orders. Alfred, married to Gertrude who shared his gravity, had started a chair factory in Alden outside the city with a loan from their father, and was making a solid success of the business. Gertrude admired Mama Kepler and flattered her with frequent questions on matters of taste. They got along very well.

"Sister!" he pulled up short and greeted Lily. "Hi, Evie—how's things?"

Lily shot him a dubious look. "You'd better stay clear of Mama, looking like that. 'Will, where is your tie, your collar, your vest, your jacket?'" she said in an excellent imitation of their mother.

Will giggled loudly. "You do that so well, Lil. Say, is she still holding court in the shelter? I just want to get a roast beef sandwich and get back to the game."

When they confirmed her location, he tried to get them to fetch him a plate from the buffet so he could avoid his mother, but they wished him luck.

"Maybe you can get one of your sweethearts to fetch for you," Eva said, teasing.

The girls finished their circuit of the grounds and then did what they did every year, crossed into the amusement park and went directly to the ice cream soda stand. They each bought a large ice cream float, Lily with root beer, and Eva with strawberry-flavored soda water. Sitting in the shade of evergreens, Lily and Eva sipped their treats and watched the human parade. A band on the bandstand was warming up for a concert. Music from the electric merry-go-round added a background of fun to the air. Every now and then the clank of horseshoes rang out from the pit nearby, followed by collective *oohs* and *ahhs* of the players.

"What am I going to do when you're away?" Eva asked, pouting slightly and poking the ice cream in her glass with her spoon.

"But you're going to school, too," Lily replied, encouragingly. "You're starting classes at Bryant & Stratton at the end of the month. So, you'll be busy."

"I don't want to go to school anymore." Eva was in a real pout now. "I have spent my whole life in school. I want to do something, something exciting."

Lily smiled. "Maybe you could run away and join the Gypsies. Remember when I asked you if you were a Gypsy?"

Eva sent her a sidelong look to show that she did remember. After a pause, she said, quietly, "Do you know where there are any?"

Lily leaned her head back and laughed out loud. "I will miss the way you can make me laugh," Lily said, smiling.

Eva looked toward the music now coming from the bandstand. They were playing, "In the Good Old Summer Time," a song that everyone had been singing this summer and last when it first came out.

"You'll find plenty of girls at Vassar who can make you laugh," Eva said morosely. "It's probably a requirement for admission."

Lily leaned over and sang with the band's melody, "*But you're my tootsie wootsie in the the good old summer time.*"

Eva tried not to smile and shook her head.

Lily stood up and held out her hand. "Come on, pal o' mine, we haven't had our annual merry-go-round ride yet. Let's gitty-up!"

Eva took the hand and allowed herself to be pulled to her feet.

They stood beside the carousel examining the options. There were the horses, which did not go up and down on this carousel but rocked front to back; there were the benches which didn't move at all; there was the 'lover's tub' which turned round and round. Lily wanted the 'lover's tub,' but Eva wanted the bench shaped like a crescent moon with a red velvet seat. And so, they selected the moon bench.

The seat was narrow and they sat very close together, the veneer sides enclosing them and curving over their heads, making an intimate space. Eva took Lily's hand as the merry-go-round started and leaned against her shoulder. Round and round, faster and faster the machine moved, and spectators began to go by too fast to identify. The music of the merry-go-round, so close to them now, was deafening, and the scene outside became a smear of color and shape. Lily was enjoying it and looked down at Eva, who had her eyes closed tight.

When the ride began its inevitable slow-down, Eva raised her head and Lily could see tears on her cheeks. She squeezed Eva's hand asking "What's wrong?" leaning close to be heard above the music. Eva straightened up and pulled a handkerchief from her little bag. By the time the merry-go-round had stopped, Eva was composed again.

"Will you tell me what's wrong?" Lily repeated.

Eva hesitated. "It's only that I know why your mother dislikes me," she said slowly.

"Why?" Lily prompted when she didn't continue.

"Because," Eva paused, and then continued in a rush. "It's because she knows how much I love you."

Lily patted her friend's hand, accepting Eva's declaration without thought or reply.

CHAPTER 2

The supper hour was past, Mama Kepler had gone to her Tuesday church committee meeting, and Lily was sitting on the window seat in her room. She wasn't feeling relaxed, hadn't felt relaxed since her trunk was picked up that morning for shipment to Vassar. Until that hour, her going to college had not been completely real; all the shopping and packing and repacking had been fun and might have been an exercise of some kind. But now almost all of her clothes for fall and winter, her notebooks and writing utensils, her dictionary and thesaurus were gone. Her room looked bare in the absence of the great steamer trunk. Three days were left until she boarded the New York Central, with no return trip until Christmas. It was unsettling, the nearness of it. Tonight, she couldn't find her excitement about college, only her trepidation about leaving home.

Taking as deep a breath as the constriction in her chest would permit, she rose and went downstairs. At this time of the evening, if he were home, Papa would be reading papers in the family parlor. But he was not there and she smelled his cigar from the front porch. She paused, fixing in her memory this moment, this ordinary moment in their family lives: Papa having a cigar on the front porch, where Mama insisted he smoke when weather permitted; the sweet breeze of mid-September that carried with it the incense of fallen leaves; the distant sounds of neighbors talking or laughing, a dog barking, a piano playing, the periodic grating of the trolley down the street. What sounds would replace these next week, in a place she had not even seen and where she knew no living soul?

She pushed open the screen door and let it close quietly, one of Mama's rules that no one dared break even when she wasn't around to know. The darkness was settling measurably sooner these days and the daylight color of the neighborhood had faded to shades of gray. Lily saw her father on the two-person swing, pushing back and forth slowly, as if in thought. She sat beside him in silence.

After a long time of gently rocking, Papa puffed on his cigar and spoke.

"So, did they pick up your trunk?"

"Yes, this morning," Lily replied to the smoke wafting above them. "The man said it should be at Vassar when I arrive."

"Good," was all he said.

The tightness in Lily's chest was beginning to ease, whether from the rocking or sitting with her father, she couldn't have said.

"I won't get there Friday until about dinner time, by the time I take a trolley to the campus," Lily mentioned to make conversation.

"Ya, that would be about right."

"You won't worry about me, will you? I'll be fine, you know."

"Ya. You will."

They sat in silence. Where Heinrich Kepler could sell a horsehair couch to a horse in his stores, he was more reserved at home. Long years of marriage to Mama Kepler had led to a division of communication and she did most of the talking at home.

"I'm an old man now," he said wistfully.

Lily started. "Papa! You aren't an old man."

"My youngest child is grown up and going away. I have to be honest. Old is what I am."

Lily shook her head. "No, Papa. An old man wouldn't have encouraged me to think about going to college. Even when Mama refused to consider it, you let me know I had a good idea."

"Your mama didn't want to lose her only girl, you know."

"But I want you to know how much I appreciate all that you are paying to send me to Vassar. I won't make you sorry that you did it. I'll study so hard—"

Her father interrupted her by a hand on her knee.

"I know, I know," he said softly. "You're a good girl and you'll do good there. I don't worry."

They fell silent again.

"Make lots of friends," Papa added, "and work together with them. Then you'll be happy at college, too."

Lily smiled into the darkness. It was so like him to emphasize the social element, the human interactions that made life worth living as far as he was concerned.

"I will, Papa. I will."

He turned to look at Lily, as if he had just thought of something.

"Speaking of friends, we haven't seen your Eva at all since—was it the picnic?"

Lily shifted in her seat. "Yes, the last time I saw her was that Sunday. I think she's been entertaining quite a bit with her aunt," Lily extemporized. "I also think that she doesn't want to say good-bye. So she may be avoiding me," she added honestly.

"Who can blame her? I don't want to say good-bye," he said reassuringly. "You go see her. You've been a sister to her. She'll be glad to see you before you leave."

"I hope so. I would hate to leave without saying good-bye to her."

"You go. You'll see."

On Thursday, the day before leaving for Vassar, Lily went to Eva's house to say good-bye. Lily had finally been able to reach Eva by phone after leaving messages nearly every hour on Wednesday. Eva, sounding distant and reluctant, had agreed to a visit on Thursday afternoon.

Eva's Uncle Walter and Aunt Martha lived in what everyone considered the "old" and therefore unfashionable part of Buffalo, too close to the rapidly expanding business section that was rolling over formerly intimate neighborhoods. A number of similar homes on Franklin Street had already been converted to boarding houses or businesses, but the Bonds seemed content with their brick home, dark with coal smoke that gave it a down-at-the-heels appearance from the outside.

Lily approached the door feeling herself almost a stranger, or at least a traitor for her excitement at leaving Buffalo. Eva had been so sad at the picnic that the rest of their time at Lein's was spent watching the baseball game in silence. Lily was at a loss as to how to respond. And she worried now that her meeting would be a repeat of Eva's feelings of being abandoned by her friend.

To her surprise, Eva herself opened the door, and smiled. She was dressed in a beautiful marine blue silk skirt with a crisp, white shirtwaist under whose high, turned down collar was a matching marine blue ribbon fastened with an enameled pin. Lily recognized the pin as one she had given Eva for graduation in June. Her dark hair was perfectly styled, as if this were a special occasion. Lily felt underdressed and smudged after her trolley ride.

But she smiled with gratitude and delight and seeing her friend look so sunny. "My goodness, but you're looking splendid this afternoon, Miss Bond," Lily said appreciatively as she entered the front hall. She put a hand on Eva's arm and added, "And a sight for sore eyes, I must say."

Eva led them upstairs to her room at the front of the house. It was the larger of the bedrooms, with a sitting room that overlooked the street. Her aunt and uncle assigned it to her and its spaciousness served as her playroom as well as bedroom, evolving over the years as she grew into a teenager and needed a place to share confidences with her friends. Lily knew the room well and could have explained Eva's mood simply by observing what had changed from her last visit.

This afternoon Eva took a seat on the small couch near the windows and Lily sat beside her. They looked at each other and grinned.

Lily took Eva's hand in both hers. "I'm uncommonly glad to see you. I've missed you, dear," she said, nodding for emphasis.

"I'm glad to know it," Eva said, smiling more broadly.

"Tell me why you didn't call or return my calls this last week and a half?" Lily asked. "That was time we could have spent together."

Eva looked down at their clasped hands. "Because I didn't know how to be with you, " she said, searching for words. "Your bedroom had that great trunk and piles of clothing, every bit reminding me that you were going away. Every conversation turned to Vassar and how much you were looking forward to seeing it. And the picnic, the end-of-summer thing we've done for years and years and now it was all going to change."

She stopped herself from continuing. "I don't want to be sad this afternoon," she said, squeezing Lily's hands. "I want you to remember me like this, happy to be with you. That way you'll write me sometime and tell me that you miss me."

They chuckled at Eva's self-promotion.

"And you are beautiful this afternoon, my friend," Lily said honestly.

Eva blushed and Lily stared in amazement. She had never seen Eva blushing and speechless. She peered at her friend. "Your cheeks are red."

"Are they?" Eva replied absently. She rose and went to her desk, returning with a small package. "I have a small going-away present for you," she said quietly, presenting it.

"Oh," Lily said, touched, holding the book-shaped present in her hands.

"You may open it," Eva encouraged her.

Lily smiled and nodded, then tore off the paper to reveal a burgundy leather-bound book of lined, blank pages. On the cover were embossed her initials, LAK, in floral letters. It was the nicest thing she had ever received.

"This is—extraordinary—," she stammered.

"I wanted you to have something not for homework or letters, but only for writing down your stories," Eva said.

"You know me so well," Lily murmured. "What kind of stories could be good enough to write in this exquisite book?"

Eva squeezed her hand. "All of them."

Lily embraced her and they held each other tightly.

The sadness of parting was swept aside and they began to catch up on their news. They chattered until nearly four, when they heard the front door open. Eva's aunt was returning from her weekly luncheon and bridge game at the Twentieth Century Club. They went down to greet her so that Lily could say good-bye. As they were nearly done in the front hall, Eva interrupted to say that there was something she had forgotten to show Lily upstairs. They took their leave of Eva's aunt and returned to Eva's room.

"What did you forget?" Lily asked when Eva closed the door.

"This," Eva replied, taking Lily's face in both her hands and pulling her into a kiss. Lily was momentarily stunned. She had never been kissed on the lips.

Eva pulled away and looked into Lily's eyes with an intensity that Lily had never seen in her friend.

"Kiss me, Lily," Eva commanded in a low voice.

Lily did as she was told, and was lost in the wonder of the sensation which began to flow through her body from her lips.

On the way home on the trolley, in her bedroom that night, and on the train to Vassar the next day, Lily caught herself brushing her lips with her fingers, reliving the discovery. She gave no thought to the line that she had irrevocably crossed, the one that left the innocence of childhood behind. The only thought that came to her was, *I had no idea.*

CHAPTER 3

L ily was the last to emerge from the trolley at the old Vassar Gate Lodge, letting the others go ahead. She followed them through the archway and involuntarily stopped at the scene before her. At the end of a long drive edged by tall evergreens was the enormity of Main, the oldest building at Vassar. Three stories tall, entirely of stone and brick, it was majestic in the late afternoon sun, like the biblical city on the hill. Woodbine vines ran along the massive building's walls, arteries blazing red in their autumnal glory. Lily was filled with awe and joy that it was built solely for the education of women. College, her college. Her Vassar.

She walked quickly, purposefully, along the drive. Passing under the porte cochere and into Main's lobby, she was once again immersed in the noise of female voices, this time multiplied many times. A bustle of activity, greetings, bumping of suitcases, bundles, umbrellas, hats, and bags of all kinds surrounded her. Eventually, she learned the direction to her room and made her way up the stairs to the second floor, where the freshmen lived. The only other class residing in the building was the seniors, on the top floor.

The long hallway on her floor was lined on either side with steamer trunks of all manufacture, some covered with labels. Most were open, their trays on the floor or balanced precariously on a corner of the trunk. Girls were coming and going with armloads of clothes and books from the trunks into their rooms.

Outside her room Lily spotted her own trunk, already delivered; it was a welcome sight. The door to her room was open and she looked tentatively inside. Seated at a table in the center of the room was a blond girl, trying the lock of a small box with a hairpin.

"Hello?" Lily greeted her. "I'm assigned to this room."

The startled girl put down the box and jumped up.

"Hello!" she said heartily, closing the distance between them in two steps. "You must be Lily," she said, thrusting her hand out in greeting.

Lily took the hand, and had it pumped enthusiastically. Her roommate certainly was energetic.

"Yes, Lily Kepler," she confirmed. "You have the advantage of me, I'm afraid."

"Bertha Jansen, Worcester, Mass," the other said, grinning, "but I prefer Bert."

"I'm very glad to meet you, Bert," Lily said, smiling because Bert was also smiling. She had a round face, with large, perfect teeth and twinkling blue eyes. Lily couldn't think of who Bert reminded her of.

"I'm from Buffalo," Lily added because Bert had mentioned her home town. "New York."

"Everybody knows where Buffalo is!" Bert laughed. "Say, are you any good at picking locks? I can't find my key to my box here. Probably left it home."

Lily put down her suitcase and picked up the little box. "I can try."

"Oh, gee, never mind that now," Bert said apologetically, and took the box from Lily. "You haven't even seen our grand suite here. Let me give you the tour."

She stepped back and waved the box around. "We have this room here, I guess it's a kind of parlor or study, and we also have two bedrooms over here," she gestured to open doors across from the hall door. "I didn't pick one because I thought we could decide that together and I also didn't unpack any books or stuff because I wanted to decide that with you, too."

Lily thanked her sincerely for her consideration but was still too dazed to be very helpful with the decisions. They eventually decided on bedroom assignments, but agreed to leave arrangement of the common room for later.

Lily did not have to work hard to converse because Bert was happy to keep up both ends of a conversation, not unpleasantly. Lily learned Bert's family was in railroad shipping, and that she was the first in her family to go to college. Her brothers had refused the idea, choosing instead to follow their father into the family business.

"Here's my sweetheart," Bert said, picture frame in hand, "Karl. He's a junior at Yale. When I graduate, we'll be married."

Lily took the photo. It showed a broad-shouldered young man, also blond, with a serious demeanor.

"He's awfully handsome," Lily offered.

"Oh, I know it," Bert replied heartily, "but I try not to tell him too often because it goes to his head. You know how vain boys are!"

Lily laughed with her.

"Do you have a sweetheart?" Bert inquired.

Lily smiled and shook her head.

"Well, you know there will be dances and such, with boys invited from other colleges, so you'll be able to meet some good lookers this year."

Lily agreed that would be likely. She was still trying to think of who Bert reminded her of. Regardless, she liked Bert. She seemed open-hearted and genuinely friendly.

After dinner, other freshmen stopped by and introduced themselves, exchanging the scant information they had about the workings of the hall, the mystery of the Lady Principal, the strictness or laxity of the rules, rumors of chafing dish parties that might be had, second or third-hand stories of past capers and scandal. As they chatted, Lily picked up the little box that Bert had been working on and picked the lock. She handed Bert the open box and was joyfully clapped on the shoulder in thanks by its owner.

That night, lying in bed, it came to her who Bert reminded her of. It was Theodore Roosevelt. She decided she could have done much worse in the roommate department and surrendered to sleep at long last.

"September 20, '03
"Dear Mama and Papa,
"I arrived here Friday just when I expected and had no trouble getting up to the college. My roommate was already here and she seems fine. Her name is Bertha Jansen and she's from Worcester, Mass.

"The Lady Principal here, Mrs. Kendrick, is our chaperone on campus. She called all the freshmen together this afternoon—nearly 320 of us—in the Chapel on the 4th floor of our building (Main) to introduce herself and tell us how things are at VC (Vassar College—everybody calls it VC). You will be relieved to know that we have many rules!

"We cannot be late for our meals because that is also the time for announcements, so the dining room doors are closed at a specific time. (Bert and I don't think we'll be missing many meals!) Every evening after supper we have Chapel, which is required, and on Sunday morning we have church services, also required. Mrs. Kendrick says these are nondenominational.

"Mrs. Kendrick spent a good deal of her lecture on the necessity for physical exercise, requiring us to do so for an hour each day. She recommends walking along the many paths on the college grounds in all seasons. But we also have a gymnasium to use in bad weather.

"Freshmen are allowed to join Phil, which is short for Philaletheis dramatic clubs, which are so very popular here, and so I will look for notice of their first meeting. It won't take much time at all.

"Well, I haven't been here long enough to be homesick. I wish you could see the campus because it's beautiful and I can't wait to explore it. Classes begin tomorrow and I am very excited about that. I'll tell you about my classes later.

"Tell Will hello from me. I hope you are not worried about me.
"Your Lily"

Lily put her pen down, glad to have her first letter to her parents ready for the post. Bert had also been writing to her family and took Lily's letter down to the mail room while Lily got ready for bed. Despite chafing against the ten o'clock rule, she had to admit that she was tired tonight at nine o'clock. In bed, she listened to the sounds of the building quieting down, of Bert moving about in her room, of a cricket. She was a freshman at VC. Her great adventure was finally about to begin.

"*September 24, '03*

"*Dear Eva –*

"*Received your worried letter Tuesday. You must not imagine that I have been done in by overwork or illness or that I have forgotten you. How could I forget you, my oldest and dearest friend?*

"*I have been entirely engaged in settling in here and getting to my classes – and trying not to get lost, even in Main, where I live!*

"*My roommate, Bert is from Worcester, Mass, and is a big Swedish girl with thick blond hair. And she is the nicest and smartest girl you ever saw. She's hearty and good-natured and everybody likes her. I do, too! She's swell and we have a lot of laughs.*

"*I hope you know that I am thinking of you and wondering how your classes at Bryant and Stratton are coming along. I hope you like your school as much as I like Vassar, but it would be hard for anyone to love Vassar more than I do. I feel as if I belong here and can't imagine what my life would be like if Mother hadn't relented at the eleventh hour and approved my coming here. And if she did in order to separate me from your influences, then I shall thank you every day of my life, for it would be because of you that I am in heaven on the Hudson now!*

"*Please let me know how things are.*

"*Ever your—*

"*Lily*

CHAPTER 4

By the second week of classes, Lily and Bert and three hallmates often traveled as a pack to dinner, or chapel, or to complete their required daily hour of exercise with walks around the lake, to Sunset Hill, or the Pines. Isabelle, the tallest of the five, was friendly with a sophomore from her hometown and was usually deputized to find out the facts of some question for the group because their fellow freshmen were clueless about the goings-on around campus, the details about a professor's quirk, the likelihood of surprise quizzes in Chem, and other important details of campus survival. They had taken to providing Isabelle with bribes of candy so that she could grease the skids of communication with the sophomore class.

One afternoon, while watching the sophomores and juniors play field hockey, Lily's attention was drawn to boisterous cheering in an adjacent section of the bleacher. She followed the sound with her eyes and noticed a girl she had never seen before, a striking girl with hair that shone golden in the late afternoon September sun. Suddenly the girl broke up in laughter at something one of her companions said, and she looked – wonderful.

She nudged Bert, who looked over at her and did a double-take.

"What are you smiling about? We're supposed to cheer for the sophomores who are at this moment losing 3-1."

Lily hadn't realized that she was. "Who is that woman, the one laughing over there?"

"I don't know, but let's ask Isabelle's friend," Bert said, forging ahead, as always. "Who's that girl?" she called over, louder than Lily might have wished.

"Oh," the friend said, in a knowing tone, moving closer, "that's Helen McIntyre. Who's asking?"

Bert, ever helpful, said, "Lily here wanted to know who she was."

"Well, she's a junior, always a lead in Phil, and last year was the object of crushes of at least half our class." She added, to Lily, "I hope you aren't thinking of having a crush on her."

Lily was caught off balance. "Certainly not," she said. "I don't believe in crushes. They're a foolish waste of time and money."

"Well," the friend commented, eyebrows raised. "That's a good way to look at it, particularly with that one. She has her own clique, accepts no crushers or sweethearts or what have you. I heard a story last year that she had a sweetheart freshman year, but somehow got her heart broken. Too bad, really. She played a man in the play last year and is smashing in formal clothes."

Later that evening, as Lily and Bert got ready for the 10 p.m. lights-out, Bert said casually, "That Helen McIntyre is beautiful, isn't she?"

"Well, she's not a Gibson girl, to be sure," Lily replied in what she thought was an offhand tone.

"I think she's beautiful, just the same," Bert repeated. "And I wouldn't blame you a bit if you were to have a crush on her."

"Bert," Lily warned.

"I'm only saying," was the last word they exchanged on the subject.

AFTER the first time she noticed Helen McIntyre, Lily began to see her daily, on the walks, in the halls between classes, and more than once per day. She almost began looking for her, and forced herself to stop it after literally crashing into classmates twice.

Helen was of slightly taller stature than her classmates, or perhaps it was the way she carried herself, more erect, her head facing straight ahead. It gave her a regal appearance. It also set her apart, highlighting something mysterious, an essence that people would not be permitted to know. But Lily also wondered if perhaps Helen was putting on a persona when not in the company of her intimates, something to titillate the underclassmen. Some girls like to play with others that way, Lily observed. Vassar, devoid of male students, had its hierarchy, and its roles. Her stature suggested a very strong personality.

Physically, she was a fine figure of a young woman. Her hair, sandy with gold highlights, was soft and permitted itself to be brought up to a pleasing puff around her forehead. Even when cheering for her team in the bleachers, her hair held its shape without dropping strands. This was a good thing because she did not seem to be fussy about her appearance; Lily never saw her self-consciously fuss with her dress or feel her hair for loose strands the way others did.

Helen's eyes were her most unusual feature. Deep-set with very dark lashes, they were grey, with hints of green. They suggested things even when Helen's face bore no expression. There was a vitality that emanated from her when she was still because of those eyes. Lily thought Helen a wide-awake kind of girl, always taking in things around her.

And yet, it was her smile, when she grinned or laughed, which was evident when she was walking with her friends, that was the feature that caught one's attention. When she smiled, her eyes crinkled, her straight nose sharpened, and her lips, neither full nor thin, turned up at the edges, and the sun broke forth from the clouds.

LILY returned to her room and dropped her books on the sitting room table with a resigned thud. Bert, in her bedroom at her desk, looked up at the sound.

"What did those books just say?" she asked, pleasantly. "I know they spoke."

Lily collapsed onto their couch and into the cushions.

"I've never flunked anything in my life. Not even chemistry or calculus. Latin was a breeze, even while taking German. I never confused the two."

She looked over at Bert, who was now leaning against the door jamb.

"I'm flunking Greek. Resoundingly," she added with emphasis. "And now I understand what people mean when they say, 'It's all Greek to me,' because it's – it's –" she paused.

"Greek," Bert completed helpfully.

Lily threw her arms over her face and moaned.

"Professor Leach called me into her office – I was one of about six students who had to see her today after we got our tests back – and said, 'You must hire a tutor, Miss Kepler, or you will surely fail to make satisfactory progress.'"

Bert made sympathetic noises. "I sort of thought you might have some trouble with Greek. It's too bad you couldn't have taken it in high school and taken German once you got here, instead of the other way around."

"And had I known – known the horrors of a language in another alphabet – I certainly would have. Now I'm trapped," she moaned, "like a rat. On a sinking ship."

"A Greek ship," offered Bert, suppressing a smile.

Lily shook her head at her roommate's attempt at humor. "Now I have to compete with at least half a dozen of my fellow dunces for whatever Greek tutors might be willing."

She sat up, blinking. "How will I know who Greek tutors are?"

"Bulletin board. I've seen some tutor offerings up already."

Sighing, Lily pulled herself up. "I may as well go look. Early bird, worm, and all that."

But there was no notice for Greek tutors on the board. And none of their hallmates had any tips on where to find a Greek tutor or whether one might post a notice looking for a tutor. Lily despaired of the ignorance of freshmen, for whom every question was a trial, more so since no one wanted to knock on Mrs. Kendrick's door and reveal her abject state. After dinner, they located Isabelle's friend from home and she promised to help.

THE next night after Chapel Lily and her friends set out for their exercise walk. Isabelle's friend caught up with them with her findings.

"I have only one name for you," she said, hand on her chest as she caught her breath. "But she's the best, several people told me. A real grind at Greek."

"Who is it?" Both Lily and Bert said at the same time.

"Well, the thing is, I don't know if she wants to tutor this year. She's a junior and very busy with Phil. But you can ask."

"And her name is???" Isabelle interjected.

"Helen McIntyre. She lives in Raymond House where the juniors live."

Bert shot a wide-eyed look at Lily, who kept walking. Bert took her arm.

"There has to be someone else," Lily said finally. "Nine hundred students and at least 300 could tutor Greek. Someone else must be available."

"Well, I checked my entire floor and that's what I came up with," Isabelle's friend said plaintively.

"Thank you for your efforts," Lily said sincerely, touching the friend's arm. "I am most appreciative that you let me know so quickly."

When they were back in their room, Bert raised the question.

"What do you have against asking Helen McIntyre to tutor you?"

Lily waved her hand dismissively. "You heard Izzie's friend say that Helen probably won't tutor this year with Phil and all."

"But you won't know if you don't ask her," Bert replied in her best Theodore Roosevelt tone. "And if you don't ask her, I might suspect that you do indeed have a crush on her."

Lily gave her a squeezed eye look.

"If your roomie can't tease you, who can?" Bert answered sweetly. "You wouldn't have to go bravely to Raymond House and track her down. We see her every night at Chapel."

Lily prepared herself to approach Helen McIntyre. She worked out how she would greet Helen, how she would quickly broach the question, and the various scenarios Helen might present, for which she prepared responses. At Chapel the next night, she rehearsed the scene in her mind. At the end, she made her way to the hall, but there was no sign of Helen.

She prepared the next night during Chapel, and afterwards she saw only a glimpse of Helen in the midst of a mass of students flowing slowly down the stairs. Lily was beginning to feel foolish, a feeling she despised as much as she did failing a subject.

The third night Lily determined to locate and speak to Helen. At the end of the service, she made her way into the hallway as quickly as possible. And there, off to the left, was Helen McIntyre, chatting with two girls. Lily took a deep breath and made her way to the group. She waited until they observed her, and almost lost her nerve when Helen looked directly into her eyes.

"Miss McIntyre," she said in a voice unlike her own, "may I speak with you?"

Helen's friends moved on and Helen looked at Lily with amused eyes and a small, almost sly, smile.

"You are a freshman if ever I saw one," Helen said, not unkindly.

"Yes, indeed," Lily confessed, aware that her heart was beating erratically. Then, picking up her rehearsed lines, she went on. "I am in great need of a Greek tutor and everyone says that you are the very best there is."

There was a pause between them.

"So, I would like to hire you," Lily finished, hurriedly.

Helen looked down, and then at Lily.

"I'm sorry," she said, sounding neither sorry nor looking it, "I only tutor my friends."

"Oh," Lily said, unprepared for this particular response. But she quickly selected the lines she prepared for a refusal. "I'm sorry to have taken your time."

She nodded and added, "Thank you," then turned to go.

When she was half a dozen steps away, Lily heard, "Wait!" and turned back to see Helen, arms outstretched, head tilted to one side.

"Aren't you going to ask to be my friend?" Helen challenged.

Lily had not prepared for such a question. She tossed her script aside and retraced her steps until she stood before Helen.

"Would you like to be friends?" she asked coolly, surprised at how well that came out.

Helen threw back her head and laughed loudly and with delight.

BERT jumped up from her desk when Lily returned to their room. She waited expectantly but said nothing.

Lily closed the door and said, "I think I'd like a cup of tea. Do you want some?" Bert only shook her head vigorously, the question written all over her face.

"Well, I'm going to have a cup," and she pulled out the spirit lamp. "I'll be out Tuesday and Thursday evenings on account of my Greek tutor session, which starts this week."

She smiled, then grinned, as Bert whooped loudly.

That night, in bed, Lily made a note to write her parents and ask for a small increase in her allowance to cover the tutoring. And she felt her heart quickening again when she recalled Helen's gray eyes smiling into hers. She hoped she could get that under control when with Helen or else she would learn no Greek.

CHAPTER 5

Lily found herself more calm than she expected as she climbed the Raymond Hall stairs to Helen's room for her first tutoring session. This was business and she had her Greek text, notebook, and pencil firmly gripped.

She knocked on the door and stood peering at the innumerable pinholes in the finish from notes that had been left. As a freshman, she didn't often have notes on her door, but presumed that as one advanced through Vassar, one would accumulate more friends and join more groups or clubs and notes would commonly paper one's door as she had observed on this floor.

Helen opened the door, smiled and gestured for Lily to enter. Lily suddenly felt as if all the air had been sucked out of the space around her, a sensation that threw her off her equilibrium. Business, she repeated silently. Serious business.

Lily saw the table in the middle of the room under the drop light, and two chairs. Helen sat down in one chair and indicated that Lily should take the other. Lily would later have no memory of crossing the room and sitting down across from Helen.

Helen looked at her expectantly and, after a pause, said, "Well, then, shall we find out where things stand with your Greek?"

At the sound of the word, 'Greek,' Lily gratefully found herself and spread out her things. She pulled out her first quiz and pushed it across the table.

"According to Professor Leach, this is where I stand after three weeks," she said, a little embarrassed.

Helen quickly scanned the quiz book, page by page, and then nodded.

Lily blurted, "I am not accustomed to failing at school work."

Helen looked at her with a bemused smile and wrinkled brow.

"No Vassar student is 'accustomed to failing,' my dear freshman. We all walked through the Gate Lodge as highly successful high school graduates. But," and her voice became gentler, "this is college. And things can be more challenging."

She leaned forward and added confidentially, "That's a good thing, though it may not seem so just now."

Helen passed the exam book back across the table. "Besides, everybody has some subject here that they believe will be the ruination of them," she reassured Lily, smiling.

Lily received the smile as if it were water to a desert wanderer, and she almost smiled back.

"Now then," Helen said, "let's see your command of the alphabet. Write out each letter, capital and small versions, and pronounce the letter as you go."

Lily opened her notebook and began to write. When she was finished, she found to her relief that she had only erred once, transposing the small letters of *eta* and *mu* as she so often did.

They worked for nearly an hour, focusing on where Lily was weakest based on her quiz results. Helen offered some mnemonic aids which Lily wrote down and promised to use.

"The thing about ancient Greek is that you must memorize, memorize, and memorize some more. When you see a Greek word, your first inclination is to translate each letter into its English equivalent. But to succeed, you must read it in its alphabet," Helen said. "And the only remedy for that is practice."

As Lily was leaving, she turned back and asked, "Will I ever become proficient at it?"

Helen raised a finger and replied, "We only need for you to *pass* the course, Miss Kepler."

Lily smiled and Helen smiled back. And Lily looked into those clear gray eyes for the first time that evening. And then she looked away so that she would be able to leave.

Two days later Lily returned to Raymond Hall for her second tutoring session. She noticed things she hadn't seen on Tuesday, like the decor in Helen's room. It was evident that it was decorated by upperclassmen because the many enormous throw pillows on the couch were a riot of color and pattern but they were tasteful, matching the damask throw covering the college-issue couch. Every wall was covered with silk brocade drapery or thick with framed and unframed prints and photos. Lily knew about the rule against driving nails into the wall to hang things, the penalty for which would be five cents per hole if the custodian saw them, but she was envious of the luxurious decoration and could not imagine why she had not taken it in earlier. This room was everything she and her fellow freshmen longed for, aimed for, and could not quite come up to. It was a look that had to be created incrementally, year by year, through bringing from home or trading with classmates or being first to buy a longed-for table or silk or rocker from seniors selling in June.

Helen responded amiably to questions about their furnishings and then called into one of the bedrooms. From it emerged Helen's roommate.

"If it's interior decoration you want to know more about, you must ask Mirabelle here," Helen said, gesturing to the girl. "She's the last word on good taste at VC."

Mirabelle was as unique as her name, with fine bones and hair that was quite as dark as her eyes. She wore a shirtwaist with a lace yoke and long cuffs, and a floor-length black wool skirt. Her dress showed a care and style that set her apart from others, but she did not appear to be fussy about it. Her hair was pulled up in the usual fashion, but a few strands curled down giving her the look of a careless beauty, for she was very pretty. Her mouth curled up at the edges, which gave one the impression she had just heard an amusing anecdote and was getting ready to repeat it.

"How do you do, Lily?" Mirabelle asked kindly, offering her hand. "I'm Mirabelle Lefcourt and I'm so glad that you have agreed to allow our Helen to tutor you. She is now able to keep us supplied with chocolate and milk, both of which I require daily."

She laughed when Lily looked at Helen and saw Helen send her roommate a look.

"You must not mind *our* Belle, Lily," Helen warned.

"Helen, let Lily make up her own mind now," Belle warned, and turned her attention to Lily. "Your name is interesting. I have hardly met another Lily these days and wonder why your parents didn't choose something more current like Rose or Daisy, or even Pansy."

Lily saw the humorous glint in Belle's eyes and knew Belle meant no offense.

"Well," Lily replied, confidentially, picking up the thread, "I understand they had quite a hard time deciding on a name for me. You see, I was the youngest and the first girl, so they had no girl names at the ready. As they told me the story," she continued, warming to the subject and encouraged by Belle's nodding attention, "they went over all the natural world as listed in the dictionary looking for something to call their only daughter. They finally set their hearts on calling me 'Rutabaga,' but had to give it up when they realized the only nicknames for it were unbecoming. You know how Americans are about nicknaming people."

"*Ah, me oui, cheri,*" Belle replied in French. "*Tro informale.*"

"*Exactement,*" Lily replied in kind. "So, when the doctor insisted they name me, they spied a pot of lilies that had been sent as a gift, and settled impulsively on 'Lily.' And so I am."

Belle broke into a wide smile and nodded. Lily saw that Helen was smiling, too. She felt as this had been another test of a sort, the social kind, though why Belle had presented it she could not guess.

As Belle gathered her books and headed to the door to leave them, Lily called to her.

"Where does the name *Mirabelle* come from?"

Belle stopped at the door and half-turned back to answer.

"It's French," she said, pausing a moment, then adding, "for *rutabaga*."

They all three laughed.

Lily nodded. "You juniors are all right."

Belle sent Helen a surprised look and was gone.

BERT and Lily were in the library on Sunday, working side by side like grinds in the great silence of the hall, a silence that was so pervasive that it rarely needed to be enforced. Lily had a Chem test on Monday, and Bert was beavering over her German text, making up lessons she missed because of hockey practice the week before.

Classmates passed their table with the soft swishing noise of long skirts and they paid no attention. Lily didn't look up until a shadow fell across her notebook. It was Helen and two others.

Helen was squinting at the table, searching over it, even leaning over to look under it. Then she looked at Lily and shrugged her shoulders. Lily sent her a bewildered look in response.

Helen leaned over and whispered, "I don't see your Greek text."

"I'm studying Chemistry this afternoon," Lily whispered back.

Helen shook her head. Her companions suppressed giggles.

"You must always carry your Greek text if you hope to pass," she whispered with a grave expression.

People were beginning to look their way.

"I will always carry my Greek text, I promise," Lily hissed.

Helen smiled approvingly and patted her shoulder. "Good girl."

She and her companions passed by.

Lily sat staring at her notebook, ignoring Bert's elbow jabs. Finally, Bert shoved a paper in front of Lily. On it was scrawled, "Your face is *so* red."

Lily's reply was to fold her arms on the table and put her head down. It wasn't the teasing that had flummoxed her. Helen's touch on her shoulder was still reverberating through her body and she didn't know what to do to make it stop so she could concentrate again.

But thereafter, Lily took up the challenge and always carried her Greek text, and she made sure to seek out Helen and wave the book at her. She brought it to a hockey game and caught Helen's attention in the stands, whipping it out, posing with it, and smiling cheerily; Helen laughed out loud. Passing on the sidewalk, positioned on the aisle in Chapel, Lily flashed the text at Helen; it became a private joke between them.

CHAPTER 6

October began to speed up as the semester and tutoring fell into a rhythm. The freshmen had their trip to Mohonk, where the entire class traveled up the river and had the day to clamber the mountain and take in the perfect autumn colors of the Hudson Valley. A Vassar tradition since the earliest days, it was exhausting good fun and served to make new friends and memories among the Vassar Class of 1907.

Lily received a grade of D on her next Greek quiz, which was an improvement. But she had not caught up to the class and that was why she and Helen worked diligently twice a week. They agreed that their goal was for Lily to graduate from tutoring at the end of the first semester.

One evening in the third week of October, as Lily and Helen were finishing a session, Belle came back to the room.

"What will you be for Halloween, Lily?" she asked, preparing to boil water for tea.

Lily looked at her, blankly.

"For your hall Halloween party," Belle added. Seeing the still vacant look, she added, "You don't know about the Halloween party?"

Lily allowed as how she hadn't heard anything.

Belle sent a cynical look to Helen. "What is wrong with the seniors? It's their duty, their sacred duty, to bring the freshmen along into our VC traditions. And, Lily," she turned her attention to the freshman, "Halloween costuming is one of the few major occasions a year where we can express our expressive selves in masquerade, impersonation, dress-up."

Belle paused to think, then began her instructions.

"You have two things to do, one of which you must do tonight. First, go find out about your hall Halloween party. Each hall has its own, so freshmen and seniors will party together on Halloween, unless," she added as an aside to Helen, "the seniors have decided not to include the freshmen.

"Next, you need to decide whom you wish to impersonate for Halloween. When you do, I will assist you in your costume. Freshmen have very little in the way of accoutrements from which they can construct costumes. Juniors have accumulated such things over the years."

"You're speaking as if we have acquired barnacles, Belle," Helen commented. Turning to Lily, she added, "But you could not be in better hands for costuming advice than our Belle. She not only loves to dress up, but she loves to dress up other people, too. That's why we have her in charge of costumes for our Phil."

Lily returned to Main with her charge and found that there was a notice on the bulletin board about the Halloween party. She and Bert had not yet heard about the costumes, but they found some hall mates who had and began making plans.

After the Halloween hall parties, Lily turned up for her tutoring session and returned things borrowed from Belle, who was preparing to leave the room when Lily arrived.

"Report, report, *cheri*," she demanded.

"So, who were you?" Helen queried.

"Emily Dickinson," Lily said. "I used one of my white summer skirts and shirt-waists and carried a scroll with a poem on it which I recited to any who asked who I was."

Helen was looking at her with interest. "Which poem?"

"Hope is the thing with feathers."

"Recite, *s'il vous plait*," Belle commanded.

"All right," Lily answered and paused, gathering the words.

"Hope is the thing with feathers
That perches in the soul,
And sings the tune—without the words,
And never stops at all,

And sweetest in the gale is heard;
And sore must be the storm
That could abash the little bird
That kept so many warm.

I've heard it in the chillest land,
And on the strangest sea;
Yet, never, in extremity,
It asked a crumb of me."

34

After she finished, the room was silent for a minute, then Helen and Belle complimented her on her selection.

Belle gathered up her cape, gloves, and books and said to Helen, "She's all yours," as she left.

As they settled in to their task, spreading out the Greek texts and notebooks, Helen paused.

"Your choice of Emily Dickinson was very unusual."

"How do you mean?"

"I can't explain it exactly, but Dickinson was a genius. She'll be immortal in American letters."

"Do you think it was too serious a choice? Or offensive to her memory?"

"Oh, no, nothing like that," Helen said quickly. "Just a thoughtful choice, I think I mean. How did the others respond to your impersonation?"

"Well, the people who read her recognized who I was. Others passed by more quickly. I wondered if maybe I made too academic a choice, perhaps."

"Not at all," Helen assured her. She shook her head, adding, "You're a very interesting person, Miss Kepler."

Lily chuckled. "Bert says that. Often. With some suspicion in her voice."

They laughed. Lily couldn't have said when the fluttering inside had stopped in Helen's presence. Sometime in October, with all the concentration the tutoring required, perhaps.

THE first hall play was upon Helen and Belle, the first of the four hall plays that year, one by each of the Phil chapters. For a week and a half, both had been occupied with rehearsals and meetings. The first week in November, three days before the only presentation of the Omega chapter's play, Lily and Helen met at four in the afternoon for their tutoring. They agreed to meet in the trunk room, a long, vaulted space in the basement of Main where girls would go to study or be by themselves with the stored trunks and unused furnishings. These catacombs, as they were called, were the only other solitary place on campus besides the attic of Main.

Lily found Helen waiting under a gas jet and they leaned against stacked steamer trunks, arranging their things on top of one.

"How are rehearsals coming along?" Lily asked.

Helen sighed. "The director is a bundle of nerves, the props are rotten, Belle forgets her lines every time she realizes that she is worried she'll forget her lines!"

"And how about your lines?"

"From time to time I remember them," Helen chuckled. "Two weeks is not much rehearsal time for any play, so you must not have high expectations for Phil plays, Lily," she warned. "Perhaps the lesson from our theatricals is to be prepared to function in any contingency in life."

She shook her head. "Whatever it is, it's surely not art!"

"Bert and I have our tickets in a special place so we won't lose them," Lily responded. "After all, thanks to you and Belle, we were able to be on line early and get tickets when they went on sale. When others on our floor learned that we are going, we've actually been offered ready cash for them. "

"I had no idea the plays were so popular," she added. "We're really looking forward to our first Phil play. Whatever it is, we will enjoy it."

Helen nodded once. "That's the right attitude. And be generous!"

Lily laughed and agreed they would. "Lots of applause and cheers!"

They completed their work in a little less than an hour and Lily began putting away her book and papers. Her text slid off the arched top of the trunk and slipped to the floor. Helen picked it up and then bent over again to retrieve a letter which had fallen out.

"Oh, my letter," Lily said apologetically, holding out her hand quickly, "I forgot I had put it there this afternoon."

Helen looked at her with interest, and pulled the envelope away from the outstretched hand.

"What kind of letter might this be that you are so quick to retrieve it?" she asked, holding it closer to the light.

"It's from my friend, Eva, at home," Lily replied, a little uneasily.

Helen turned the envelope over, then held it up for Lily to see.

"What does '45 days' mean?"

Lily sighed. "I believe she means that I will be home in forty-five days."

Helen lost all interest in the letter and absently handed it over, her eyes never leaving Lily's.

"She obviously is eager to see you. Does she write often?"

Lily didn't know why she felt compelled to answer. She nodded.

Helen paused, as if contemplating whether to ask the next question.

"More than once a week?" she asked quietly.

"She used to," Lily replied in the same quiet tone. "But a few weeks ago she began spending time with a beau and so now it's been about once a week."

"And do you write her often?"

Lily shook her head. "I told her from the beginning that I didn't have enough time from my studies to be a frequent correspondent."

Helen ran her fingers over the strap on the trunk. Not looking up, she asked casually, "Is Eva your sweetheart?"

Lily started. "Oh, no," she said quickly, "goodness, no. We've been friends since we were eight and have shared almost everything."

Helen wrinkled her brow and suppressed a smile. "Well, then you don't mind that she has a beau."

Lily shook her head. "No. I was glad to hear that she had met someone because she was so lonely and didn't like her classes at Bryant & Stratton. I think that was why she wrote me so often," she added.

Helen said apologetically, "I've been a real interrogator, haven't I? Pay no attention to me. Too many dramatic scenes lately!"

THE Phil theater was located upstairs in the gymnasium in a large room used for tennis and basketball. It had a stage set into a wall faced with wainscoting. Over the stage the Greek letters *Philaletheis* were spelled out. Lily and Bert arrived early and waited in line until the ushers opened the doors. They secured seats in the third row and smiled victoriously at one another.

Belle and Helen had described the play to Lily during one tutoring session. The chapter had chosen J.M. Barrie's *The Little Minister,* for their hall play this year. Belle had the role of Babbie, a young woman who pretends to be a gypsy girl and is very free spirited but who in reality is the adopted daughter of the Earl of Rintoul. Helen had declared Belle to be not only the star of the show, but also the epitome of Babbie.

"Oh, I dinna ken o' that," Belle had answered in the Scottish dialect they had been learning for the play. She turned to Lily. "The play's called, *The Little Minister,* and there sits the namesake," she said, gesturing toward Helen.

And that is how Lily found that Belle and Helen were starring in this play. She didn't even have to persuade Bert to spell her in her queue-standing task to get the tickets. Bert was as interested to see the play as she.

Eventually, the room filled, chairs stopped scraping on the wooden floor, and the deafening chatter of 200 girls began to ebb. The college Glee club sang two songs and then it was time for the play to start, set in Scotland in days gone by. Gavin Dishart, a minister, was hired by the local kirk elders in the hamlet of Thrums to replace their retiring man of the cloth. Shortly after he moved into the parsonage, he went walking in the woods and meets the "Egyptian," as Babbie was called in her gypsy costume.

Belle was immediately bewitching when she appeared on stage, as she should have been in her role, and Lily saw that the part seemed an extension of her normal personality. Everyone else was enjoying her, too. And then the minister appeared on the path in the woods.

Bert clutched Lily's arm but the latter was heedless of it. Lily was staring wide-eyed at the young man who had entered from stage right. It was Helen, her hair covered by a dark, short wig, and wearing a perfectly cut dress suit, including striped trousers, stiff shirt and white cravat around her neck. She carried a top hat. Helen had come across Belle/Babbie and they were speaking, but Lily wasn't following any of the dialogue. She was entirely absorbed in how utterly debonair the "little minister" appeared.

"She's so handsome!" Bert whispered, leaning close to Lily's ear. In a daze, Lily turned to look at her, and Bert suppressed a grin, apparently at what she saw in Lily's face.

By the middle of the play, Lily had composed herself so that she could follow the action. Babbie and Gavin were clearly attracted to one another but the relationship seemed doomed because Gavin, as the minister, couldn't choose a gypsy for his beloved. And then came the scene where the little minister threw aside the opinions of others and declared that he would choose Babbie, no matter what his congregation and the church elders might say. He and Babbie were sitting on a bench in the woods during their mutual expression of love and then he leaned over and kissed her on the lips.

For a moment, Lily thought she would slip out of her seat. She was staring open-mouthed at the event, gripping the seat of her chair to steady herself. Dimly she heard the audience gasp and then applaud wildly. And then Babbie pulled Gavin's face to hers for a second kiss. The audience cheered.

The rest of the play went by in a blur and then everyone was clapping and the cast was bowing. All the chapter members who worked behind the scenes crowded onto the stage in front of them. Helen and Belle emerged from the crowd, hand in hand, laughing and smiling happily, relieved expressions on their faces. Helen tipped her hat and the audience cheered. The evening was ended.

Bert took Lily's arm. "We can go now," she said, chuckling. Lily became aware that every muscle in her body was rigid and she had to make an effort to pull on her coat.

Lily paused on their way out and looked back toward the stage. Helen and Belle and other members of the cast and crew were still on the stage, chatting and laughing with members of the audience who were bunched up on the floor around the platform.

"Did you want to congratulate your friends?" Bert asked.

"Oh, no," Lily said quickly. "Let's go."

Bert looked at her oddly but led the way out of the theater.

The evening was cold as they followed the crowd along the sidewalk from the gymnasium. Everyone walked briskly, not just because of the temperature but because the hour was late and they were nearing the evening's curfew.

Back in their room, Bert and Lily were immediately visited by half a dozen hallmates who had not been able to get tickets and who demanded a recounting of the evening. Lily said little and no one noticed because Bert was most entertaining in relating the story.

Finally, the lights-out gong sounded and the visitors left. Bert and Lily got ready for bed and they put out the light. Bert stopped in Lily's doorway.

"What did you think of the play?" she asked. "You didn't say much."

"To be honest," Lily confessed to her roommate, "I didn't pay attention to parts of it."

"But you were paying attention when Helen kissed Belle," Bert said. "I saw your face."

"Yes, they never mentioned to me that there would be a kiss," Lily said. "It was quite a surprise."

"I'll say this right now, and never deny it," Bert said, "Helen can put on that suit and kiss me any day of the week. I'd consider myself lucky."

Lily laughed in the darkness.

"Took the words right out of your mouth, didn't I?" Bert said slyly. "Goodnight, roomie."

And she left before Lily could find anything to say. It was a long while before Lily fell asleep.

CHAPTER 7

The next Tuesday Lily arrived for her tutoring session to find Helen and Belle's room cluttered with leftover odd bits from the play and a party they had in their room after the performance. Flowers in any container that would hold water were here and there in various stages of wilting. Lily stood looking at their study table now littered by an open box of Huyler's chocolates and another from Smith Brothers in town.

Helen quickly moved to clear the table. "Have a Huyler's," she urged, cheerfully, holding out the box. "We've three more boxes in the closet."

Lily took a piece and sat down at the table. Belle was getting ready to leave and approached Lily.

"This is some of the loot your tutor collected the morning after her performance," she said confidentially.

"Oh, now, Belle," Helen interjected, "only some was for me. You were deluged with flowers and dainties, as well."

Belle put an arm around Lily's shoulder and leaned close, as was her habit.

"You should have read the notes accompanying the gifts, Lily," she said confidentially. "They were attached to gifts expressly directed to our 'little minister' here. And I must say a few made even me blush!"

Lily looked across the table at Helen, wondering what those notes might have contained. Helen simply frowned.

"I don't take such things seriously," she muttered, shaking her head. "Although Belle likes the chocolates, don't you, 'Babbie'?"

Belle laughed and shook her head grandly. "She wears the mantle of fame so easily, does she not? That's why we love her!"

She looked around. "Helen, do you have my Thackery in your room?"

Helen allowed as how that might be possible and stepped into her room. Belle leaned close to Lily.

"There was only one kiss in the stage directions," she whispered hastily, "the second was for you, dear Rutie."

Lily blushed deeply as Helen returned empty-handed.

"I do not have it—" she said and, taking in the scene before her, added "—what's been going on?"

Belle ignored her and threw on her cape with a flourish.

"Later!" she called gaily and was gone.

Helen resumed her seat at the table and watched Lily assemble her text and papers.

Lily cleared her throat. "We're on noun drills this week," she said quietly, looking at a spot in the center of the table where the light was brightest.

Helen sat back in her chair. "Look here," she began in a firm voice.

Lily looked over at her, eyes wide.

Helen seemed to be having a hard time finding words.

"I don't hold with talk of stage stars or adoring fans," she said haltingly. "We gave a play, I had a part, and now it's finished. Don't get me wrong, I like playacting, but it's for fun. That's all I mean."

"I understand," Lily responded, unable to think of anything else to say.

"Next year, I'm going to put in to direct or stage manage," Helen said, "give someone else the opportunity to collect flowers and candy."

"Oh," said Lily, honestly disappointed, "that will be too bad. You are very good, you know. "

"Well, thank you," the other said, sincerely. "I wasn't sure if you approved the performance because you left right away afterward."

"Oh," Lily said again, surprised that it had been noted. "There were so many crowded around you and Belle."

They were silent a moment. In the hall outside the room a clutch of girls passed noisily.

"You cut a fine figure in your suit," Lily added truthfully, "as you could tell by the audience reaction."

"Oh, that's just because most of the girls are boy-crazy and haven't seen one on campus since September," Helen said dismissively. "The suit is my brother Harry's."

Lily nodded, though she believed the audience's exuberant reactions were something else than that. "Will you keep the suit?" Lily asked, trying to sound as if she didn't care.

Helen smiled and nodded. "Yes, it's mine. I like wearing it, if you want to know the truth. Walking about in it gives me a little taste of what it must be like to move around the world without a corset and petticoats. One feels so free in trousers, truly. I think if more women tried them on, we might just decide to wear them all the time."

Lily liked the idea. "I tried on my brother Will's clothes once a couple of years ago," she began and then stopped herself because she had been with Eva when they both dressed as boys one afternoon. "I liked it."

Helen smiled, meeting Lily's eyes. Lily glanced down at her papers.

Helen sighed. "Was it verbs drill you said?"

"Nouns," Lily replied. "Will you tell me what was in the notes that made Belle blush?"

Helen raised an eyebrow. "If you will tell me what Belle told you that made *you* blush."

Lily smiled a little and then repeated, "Nouns drill tonight."

They settled into their work.

HOCKEY season had finished and Bert was now beginning basketball practice. She would run from the gym across campus to their room in Main in her damp gym suit each day in the cold November darkness. It was only reasonable that she come down with a cold and she did. For several days, she tried to muddle through but it settled in her chest and her coughing became worrisome to Lily at night. Finally, on Thursday, Lily returned from classes at the end of the day and found Bert in bed, feverish. She sped directly to Mrs. Kendrick's room and asked for advice. The Lady Principal recommended that Lily get Bert to the infirmary without delay.

Bert didn't want to go, but Lily had Izzie come in and between the two of them, bundled her up and helped her down the sidewalks to the infirmary. The nurse on duty took one look at her and had the girls take her into the ward. Then she telephoned the doctor to come to campus. The dinner hour passed and the doctor had not yet arrived, so Lily persuaded Izzie to go back to Main. And then she realized that it was Thursday, a tutoring night, so she asked Izzie to get word to Helen that she couldn't make it on account of Bert. Izzie promised to do it before she had a morsel to eat.

The doctor arrived, sending Lily out of the ward to wait in the hall. Then he came out and told her not to worry, that it was just a chest cold and they would keep her for a day or two until she was better. Lily was not persuaded but the doctor clapped her on the shoulder a couple of times and told her to go along and take care of herself, adding that Lily could stop at the end of the day tomorrow to check on her friend.

The next day after breakfast Lily returned to her room to find a note pinned to the door. It was from Helen. She quickly closed the door behind her, her heart fluttering unexpectedly, and read the contents.

"Lily, I was sorry to hear that Bert is in the infirmary.

"If you want to make up the tutoring session, I am available tomorrow—Saturday—morning from 9 to 10.

"It would be preferable if I came to your room. Helen"

She sat down, note in hand, pondering this. On the face of it, the note was a simple offer by a tutor to a student to schedule a make-up session. But she knew, and Helen knew, that Lily had progressed to the point where such a session was not absolutely necessary. So why had Helen come to her room this morning to leave a note to schedule an hour together on Saturday?

She penned an acceptance of the offer and stopped by Helen's room between her morning classes. As she expected, the door was closed and no light appeared in the transom, so she pinned the note and went away, smiling to herself.

Saturday morning Lily bustled around the room after breakfast, picking up and trying to artfully arrange her and Bert's slender quantity of pillows and throws to make the room look tidy and as attractive as possible. It had none of the style or softness that Belle and Helen had wrought in their room, but she had to admit it was slightly better than some of her hallmates.' She had stopped at the store downstairs and bought a tin of milk and some biscuits in case Helen wanted a cup of tea, though their regular tutoring sessions never involved such social niceties. She was falling back on her mother's training to be a good hostess, though she couldn't have said why. The last thing she did was to set the door ajar, the sign that the inhabitants were receiving guests.

And promptly at nine, Lily jumped at the small knock on the door which was followed by Helen peeking into the room.

"Good morning?" Helen said softly. Saturday morning breakfasts were half an hour later than weekdays and everyone kept a low tone in the halls until nearly lunch.

Lily replied and welcomed Helen as if she were a guest, gesturing where she should put her coat. She offered Helen tea which she accepted, and Lily suddenly had a vision of setting the room on fire if she was careless with the alcohol lamp. She put the water kettle on and watched the burner intently.

Helen was walking around the room, looking at the prints they had stuck on the wall with small tacks, and the books in the bookcase.

"How is Bert doing?" she asked.

Lily replied that she had not been permitted to see Bert the day before but she was going to visit later in the day.

"But you're coming to the Junior reception tonight, yes?" Helen asked, turning to her. "It's the only one this year given to Freshmen by Juniors."

"I'd forgotten about it," Lily replied honestly.

"Well, I've saved a dance for you, so I hope you will come. Otherwise, I'll be a wallflower," she said, smiling slyly.

"Oh," was all Lily could muster in response. The tea was ready and she brought the pot to the table that would serve as their work space.

"Your room is very nicely decorated," Helen said pleasantly.

Lily poured the tea and shook her head. "We've not much in the way of decorations, I'm afraid. What you see is what I was able to have my family send me from our store."

Helen stirred milk into her tea. "Oh, you will accumulate things quickly enough, believe me. Especially in June when everyone is cleaning out before going home. There are all kinds of flotsam that seem attractive then, especially as most are at fire sale prices and the rest are free."

Lily opened the box of biscuits and offered them to Helen.

Helen leaned back in her chair and smiled. "When I came here I had my trunk and six books. I was practically weightless. And now I can barely get from my bed to the door some days, for the accessories and books."

"What books did you bring?" Lily asked, interested.

"A regular dictionary, a German dictionary," she squinted, recalling, "and I blush to admit it, but a volume of Emerson. Although I like him well enough, I think I brought it to make an impression of serious academic purpose." She laughed. "College teaches us many things. Among which is how to laugh at ourselves."

Helen took a biscuit. "What books did you bring?" she asked, smiling. "Besides your Emily Dickinson."

Lily nodded. "I confess that I did bring Miss Dickinson. And my dictionary and thesaurus."

"That's it?" Helen was mock surprised.

"Notebooks and pencils, too," Lily offered. "I came as a *tabula rasa*."

"As our Belle might interject were she awake and present," Helen replied, "if you came here with that attitude, there's no telling what might be written on your *tabula* before you graduate."

They both laughed at that.

After a few minutes of such conversation, it occurred to Lily that they were not moving any closer to beginning their tutoring session. She felt comfortable enough in her own room to ask the question on her mind since the day before.

"Miss McIntyre," she began, which caused Helen to look at her with those grey eyes, curious now. Those eyes, Lily thought, looking at her cup.

"Why did you offer to reschedule the tutoring session? Unless you think I need it more than I realize. Or are you going to tell me that Belle needs more chocolate?"

That put Helen at her ease, and she chuckled at the comment.

"I suddenly found myself having to study Thursday evening." She looked at Lily. "I wanted to make sure you knew I was available for another session."

Lily smiled wryly. "I hope you caught up on your reading. I think we can wait until Tuesday for our next session."

"So, are you canceling our make-up tutoring session, Miss Kepler?" Helen asked, smiling.

"I am," Lily smiled back.

"I was hoping you'd say that because I have a Miscellany meeting at 10:30, which is—" she looked around.

"Fifteen minutes from now," Lily stated.

"Oh," Helen said, "darn. I was enjoying these biscuits," she added, raising her eyebrows.

She got up and began getting ready to go.

"Will I see you tonight then?" Helen asked in a neutral voice. "There's that dance with your name on it."

"I would probably step on your toes," Lily murmured.

Helen raised a finger. "Not," she said emphatically, "if I step on yours first."

She looked at Lily questioningly.

"I don't know," Lily said, trying to find a way out of a frightening scenario. "I planned to spend some time with Bert if she's well enough."

Helen looked at her, and Lily could not interpret her expression. "I understand."

She turned to go. "Thank you for your hospitality, Lily," she said, nodding. She smiled and was gone.

Lily sat down, suddenly feeling miserable. It took a few minutes before she realized why. She was simultaneously terrified and tantalized at the prospect of being in Helen's arms on a dance floor.

At four o'clock, Lily was in the reception room of the infirmary. The nurse seemed to expect her and greeted her kindly.

"Your friend is much better today. She had a big breakfast and her color is good."

Lily asked to see her. The nurse went down the hall to the ward and returned, smiling. Bert was awake and able to have a visitor.

Bert was the only patient in the ward which had eight beds. She was sitting up but propped against several thick pillows. She smiled weakly as Lily approached.

Lily stood over her roommate, beaming, until Bert finally told her to pull up a chair. She took Bert's hand, something she had never done, and they held fast to each other, grinning.

"I was so worried—" she began and Bert said, "I told you and Izzie it was just a cold—" and they talked over one another for a few moments, and then laughed. Or Lily laughed, and Bert lapsed into a coughing fit.

"Don't worry about me, Lil," she said after it subsided. "The doctor says I can leave tomorrow evening if I continue to improve."

Then she added, looking askance at Lily, "Then again, I may take a turn for the worse because the food is really good here and the nice nurse brings it to me on a tray."

Bert asked for news and Lily shared what little had transpired since Bert was hospitalized. She mentioned the Junior reception.

"Oh, Lily, you have to go," Bert said emphatically. "You can mingle with Helen outside tutoring."

Lily looked abject.

"Oh no, what's happened?" Bert asked.

Lily sighed, something she had been catching herself doing lately. "Helen said she's saving a dance for me."

Bert's eyes grew big like Christmas morning. "That's swell, I'd say!"

"I can't dance with her, Bert," Lily pleaded. "I'd be too afraid."

Bert cocked her head and looked thoughtful, an infrequent expression for her.

"Oh, Lil, you really are carrying a torch, aren't you? All this time I was kidding you, and it was real." She looked sorrowful. "Does she know how you feel?"

Lily shook her head. "I think she believes that my friend Eva and I are sweethearts and when I told her I would probably spend the evening with you if you were well enough, she just said she understood."

They were silent for a minute. Then Bert slapped the mattress between them.

"I am too weak to spend any amount of time with visitors. Right at this moment, I can feel my strength ebbing. You are going to have to leave now, Lily."

She looked at Lily sternly; Lily shrank under her gaze.

"Fortunately, my poor condition will give you plenty of time to get ready for the Junior reception. And you know if I weren't in here, you'd be going if I had to carry you to Raymond and put you down in front of Helen."

Lily nodded.

"This is a good thing for you to do, Lily. This is college, where you take chances so you can gain knowledge and grow to be a strong and productive woman and mother. Look at it as an assignment that you must complete."

"You're beginning to jabber, Bert," Lily warned.

Bert grinned. "I am a good influence on you, don't you agree?"

Lily smiled in spite of herself.

At 7:30, Lily, Izzie and the rest of their little band, dressed in their finery, entered the handsome Raymond Hall dining room, transformed for this November night into a summer bower. Every other chandelier was lit giving the room a twilight quality. Streamers crisscrossed the big room's ceiling, draped loosely to make the ceiling lower and the space seem more intimate. Flower-bedecked tables were scattered around the perimeter, a small instrumental ensemble was perched in a balcony designed just for such purposes, and a wide empty expanse yawned in the center of the room—the dance floor. Refreshment tables were in one corner and juniors were everywhere, greeting freshmen as they entered, laughing and chatting with each other. They knew they belonged here and their easy confidence contrasted with the freshmen, bravely smiling, moving uncertainly, clotting together for safety.

The music started, dancers began to take the floor, juniors extending a hand to freshmen as was the custom. Lily sought the farthest corner of the room. Her friends followed, except for one who straggled and was chosen to dance. As the evening wore on, the rest of her group felt comfortable enough to loiter around the edge of the dance floor or refreshment table and eagerly accepted an invitation to dance. Lily furtively looked for Helen and didn't see her.

And then, when she was checking her watch to see how much longer until the event was finished, when her friends were safely around her at the table, she felt a hand on her shoulder. The same electric current ran through her as that day at the library, and she knew without turning to look who it was. And then a voice softly spoke close to her ear.

"I hope your presence doesn't mean that Bert is too sick for visitors."

If someone had told Lily that she was levitating, she would have believed it. She forced herself to turn to look up at Helen.

"No, she's actually much better," she said, sounding almost normal. "Thank you for asking."

"I'm so glad to hear it," Helen said, smiling beautifully. "Now then, Miss Kepler, may I have the next dance?"

Lily stared at the offered hand, and watched her own hand extend to it in return. Helen exerted the slightest pressure and Lily rose from her seat.

As they neared the dance floor, Helen stopped and put her hands on Lily's shoulders, looking into her frightened eyes. Then she stood back.

"You know, it's too hot in here to dance. Will you step out with me?"

She offered her arm and Lily automatically slipped hers through it. Helen led them out into the corridor and walked them slowly to one of the reception rooms. Just one of the couches in the dimly lit room was occupied by two people; Helen guided them to a window seat in the shadows.

They sat side by side in silence for a while. Lily felt her breathing slow and some semblance of calm return.

"Thank you," Lily said, "It really was quite close in there."

Helen smiled. "Yes, one gets so warm dancing."

Lily realized that Helen had reacted graciously to the panicked response she had observed in Lily. She also realized that Helen was able to read her face and body language. It thrilled her and at the same time frightened her a little.

They sat until they heard the sounds of chattering girls exiting the dining room. The dance was over.

"Well, I guess I should go," Lily said, wishing she could think of something else to say.

"Yes," Helen responded, sounding a little hesitant. "I hope you enjoyed yourself, even if you didn't dance at all."

"You noticed that?"

Helen laughed. "Yes, I did. Do you dance?"

Lily shrugged. "Yes, not very often and probably not very well."

"Well," Helen replied, "I'll be the judge of that."

"Are you going to tell me I owe you a dance?"

"I guess I don't need to, do I?" Helen's voice was playful.

CHAPTER 8

The next Wednesday after Chapel Lily found Helen waiting in the hall for her to exit. She accompanied Lily and Bert back to their rooms so that Lily could get her coat and gloves. Helen had asked her to take an evening exercise walk with her. Lily quickly put on her boots and gathered her things in hopes that Bert's banter would not be too revealing. Bert was without guile and in her cheerfulness was liable to say whatever came to the front of her mind.

But Helen initiated the exchange, inquiring after Bert's health which, except for a hearty cough that echoed through the Chapel, had improved greatly. Bert inexplicably waved goodbye to Helen and Lily as they left, and called, "Bon Voyage!"

Helen laughed as they went downstairs and Lily just shook her head.

"She's a uniquity for VC, Lily," Helen said heartily. "I hope you know how lucky you are to have landed in a room with your Bert."

Lily sighed elaborately, as if to emphasize her trials with her roommate. "In spite of her foibles, I do care for her greatly."

They were outside now, and Helen guided them in a direction she apparently wanted to go.

"Oh, my, it's gotten much colder than this afternoon," Lily said suddenly when they walked out of the shelter of the building and the wind made itself felt.

"Yes, and there's a new moon tonight," Helen said, as if Lily could see a connection between those observations. "I want to take you to the top of Sunset Hill and show you the constellations."

Lily knew that particular hike was a long and even breezier one and she pulled her collar closer, wishing she had thought to bring along a wool hat for her bare head.

"I've been waiting for the right conditions to take in the heavens and get some practical application for my astronomy course," Helen said enthusiastically. "I'm so glad you agreed to come along."

"Ever ready for an academic field trip," Lily muttered with false heartiness, hustling keeping up with Helen's brisk step.

Helen laughed happily. "Step lively now!"

They were on a path that ran up to Sunset Hill among pines. Without any moonlight, the path was invisible to her.

"How can you see where to go?" Lily inquired, squinting into the darkness.

Helen took her arm to guide her. Lily could feel Helen's exhalations as a faint warmth on her neck.

"You must remember that I've been walking these paths for two years," Helen replied. "I could walk them blindfolded."

"And you might as well be, for all that one can see," muttered Lily.

"Are you taking a carping tone?" Helen asked with mock suspicion. "And we on our great and inspirational November trek to the stars?"

Lily chuckled in spite of the cold. "Not carping. Most appreciative."

Helen squeezed her arm and Lily could see her grin in the starlight as they emerged from the evergreen trees into a small clearing at the top of the hill. Down the hill to their right were the college buildings they had left behind, their windows yellow pale beacons, like a journey's end to weary travelers. Around the rest of the countryside were occasional winking lights of scattered houses. A faint light on the horizon beyond the campus would be the streetlights of Poughkeepsie. On a night like this, Lily thought it all looked like a storybook world, real to some but a curiosity to her on this hill, removed from it.

And then Helen put her arm around Lily's shoulder, bringing her abruptly back from her momentary reverie. "Look up," Helen was saying, pointing with her free arm.

Lily looked up.

"Ursa Major," Lily said.

Helen was taken aback, but Lily continued.

"Ursa Minor," Lily pointed, "Arcturus, Sirius, Orion." She turned to look at Helen, who had pushed out her lower lip.

"You already know the constellations," Helen said. Then she challenged, "Where is Cassiopeia?"

"I have no idea," Lily declared frankly. "Show me."

Helen glanced at her to verify her sincerity, then leaned close to Lily's face and extended her arm straight up. "What we can readily see is a 'W' shape right along there," she said, tracing it with her hand. "Do you see it?"

Lily nodded. "Yes. What is the image?"

"Well, it's Queen Cassiopeia sitting in a chair. Poseidon put her there because she was very vain. The chair revolves around the Pole Star, so half of each year she is upside down in her chair."

She looked at Lily, who was following her commentary. "I suppose that was some kind of Greek god revenge humor," she shrugged.

Lily laughed and thanked her for the new information.

"But," Helen continued, "there is a relevance to our tutoring."

"Oh, no," Lily murmured.

Helen laughed. "Do you know what her name means?"

Lily just looked expectantly at Helen, still so close beside her.

"'She whose words excel,'" Helen enunciated.

Lily nodded. "I like that. I would like someone to say that about me someday."

"But not if you have to sit in the heavens in an upside-down chair."

Lily had to agree that would be a price too high. Then she shivered involuntarily. The evening's temperature was making itself felt.

Helen, still jocular, leaned close to Lily's ear and asked, "You're trembling. Are you afraid?"

"Certainly not!" was Lily's instant reply.

Helen stepped back and laughed out loud, the same full laugh she had set free the first time they spoke.

Lily rubbed her arms. "Helen McIntyre, I'm freezing, if you must know. You didn't tell me we were going to stand still on a hilltop tonight. I thought we were going on a brisk exercise walk."

Helen made an apology, offered her arm, and they started back down the un-lighted path through the Pines.

In the darkness, Helen said, "Actually, there was another reason I wanted to talk to you alone tonight."

She paused, and Lily noticed it.

"You mentioned last week that you're not going home for Thanksgiving. Have your plans changed?"

"No, I'll be staying here. Bert was very apologetic about not asking me to go to Worcester with her but she'll be spending most of her time with her sweetheart."

"Understandable," Helen agreed. "Well, I've contacted my family and it happens that my brother Harry will be entertaining his friend from Yale for a couple of days and I thought that we all could have a swell time if you were to come home to Glens Falls with me."

"Oh," was Lily' s surprised response.

"Harry is a freshman at Yale," Helen rushed on, "and my only brother and if I do say so, he's a corker. You'd not be bored. We play games, tell stories. Oh, and my parents are interesting and personable. My mother said they'd be most glad to have you. I think you would enjoy yourself." She was winding down.

Lily felt as if a large wave had just washed over her and she was working to get her bearings again.

"I would like you to come," Helen added. "If you don't, I'll probably have to spend most of the time catching up on my reading—or my astronomy—because Harry and his friend will be off racing cutters up Broad Street. You don't want to be responsible for that, do you?"

Lily smiled wanly, though Helen couldn't see it. "I was going to catch up on my own reading on campus."

"See, that's the thing, Lily," Helen said authoritatively. "One of the things you have to learn about college is not to study too hard. It just drains all the fun out of the experience."

They had almost walked out of the woods.

"Besides," she said confidentially, "I doubt that you have much reading to catch up on. I think I can say with some accuracy that you are one of the more conscientious freshmen I've seen. Even Belle has commented that you could use some more non-academic activities."

They were nearing the buildings now, the path ahead of them lit by the occasional streetlight and reflected light from windows. Helen went ahead two steps and turned back, arms spread.

"You could call my invitation a *non-academic field trip*! What do you think?"

Lily stopped and looked at the beautiful woman before her, her arms still spread wide, her face a hopeful question mark.

"Say: *Yes*," Helen hinted.

Lily smiled and didn't even try to stop herself.

"Yes," she replied. "I'd be pleased to accept your very kind invitation."

Helen didn't hear the last part of her acceptance because she whooped loudly, creating an echo that ricocheted from Rockefeller to Main.

That night in bed Lily replayed the vision of the world as seen from the top of Sunset Hill. She felt herself soaring over that world, full of joy.

THE McIntyre home at 162 Warren Street overlooked a gentle slope that ended eventually at the Hudson river which divided Glens Falls from South Glens Falls. It was a newer home, a great brick Queen Anne complete with a two-story turret on the right balanced on the other side by a bay window on the second story under a peaked dormer. As if this syncopation were not sufficient, between the two features, in the cleavage of the Queen's bosom as it were, was an eyebrow window in the roof. It was a big house without a symmetrical aspect anywhere, the kind of house the Keplers would never have built because they would have seen it as a noisy structure, lacking the restfulness of uniform lines, and profligate in its waste of materials on architectural gewgaws. Lily was dazzled by it immediately.

In the wet, raw November day, a snowless Thanksgiving, she and Helen carried their suitcases up the front steps just before noon on Thanksgiving Day. Helen, grinning happily, held the door open for Lily. Agnes, a girl of around sixteen, came out to take their coats, directing them to the family sitting room where Helen's father was enjoying his paper.

He rose from his seat by a brightly blazing fire and came to greet them, embracing Helen warmly and shaking Lily's hand. She thought his eyes kind and cheerful and felt comfortable at once. They sat around the fire in upholstered chairs that looked as if people sat in them often, and warmed themselves. Helen and her father exchanged small talk about the trip. Lily relaxed into her chair and watched them. To Lily, he seemed a quietly gregarious man, average in height, with the usual roundness of so many middle-aged successful men and the receding hairline to go with it.

Helen had given her brief sketches of her family on the train ride from Poughkeepsie that morning. Mr. McIntyre had built on his father's financial success during the Civil War, when grandfather McIntyre had secured a contract from the U.S. Army for the manufacture of tin cups and plates and canteens for the Union troops. Helen's father, educated at Yale on those profits, returned to Glens Falls to become a vice president of the First National Bank of Glens Falls and a director of the Glens Falls Insurance Company.

After a few minutes, Agnes brought tea for Helen and Lily. Helen immediately focused on the plates on the tray. They hadn't eaten since their early breakfast at the college.

"Oh, Agnes, " Helen said, holding up a biscuit with a sigh, "are these Margaret's almond scones?"

Agnes smiled and verified that.

Helen took two and urged Lily to do the same. "You will love these," she assured Lily. "They have almond paste in the batter and toasted slivered almonds, as well. Margaret has been our cook since I was born practically, and she knows these are my favorite."

Lily tried one and agreed they were excellent, laughing at Helen who was dunking hers into her tea cup.

"Go ahead," she urged Lily, "it makes the tea taste like almonds."

Lily was tempted to try it but saw a handsomely dressed woman enter the room, and fell back on her manners. Looking at Mrs. McIntyre, Lily could imagine Helen in twenty-five years, so similar were their features.

"Mother!" Helen exclaimed, and rose to embrace her. "I expected that you'd make a grand entrance after you were quite ready."

Mrs. McIntyre kissed her daughter on the cheek and then held her at arm's length, inspecting quickly. Then she turned to Lily and extended her hand.

"I am so very glad you could join us for the holiday, Lily," she said graciously, not waiting for an introduction. "We enjoy having young people in the house."

And Lily sensed that she meant it. On the train, Helen had said that her father declined to select one of the local girls when he decided to marry, electing instead to cast his net into New York City. She said that he related to her the story of spotting his future bride at a crowded but dull party in the high season one winter. She was laughing and he was immediately smitten. Lily was struck by that, recalling that the first time she noticed Helen, the girl was laughing.

Mrs. McIntyre was commenting on Helen's attire. "What are you wearing—a golf skirt?" she nodded at the ankle-length skirt. When Helen assented, her mother added, "Winter is approaching, dear. Why not wear your regular gabardines?"

"This is what everyone wears at college, Mother," Helen replied in a sing-song voice. "They're very practical for walking outdoors in all weathers because these shorter skirts stay cleaner."

Mrs. McIntyre gestured in surrender. Looking at Lily, who was wearing a regular-length skirt that reached to her instep, she said, "You mustn't mind me. I'm just an old relic, out of step with the 'new woman!'" And she laughed.

Helen poured her a cup of tea and they all sat down again.

"Have some sandwiches, girls," Mrs. McIntyre urged them, nodding to the plate of little triangular, crustless items. "You must be hungry from your journey and we won't be eating until around 5 or 5:30."

"When's Harry coming?" Helen asked.

"What did his note say, Father?" Mrs. McIntyre asked.

"What?" he said, looking up from a paper. "Oh, he said he would be arriving at 1:20 from Albany so we'll see him sometime after that," he added genially. "Unless he runs into pals at the station."

"Both my chicks home," Mrs. McIntyre crooned. "Your father is tired of hearing me say it, but this fall has been more difficult because with Harry gone the house is so quiet." She leaned toward Lily and added, "Last year it was clump-clump-clump, then bang went the door, all year. He and his pals were up in the attic every weekend playing Ping-Pong."

Lily looked at Helen. "What's Ping-Pong?"

Helen rolled her eyes. "Think of tennis. Then shrink the tennis court to a very small table, on which you volley a very small ball with very small paddles. It's a new game, and simply captivated my baby brother and his friends. When I was home last summer, you'd hear crack-crack-shriek or groan which was your clue that someone won a point. All afternoon this went on. They moved the table outside to the veranda in the back, so there was no escaping it."

She shook her head. "I'm sure he'll be playing when he comes home. We should make a bet on how long it will be before he picks up a paddle."

Mrs. McIntyre frowned. "We don't gamble, dear. Besides, it shouldn't take too long come tomorrow because Harry's classmate Tom is coming up from Albany to spend the night."

Helen helped herself to another sandwich, and sighed dramatically. "I must admit, I will still be glad to see him, despite his obsession."

During their almost three-hour rail journey that morning, Helen had described her brother Harry as "high spirited, not in the manner of a young thoroughbred, but more like a large puppy, a large drooling puppy with muddy paws." He was a freshman at Yale and liked athletics, fast horses, and girls. "As a matter of fact," she added, "he will probably be smitten by you. And you will find him very charming." Lily filed that away to think about later.

HELEN and Lily spent some time chatting with Mrs. McIntyre and then went up to their rooms. Lily was shown to a guest room across from Helen who had her old room. She unpacked her dresses, laying out the dark brown wool skirt and the ivory tucked waist for Thanksgiving dinner. It was the best she had brought from Buffalo and hadn't been worn much. She dressed somewhat distractedly and jumped when Helen knocked to see how she was coming along. Helen had already changed and done her hair up freshly. Lily was dressed but fumbled with her green velvet neck ribbon.

"Need a hand?" Helen asked, moving to assist. Lily gave her the ribbon and Helen quickly fastened it. She stood back and smiled.

"You are a picture, Lily," she said, admiringly. "That green sets off your hair brilliantly."

"My hair which I still have to do," Lily said, pushing at her sagging topknot. She pulled out her brush and box of pins and sat at the dressing table.

Helen sat at the end of the bed and leaned against a canopy post. "May I stay while you do?"

Lily laughed. "Of course."

Helen solicited Lily's impressions of her family so far and Lily said how much she liked them and how much Helen resembled her mother.

"I suppose I do resemble her, and in more ways than one," Helen confirmed. "We both have strong opinions, although these days not the same opinions! But my mother was raised a Unitarian and eyebrows were raised when my father brought her to the Presbyterian Church in town. Presbyterians are not accustomed to women who are accustomed to being listened to. "

Lily looked at Helen's reflection in her mirror. "What happened?" she asked, tucking pins into her hair rapidly.

"Well, I wasn't actually there, not having been born yet," she confessed, "but eventually a compromise was reached which had my mother making suggestions less and the Presbyterians appreciating her gifts more. That's how the story was told to me."

They both laughed.

"She would have fit right in at Vassar," Lily commented.

Helen nodded. "I think she was glad I wanted to go to college. What about your mother?"

Lily was finished with her hair and pulled open her bag to fish out the long necklace and earrings she had brought to wear.

"My mother is a different story, I'm afraid," Lily said tentatively, untangling the necklace. "I think she has a vision of social progression whereby she has attained a certain level in her society, and her children are expected to achieve a higher level of social standing."

She turned to face Helen, adjusting the loops of the necklace. "My family is solidly middle class, and my mother isn't satisfied with that. So, my wanting to go to Vassar, which I first wanted to do at the end of my sophomore year, was simply irrelevant to her. She said more than once, 'This is not what I had in mind for you, my only daughter.' "

Helen looked dubious. "What *did* she have in mind?"

"What else but that I meet a wealthy young man of a higher social standing and persuade him to marry me. The sooner the better. If possible, a Rockefeller or Carnegie."

Helen smiled at that and then asked, "How did you do it? You're at college and unmarried."

Lily sighed, debating quickly how much she should say. "Someone told her that Vassar girls socialize with Ivy League boys and that may have helped."

Helen laughed out loud. "She doesn't know that we have only two dances a year where boys are invited?"

"No," Lily smiled, "and I'm not likely to mention that. You see, she is already predisposed to believe that I spend too much time with my closest friends."

Helen looked at her with curiosity. "What do you mean?" she asked.

"Well," Lily began, "you already have become acquainted with my childhood friend, Eva. Eva insisted that she was responsible for my mother suddenly deciding in January to allow me to apply to Vassar. There may be some truth to that. I think my mother thought Eva was occupying spare time that I could have been spending cultivating friendships with young men."

Helen bit her lip and slowly shook her head. "Just to see if I understand Mrs. Kepler's reasoning, may I restate? In order to separate you and your friend Eva, your mother agrees to send you to a college where you will be swimming in an ocean of young women just like you?"

Lily pursed her lips to keep from laughing out loud, nodding.

They prepared to go downstairs and Helen took Lily's arm as they left the room. She leaned over conspiratorially. "I hope your mother at least appreciates that many of the girls with whom you keep company are very wealthy and of high social standing. She has achieved part of her goal, at least."

Their laughter echoed down the stairway.

They had barely returned to the sitting room when everyone heard the front door open. Harry had arrived and, in an instant, appeared in the sitting room archway.

"Where's the band? I thought there would be a small brass band outside to welcome the prodigal son home!"

He laughed along with his family and then he strode to his mother, embracing her in a big hug. "Hello, Mater!" he said heartily.

Mrs. McIntyre protested faintly at his grip but beamed and greeted him.

Harry then crossed the room to greet his father, who rose to shake hands and welcome Harry home. Harry was slightly taller than anyone else in the family, slender and wiry, with dark curly hair that looked at once unruly and attractive. He shared his nose and smile with his sister but his jaw line was wider, which allowed him a truly big grin.

The handsome young man then bounded back to stand before his sister. "Give me a hug then, big sister," he demanded.

Helen complied and said sympathetically over his shoulder, "I'm so sorry for your loss."

Harry pulled back and made his face the look of despondence. "Oh," he said, with mock sorrow, "thank you, but I can't talk about it yet."

"Harry, what are you talking about?" his mother asked, frowning. "And why don't you take off your coat, for goodness' sake?"

Harry complied and turned to find Agnes in the doorway waiting for his wraps. As he handed them over, his sister answered the question. "Mother, Yale lost last Saturday to Princeton, 11 - 6. Since both were undefeated, that means the Princeton Tigers will surely take the championship."

Mr. McIntyre said "Hmmph," eliciting a penitent look from Harry. And, in a flash, he changed demeanor and stood before Lily. He held out his hand and waited until she put hers into it. Then he held it and looked soulfully into her face.

"I want you to know that I do not play on the football team and therefore I am blameless for the recent debacle. I also wish you to know that I have in the past — once—" he noted with a glance at his sister, "accepted an invitation to the Founder's Day dance and so I can say with some confidence that most Vassar girls have not been especially blessed by Mother Nature when it comes to physical beauty. But somehow my sister manages to bring home the most beautiful girls in the student body. You, stranger, are the very apex, the pinnacle, of young beauty," he finished with a flourish, bending at the waist to kiss her hand.

"Harry, if you don't stop now, Lily might think you are serious," Helen warned. "Or just plain crazy."

She moved to Lily's side. "Harry, this is my classmate, Lily Kepler," she said, properly introducing them. "This gasbag is my baby brother, Harry."

Harry looked hurt. "How do you do, Lily? You may ask anyone and you will learn that I only tell the truth about what I see. I am genetically incapable of lying."

"Oh, Harry," his mother admonished, "Lily is our guest and I want her to feel at ease. What you need is a sandwich and some tea to help you think clearly. Or at least make it impossible to talk for a few minutes so your brain can catch up!"

Harry stared open-mouthed at his mother, who gave him a sound kiss on the cheek as she passed out of the room with the teapot, muttering, "*Genetically incapable*! Good heavens!"

The Thanksgiving holiday had begun. After the family had chatted for a while, Mrs. McIntyre glanced at the clock and touched Helen's arm.

"Will you see if Grandmother McIntyre is ready to join us? It won't be long until dinner."

Helen rose and excused herself. Mrs. McIntyre turned to Lily. "You have one more McIntyre to meet, Lily," she said sympathetically, "my husband's mother. She lives with us and has been enjoying her afternoon nap."

"I shall be pleased to meet her, I'm sure," Lily said, respectfully.

Mrs. McIntyre reached into the shelf of the table beside her and pulled out a leather-bound photo album.

"She's a woman of grace and dignity and we love her for her lifetime of kindness," she said. "We are patient when she has lapses of memory," she added and Lily heard a caution in that. She made a note to herself.

"Come sit beside me," Mrs. McIntyre said, giving a quick nod. "You can look into our rogue's gallery."

Lily moved to sit next to the woman, who was opening the album.

"This is my husband, eons ago," she laughed. "Don't you think Harry takes after him?"

Lily agreed.

"Harry doesn't think so, of course, because he can't imagine losing all his curly hair one day!"

She was turning pages. "Here is Helen when she was four, I think," she held the book so Lily could see.

"What a happy child," Lily commented.

"Yes, smiling even though she had to hold the pose for the exposure," Helen's mother said. "That should have been a warning to the world that she loved performing."

They chuckled.

"Have you seen her in a play yet?"

"Yes," Lily confirmed. "Their hall play was two weeks ago. She was quite remarkable."

"Everyone says that," the other sighed, shaking her head. "I can only hope that she won't write to us one day that she has decided to go on the stage!"

Over the next few minutes Lily was toured through McIntyre family photos by Mrs. McIntyre's maternal wit.

"Oh, here's one from two years ago, taken over Thanksgiving," she said, with some surprise. "I had forgotten it was in here."

Lily saw a photo of Helen and another girl, posed with the girl seated and Helen with her hand on the girl's shoulder. She assumed it was a Vassar girl but didn't recognize her.

"Is she a Vassar student?" Lily asked.

"She was the year this photo was taken," the other explained. "But I understand that she did not return after freshman year."

"Oh," Lily said, looking closely at the pretty girl, smiling very slightly at the photographer as if she knew a secret. "That must have been a great disappointment to her," she added, trying to imagine what it would be like to have only one year at Vassar.

"I should say," Mrs. McIntyre replied. "Helen was positively morbid the entire summer after freshman year in sympathy for her." She looked into the distance. "I cannot remember her name for the life of me. I think her people were from Cleveland."

Just then, Helen returned, walking slowly with an elderly woman on her arm. The petite woman, thin and a bit stooped, wore a black watered silk skirt and black lace-trimmed waist. She carried herself with dignity and glittered from a number of long necklaces in black faceted beads. And she smiled when she saw Lily.

"Grandmother, this is Lily Kepler, my classmate from Vassar." Helen said. "Lily, this is my grandmother McIntyre."

"Hello dear," the old woman said. "Welcome."

"Thank you," Lily answered. "How do you do?"

Grandmother McIntyre looked around and then back at Lily, a glint in her eyes.

"Still here," she said with spirit. "No one is more surprised than I!"

Agnes appeared to announce dinner.

The McIntyre dining room was a picture of loveliness. The group entered to see the gas chandelier casting a golden glow over the table, its cut glass prisms giving the fixture a twinkling appearance. The table, covered with a snow-white damask cloth, was set with gold-edged china and crystal goblets. In the middle of the table, a large arrangement of orange and gold chrysanthemums pronounced the season. Lily thought of how her mother would have approved of this display of fine living, and how similar it was to the holiday table set for her family, the scene from which she was absent this year. It gave her a momentarily pang.

From her place at the foot of the table, Mrs. McIntyre directed Lily to sit at her right, beside Harry. As Harry pulled out her chair, Helen was doing the same for her grandmother on the other side of the table. Mr. McIntyre took his seat at the head of the table, closest the room's bay window and farthest from the crackling fire behind Helen's mother.

When they were seated, Mr. McIntyre said grace and almost immediately upon his "Amen" a door swung open and Margaret came in with covered tureen and warmed soup bowls. Mrs. McIntyre ladled oyster stew to be passed along the table, first to Mr. McIntyre and Grandmother McIntyre.

That course finished, Agnes appeared and collected the bowls. And then Margaret brought the turkey in. Everyone made sounds of admiration and anticipation over the golden bird which she placed before the family patriarch. He stood, picked up the utensils and began to carve.

Agnes entered with steaming bowls of mashed potatoes and roasted beets. The door swung almost continuously as Margaret returned with bread stuffing and squash. Gravy, the cranberry jelly and pickles followed. Plates were passed up the table for turkey, and the accompaniments passed with much cheerful banter about the food and schools. Harry had to endure another ribbing about Yale's loss to Princeton, this time from his father. Harry replied that he had to suffer critical comments on behalf of the Eli football team from a stranger on the train from New Haven and again at the Glens Falls station from an old Academy classmate. Helen offered sympathy and promised not to say another word. Grandmother McIntyre seemed to think that there had been a death she had not been told about until it was explained that the sorrow was for a sporting event.

Harry was asked to pour the Riesling for those who wanted it, which he did with a flourish. Lily, unaccustomed to alcohol, nonetheless followed Helen's example and assented when Harry asked. The evening felt full of magic for her even before she had a sip of wine. From time to time, she would look across the table at Helen and often as not find Helen already looking at her, eyebrows raised in question. She smiled in response.

Grandmother McIntyre addressed Lily. "Where are your people from, young lady?" she was asking.

"Buffalo," Lily responded.

"Oh," she answered, "booming Buffalo."

Lily agreed.

"Are you married, dear?" she asked.

Lily blushed. "No. I want to finish college before I think about that."

The old woman leaned forward and said in loud whisper, "My grandson is single."

Everyone laughed and Lily blushed more deeply. "That's what I understand," she said, nodding and smiling.

Agnes entered the room and began to clear the table.

Mrs. McIntyre easily changed the topic by engaging her mother-in-law in telling remembrances of Thanksgivings past.

When the pumpkin and mince pies were brought out, Lily was feeling warm and lighthearted from her wine. She declined the offer of sherry and had coffee, hoping to keep all of her wits close by.

Mr. McIntyre inquired about Lily's father's business interests.

"Our family sells furniture and household furnishings," Lily said, without embarrassment. "We have two stores and my brother Will has come into the business. My other brother owns a furniture factory and sells some of his products to our stores."

Mr. McIntyre nodded. "That sounds like a good business for a place growing as fast as Buffalo. Lots of money to be made by those who work hard."

Lily nodded appreciatively. Helen's father recognized that the Keplers were the makers of their fortune, not inheritors, and his comments respected that.

"It was especially good business for Lily and her roommate because they got their room furnished in fine fashion from the family business," Helen said heartily.

They all repaired to the sitting room after they were finished and sat more quietly in their post-prandial hour than before. Grandmother McIntyre was the first to excuse herself, and then Helen's parents said good-night.

The young people lounged in their seats as much as their formal clothes permitted. Harry suggested a game of cards, but Helen begged off for her and Lily, noting that they had arisen earlier than Harry in order to travel home that day.

"So, who is Tom that he is visiting tomorrow?" Helen asked.

"Oh, Tom's first-rate," Harry said with enthusiasm. "He loves a good time and I promised him a Ping Pong tournament. I'm going to call a couple of last summer's champions tomorrow and see if we can create some real competition."

Helen raised her eyebrows. "None of those 'champions' attend Princeton, I hope."

Harry sent her a weary look.

"I couldn't help it, brother," Helen smirked.

"Say, Lily, do you play Ping Pong?" Harry looked at Lily, propped up by the corner of the couch.

"No," she answered. "I only just learned of it today. It must not have made it as far west as Buffalo, yet."

"We must address that deficiency *tomorrow*," Harry said, interested. "You could become a Ping Pong ambassador to Buffalo. We could give you a certificate to take home when you go."

Helen pulled herself out of the couch.

"What we *must* do is go to bed," Helen declared. "A *Ping Pong ambassador*? The workings of your mind astonish me, my dear, dear brother. Come on Lily, you can dream of your Ping Pong *certificate* tonight."

"What did I say?" Harry asked in mock surprise.

Helen and Lily had reached the doorway. They stopped and Lily spoke up.

"Harry, I do believe that you are out standing in your own field," she said, breaking up Helen at once.

"And I thank you for that, Lily," he said in a grateful voice. "A prophet is unappreciated in his own land."

The girls laughed in unison as they left him. When they approached their rooms, Helen asked Lily to come to her room for a bit. Lily sat in a chair beside Helen's dressing table and they began pulling hairpins, each letting down her hair.

"Are you enjoying yourself so far?" Helen inquired.

"Oh, yes," Lily replied sincerely, "you have a wonderful family."

"Don't mind Harry, he's ebullient and loves to talk."

"I think he's very sweet," Lily said quickly. "He reminds me of my brother, Will. Except that he's better looking than my brother."

Helen glanced at her briefly and then began to run her fingers through her long hair to avoid tangling it with her brush.

"He seems to like that you bring home classmates he finds attractive," Lily commented

Helen just smiled and shook her head.

"Who was the girl you invited for Thanksgiving freshman year?" she asked in what she tried to make a casual manner.

Helen stopped brushing her hair. "Why do you ask?" she said, not looking up from her brush.

Lily was sorry she brought it up. Helen's face had become a mask.

"Oh, I was just curious because your mother showed me the album photo of you and another Vassar girl from Thanksgiving," she said, hurrying her words to get through what seemed to be a sensitive subject. "It's nothing, just my chattering. I probably caught verbosity from Harry."

Helen nodded and smiled a very small smile. But she didn't look at Lily. Lily gathered up her hairpins and said goodnight. And she vowed that she would stay clear of the subject in the future.

CHAPTER 9

The next morning at breakfast Margaret related that Helen's father had gone to work, her brother Harry had not come down, and her mother as was her habit had taken her breakfast in her room. Helen and Lily had the dining room to themselves. Once again, the air was filled with the aroma of roasting turkey and, when questioned, Margaret indicated that it was her own family's turkey that was in the oven.

The girls enjoyed a hearty breakfast, eschewing the offer of oatmeal, Vassar standard breakfast fare, for eggs and sausage and fresh biscuits. Afterward, they retrieved homework and sat in the sitting room before a fire that took away the damp chill of the November morning. Lily followed Helen's lead; the latter was reserved this morning and Lily, trying not to imagine why, made little conversation. She didn't mind the quiet, even though she read her text only sporadically. Her attention was flitting, her mind window-shopping. She thought of what her family would be doing this morning and realized that she probably would be seated in the Kepler family parlor, in the comfortable rocker near the radiator, with the same book as she now had in her hand. She thought about Eva, and wondered how serious she and Frank Marshall, the "handsome, fun-loving" beau she wrote about, were becoming. And she realized that she wouldn't be at all surprised when she went home at Christmas to find that Eva was planning a future with Frank. Eva didn't like being alone, she had no interest in a career, and a beau who might become a husband would be the most reasonable course for her to pursue.

Lily thought about Helen, glancing over at the girl in her easy chair, feet drawn up and head tilted to one side as she read. She remembered Bert commenting on how attractive Helen was and that she had made some short reply about Helen not being a Gibson Girl. Bert probably wasn't fooled by that remark; she had proven to be an excellent observer of human nature. The truth was that Lily was thrown off balance by Helen's beauty and until recently refused to admit to herself that looking at Helen, in repose as she was now, made her catch her breath. Every time, just like the first time.

And she wondered what the future held for someone with those feelings. In another year, Helen would graduate, move on and probably marry within the year. What would Lily do with those feelings in that eventuality? She blinked to close that subject and once again tried to focus on her reading.

Before long, a noise on the stairs signaled that Harry was up. He put his head into the sitting room to say good morning and then went to have breakfast. Afterward he brought a cup of coffee and joined Helen and Lily.

Sitting down with a sigh, he was all energy and good humor.

"Don't you feel like living after a real home-cooked breakfast?" he exclaimed.

Both girls assented at the same time. College food was the same everywhere.

"What is Vassar planning today?" he asked, taking up his cup.

Helen put her book down and looked over at Lily.

"We have no firm plans so far," Helen replied. "What is Yale planning?"

"Well," Harry said, cocking his head the same way Helen did when thinking out loud, "we have to achieve our quorum first, and we will around noon when Tom gets in. And then I thought we might do some things together. What say you, sister?"

Helen looked at Lily, who shrugged to signify *why not*? and said, "If it's interesting, we'd be game."

"Of course, what I'd really like to do we can't do, unless a meteorological miracle happens."

Helen leaned in Lily's direction. "Harry means that he's dying to go sleighing but can't because there is no longer any snow."

"And I can't understand it. Last week it was so cold I had icicles on my eyelashes, and just like that, it's all melted and my hopes are dashed." He tried to look sad.

"Of course," he said, brightening, "we have the promised Ping Pong lesson, Lily."

Lily smiled and nodded.

"But not all afternoon," Helen interjected. "Besides, you could take us all for a drive today. It's not too cold and we can show our guests our local natural wonders."

"Oh," Harry crooned, "Cooper's Cave. Have you heard about it?"

Lily allowed as how she hadn't.

"Sister, a ride may be just the thing for outdoor enjoyment and fresh air," he declared.

"And you may take us to Glen Street because we're going to buy chocolate," Helen added.

Lily looked at her curiously.

Helen smiled. "Lily and I will make you boys some genuine Vassar fudge."

"But not in a chafing dish over a spirit lamp," Lily pleaded.

Helen laughed. "No, we'll use an actual stove. Margaret will be off the rest of the day so we won't be a bother in the kitchen."

TOM was a good deal shorter than Harry but his broad shoulders and thick neck were the features one noticed first. He had dark hair that he wore close trimmed and matching dark eyes that crinkled deeply when he grinned. He had the beefy figure of a fullback or a wrestler, but a high-pitched laugh, which is what the girls heard before they saw him.

After lunch, Harry and Tom left to fetch a carriage for their ride. Helen reminded them to bring back a covered vehicle. They did and the foursome set out for a ride, Helen and Lily riding under the canopy with a lap rug and Harry and Tom in the driver's seat, partially exposed to the weather.

They headed out Warren Street away from the village center and circled the village through its residential streets, winding north into higher elevations until they reached Glen Street. The wind picked up as they descended toward the business section and the river and the girls tucked the lap rug more snugly around their ankles. Helen reminded Harry to stop at Smith's for chocolate and he pulled up to the curb in front of the store. Helen and Lily went in and made the purchase.

Then they were off to the river and Cooper's Cave. Rattling across the river on the Iron Bridge, Harry pulled the carriage off the street and stepped out near the falls that gave the village its name. Helen got out as well and turned back to Lily, holding out her hand to assist her in getting out of the carriage.

Lily looked at Harry with his hand outstretched on the left and Helen on the right. Feeling herself in an awkward position, she took Harry's hand quickly and was helped out of the carriage.

"Noisy, isn't it?" Tom called as they stood looking over the frothy cascade.

"Not in summer," Harry called back. "Are you cold?" he asked Lily, solicitously.

Lily allowed that she was a little. Harry led the group to a spot on the bank where the so-called cave was visible.

Leaning close to Lily, he said, "It's not a true cave, but a hollowed-out rock formation."

Lily nodded in agreement.

"But James Fenimore Cooper passed through here and later used it in his novel, *Last of the Mohicans*. So, we call it Cooper's Cave."

Lily smiled at him.

"We have some claim to fame, however minor it might be," Helen said from behind them.

With that, everyone agreed that they were surfeited with fresh air and could return to the McIntyre home at once. The boys dropped off their passengers and left to return the carriage.

Back indoors, Helen and Lily went into the warm kitchen and commenced making fudge. Margaret had left the stove good and hot so they poked into cupboards until they located the sugar. Lily found cream and butter in the icebox and let Helen take charge of the cooking.

Lily sat at the heavy kitchen table, noting that it was bleached and scrubbed clean, left in proper condition by Margaret before she left to spend the day with her family. She cupped her hands around the tea pot she had just filled and began to feel warm through.

Helen was stirring the chocolate mixture continuously and looked over at Lily. "Will you be pouring that tea soon or just warming your hands?" she asked pleasantly.

"I'd be happy to pour you a cup," Lily said, and carried the cup to the stove for Helen.

"What do you think of Tom?" Helen asked.

"I think he's awfully nice," Lily said honestly. "He isn't sarcastic but still quite funny. That's unusual in young men, in my experience."

Helen reached for her cup in her free hand. "And you have a lot of experience from which you are drawing?"

Lily laughed and returned to her seat at the table. "Hardly. I was just recalling my high school classmates, always making cracks at girls."

Like the experienced fudge maker that she was, Helen stirred just long enough to get the proper consistency. They turned out the pound of fudge into a shallow pan and put it in the icebox to harden.

As they left the kitchen, Harry and Tom blew in, their cheeks and noses red from the walk back from the livery. Helen made them tea and they gathered in the sitting room around the fire.

"So, where's our famous Vassar fudge?" Harry asked, stoking the fire and adding coal.

"It has to harden so we need to wait a half an hour or so," Helen replied.

Both boys groaned as if on cue.

"What will we do for half an hour?" Tom asked.

"Music," Harry said, raising a finger.

"Yes," his sister agreed, and they both made for the Victor, the family's phonograph.

"Rags," Harry said as they both searched through the thick phonograph records in their heavy paper sleeves.

"Here," Helen said, holding up a record. "'Breeze from Alabama.'"

"Right! Put her on," he said, and began turning the crank to power up the Victor.

The introductory notes of the ragtime piece began and they looked at one another, eyebrows raised. Then Harry drew Lily from her seat, and Helen pulled Tom up to dance.

"I'm not very good at modern dances," Lily apologized as she put her hand in Harry's. "We're rather more traditional at school in our dancing."

The ragtime piece had launched into its trademark syncopation and Harry began to bend to and fro to the rhythm.

"It's just a one-step, see?" he said, and it was easy after all. Then at a certain point, he twirled them around and began the rocking motion again.

They bantered with Helen and Tom who, despite being a head shorter than Helen, carried on beamishly.

The song ended and Harry pulled the needle from the record.

"I vote for another," he said heartily.

"Alright then," Tom said, stepping over to Lily and offering his hand.

Harry was putting on the "'Cleopha March and Two-Step'" and caught Tom's gesture out of the corner of his eye.

"Wait, are you going to force me to dance with my sister?" he whined.

"It's just trading partners, brother," Helen commented with a small smile.

He danced with his sister and everyone added embellishments to their styles, laughing approvingly at each other.

Lily went to the record box after the number was finished and looked through the rags. "This is my favorite," she said, handing Harry the record. "'The Easy Winners.'"

Harry put on the record and gave the crank a few turns. Then he made sure to select Lily as his partner, quickly grasping her hand and cracking up the others.

They danced to the slower ragtime piece and halfway through, Harry felt a poke on his shoulder. He stepped back and was surprised to see his sister.

"I'm cutting in," she said, and then stepped in between Harry and Lily, taking her hand and the lead.

As they danced, Lily smiling incredulously, Harry and Tom stood by.

"Dance, boys," Helen called over to them.

"We don't know who should lead," Tom called back, in fun.

"You notice that my sister *always* leads," Harry cracked.

Then the boys took up the challenge and danced the one-step in an exaggerated fashion. When the dance ended, everyone applauded each other.

Helen and Lily went to the kitchen to get the fudge. It was fine for cutting, firmer than at Vassar where fudge was invariably eaten before it had begun to harden.

Lily held a plate while Helen cut the fudge into pieces. "You got your dance, after all," Lily said quietly.

Helen licked a fudgy finger and smiled slyly. "The dance I asked you for was a waltz," she said. "So, I'm still owed."

The young people lounged before the fire, now burning quite warmly, enjoying the fudge.

"Smith College girls also make fudge," Tom commented languidly.

"Base imitators," Helen commented back in the same tone. "This is the real McCoy."

"Or the real McIntyre," Lily added, provoking a chuckle.

After they had polished off the entire plate, Harry suggested that they all adjourn to the attic for some Ping Pong. Helen urged them to go on ahead and warm up the table, promising to come along in a little while.

Alone before the fire, Helen and Lily took the best seats.

"Not to deny you Ping Pong time, but the less whack-whack-whack we have to endure, the better, as far as I'm concerned," Helen said, stretching her legs onto a hassock nearest the fire.

The heat made Lily's muscles loose. "Do you think you'll get married soon after graduating?" she asked.

Helen didn't answer for a moment. "I'm thunderstruck, Lily," she said to the fire. "Graduation is in a year and a half. I have no prospects in mind, haven't given it a thought. Why do you ask?" she finished, glancing over at Lily.

"I was just wondering. It seems to me that graduation is like some kind of demarcation that spurs girls to get married. A number of my high school classmates were married in the summer and fall this year."

Helen was silent for a moment. "Do you think you'll marry after *you* graduate from Vassar?"

It was Lily's turn to be silent. "I can't picture myself married," she confessed.

"Well, that will change when you meet the right man," Helen replied.

"I don't..." she hesitated, "I don't know if I want to be married."

They were silent.

"That's heresy, isn't it?" Lily commented.

"Most people get married," Helen said. "But not everyone. Women who pursue careers often don't marry because they wouldn't be able to work full time if they have to keep house and raise children."

When Lily didn't respond, Helen asked, "Do you have a career in mind?"

"No," Lily sighed. "Is that the very essence of a freshman—to know not what you want to do or why?"

Helen didn't reply but rose from her chair and went to the Victor. She pulled out a record and wound up the machine, then lowered the needle onto the platter. A waltz began.

"Miss Kepler," she said, standing beside Lily's chair, "may I finally have this dance?"

Lily took the proffered hand and stood. She smiled, took a deep breath and found that she could do it. They danced the waltz, back and forth, round and round, until Lily was grinning and Helen was laughing.

After their evening meal, the four young people made popcorn and carried refreshments up to the attic for Harry's much-anticipated tournament of champions, a get-together of his old pals. The girls played only briefly, for collegiality, and then sat on the sidelines while the serious competition began. Harry had made an elimination chart for the ten players and the evening grew long before the final round was played. Lily sat with Tom on a trunk for some time as he interviewed her.

"So, is Helen your roommate at Vassar?" he asked.

"Oh, no," she said, "she's my Greek tutor. I didn't take it in high school and was simply flunking it so I asked around and her name came up."

Tom was gazing at Helen across the room, shaking his head. "See, that's what I have against men's colleges and women's colleges."

Lily looked at him when he didn't continue. "Yes?" she said above the noise of cheering for a point scored.

He looked pained. "If we were coed at Yale, I'd hire Helen to tutor me."

"In what?"

"Anything at all," he replied wistfully.

Lily laughed. "Tom, I do believe you are soft on Harry's big sister."

He looked seriously at Lily. "Who wouldn't be, can you tell me?"

She looked at him, frankly. "No, I can't," she said, surprising herself.

After the evening ended, past eleven, Helen stopped at Lily's room and was invited in. She closed the door and sat in a rocker, removing hairpins. Lily brushed her hair and filled her in on Tom's wish to have Helen tutor him.

Helen leaned back in the rocker, laughing quietly. "The poor boy," she said.

Lily frowned. "Why do you say that?"

"Well, because, it's so impossible," Helen said dismissively, smiling. "He's the same age as Harry, for heaven's sake."

Lily very nearly said that she was the same age as the boys, but stopped herself at the irrelevance of it. "He seems awfully nice, is all I meant," she said instead.

"And so he is, my dear," Helen assented, "but he's not particularly strong-willed." She looked off into the distance and sighed. "And whoever is to win my heart must be very strong, inside," she added, tapping a hand on her heart.

Lily looked at Helen's reflection in her dressing table mirror. "You mean someone stronger than you?"

"Oh, I'm not strong," Helen said quickly, sitting up. "Not strong at all."

Lily gathered up her hairpins from the dressing table one by one and put them into her box. She hadn't imagined Helen as anything but strong and confident.

Helen rose and began to leave.

"I came in specifically to warn you," Helen said, her hand on the door knob.

"Harry spoke to me tonight in the attic about you. He wanted to know if you had a sweetheart somewhere or were otherwise spoken for. I told him I wasn't certain. Told you he'd be captivated by you."

Lily looked into those grey eyes with her worried face. "I'm not looking for a beau or suitor," she said in quiet earnestness.

Helen smiled, holding Lily's look with her own. "Leave it to me," she said. "Sleep well."

SATURDAY morning was a quiet rising. Lily arose and dressed and then sat in her room and read until she heard Helen open her door. They went down to breakfast together. The boys were nearly finished eating but loitered to chat with the girls. Lily noticed that Tom glanced only furtively at Helen, not meeting her eyes even when she spoke to him, and she felt sorry for him. She knew exactly how he felt, with feelings strong and unexpected bunched up in the chest, and no time to decipher them or make a plan of action. And no hope of having the infatuation returned. Helen had said that Tom wasn't strong-willed enough for her. She wondered if it was possible for strong-willed people to have feelings that made the knees weak and the tongue tied. She looked over at Helen who was bantering with her brother, and wondered if she had ever had those feelings.

Helen caught her looking across the table and said, "Are you interested?"

Lily blinked, focusing on the present again. "Interested in what?"

Harry gave her a nudge. "Not awake yet, are we?"

Lily demurred. "I was daydreaming, a vacation luxury."

"I'll give you that point," Harry replied amiably. "Sister suggested that we spend our last morning together with a game of euchre. Do you play?"

"I do play, Harry," Lily nodded, "and would be pleased to play."

"Girls against boys," Helen said firmly. And the boys agreed, with some relish, giving the impression that they considered themselves superior in euchre strategy.

That confidence proved false by the end of the first hand. As Helen gathered the cards to shuffle them, she looked across the table at her partner.

"You most certainly do know how to play euchre," she said to Lily, impressed.

"I play sometimes with my brother Will and his friends if they need a fourth," Lily said innocently.

"Tom, gloves off," Harry called to his partner, eyes narrowed.

"Right," Tom replied, looking as if he were preparing for battle. Helen and Lily just laughed at them.

By the end of the morning, they disagreed on the score and everyone surrendered good naturedly. They were able to agree that their time together over the last day had been enjoyable. Harry and Tom left to pack and get ready to leave for Albany, where Harry would spend the night with Tom's pals before they returned to Yale the following day.

After dinner, the boys gathered up their coats and satchels and said good-bye to Mrs. McIntyre, Helen, and Lily in the reception hall.

"Lily," said Helen in a formal tone.

"Yes, Helen?" Lily replied in the same tone.

"Who won?"

"We did, Helen," Lily answered, looking quietly official.

Harry stood shaking his head dramatically. "This is a fine send off, Mother," he appealed to her. "If the train derails and we're smashed to atoms, this will be the last word I remember from my sister."

His mother gave him a hug and kissed his cheek warmly. "I wonder that you haven't joined a theatrical group yet, dear," she said in a mock puzzled tone. "You're such a natural melodramatic!"

Good-byes were exchanged all around and then they were gone. The house seemed to exhale. Mrs. McIntyre turned to Helen and Lily.

"What will you girls do this afternoon?"

Helen said they planned to do some reading for school. Mrs. McIntyre turned to go upstairs.

"Well, take some rest this afternoon some time so you'll be fresh for our evening out."

"We will, Mother," Helen promised.

They went into the sitting room and pulled the coziest chairs up to the fire and settled into their reading. After a while, it became apparent that they had neglected to add coal to the grate because the room was becoming chilly, so Helen got up and tended to that, and then offered to make hot chocolate for them. Lily offered to help, but Helen handed her a lap rug and said she would be back shortly.

Lily put her book down and took a deep breath. She had hardly been alone these several days except to sleep. Not that she had minded, given the company, but she was unused to it. At home she would spend hours reading or writing poetry or stories alone in her room. Her mother was usually out in the afternoons for some committee or organization of which she was an officer and Lily regarded that as a good thing because her mother thought Lily spent too much time reading, studying, or chatting with Eva.

She threw off the lap robe and walked around the room. There were books in a glass-fronted case, books on the piano, a newspaper on a marble-topped table beside a chair, a Harper's and Munsey's on a footstool. She felt entirely at home in this house where reading was as natural as breathing.

Lily came upon the little table with the shelf that held the photo album Mrs. McIntyre showed her Thanksgiving Day. She looked at it, then bent and pulled it out, laying it on the table top. Smiling, she reviewed the photos and remembered the mother's narration. And then she turned to a page where the photo on the right-hand side was gone. She turned back pages and forward and was certain which photo was missing, the one of Helen standing beside a seated girl, the photo taken two years previous.

Helen came into the room with a tray containing two steaming mugs and saw Lily standing over the album. She put down the tray and brought Lily her mug.

"Are you looking at my baby pictures or Harry's?" she asked playfully, and then looked down to see the empty frame.

Lily placed a finger in the empty rectangle and traced its edges, looking up when she was finished. Helen went back to the tray, picked up her own mug, and returned to her seat. Lily joined her. They sat warming their feet before the fire and their hands around the thick mugs, not speaking.

"This is delicious hot chocolate," Lily offered quietly. "I think you are a chocolate wizard."

"Julia Fremont," said Helen.

Lily wrapped her mind around the name.

"That's the answer to the question you asked the other day."

"Yes," Lily said. She had figured that out.

"And that's all I have to say," Helen said quickly.

Lily pursed her lips. "Her smile suggested to me that she was—untrustworthy," she said, choosing her words carefully. "And that's all I have to say."

She glanced sideways at Helen who was looking into the fire and who very slowly began to smile.

At length Helen said, "To paraphrase, you freshmen are all right."

Lily smiled broadly. And the subject was closed.

They each read in the warm room until Lily began to feel sleepy. She put her book down and thought she would just close her eyes for a minute. The next thing she knew was that the room had grown dim and someone had covered her with the lap rug. Peering over at Helen's chair, she saw the other curled into a corner of it, covered with a blanket. Leaning back and closing her eyes again, Lily felt awash in an intimate moment. She allowed herself to imagine that she and Helen were always together and every afternoon they read until they napped. If it was a dream, she never wanted to awaken.

Mr. and Mrs. McIntyre had arranged for Helen and Lily to join them in a theatrical evening at the Empire Theatre downtown. Fitch's *Cowboy and the Lady* was playing and Helen had a great deal to say about Clyde Fitch, her favorite playwright after William Shakespeare.

"Did you know that Maxine Elliott played Mrs. Weston, the lead in the play we're going to see, when it was in New York?"

Finally, during the carriage ride to the theatre, her mother leaned over and said,

"Helen, dear daughter, you have prepared us so well for our evening, won't you stop to take a breath now?"

Helen hung her head and then sat back happily, giving her shoulders a shiver of anticipation. Lily smiled at Helen's delight.

Helen looked at Lily, seated beside her, and leaned against her. "I love a good story, well-acted!"

Lily readily agreed.

Darkness embraced the streets of Glens Falls and transformed them from the gray, wet, nearly-winter streets Lily recalled from the day before. The gaslights cast their golden halos, reflected in the wet cobblestones and the store windows, and the evening fairly glistened from all sides. The McIntyre's carriage pulled up to the four-year old Empire Theatre and Lily gazed wide-eyed at the three-story building, the name outlined loudly in electric lights. Well-dressed patrons were approaching on the sidewalk and she smiled in anticipation.

They waited in the two-story lobby with its mosaic floor spelling out the theatre's name while Mr. McIntyre stabled the horses nearby. Their evening's entertainment, *The Cowboy and the Lady,* was given in the biggest venue in the building, the opera house. They entered the cavernous room along with over a thousand people, all of whom were finding their seats, greeting friends and neighbors; the hubbub was tremendous.

The play was a light-hearted comedy, a modern play where sophisticated, beautiful Mrs. Weston desires to leave her philandering husband rather than continue to be mistreated. The husband is killed during an indiscretion so she needn't obtain a divorce. She is then free to fall into the arms of, in this case, the cowboy on whose dude ranch she has been staying. It was set in the west and all the characters wore chaps and bandanas and spoke rustic slang the writer thought appropriate for people who lived there.

Early in the play, a young girl named Midge is asked by the hero to sing "that little song" and she sings, "I love a lovely girl, I do, and I have loved a girl or two. And I know how a girl should be loved, you bet I do."

Lily sat very still when Midge sang the song, which was repeated later in the play and then the melody was whistled by another character. She was afraid if she moved, people around her, even strangers, would be able to tell that she loved a lovely girl.

At the intermission, Mr. McIntyre stepped outside to have a cigar with other gentlemen of his acquaintance, and the ladies stood in the hallway enjoying a glass of sparkling water. The mother of a classmate of Helen's stopped to exchange news, noting that her daughter was absent because she had preferred to go to New York with her Smith College friends.

"Honestly," she said to Mrs. McIntyre, with an eye toward Helen and Lily, "don't you think our children, when they reach a certain age, would like to lock us away so they can finish raising themselves?"

She laughed and Mrs. McIntyre smiled agreeably.

"You know that we live in a new century now," Helen's mother replied. "More has changed than just electric lights and automobiles."

When the woman moved on, Mrs. McIntyre turned to the girls.

"Do *you* want to lock me away?"

Helen put an arm around her mother. "Of course not, Mother!" she said, giving her a squeeze. "We think you're ripping. And I wouldn't want you to miss my opening night on Broadway!"

Mrs. McIntyre feigned horror and they were laughing when Mr. McIntyre returned. Helen took Lily's arm as they headed back into the opera house, leaned over and hummed the melody of the song. Lily blushed in response. Helen laughed, enjoying herself.

WHEN the evening ended and Helen and Lily had mounted the stairs to their rooms, Helen hissed and cocked her head toward her own bedroom. Lily took the hint and followed her.

Helen took off her shoes and unbuttoned her waist, and pulled it off, threw off the corset cover and unhooked her corset and threw it down. Covered only by her chemise, she sighed and flopped onto her bed, tucking her hands behind her head. Looking at Lily, she took up the melody of that song again, "la de da di-da di-da."

Lily sat in an upholstered chair and unbuttoned her high collar, avoiding looking at Helen.

"We should do that play at Vassar, what do you think?" Helen said. "It would only cost twenty-five dollars in royalty. I could play Teddy, the hero."

Lily grimaced. "But you wouldn't be able to wear Harry's suit. You'd have to wear chaps and a bandana around your neck and a big ten-gallon hat."

"You don't think I would appear heroic in that costume?"

Lily chuckled. "I am on the wardrobe committee for my Phil chapter so I think about how hard it could be to outfit the cast."

Helen dismissed that. "Minor challenge, that. I could also play Mrs. Weston. But in any case, the song alone would become a campus hit." And she la-di-da'd the melody again.

"I don't know why you think so," Lily mumbled, still uncomfortable about the lyrics' relevance.

Helen rolled over to face Lily. "Don't you see how hysterically funny we could make the play?" she asked. "The song would be sung all over campus, by crushes, sweethearts, by people poking fun at sweethearts who spend too much time alone together. It would be a killer," she finished with glee.

Lily was taking in the information that there were multiple pairs of sweethearts on campus and they were called out if they spent too much time by themselves. These details had not yet reached the freshman class grapevine.

Helen pulled her pillow closer and relaxed into it, gazing lazily at an unresponsive Lily.

"Oh, say," Helen said, "I had a minute to talk to Harry today about you."

"Oh?" Lily said, surprised.

"Yes, you'll recall our conversation last night? Well, I told him that you had a devoted beau in Buffalo and wouldn't dream of being untrue."

"What did he say to that?" Lily said, wonderingly.

Helen snorted. "He said there couldn't be anyone in the entire city of Buffalo better qualified to be your beau than he."

Lily looked alarmed.

"But it's alright," Helen hastened to add, "He believed me and withdrew from the field, like the gentleman he is. So, you're off the hot seat on this one."

"I appreciate your persuading him," Lily said sincerely.

Helen turned onto her back and looked at the ceiling. "He really is a gentleman, inside the exuberance and braggadocio. I tried to make the lie as small as possible so as not to hurt his feelings. He's my baby brother."

Lily nodded. "I should go," she said.

Helen sat up and wrapped her arms around the bedpost at the foot of the bed. The outline of her small breasts was visible through the thin fabric of the chemise. Lily looked only once and then shifted her eyes to Helen's face. She couldn't translate the latter's expression.

"Are you glad I talked you into coming home with me?" she said, her face screwed into a question.

"Oh, yes," Lily said quickly, with warmth. "I've had a splendid time and don't know how to thank you."

"Ah," Helen said, raising a finger, "but it is I who should thank you for spending these three days with me."

"But why?" Lily asked, surprised.

"A lot of reasons," was all the cool reply she received, with a shrug.

THE next day was Sunday, and Lily accompanied Helen and her parents to services at the Presbyterian church. Then they came home to a roast beef dinner and before long it was time for the girls to leave for the station. Helen's mother came from the kitchen with a package.

"Some supplies for your larder, dear," she said, handing it to Helen.

"And possibly some of Margaret's spice cake?" Helen asked coyly.

"Of course, dear!"

Helen handed the package to Lily and rushed into the kitchen calling the cook's name. Mrs. McIntyre looked at Lily and just laughed.

"I owe you many thanks, you sweet girl," she said, giving Lily a hug despite the intervening package. "Tutoring you seems to have been a real tonic for Helen."

"Well, I've certainly improved my Greek, thanks to her," Lily replied earnestly. "I won't have to have tutoring after this semester."

Mrs. McIntyre put a hand on Lily's arm. "The Helen who walked in this door three days ago is the daughter I haven't seen in over a year. I hope you will remain friends after your tutoring has finished. And that you will come to visit us again, I mean that."

Lily could only mumble, 'Thank you,' and put her free arm around the mother's neck.

As the train from Albany began the trip along the Hudson, Helen was reading while Lily stared out the window without seeing anything. She was sifting information, sorting fragments and replaying Mrs. McIntyre's last comment over and over.

CHAPTER 10

Lily awoke Monday morning to the whirlwind of school again. The gong woke her up for breakfast and she got out of bed in a cheerful mood that more resembled Bert's demeanor than her own mumbling morning mood. She felt light as a feather as she dressed to go down for breakfast and even the sight of her history text, with so few pages of the assignment read, didn't dampen her spirits.

And then she picked up the morning mail. Lily had two letters, one in her mother's handwriting. Her heart sank to see it, because she knew what it would say.

Her mother castigated her for not writing in nearly two weeks. Lily thought back and recalled writing to her parents immediately after Helen had asked her to go to Glens Fall. How had she neglected to write again nearer Thanksgiving to wish them well and tell them she would be thinking of them on the feast day?

In the beginning of the semester, she had written home almost twice a week, long letters filled with descriptions of the campus, the food, the entertainments, and brief mentions of her classes. But by early November, she had let the frequency slip to once a week, and her letters were shorter, less effusive. She couldn't recall the last time she signed her letters with a phrase suggesting that she longed to see her family.

And she realized this morning, with the short letter communicating her mother's pain at being forgotten by her only daughter, that something significant had happened since she arrived at Vassar. The college was her home now, the center of her universe. The smell of the first-floor hallway near the dinner hour, of wet wool in classrooms on rainy days, the knocking and groaning of the steam pipes in Main that sometimes woke her in the morning before the breakfast gong—all of these made up her reality. She could no longer hear the sounds of classes passing at Central High; her mind was filled with the nuanced sounds of morning classes changing in Rockefeller and afternoon classes in Main. The paths across campus, through the pines, around the lake, were more familiar to her now than those in Humboldt Park in Buffalo, a park where she had played since a small child.

Bert and Izzie and the rest of the gang had surely always been her friends, and she could read their moods by the way they walked or tilted their heads, the tone of their laughter or the depth of their sighs. Eva, whose unopened letter was the second one she received this morning, seemed almost alien to Lily now. They had never shared a love of learning. Vassar classmates might talk heatedly for an hour on suffrage, settlement work, Philippines policy, unionism, and then have an impromptu spread with everyone contributing whatever they had on hand, be it crackers, olives, a tin of smoked oysters, or the prized chocolate. The laughter and warmth were not contradictory to the previous opposing positions, but the ordinary way of things here.

Lily opened Eva's letter and was relieved to find that Eva was more interested in relating the progress of her relationship with Frank Marshall than noting the absence of letters from Lily. She said that she had so much to share with Lily that she could hardly wait to see her at Christmas and begged to know the exact date she was coming home.

There was an hour before her first class of the day; Lily sighed as she pushed the history text to one side of her desk and took out stationery. She had time for an apologetic note to her parents and possibly one to Eva.

LILY stepped off the trolley onto slushy Main Street in downtown Poughkeepsie. Minute snowflakes drifted lazily like ashes from a fire. She shivered in the chill and pulled the collar of her coat across her throat.

It was the second of December. Classes let out for the Christmas break in two weeks. What she had in mind as a gift for Helen was yarn for a knitted wool cap for winter recreation and in Vassar's rose color if she could find it. And she need-ed to buy the yarn today if she was to finish it in time to give the cap to her for Christmas.

Earlier she had sat at her desk and made a Christmas gift list. She decided to buy her father a mechanical pencil because he often had trouble finding a pencil when he wanted one and because he liked gadgets. And that was all she had in mind as she window-shopped along Main Street, quite busy this time of day.

Lily had only been into Poughkeepsie twice since September, both times on excursions with her clot of fellow freshmen as they explored their environs. They were told to make sure to stop at Smith Brothers for a snack or confection and so they did. Luckey Platt & Company had been recommended as the most comprehensive department store in town, so they trooped through its many floors, compiling wish lists of things they wanted for their rooms. Although Lily's friends were probably wealthier than she, all of them had finite allowances from home, which was a relief to her. None of their group thought they could buy anything that struck their fancy, unlike a few on their floor who made a show of their disposable income. But, rather than dislike those spendthrifts, they were delighted to share in the sumptuous spreads to which their generous hall mates invited them which often included cakes ordered from Frost's in town.

She headed for Luckey Platt's in hopes of finding the wool yarn and possibly something affordable for her mother at the same time. The revolving door passed her from the cold streetscape, smelling of electrical sparks from the trolleys and horse manure from the carriages into a suddenly warm space redolent of pine. The first floor of the department store, brilliantly lit with myriad electric bulbs from its high white ceiling, was in fulsome holiday display. Around each of its support pillars was twisted holly or pine boughs, their dark green dotted with bright red glass ornaments. Lily couldn't help but smile at the scene as she paused to take it in.

She had caught the attention of a floorwalker who suddenly stood before her, a condescending smile on his close-shaved face. He clasped his hands together in front of his checked silk vest which fairly gleamed from his black suit coat.

"Good afternoon, madam," he said, his evaluative glance including her golf boots. "How may I assist you today?"

Lily asked for the location of the yarns and was directed upstairs. There was no shade near Vassar's rose, but she chose something in the same color family. She thought it would look good in a cap close to Helen's face, setting off her complexion and especially her eyes.

That settled, she wandered the store and nearly bought a pretty box of stationery for her mother before she realized how ironic that would be from the daughter who forgot to write. She eventually purchased a small pressed glass dish suitable for her mother's dressing table, useful for holding rings or a brooch.

The store had so many beautiful things, all attractively arrayed on tables or under glass cases. Lily began to calculate how she could save more money to afford the gifts she wanted to give. In addition to more economies, she realized that she could terminate her tutoring sessions and use that money. She immediately returned to the campus.

"YOU'RE sacking me?" Helen said, with feigned hurt, during their regular Thursday evening session.

"Well, you know I really am caught up in my Greek, now," Lily said reasonably, "and I could use the money for Christmas presents."

"Oh," the tutor replied, drawing out the word, "it's about the money. Belle, dear roommate, there will be no Christmas for you this year. I'm unemployed."

Belle appeared in the doorway of her room, a man's plaid flannel bathrobe tightly cinched at the waist and felt slippers on her feet, a far cry from the usual oriental vogue she displayed.

"What do you mean 'no Christmas for you?'" she said. "You have my list."

"I know," Helen said, still in her drawn-out tone, "but you'll have to keep Tiny Tim in mind and bear the hard times bravely."

Lily was shaking her head. "You both are such teases."

Belle pulled the neck of her sorrowful robe closer and sent Lily a pouty look. "It's easy for you, Miss Rutie, you who forgets how I've sacrificed this semester every Tuesday and Thursday so that you and your tutor would have a place to be alone." She paused. "For tutoring, or so I'm told."

Lily glanced over at Helen to see her send a pursed-lip look at Belle, who in return simply smirked and shrugged her shoulders.

"Some gratitude, that's all I can say," Belle muttered and returned to her room, closing the door dramatically.

Lily sat quietly, and finally Helen reassured her. "We were indeed teasing you. But wasn't it worth it just to see Belle in her natural plumage?"

Lily chuckled. "She *was* a picture."

They sat at the table without speaking.

"So," Helen said, finally.

Lily nodded. "So."

"We don't have any reason to—" Helen said, opening her hands, hands that Lily had so often watched across the table under the drop light when she was explaining something. Pretty hands, with long artistic fingers, hands that Lily had wanted to touch for weeks.

"We could—" Lily blurted out, snapping out of her reverie without knowing what she meant to say, "I mean, we could sometimes take our exercise walks together. To keep—"

"To catch up," Helen offered.

"Exactly," Lily confirmed, nodding. "I wouldn't want to miss any high jinks that you and Belle have."

They fell silent again. At length, Lily felt that she should probably leave. She put her hand on her books.

"I have some reading—" she said, quietly.

"Oh, sure," Helen said quickly, rising from her seat.

Lily pulled on her boots and put on her coat. "So," she said, buttoning her coat, "do you think you'll be free for a tramp next Tuesday after Chapel?"

Helen smiled and this time, she smiled into Lily's eyes. "As it happens, I have nothing scheduled for that hour."

Lily held the tissue-paper package under her arm as she walked the familiar path from Main to Raymond Hall the night before the exodus for Christmas vacation. She had arranged to meet Helen in her room; the other had readily assented. Perhaps each suspected that the other had a gift. Lily was uncertain if her gift was good enough.

The feeling had been slowly creeping into her consciousness over the last week, after she had finished the knit cap. The wine-colored yarn had made a very pretty cap, but in the last week she fretted over whether to add crocheted strings to the ear flaps so the cap could be tied under the chin or conversely tied on top of the cap if the warmth of the little ear flaps was not needed. Unable to decide, she went into town to finish her shopping and found a pin in the shape of a half-moon inset with a tiny ruby when she was shopping for earrings for Eva. Helen had mentioned once that her name was Greek in origin, meaning *moonlight*. She bought it and pinned it on one side of the cap.

But then she revisited the strings idea again this week and ended up staying up after hours making them, fashioning little pom-poms on the ends. And that is the gift she wrapped in tissue paper and tied with a piece of satin ribbon obtained from Izzie's roommate.

She and Bert had already exchanged their gifts. Bert was very pleased with her Conklin's self-filling fountain pen. They laughed over the two shirtwaists and one skirt she had ruined thus far in the year with her old pen; she was also unable to read pages 74 through 88 in her Chem text because of an unexpected ink explosion. Lily wished her good luck with the new technology.

Bert had given Lily sheepskin booties for wearing in the room when she studied. It was the kind of gift that a family member would give, one who cares for your comfort. Lily put them on immediately and didn't take them off until she went to bed. They were exactly what was needed against the drafts that seemed continuous along the floor of their room.

Giving Helen her gift was nearly the last thing Lily had to do before leaving for home the next day, home that she hadn't seen since the 18th of September. The excitement of seeing her family nonetheless paled in comparison to seeing Helen tonight and giving her the small tissue package. She felt sure at this point that, if Helen didn't care for a homemade knit skating cap, she would nevertheless appreciate the thought behind it. Lily could do no more.

On the stairs she met Belle rushing down.

"Are you finished packing?" she demanded of Lily.

"Almost," Lily admitted.

"*Zut!*" Belle said in profane French, throwing up her hands and rushing past her.

Lily scratched at Helen's door and was called in. The room was in a state of extraordinary dishevelment; Helen was standing by their couch, hands on her hips, surveying a portion of the jumble of clothes. She twisted to greet Lily.

"Hello," she said, "be careful where you step. I'm afraid this is what 'I-can-wait-until-the-last-possible-moment-to-pack' looks like, doubled," she laughed ruefully. "How is your packing coming along?"

"I still have some left to do," Lily said diplomatically, given the scene before her. "I wish I had brought a second satchel."

"Yes, those are handy for shoes and boots and whatever won't fit into the suitcase," Helen said ruefully. "I wouldn't need to take much, unlike Miss Mirabelle here," she said, gesturing to the laden table and chairs and every other available surface, "because I don't have as many social obligations as she. She's taking a trunk home."

She cleared the couch of clothes and invited her guest to sit. Lily took off her coat and studied where to put it until Helen, laughing, took it from her.

They sat side by side on the couch and Lily presented Helen with her gift. Smiling, Helen held it on her lap for a moment and then put it down and went into her bedroom, returning with a package which she gave to Lily.

"Oh," Lily said, surprised, and relieved that she had been right to act on her desire to give Helen a Christmas gift. She looked at Helen. "You open yours first," she said.

"Alright," Helen said agreeably, "I like gifts, don't like the suspense!"

She pulled an end of the ribbon and the bow released. Unwrapping the paper gently, she saw the wool and the pin first and then lifted up the cap, its little pom-pom strings dangling.

"It's a skating cap," Lily offered helpfully. "You said there would be skating on the lake in January and February. I thought this might be warm. I tried to get the wool in Vassar rose—"

Helen cut her off. "Lily," she said warmly, "I love it." She paused, slipping her hands inside the cap and flaring it. "Even more because you made it."

"Really?" Lily said, taken a bit aback by Helen's voice. "The pin reminded me of moonlight, what you said your name meant in Greek."

Helen ran her finger over the pin, gleaming in the gas light. She nodded and then looked at Lily, smiling with a shyness that Lily had never seen.

"Open yours," Helen urged.

Lily tore open the paper and a long muffler with alternating rose and gray color blocks tumbled out. She laughed as she gathered it in.

"You said you forgot to pack a muffler," Helen said. "Now you have a true Vassar muffler and wherever you go, people will see the rose and gray and recognize a VC girl."

Helen picked up an end and looped it around Lily's neck. Lily laughed, and lifted the cap up to put it on Helen. The latter took it and pulled it on, leaving its strings untied.

They laughed happily. And then Helen reached into her pocket and pulled out a small jewelry case, placing it on the couch between them.

"This is so you will always remember this semester," Helen said quietly.

Lily looked at the box without touching it.

"Go on, open it," Helen said.

Lily pried open the hinged box. Inside was a small silver object on a silver chain. Pulling it from the box, she looked at it for a long moment and then looked at Helen, mouth open.

"It's a *lambda*, a lower-case *lambda*," she said with delighted surprise.

"Your initial," Helen replied, shrugging diffidently. "To remind you of our Greek sessions."

"But how did you ever find anything like this?" Lily said, amazed.

"As for that," Helen said easily, "we live in a college town. To fashion a Greek letter is ordinary work for our local jewelers."

Lily tried to unfasten the clasp to put the necklace on but her hands were trembling. She had to give it up and hold out the necklace to Helen for help. What was a casual task did not seem so casual to Lily when Helen leaned closely and held her arms around Lily's neck as she fastened the clasp. And it seemed to her that Helen felt something in that physical proximity, as well.

Helen sat back and looked at the necklace, avoiding Lily's eyes, which were on her. "That looks just as I hoped," Helen said quietly, trying to smile.

And then Lily did something that would later cause her to wonder how she could have done it. She took Helen's hands in her own and found her fingers immediately clasped in response. She and Helen sat very still, looking at their hands. Lily was trying to breathe; she had no idea if Helen was experiencing similar feelings.

"Write to me?" Helen said, almost a whisper.

"Yes," Lily said to the hands.

And then the door opened wide. It was Belle, blowing into the room with an armful of clothes and accessories. She stopped when she saw Lily and Helen and then tossed the articles onto a pile of clothes where they immediately became indistinguishable from the rest.

"What is this?" she said, breathlessly. "I am gone only minutes and—" she paused for dramatic effect, "presents have been unwrapped!"

She stepped closer to the couch. Lily and Helen had quickly pulled their hands back when the door opened, but that was all they had time to do. Belle laughed heartily.

"You are both dressed for a winter's trek, have you seen yourselves?"

Lily and Helen had to laugh as they took off their gifts. Belle demanded a narration of gifts given and received. When Lily held up her necklace, Belle squinted and frowned.

"What is that? A twig?" she said, turning to Helen.

"No, Belle, it's a wonderful thing," Lily said quickly. "It's a small case *lambda*, the Greek letter 'l'. It's my initial."

Belle gave Helen a long, baleful look. "I always suspected that, at the very bottom of your secretive heart, dear Helen, you were a grind," Belle said heavily. "And here is proof. Giving your tutee a silver reminder of her academic difficulties."

"But, Belle, I love it, " Lily said passionately. "I do."

Belle sent her a sympathetic look. "*Cheri*, we have known since you first entered this room that you are a grind, and you make no secret of it!"

"Pay no attention to the harried woman, Lily," Helen interjected. "She would be honored if she had a hand-crafted silver necklace."

Belle turned to the piles around the room that apparently were hers. "What I really would like," she said, her arm sweeping the disaster, "is a small army of elves to select which ensembles I need to take to New York and then to pack them!"

Lily took that as her cue to slip away. She put on her coat and Helen hastened to loop the new muffler around her neck. They looked at each other, the intensity of their earlier moment having receded, and smiled. Lily pocketed her little jewelry box and turned to Belle, now knee deep in skirts.

"*Joyeux Noel*, Mirabelle," she said fondly because she very much liked Belle and would have gifted her for Christmas if she had unlimited means.

Belle stopped, dropped the clothes on her arms and climbed through the tangle to put her arms around Lily. She squeezed the freshman tightly.

"*Joyeux Noel, cheri*," Belle said heartily, and kissed Lily on both cheeks after the French fashion. Everyone laughed.

"*Bonne Annee*, " Lily said, glancing at Helen who was grinning at her. "Happy ought-four!"

CHAPTER 11

Lily was ready early in the morning after breakfast. Main's hallways were a continuing cheerful chatter of, "Merry Christmas," "See you in ought-four!" "Be seeing you," "Have a good rest up for Mid-years" as the students lugged their suitcases to the building's single elevator or down the stairs. Everyone converged on the porte-cochere under the library, preparing for the chilly walk to the Gate Lodge and the electric trolleys. Lily gave her new Vassar muffler an extra loop and began her journey home to Buffalo.

After Albany, she was able to secure a window seat where she could lose herself in her thoughts of the night before. She slipped an ungloved hand to her throat and caressed the silver *lambda*. Helen had ordered it made especially for Lily. She still had trouble believing it because it was too wonderful. The miles sped by unmeasured; even the clickety-clack of the steel wheels on the jointed rails, the chill of the rail car, the conversation of other passengers all failed to penetrate the aura of pure joy that surrounded her.

Only when the train neared the factories at Depew, so close to her destination, did Lily force herself to come down from her cloud. Her mother's letter said that Will would be at the station to take her home. Although she looked forward to seeing her ever-cheerful brother, she began to feel a wariness about seeing her mother, and even Eva. She felt a need she couldn't have explained to protect her happiness by putting on a mask. She hoped it was a convincing one because the two people who knew her best could usually read her face like an open book. The last thing she did was to tuck the necklace under her collar.

Suddenly the car became dark and Lily knew they had entered the cavernous, covered Exchange Street station. And then all was commotion as people gathered their luggage, packages, children and made their way out, spilling onto the platform like a swarm of bees from a hive. Once free from the crush, Lily looked about for her brother. The interior of the station area was a veritable hydra-head of numerous trains on adjacent tracks, and the roof, platform and walls were as uniformly soot black as if they had been painted that lifeless hue. Despite the bustle of people shouting to one another, the periodic sharp discharge of steam from engines and the whistle of conductors, Lily thought the place gloomy. Train stations were a place of separation, of good-byes, as well as hellos.

And then there was her brother, waving his derby and striding quickly along the platform.

"I swear, you were almost in the last car," he said, catching his breath, but grinning. "This was a long train!"

Lily smiled and held out her suitcase for him to take.

"Hello, brother!" she said happily. "I'm so glad Vassar let us out today. Imagine if I had to come home next week."

They didn't hug in greeting. Their family didn't engage in such displays of affection, and neither did their fellow German-American friends. Good words and good deeds were the measure of affection that counted. How different it was from the effusive affections exchanged at college among her classmates at sports events and over hot chocolate in their rooms.

Will had her wait in the station lobby while he fetched the horse and buggy from a spot on the curb that he suggested was so far away as to be halfway to their home. Theirs was a slow ride through the congested city traffic.

"People won't stop moving to Buffalo," Will said cheerfully in their stop-and-go journey. "Even the trolleys are jammed these days."

"How are things at home?" Lily asked.

"Oh, fine," Will replied. "I think Mama is looking forward to seeing you."

"That's good, because I did omit writing one week at Thanksgiving, and she took me to task for that."

Will just laughed. "You know that she wants things to go along just so. You're too far away for her to know everything that goes on. Besides, she has my future to worry about!"

Lily laughed. "Is she still hunting up a good wife for you?"

Her brother shook his head and groaned. "She found three this fall, inviting one after the other to Sunday dinner. Oh, Lily, please don't take offense, but after meeting these, I can't say that women are the *fairer* sex anymore!"

She gave him a hard nudge that made him giggle. "They probably came from solidly prosperous families," she asserted.

He nodded. "Yes, they did. Good German girls."

"Girls like these don't come along every day," she added in an authoritative tone.

He nodded, tickled. "And I am so grateful for that!"

"So, do you have a girlfriend?" she challenged him.

"Well," he fudged. "There's a girl in the store, in the office, that I talk with every day."

Lily looked at him and thought he was almost blushing.

"I can tell you like her," Lily said helpfully, "but have you asked her for a date?"

He shrugged. "I'm trying to think of how to proceed. See, she's Irish Catholic."

Lily groaned and he quickly added, "But she's as nice as anything and so pretty. You'd like her right away, Lil."

"I probably would, but you are playing with fire. Does Papa know?"

He raised an eyebrow. "Papa knows everything that goes on in both his stores, believe me. But he hasn't said anything to me."

"You should talk to him," she said encouragingly. "You know he's more open-minded than Mama."

Will nodded. "I figure I'll take my time. Maybe she'll give me the cold shoulder one day soon, who knows?"

They had to stop again, this time to let a trolley cross at Seneca Street.

"So, have you met anyone prosperous and eligible?" he said, half-jokingly.

The wagon resumed its journey. Lily looked at the shops slowly passing by.

"Lots of prosperous, eligible people," she said lightly. "They all just happen to be girls!"

Will laughed loudly.

"Maybe you should come to Vassar and meet some of them, brother," she added. "You might forget your 'Wild Irish Rose.'"

"Mae," he said, clucking to the horse to set it in motion. "Her name is Mae."

Lily heard the serious tone and understood more about his feelings for the girl.

"So," she said, changing the topic, "Mama's been too busy with you to worry about me forgetting my family."

"Sure," he replied dismissively. "And if she started worrying, Papa would eventually end the subject by reassuring her that you are 'a good girl,'" he added in their father's slightly accented voice.

Lily chuckled.

"You know that Papa thinks you're solid gold, like that statue of Maud Adams," he kidded her.

She did know, and knew that her father's suasion had won Vassar for her. Knowing what she knew now, barely three months into her college career, Lily could not imagine how to repay his faith in her.

Eventually, Will pulled the buggy to a stop in front of the Kepler house. Lily took in the sight of home while Will pulled out her suitcase and came around to help her out. It looked just the same as when she left except that snow covered the front lawn and a fresh evergreen wreath with a red bow hung on the front door. It felt like home, but not quite home, a feeling she could only recognize but not explain.

Will brought her suitcase into the front hall and then took his leave. He was returning to work and would be home for a late supper because these were holiday shopping days for the store. All those new residents needed furniture and the less-new residents wanted to replace their old furnishings with new, better quality things to reflect their success.

The house smelled wonderful, of braising and baking. The kitchen's swinging door opened and Lily's mother hurried down the hall toward her, wiping her hands on her apron.

She hugged her daughter tightly in greeting, surprising Lily, who hugged her back.

"You look thin, dear," Mama declared, holding Lily at arm's length to inspect her up and down.

"I'm not any thinner than when I left," Lily protested, unwinding her muffler. "And I should be putting on weight with all the fudge and hot chocolate I consume!"

"What is this?" Mama took the scarf Lily had taken off, holding it up dubiously.

"It's a muffler in Vassar colors, rose and silver gray," Lily said. "It's wondrously warm."

Her mother hung the scarf over a peg on the hall mirror. Then she looked at Lily's feet.

"Oh, what are those awful things?" she moaned.

Lily pulled up her skirt hem. "Golf boots. Everyone wears them on campus because we have to be outdoors so much of the day. They're awfully comfortable and keep my feet pretty dry."

Mama frowned. "They look like something factory girls would wear."

Lily sat down and unbuttoned them. "Factory girls couldn't afford them, Mama."

Her mother clasped her hands, as if to restrain her criticism.

"Are you hungry?" she asked. "I kept the pot roast from dinner warm because I was sure you hadn't eaten."

Lily stood up. "I am most hungry, Mama, especially for your pot roast. All I had on the trip was a roll I saved from breakfast."

Her mother was very happy and led her daughter into the kitchen.

"Sit down," she ordered, and Lily was happy to obey.

She could see that her mother and Trude, the family's part-time cook, had been baking stollens and kuchens and anise-flavored springerle cookies. The kitchen was redolent with the sweet smell of yeast dough, cinnamon, anise; finished baked goods lined the sideboard. Lily's mouth watered in anticipation. Nothing her classmates could conjure up for a spread compared to these gustatory pleasures.

Mama placed a bowl of pot roast before Lily and two baking powder biscuits. Lily ate it hungrily, then had tea and a few of the cookies for dessert. And then she realized that she had been traveling for over six hours, not counting the trip to and from train stations. All she wanted to do was sleep.

Fortunately, her mother had anticipated that and ordered her to her room for a nap. She said that the house would be quiet soon because Trude would be leaving and she had to go out for a while. Lily carried her suitcase up to her room and, when she saw her bed, dropped the case and decided to unpack later. Her mother had laid out a fresh flannel nightgown and Lily changed into it. The bed was unfamiliar for a few minutes. Her body was finally lulled into sleep by its memory of the gentle rocking of the train and the hypnotic clickety-clack of the rails.

At some point, she thought she heard the sound of a telephone ringing and ringing and no one answering it. It occurred to her that perhaps it was Eva phoning to see if she was home yet, but she had no strength to wake up and go downstairs to answer it.

Her room was dark when she opened her eyes later, and Lily realized that it was evening. She heard voices downstairs, men's voices, and roused herself to get dressed. It would be supper time and her father would be home. *Everybody's home now*, she said to herself, and smiled.

THE next morning Eva arrived at exactly the time she promised. She threw her arms around Lily even before the latter had finished closing the door.

"Oh, Lily," Eva gushed, "I'm so glad to see you at last!"

Lily hugged her back. "And I you, dear," she said, meaning it.

Eva took off her things and they passed into the family parlor in the rear of the house. Lily's mother was there at her desk, taking care of correspondence as was her morning habit. She greeted Eva warmly which prompted Eva to go directly to her and give her a hug. Lily watched in some amazement.

"Why, Eva," Mama said, "it's been months since we've seen you. You look so lovely—is that a new dress?"

Eva demurred, and Lily's eyes grew large. "It is, Mama Kepler," she said, pleased, "and Lily didn't even notice."

Lily sat on the settee and Eva sat beside her.

"You mustn't mind Lily, dear," Mama said. "Apparently college girls don't care much for fashion."

Eva looked at Lily and smiled, her eyes twinkling. Just then, Trude came in with a large tray which she put on the table used for playing cards and doing puzzles. On the tray was a large pot of tea and a plate of kuchen.

Lily went to the table, glad for a change of topic. "I'll be mother," she said with forced cheerfulness. "Tea, Eva?"

They enjoyed the fresh-baked kuchen, a coffee-cake with cinnamon and brown sugar sprinkled on top of the sweet dough. Eva, never at a loss for words, chattered away, filling up the space between Lily and her mother.

"I never have kuchen except here and I love it so," she was saying. "Is this your own recipe?"

Mama smiled and nodded. "And I made it myself this morning, while Lily was still sleeping the day away."

Eva turned to Lily. "You had such a long journey yesterday," she said sympathetically.

Lily smiled and remembered that Eva had ever been on her side. She merely nodded in reply but she was grateful.

"How are your studies going at Bryant and Stratton?" Mama was asking.

"Well," Eva began, eyeing the plate of kuchen out of reach on the table. "I wasn't very happy there, so I quit everything except bookkeeping."

Lily shook her head. "And this is the girl who can't stand math."

Eva raised her eyebrows slightly. "The class turned out to be quite educational," she added coolly, not looking at Lily.

"Well, you gave it a try," Mama said encouragingly. "Most girls are not cut out for great amounts of study after the basics."

Eva smiled sweetly. "I'm letting Lily take care of that for both of us!" She leaned toward Lily. "Are we passing everything?"

Lily laughed. "Yes, we are."

Mama changed the subject. "I understand you have a beau. Tell me what he's like, won't you?"

It was a subject on which Eva had a great deal ready to say. "The first thing you notice about Frank Marshall is his good looks. And then you notice his wonderful sense of fun. Wherever he is, people enjoy themselves. It's a talent he has."

Mama was nodding, following Eva's commentary but obviously withholding approving sounds until she heard something meaningful.

"I should mention that he has a good job at the Buffalo Savings Bank," Eva went on quickly. "His family is from Connecticut; they are related to the Sydney Shepards. I'm sure you know them."

"Oh, yes," Mama replied. She was beginning to approve. The Shepards had a profitable factory in tinware and were invited everywhere in fashionable Buffalo.

"Well, Mr. Shepard secured a position for him at the bank."

"What kind of position?" Mama asked.

Lily interjected. "He's a teller, Mama."

"But," Eva hastened to add, "he said he's expecting to get a promotion in the next couple of months. And then he'll be on his way."

Mama frowned slightly. "What made him leave Connecticut to come to Buffalo to be a bank teller?"

"He is the youngest of three brothers," Eva explained. "There were no prospects for him in the family business after he graduated from Brown University. So, he came here and you know that opportunities abound in our city for clever, industrious men willing to make their own way."

Mama nodded, more firmly. "Yes, indeed." And then she added, "Are you two very serious?"

Lily looked over to see Eva actually blush.

"Well," Eva replied breathlessly, "I believe we are."

Mama sat back in her chair. "I think that's wonderful, dear. Truly wonderful," she repeated, her approval now complete. "Lily, pour me more tea. And pass Eva the kuchen. She's been longing for another piece."

Lily did as she was told, feeling much like a spectator at an unfamiliar sport. Her mother, who had hardened her heart against Eva all the last year of high school, was now embracing her as a daughter. And a daughter who had fulfilled a mother's hopes, at that.

"So do you think you'll take a bookkeeping position after your classes are finished?" Mama asked.

Eva looked at her hands. "I hope I won't have to. If I were to marry, that would be impossible, and unnecessary, of course."

Lily sat up. "But it is important to have a skill in case something should happen to one's husband."

"But, dear, if one marries well," Mama said, enunciating each word carefully, "there would be sufficient income to care for the widow in such an unfortunate circumstance."

"Not always," Lily said stubbornly. "Remember how hard things were in the 90's when people didn't have jobs and Papa couldn't sell much furniture."

Her mother looked at her. "You're not making any sense, Lily. There were no jobs for *anyone,* men or women."

"Women can always find work," Lily said evenly, "especially if they are educated."

Eva stepped into the conversation. "Lily has a point, you know," she said gently. "You have seen many women who have been left destitute due to circumstances and without any skills to help themselves."

Mama seemed mollified. "That's true, Eva. But my generation never thought of supporting themselves. Perhaps we were foolish like that. And there were no colleges for women. You used your wits to do the best you could by marrying a smart man."

"And you succeeded, Mama, with Papa," Lily said.

Mama smiled with some pride. "I did, didn't I?" She looked at Eva, benignly. "And now you may be on your way to marrying well, too."

Eva smiled sweetly. "I can't say. But my Frank has a bright future ahead of him at the bank. All the higher-ups like him, he says."

Mama folded her hands on her desk and sighed, looking at Lily. "But what are we going to do about you, Lily?"

Lily stiffened a little. "I don't think we need to do anything about me, Mama. I'm completely happy at college, learning a great deal."

"With no one but girls to socialize with."

"Oh, but the girls have brothers, don't they Lily?" Eva said quickly. "She's already met two Yale boys."

Mama looked surprised. "Is that so? You didn't mention it in your letters."

Lily tried to sound offhand about it. "It was at Glens Falls. Helen's brother Harry came home for Thanksgiving and the next day his friend Tom came up from Albany. We had a lot of fun."

"Well." Mama was silent, sipping her tea, and Lily wondered if she was recalling the letters Lily had failed to write around that time and which might have contained some of these details. "I don't understand young people of today," she said, almost to herself. "Wanting things, feeling free to travel unchaperoned, studying ancient Greek. Who speaks it? I ask myself."

The hall clock struck eleven. Mrs. Kepler looked at the watch pinned to her bosom and started.

"I need to get these letters in the mail and so I am shooing you both away. Take kuchen if you want," she called after them as they left her at her desk.

Once inside Lily's bedroom, Eva closed the door, and leaned against it, looking at Lily with a sly, expectant look.

"When did you and my mother become friends?" Lily whispered loudly.

Eva giggled. "I'm as surprised as you! Isn't it too wonderful?"

And then Eva crossed the room and stood before Lily. Still smiling, she reached for Lily and pulled her into a kiss. Lily was prepared this time and kissed her back. She had thought often about kissing since Thanksgiving. She had decided that she liked kissing and wanted to do more of it. The kiss went on and on, Eva kissing with her head tilted to one side and then changing her head to the other side. Lily followed everything and reciprocated. When they finally stopped, both were breathless.

"Wow," Lily whispered finally.

Eva smiled raggedly, running her hands across Lily's shoulders and down her arms, taking Lily's hands in her own. "You have no idea," she said, breathing hard. "There are much bigger *wow's* than this."

Lily shook her head. "What does that mean?"

Eva looked at the ceiling and then back at Lily. "It means that I have so much to show you. And I can't wait for you to come over to my house."

She looked at Lily's baffled expression and smiled slyly. Putting a hand on Lily's cheek, she said, tenderly, "It's lovemaking, Lily. And there's no one in the world that I want to share it with than you."

After Eva left, having arranged to meet at Eva's on Tuesday afternoon, three days away, Lily lay on her bed wondering what else besides kissing there was to lovemaking. And she thought about Helen, about kissing Helen just the way she and Eva had kissed. The thought roused butterflies in her stomach and she shivered in the imagining of it.

ON Sunday, after church and their standard Sunday roast chicken dinner, all of the Keplers gathered in the front parlor to decorate their Christmas tree. This was a family tradition and one that Mama Kepler cared deeply about. Alfred and his wife, Gertrude, came to Sunday dinner on this day expressly for the decorating ritual. If Gertrude who, like her husband, would never be called by a nickname, had any notions of one day establishing traditions in her own household, she did not hint of them. When children came, there would be changes, surely, but for now all family traditions rested with Alfred's parents.

Alfred, with his factory in the country, had been assigned the task of procuring a suitable evergreen and, as always, completed his mission promptly and with good taste. The tree was nearly as tall as the high ceiling in the parlor and the men fussed over cutting the trunk and nailing it to the wooden stand. Then Mama tilted her head and crossed her arms, judging its angle and looking for its best side.

At last, the tree was committed to a final pose and everyone sat down and rested for a minute, it being, as Papa drolly noted, the official day of rest. Lily had opened the ornaments box and was poking into it, pulling out glass and tin ornaments, looking for the favorites of her childhood.

"Well," Mama said, standing purposefully, "let's decorate, everyone. Lily, find the garland. That goes first."

Lily felt around the packing paper until she felt the long tangle of glass beads. She pulled a handful out and loaded up Gertrude's lap until she had retrieved it all.

"For you, sister!" she laughed.

Alfred helped his wife untangle the gold-beaded garland and they both wound it around the tree. Mama Kepler had nothing but praise for their artistry, as was consistent with her mood. As she used to point out when her children were small and given to bickering, it was Christmas and a time to be of good cheer and to get along.

Papa had lit a pipe and was sitting in an armchair watching his family all around him. Lily smiled to see him content. She herself was full of love this day, not the least of which was love for her family, so much more appreciated now because she had been away for three months. There was another love on her mind as well, and she basked in its glow. It was as close as the necklace she wore under her shirtwaist.

She began to feel sentimental as ornaments from her childhood passed through her hands from the box to Gertrude, Mama, Will and Alfred. Being away had given her a new perspective on the passing of the years of her life, and the past now seemed to her almost irretrievably distant, and separate from her life now.

"Do you remember," Lily said, "when we were little we didn't have these kind of garlands or even nice glass ornaments? We used to string popcorn for garlands."

Mama nodded. "Oh, yes, we didn't have a lot of money in those days, only three little children who always needed shoes."

"When we decorated back then, I always associated the smell of popcorn with Christmas," Lily said wistfully.

"Why don't we make popcorn?" Will said. "We don't have to string it, just eat it!"

And so, he and Lily made popcorn and everyone enjoyed it. When Lily went to sleep that night, the house smelled of Christmas.

CHAPTER 12

Lily approached the Bond townhouse on Franklin Street along a slate walk that had been recently swept clean of snow. Aunt Martha herself opened the door when Lily rang. She was pulling on her coat, preparing to leave the house. She was not naturally an effusive person and her unadorned face gave her a pensive, even aloof impression. But when she smiled happily, as she did now at seeing Lily, Aunt Martha was a good-looking woman.

"Oh, my dear Lily," she said, giving Lily a quick hug, for she was a reserved woman. "I'm so glad to be here yet to see you!"

Lily agreed that she was glad as well. Aunt Martha put on her hat and was adjusting it in the hall mirror when Eva appeared at the top of the stairs. She called a greeting and came down, wearing a flannel kimono-style robe with a floral pattern of pale pink flowers on a blue background.

"Eva, you can't come downstairs in your robe," Aunt Martha admonished Eva, but not very sternly. Eva had never been admonished very sternly by either of her guardians. "What if someone should come to the door right now?"

"I'd hide behind Lily!" she said gaily, her dark eyes sparkling at her friend.

"What a pretty kimono," Lily said, admiringly. It was a perfect complement to Eva's dark hair. "Is it new?"

Eva lifted the wide arms to show them off. "New to you, Miss Kepler. I've had it for ages."

Aunt Martha was pulling on her gloves and rolled her eyes. "She bought it last week," she said to Lily, "in honor of your return for the holidays."

Eva pursed her lips and put her hands on her hips. "I bought it because I needed something warm for the winter," she protested.

But Aunt Martha had already opened the door to leave. "All right dear," she called. "I'll be back around four. Good-bye, Lily. You must come to dinner while you're home and tell us all about college."

Lily said she would and Aunt Martha was gone, leaving behind a cold gust of wind in the hall. Lily looked at Eva, smiling. They were going to exchange Christmas gifts today.

"She has to tell everything," Eva muttered. "Well, for goodness' sake, take off your things!"

Lily removed her hat and coat and gloves and sat down to remove her boots. The Bond's maid appeared and took Lily's things.

Eva turned to lead Lily upstairs to her room and suddenly paused, turning back. "Virgie, if anyone calls, I am not at home," she called to the woman.

"Yes, ma'am," Virgie replied, hanging up Lily's coat and draping her Vassar muffler around it. "Will you be wanting tea?" she added, in a weary tone that suggested she hoped it would not be wanted.

"No, Virgie," Eva said, already on her way up the stairs.

After Lily had passed into Eva's room, Eva closed the door and turned the key in the lock.

"Do you really like my kimono?" she asked, coyly.

Lily nodded. "I do indeed. And you look warm as well as lovely."

Eva tried to look modest and abashed, but she was never very good at it. Lily looked around the room that was as familiar to her as her own. It looked the same as it had that day in September when they said good-bye. She watched Eva cross the room to her desk. On it was a pile of small envelopes and cards.

"I haven't finished the invitations to my party yet," she said, gesturing to the pile. "I'm having all our old crowd, so they can meet Frank and vice versa." She looked at the desktop and raised a finger. "And Uncle Walter asked if I would invite Roger Hudson, someone he lunches with often at his club. I think he wants to introduce Mr. Hudson to a crowd closer to his age in hopes of putting him into circulation or some such thing. I don't know what he hopes, honestly!" she laughed and threw up her hands.

Lily laughed and allowed herself to be led to the couch near the big bay window. She brought out her small box.

Eva immediately held out the box in her lap, and Lily proffered hers. They exchanged boxes.

"You go first," Lily said.

Eva made no objection at all but pulled the ribbon from her box. She lifted the top and gasped. Inside, on a bed of cotton batting, was a pair of pearl earrings. Each consisted of two pink pearls, a smaller one atop a slightly larger pearl, with a rhinestone band between them like a belt. They looked like miniature pink snowmen and were designed to swing freely on their screw back findings, which were also accented by a rhinestone. Lily had known as soon as she saw them how well they would look next to Eva's dark hair. And she knew Eva would love them.

Eva was also greatly touched. Things like this meant a great deal to her and Lily was not surprised to see Eva's eyes grow moist.

"You should put them on," she suggested gently.

Eva replied by throwing her arms around Lily. "Thank you, darling," she said in a tight voice. "You knew just what I wanted. You always do."

Then she sat back and blotted her eyes with her kimono sleeve. "Now, you open yours," she ordered.

Lily opened the small box to see a silver heart on a silver chain, the second necklace she had been gifted this Christmas. She lifted the necklace and could see engraving. Holding it to the light, she read, "Lily." She smiled at Eva and was readying her thanks when Eva spoke.

"Turn it over," she said.

Lily did so and saw engraving on the other side, also. It read, "Eva." Now her heart sank at Eva's likely meaning. She stared at the heart to avoid meeting Eva's gaze as she tried to think of what to say.

Finally, she swallowed. "This is a beautiful gift, Eva. Thank you." She tried to smile.

Eva apparently didn't suspect that Lily might feel anything other than simply being overcome by joy at receiving her gift. "I want you to wear it and know that it carries my heart," Eva was saying. But she was also working on Lily's collar.

"What are you doing?" Lily asked, mildly.

"I'm taking off your darned collar," Eva said, squinting to find the button on the back of Lily's shirtwaist. "I want to put your necklace on and see how it looks."

She tossed the collar aside and began to unbutton Lily's shirtwaist. Lily sat patiently, glad she had the presence of mind to remove Helen's necklace when she dressed today. Eva leaned close to fasten the clasp of the necklace. The heart rested in the hollow of Lily's neck. Eva bent and kissed the heart, and then kissed Lily's bare neck gently, slowly. Lily could feel the softness of Eva's lips and the warmth of her breath.

When Eva looked up at her, Lily could see a vulnerability in her friend's eyes that she had never experienced. She knew at that moment that she could break Eva's heart with a word. And she knew that she lacked the courage to do it.

Eva was looking at her. "What are you thinking?"

Lily tried a smile. "How much I like my gift," she said. "How pretty you are."

Eva took a deep breath and squeezed Lily's hands. Then she stood and pulled Lily after her, leading them to her bed, the bed where they had spent countless rainy afternoons reading or making up stories or imagining what their lives would be like and who they would marry when they grew up. It was the full-size bed that Eva had received for her twelfth birthday as part of a suite of furniture she was allowed to select for her large bedroom. Lily had spent many nights beside Eva in this bed, children innocent of carnal desire. Now they lay down beside one another again. As she had done often in recent years, Lily pulled one of the throw pillows under her head as she lay on her side facing Eva.

Eva was lying on her back but looking into Lily's eyes. Her lips seemed to tremble as if she were going to cry, but she reached over and pulled Lily into a kiss that was at once passionate and unyielding. Lily felt the intensity of it and was swept along as if by a current as wide and strong as the Niagara River's. She couldn't stop kissing Eva and may not have been permitted to had she wanted to stop. This was new, this urgency, and she felt her heart thumping as she pulled Eva closer.

Eva was the one to break their kiss. Both were breathing hard, Eva's chest heaving as she lay back gazing at Lily with soft, almost unfocused eyes. Lily was on one elbow, breathing open-mouthed, searching Eva's face for some understanding of the moment. Her body seemed to be vibrating like a tuning fork from the inside out. Then Eva smiled and stroked Lily's cheek lightly.

"Isn't this wonderful?" Eva murmured.

"What is?" Lily asked helplessly.

Eva ran her hand along Lily's neck and under the unbuttoned top of her shirt-waist. Her hands felt warm and possessive on Lily's skin.

"It's lovemaking," Eva whispered, pulling open her kimono to reveal a silk dressing gown. Her breasts lay full and naturally without the artificial constrictions of a corset. Then she ran her hand along Lily's arm, following it with her eyes.

"I have worried that you had become enamored of someone at Vassar. That you had a sweetheart you made love with. And I've wanted to make love to you for so long, Lily."

"Evie," Lily said, drawing out the word as she did whenever she used the nickname. "We're both changing now that we're out of school. You have Frank—" but Eva put her fingers on Lily's lips.

"Shhh," she replied and pulled Lily into a kiss again.

And when the tuning fork inside of Lily began to hum again, she felt Eva gently but firmly cover Lily's hand and move it from Eva's shoulder to her breast, where she squeezed the hand by way of instruction. Lily had never felt another's breast and was amazed at the elastic softness of it, and the visceral way Eva reacted when Lily gave it a gentle squeeze. Then Eva moved Lily's hand to cover the hard nob and showed her how to pinch it. Eva had stopped kissing Lily and lay back biting her lip with her eyes closed, turning her head this way and that. Lily watched her fascinated and realized that she, too, was trembling and breathing hard.

Then Eva looked into Lily's eyes with something like fierceness and roughly pulled Lily by the neck into a brief kiss. Eva broke off the kiss and pulled Lily's head to her breast, hissing, "Kiss hard." Lily felt Eva push the hard nob into her mouth and she kissed the breast again and again until the silk covering it was damp from her kissing.

Eva pulled Lily's hand along her body and pushed it between her legs, then she closed her silk-covered thighs tight around the hand, saying, "Oh," in a sound halfway between a sigh and a groan. Her body began to stiffen as she rocked her hips up and down, slowly at first and then in short, rapid motions. And then suddenly, her body convulsed.

Lily moved back in some alarm as Eva's body arched, small whimpering sounds escaping from her lips. Lily didn't know what to do so she simply witnessed her childhood friend writhe until Eva lay more quietly, trembling intermittently.

Lily put a hand on Eva's shoulder. "Are you all right?" she asked, feeling somewhat foolish.

Eva tried to chuckle, but another tremor passed through her body. She could only smile raggedly. "Yes," she gasped. "Indeed I am, my darling."

When her body was still, Eva gazed up at Lily, still on one elbow beside her. "You don't know what that was, do you?" she asked, voice lazy with satiety.

Lily shook her head. She felt like a freshman, as if she were back at Vassar and it was the first week of school.

"Ecstasy, Lily," Eva said. "When you feel passion and it builds and builds, there's a point where you can't bear it anymore, and then you reach your ecstasy."

Lily didn't say anything, taking in this new information.

Eva reached into Lily's shirtwaist and hooked a finger over the top of Lily's corset.

"I will show you how to find yours if you'll take off this blasted corset," she said slyly. "You know how I've always hated those cages."

Lily smiled a little. "You've hated corsets since the first one Aunt Martha bought you, which you hid behind your dresser."

Eva gave Lily's corset a little tug. "Let me make love to you," she breathed.

But Lily did not want that intimacy with Eva and changed the subject. "Where did you learn about lovemaking? And passion and ecstasy?" she asked frankly.

"Why do you ask?" Eva tried to affect a small pout.

"Because for ten years we've always known everything together and I don't know anything about this. Something happened this autumn, didn't it?" she asked, but it wasn't a question.

"It was nothing, Lily," Eva said firmly. "It has no bearing on my love for you."

"Frank?" Lily was at sea about what constituted *nothing*.

"Lily!" she said, shocked. "Frank Marshall wouldn't try to lay a hand on me. And I wouldn't permit it, if he did. I'm hurt that you would think such impropriety."

Lily was unperturbed at the rebuke. She simply waited, holding Eva's eyes with hers.

Eva sighed, resigned to telling. "You know I didn't quit bookkeeping."

Lily nodded.

"Well, there was a girl in my class," she said, then added hastily, "a very common sort. But I would catch her looking at me every now and then, and eventually she found some excuse to speak to me about some assignment or the boring teacher. I finally realized that she was flirting with me."

She looked at Lily, who was still waiting, and she sighed again. "You know I was so bored with school, and I hadn't met Frank yet. So, we spent some time together after class."

"And then you kissed her," Lily offered, recalling the kiss Eva had extracted from her when she left for college.

"No," Eva denied in a pouty tone. "She kissed *me* in the coatroom one day. And then she told me about things that girls can do to pass time together."

She looked at Lily, who hadn't moved.

"Oh, stop looking at me like that!" she said in a wounded tone. "We're grown up now, Lily. We have passions, longings. I was so lonely."

She paused. "Janie did me a favor. She taught me how to show my love, how to—" she shrugged a little, "relieve the longing."

"We weren't sweethearts, Lily. Not even friends. I wasn't untrue to you," she said defensively, and was finished.

They were silent. Lily was thinking about Helen and what constituted being untrue.

Eva tugged at Lily's sleeve. "Please say something," she said softly. "What are you thinking?"

Lily smiled ruefully and slowly shook her head. "I'm thinking that at college we don't learn anything *useful* at all!"

They both lay on the bed and laughed themselves silly.

WHEN Lily got home later, the afternoon mail had brought her first letter from Helen. She stared at it in the tray on the hall table, breathless. And then she hurried upstairs with it and sat on her window seat for some time, gazing out into the darkness, wondering if she was being disloyal. And, if so, to whom?

CHAPTER 13

Christmas Eve was cold, the kind of cold that makes the hairs inside one's nose tingle with frost. The cold encouraged the Keplers to crunch along the sidewalk to St. Peter's Evangelical church on Genesee Street with more purpose this night than getting to services on time. Lily looked up as they neared the edifice, impressed as she always was to see the soaring steeple faintly illuminated by the city lights. St. Peter's had the tallest steeple of any church on the East Side of the city, nearly two hundred feet tall, the tapered portion above the illuminated clock stretching to the slenderness of a needle or so it seemed from the street. The St. Peter's congregation was very proud of that steeple and Lily's mother was proud of their membership in the congregation. She and Lily's father had been married in that church and Lily and her brothers had been baptized and confirmed in it.

When Papa and Mama Kepler, Will and Lily entered the pointed Gothic doorway, they instantly passed from a cold night with all its potential for isolation and danger into a hive of warmth and community. The electric lights cast a golden warmth around the crowd slowly being digested by the vestibule. People greeted each other with quiet heartiness but with genuine good cheer. This was a good night to be Christian, the eve of the most joyous holiday of the faith, the birth of the man who came to save the world by saving its souls.

Lily felt enveloped by familiarity, with all the *familial* feeling that word implied. Everywhere around her were people she had known all of her life, and tonight she felt as if she had put on an old pair of shoes, discovered in the back of her closet, and remembered how comfortable they felt. Chapel at Vassar could not compete with this feeling, with its ecumenical style and sermons aimed at improving young women's minds and spirits. Around her were stolid German-Americans, some of them third-generation whose families went back to the 1830's in Buffalo. The men with their big bellies and mustaches like boar's bristles, the women with their long, pointed noses and extra chins, the children with their stocky arms and rosy cheeks, all were her people. The large Jacob Dold family was making its way down the aisle to their pews. Tomorrow, Lily and her family would have a Dold ham for their Christmas dinner. The cheesemaking Hasselbecks were already in their pew. Lily recognized Julius Binz and Jacob Scheu, brewers, greeting people. The Kurtzmanns, owners of the piano factory, smiled and nodded at the Keplers as they passed by. Bakers, furniture makers, foundry owners, men who made radiators, umbrellas, baby carriages, all filled the 700-seat church this evening. They were hard workers, prosperous, glad to be German and American, deferring to no other group.

The Keplers took their accustomed seats and loosened their coats. They didn't remove them because the cavernous church was almost impossible to heat. Mama Kepler would not have wanted to remove her coat in any case, with its fur-trimmed neck and cuffs. She was not the only matron with expensive outerwear purchased for churchgoing. Lily glanced at her mother, who looked over at her and smiled happily, as if to say, "Everyone should see my fine children here with me."

The organist played out of sight above and behind the congregation in the balcony. It stopped as Reverend Mueller emerged from a door behind the pulpit and stepped up into it. He was a youngish man as ministers went, having been called six years ago when the venerable Reverend Hassauer finally stepped down and then expired within the year, possibly from a sudden lack of purpose. Reverend Mueller had a round face, his stiff hair parted severely, as if he had struggled mightily with it and prevailed only with the aid of a firm comb and a little pomade. He had the requisite mustache but kept it trimmed so as to avoid having his flock watch it bob up and down as he preached, or so Lily presumed.

Spreading his arms wide in a pastoral embrace, looking unwittingly like a dark angel in his gown and wide sleeves, Reverend Mueller intoned the greeting for the Christmas Eve service.

"The angel of the Lord came upon them, and the glory of the Lord shone round about them... And the angel said unto them, Fear not: for, behold, I bring you good tidings of great joy, which shall be to all people."

All of the Christmas story as Luke told it was inscribed inside her mind from her earliest days. She fell into her habit of following along with the service and then letting her mind wander, returning when it was time for the next hymn. Reverend Mueller had no surprises in his selection of hymns tonight. His first was *Stille Nacht* sung in German because it was a crowd pleaser. Everyone, regardless of age or ability to speak German, could sing "Silent Night" in its original language.

As the service wore on and the sanctuary grew warmer, Lily opened her coat and relaxed. She touched her breast near her neck, feeling the small shape of Helen's necklace under her shirtwaist. She wondered if Helen was at Christmas Eve service at the Presbyterian church in Glens Falls right now, sitting beside her parents and Harry. Could Helen be thinking of her? The thought made her sigh, which made her mother glance over at her. Lily tried to look reverent.

But she was thinking about what she had written in response to Helen's letter, about how she would manage to accomplish her goal if Helen was willing. After returning from her afternoon at Eva's and finding Helen's letter, Lily had waited until the next day to reply. She needed to digest the events at Eva's and when she awoke the next morning realized clearly what she wanted to do. She wrote to Helen, asking if she would be able to return to Vassar Sunday evening instead of Monday when everyone else would be returning. The reason she gave was that she had something she wanted to show Helen. She couldn't find any appropriate words to explain what she had in mind, although she knew exactly what that was. At the end of the letter she wrote, tersely, "I miss you," as part of her closing. Her hand tingled as she wrote it and her heart skipped a beat. She stared at the telling phrase for a while, wondering if she should write a new copy without it, and then folded the letter and sealed it.

Reverend Mueller was calling the congregation to sing, "It Came Upon a Midnight Clear," the carol that always brought out the worst in the reedy sopranos in the congregation as they yearned for the high note at the start of each verse. She thought the sound was so like that of a bagpipe inflating that she invariably smiled when it was sung. She smiled this night, as well, and her mother smiled in response.

If Helen was agreeable to returning to Vassar a day early, Lily knew her challenge would be to convince her parents of the necessity of her leaving on Sunday. She would need a premise that would be accepted, something to do with her studies. Lily would work on that.

Tonight, she gazed at the candles burning on the altar but in her mind's eye she was seeing Helen's face that night when they exchanged gifts. They were clasping hands tightly and she was searching her memory to recall Helen's face the moment before Belle burst into the room. Was it a fierce look? No, it was an intense expression, as if she were worried—no, struggling. Yes, her face said that she was struggling with something. She saw Helen's lips tremble, then purse tightly. Then Lily saw Helen's chest heaving.

Lily sat back in her pew and exhaled, eyes wide open. And then she smiled, probably with the same smile she had in Sunday School a dozen years ago when she found out that Mary and Joseph had a little baby and, wonderfully enough, on the same night St. Nicholas visited her house.

She wanted to kiss me.

The final hymn of the night was "Joy to the World." Lily sang happily and slipped her arm through her mother's, spreading the joy.

THE next morning, Christmas came quietly in the Kepler house. When Lily and her brothers were small, they were always up early, unable to stay in bed after day broke and ever hopeful that they would come downstairs and find the family rule on opening presents before breakfast swept aside. It never was when they were small but after moving into the big new house on Humboldt Parkway six years ago, Mama had decided that they were sufficiently mature to open presents before eating, provided each had dressed neatly in his or her bathrobe and had combed hair and brushed teeth. But by that time, they had reached the age of insouciance and irony, and so the privilege held less zest.

Lily lay in bed after waking, listening to faint sounds from the bathroom and slippered footsteps on the stairs. The quiet was extraordinary, something that hardly existed in Main at Vassar. And this morning, she also heard no street sounds, not a single set of sleigh bells jingled by her window. She touched her necklace and whispered, "Merry Christmas, Helen," and basked in her happiness.

When she knew her parents were moving about downstairs, she arose and put on her robe and casually put up her hair. There would be time later for a proper toilette and dressing, before her brother Alfred and his wife, Gertrude, arrived for Christmas dinner. Gathering the gifts for her parents, Lily went down to celebrate her eighteenth Christmas.

It was a truly pleasant morning, even her mother was relaxed and jocular, allowing herself to be teased without raising a finger of objection. Her father had that effect on his wife when he was able to spend time at home and was free from worry about the stores. Lily, who felt the burden of being the only daughter of a strong-willed mother with specific plans for her, sometimes wondered what her warm, humorous father had seen in Elda Vogt long ago. But on mornings like this, when the family sat around in their bathrobes drinking coffee and eating fresh kuchen, Lily saw her father gaze at her mother with soft, crinkled eyes that smiled with love. She didn't understand it, but carefully filed it away as something important to remember.

The handful of presents under the tree were wrapped in the customary plain paper or tissue, tied with string. Each giver retrieved and presented his or her gift to the recipient. Lily's mother made a big fuss over the pressed glass dish, saying that she had been needing something on her dresser for her rings. Lily in turn opened a large bundle that contained a black shawl of the softest alpaca. It was crocheted and the border stitched in a star effect. She opened it and flipped it over her shoulders, smiling with delight at how instantly warm it felt.

"You said how your room at school was so cold," her mother commented. "I thought you needed something warm around your shoulders. It only came in black or cream."

Lily agreed and added, "It's beautiful as well as warm."

Her mother handed her another bundle, and Lily opened it to discover flannel pajamas. She held them up and looked at her mother, shaking her head in amazement. Never had her mother given her anything so modern. She saw her mother shrug and chuckle, pleased with herself at the effect the gift was having. Lily loved them, thick white flannel with pink stripes and frogs along the front of the top to receive the large pearl buttons.

Lily went to her mother and gave her a hug.

"Well," her mother was saying, "they said at Flint and Kent's that these are popular for sleeping or lounging. I thought you could keep your legs warm when you study."

Lily was simply grinning in response.

After Will opened his presents and Papa Kepler his, Lily and her mother picked up the wrapping papers and string, folding everything to be used for other purposes later. It was time to help Trude finish preparations for the dinner and then get dressed.

When she was about to leave the room, Lily saw her father working his mechanical pencil intently. She smiled and then impulsively went to him and threw her arms around his neck, kissing his cheek loudly. He feigned surprise, and they both laughed. He waved his pencil and nodded positively. It had been a good idea.

Alfred and Gertrude arrived in their sleigh at the appointed time, their cheeks rouged with the cold. When they later took their seats around the dining room table, the scene was that of a prosperous, healthy, bourgeois family. Mama's best lace tablecloth was beneath the family's best dishes; the silverware had been polished to a gleam. Relish dishes of brilliant cut glass made their rare appearance holding the deep green sweet pickles, pickled cauliflower, spiced cold beets. Papa stood and sliced the large smoked ham, studded with cloves and browned with glaze; a great bowl of fluffy mashed potatoes was passed. There was Papa's favorite jar of horseradish mustard, bright yellow and silky, made by old Mr. Gentsch and his sons and sold at his factory's store on Broadway. Green beans, canned last summer, made their appearance dressed with a bacon-vinegar dressing, as did boiled carrots, sliced in rounds and glossy with butter.

It was a happy day for all the Keplers. Lily had her family, and the prospect of a deeper friendship with Helen. Will had confided to Lily that his Mae had received the small gift he had given her with a smile that gave him encouragement. Alfred and Gertrude had announced that they were to become parents in the new year. And Mama and Papa Kepler had all of their family around them. It was a day to be remembered.

CHAPTER 14

Eva's party was in four days, a point which she made breathlessly on the telephone the day after Christmas. She called to confirm that they were shopping that morning for a new dress for Lily to wear to the party. Lily's mother had been almost cheerful about the prospect of her college daughter shopping for pretty clothes and gave her a surprising amount of money for the task. She had long ago given up shopping for clothes with her daughter, having been persuaded that her tastes were hopelessly out of date. And so the stylish Eva, her shopping pal, would walk Main Street with Lily on Saturday.

When the doorbell rang half an hour later, Lily headed for the stairs and suddenly stopped, feeling her neck. She was wearing Helen's necklace and rushed back to remove it. As she was putting it away, Eva knocked on her doorway and entered, calling a bright, "Good morning!" Lily whirled to smile in greeting, hoping she didn't look startled. Or guilty.

She showed Eva her gifts and Eva promptly wrapped herself in the alpaca shawl, closing her eyes with pleasure as the wool quickly warmed her.

"You always know which of my things are the most comfortable," Lily said, smiling. "You have an uncanny knack."

Eva looked at her friend, eyes dreamy. "I always want to be wrapped in comfort," she said. "I told Frank that anyone who wanted to marry me would have to be able to do that." She took off the shawl and folded it gently. "Or words to that effect," she shrugged, smirking.

Lily said, "I'm ready to go," and whispered how much her mother had given her to spend.

Eva raised her eyebrows and pursed her lips. "I think we should stay on the trolley until Flint and Kent's. Why waste time on the other stores with that sort of allowance?"

Lily laughed and started toward the door to her room. Eva headed her off, pushed the door mostly closed, and turned back to face Lily.

Lily gave her a look and nodded toward the door in caution.

"Just a small kiss for good morning," Eva whispered as she wound an arm around Lily's neck and pulled her into a kiss that took Lily's breath away in its sensuality.

As they descended the stairs, Lily followed Eva and wondered what was happening to her. She was becoming a stranger to her old self, a self that was happiest in reading or playing the piano or writing stories or being with friends. Her body had hardly made itself known until now and almost never interrupted her pursuits unless she was sick or tired. But now she had trouble concentrating on anything for very long. She dreamed during the day and the night, wondering and desiring to kiss Helen, embrace her, make love.

Their shopping trip was successful. Eva was able to devote all of her attention to Lily's quest because she had purchased her own new outfit two weeks earlier with her aunt, whose greatest pleasure it seemed to Lily had always been dressing her beloved charge. Eva first spotted the dark green velvet shirtwaist with a plaid silk ribbon trim along the front. It came with the requisite high collar, but a soft collar and of the same green velvet. And it also came with a matching plaid silk tie, to be tied either as a bow or four-in-hand. When Lily tried it on, Eva tied it four-in-hand, declaring it the only stylish alternative. She gave it a tug and winked slyly, making Lily smile and blush.

Lily needed a new skirt in any case and so they selected a seven-gore skirt in grey serge. It looked sleek and smooth when paired with the green velvet shirtwaist whose sleeves puffed loosely and tapered to three-quarter length. Both articles of clothing would need minor alterations to be closely fitted as fashion required, but Lily knew her mother would gladly do that. It would give them something to do together Sunday afternoon. If not for that activity, Lily would sink onto the window seat in her bedroom with a book, ostensibly to read but actually to daydream about kissing Helen.

MONDAY, the day before the party, found Lily deputized by Eva for the party favors shopping trip. They went up to Knox's 5 & 10 for supplies. Lastly, they stopped at Fowler's and Eva picked out two dozen chocolate bonbons and then had the girl put in four more, for the "help," she said to Lily with a wink. Thus laden with bag, box, and packages they walked to Eva's on Franklin Street.

The girls had dinner with Aunt Martha and Uncle Walter and then cleared the dining table for their afternoon work making the party favors.

They worked to insert charms into walnut halves, gluing two halves together with a ribbon attached. Each guest would choose one to take away.

"What kind of charm do you think Frank would like?" Lily inquired. His personality was still essentially a blank slate to her because Eva's comments about him were vague or anecdotal.

Eva looked thoughtful, then picked up the miniature team of horses. "I think he would like this one," she said. "See how smartly they are trotting? He would want that in any team he owned."

"Would you like to marry him?"

Eva raised her eyebrows. "I think I would," she said, putting the horses into a shell. "You wouldn't mind if I did, would you?"

Lily held the glued walnut halves together for a minute to make sure of the seal. "Of course not, Eva. I hope you wouldn't think that of me."

Eva was lining up the finished favors, straightening their ribbons idly.

"Well, I wouldn't mind if you were a *little* bit jealous of Frank," she said slowly, tilting her head so that she gave a wistful, pathetic appearance.

Lily laughed and shook her head. "Oh, Eva. You make me laugh! You should have your picture taken with that look and put on cards. Then you could hand out a card to people when you want something."

Eva sent her a look of shock and dismay, which made Lily laugh more. And then Eva began to chuckle, too.

They finished the favors in good cheer and Eva found a bowl for them to arrange the nuts heaped up with ribbons streaming down artfully. Then Eva found Virgie and ordered some tea for them to have with their bon bons. They wandered into the second parlor.

"Tomorrow, we'll open the door between these parlors and bring in chairs from the dining room, so we'll have plenty of room for everyone. And for our games, of course," Eva narrated, nibbling on a bonbon.

They discussed the games to play at the party.

"Charades, for sure. Everyone loves that. And I think Squeak, Piggy, Squeak!, also," Eva replied, taking a seat on the settee nearest the radiator. "It will be good for laughs because there's a forfeit."

"People made such fools of themselves at the last party," Lily recalled. "Can your Frank make fun of himself?"

Eva waved her off. "Don't worry about Frank. He loves a good time."

Virgie came in with the tea tray and the girls helped themselves. Lily ate her bonbons by halves, slowly savoring them as she sipped her tea.

Eva nudged Lily's foot. "I think I always imagined when we were small that we would both get married at the same time and live next door to one another."

Lily smiled a small smile. "Perhaps I won't get married. That would ruin your childhood plans, wouldn't it?"

Eva looked at her friend with genuine puzzlement. "Everybody gets married, Lily."

Lily was shaking her head before Eva finished. "No, not everybody."

"Well, you probably have old maid professors at Vassar," Eva allowed, "but one can't count them."

Lily pursed her lips. "Of course, they count, Eva," she said. "For all I know, I could become one of them."

Eva gazed at her in amazement. "Why ever would you want to?"

"Because," Lily explained patiently, "if I don't marry, I will need to support myself. And in that case I might decide to teach."

"But you're pretty and not the old maid type," Eva persisted. "You can easily marry."

Lily took Eva's hand and spoke slowly. "I might not *want* to marry."

Eva was quiet for a minute. "You could change your mind," she offered in a questioning voice.

Lily chuckled and shook her head. "Yes, I could change my mind," she said, surrendering.

Eva changed the subject back to the party and reviewed their timetable for the next day.

"I'm having my hair done in the early afternoon," she enthused. "Wait until you see it! I've been saving a magazine sketch for Mr. Foster to copy."

She asked Lily to come around 5 o'clock so they could dress together. Lily shook her head.

"Mama wants me to dress at home so she can see me as I will look at the party, with my hair properly done and my perfectly fitted waist and skirt. She's going to have Will bring home a wagon so he can drive me over."

Eva tried to look glum but that lasted about five seconds. "All right, but come over by 6:30 then, so you can help me finish dressing. Will she let you out of her sight that early? People will be coming at 8:30."

Lily allowed that she would be there.

"When guests arrive, you stand beside me and receive with me. Virgie will take coats and you can move our guests into the parlors. We will have to look out for Mr. Hudson who won't know anyone and introducing him around will have to be your job."

Lily nodded. "What about Frank? I thought he might be receiving with you."

Eva shook her head. "He's a guest and I will introduce him to our friends so everyone will become acquainted."

Lily observed how Eva's energy seemed gathered behind her eyes, ready to spring loose.

Eva grasped Lily's hand, squeezing it. "I love parties. I love to give a party."

"I know you do," Lily replied indulgently, knowing how Eva loved to be the center of attention.

"If only everything goes just right, Lily," she said with a touch of anxiety. "We're having cream puffs with lemon custard filling. They have to arrive late tomorrow so they're not soggy. The bakery has specific instructions not to make them early in the afternoon."

"I'm sure they will be fine. Your parties are always a success. Everyone knows that."

Eva gave her a grateful face. "It will be so pretty here tomorrow night. Aunt Martha and I will be decorating with pine boughs and red carnations tomorrow morning. I just can't wait!"

THE next day Lily spent much of her day preparing for the party. She unboxed her satin party slippers, which she would put on once at Eva's because they could not be worn out of doors. She laid out a fresh chemise and drawers, white silk stockings, corset cover and two linen petticoats. Her mother had finished altering her new green shirtwaist and gray skirt on Monday and they were hanging, perfectly pressed, on the door to her closet. She spent a good deal of time selecting earrings which would sparkle but also match the silver necklace Eva had given her; she finally settled on a pair of crystal earrings with silver fasteners.

She was looking over the scene on her bed when she heard the mailman's heavy foot on the front porch below her window and knew the morning mail had arrived. She flew down the stairs and snatched up the envelopes from the hall floor moments after they had come through the slot in the door. And there in the pile was the awaited response from Helen. Tossing the rest of the mail onto the hall table, she scooted back upstairs to her room to savor her letter.

Lily tucked herself onto her window seat and pulled a throw over her legs. She wanted to get comfortable first because the envelope seemed thick with pages. She held it in her hands, conscious that she was trembling with the joy of the unopened envelope and the anticipation of yet more joy from the words to be read. And then she opened it.

Helen said that she certainly could return to Vassar on Sunday night rather than Monday and expressed curiosity about what Lily had to show her. Much of the letter was devoted to describing how her family had spent the holidays thus far. Lily laughed to read that Harry had already had two Ping Pong tournaments with more to come. Helen begged Lily not to introduce it among her Buffalo friends.

And then Helen wrote, "I am seeing a number of my old friends, a good percentage of whom are married. O, Lily, how many times can drapery fabric be dissected before the subject is threadbare—pun intended? At times like that, I recall the happy hours we spent here in the parlor just a month ago. And I miss you."

Lily sighed when she read the last words and then looked out of her window at the gray winter scene. Helen missed her, too. She could almost hear the hum of a perfectly tuned universe. In a minute she would re-read the entire letter as she would later do many times, but at this moment she dared to imagine that she and Helen shared the same feelings.

WILL was a little late bringing the wagon home and apologized to Lily, who was pulling on her coat in the front hall when he entered. He picked up her overnight satchel and left her to say goodnight to her mother. Her mother was beaming, her head tilted and hands clasped, looking like the mother of the bride.

"You make sure to tell Eva how much I like the shirtwaist," she said.

"I will, Mama," Lily assured her as she took her Vassar scarf from the hall tree and looped it around her neck.

Her mother groaned to see the attractive image marred by the long rose and gray muffler, but Lily ignored it and gave her mother a kiss.

"And Eva will immediately notice your expert tailoring, Mama. Good-night to Papa, too! I'll see you tomorrow sometime before supper!"

Lily hurried to the wagon and Will helped her into the seat beside him.

"I know, I know," he was saying as he clucked to the team and gave the reins a little snap. "I'm sorry to be getting home later than I planned. There was a lot of traffic on South Park."

"What on earth were you doing way over on South Park?" Lily frowned because that was in South Buffalo, a long way out of the standard delivery area for the stores. And then it came to her.

"Will," she said, drawing out his name.

"I was only giving Mae a ride home, which I can see you already guessed," he said with some embarrassment.

"You had better catch me up if things have progressed to giving her a ride home in a store wagon, brother!" She was in a teasing mood from the letter from Helen and the excitement of the evening's party.

Will was deftly handling the horses, picking through traffic and taking least traveled streets, using the dry pavements to his advantage. In the dim light of passing streetlights, Lily could see a bashful, wistful smile on his young face. As was his habit, he was wearing his derby a bit farther back on his head than older men, as if to say, "I've a long time to be serious and that time has not arrived."

"Today was only the first time I've given her a ride," he was explaining. "I was taking the wagon to drive you and thought I could use it to spend some time with Mae. We never get much time to talk."

"And what does she say about her family's notions of a beau for their daughter?"

"Well," he hesitated, "I guess they were of two minds when she began working for us, because it was across town in a German neighborhood. They were proud of her for being smart but would have been happier if she had got the same job in the big office at Larkin's, closer to home. And—"

"And able to dodge the temptations of meeting a German Protestant boy," Lily finished.

Will nodded. They were approaching Franklin Street.

"Does she care very much for you?" Lily asked tentatively.

Will looked over at her and nodded, his lips pursed in a small smile.

She knew better than to ask how her brother felt. He had never been serious about any girl before.

Will pulled up in front of Eva's house and tied the reins. They sat for a moment quietly.

Lily said, "I can't speak for her family, but I think your main ally in our family could be Papa. He's got a soft heart and probably already has made his own observations about you and your Mae."

Will nodded.

"But it's not going to be easy." She felt certain that Will would be willing to convert to Catholicism if that was what it would take to marry Mae with her family's approval, but the uproar that would cause in the Kepler household challenged the imagination.

Will sighed. "I know."

Then he climbed down and came around to help her to the sidewalk. In a gallant gesture, perhaps in thanks for being able to talk to a sympathetic family member, he insisted on taking her arm and carrying her satchel to the door.

"It's lit up like daytime," he grinned as they approached the house, each downstairs window and the front hall glowing into the winter night.

"Indeed!" she replied.

Virgie opened the door and stepped back to admit Lily. "She's in her room," the girl said, adding in a resigned tone, "and been asking after you every five minutes."

Lily gave Virgie her coat and muffler. "I know, I'm late," she said, picking up her satchel and heading for the stairs.

Lily found Eva standing in the middle of her bedroom, Aunt Martha buttoning a petticoat around Eva's tiny corseted waist. Eva gave her a desperate *where-have-you-been* look.

"I'm sorry to be late, it couldn't be avoided, dear," she said in placating tones. She put her satchel aside and approached her friend. "How wonderful your hair looks!" she said admiringly. Eva's dark hair had been piled high with long loose curls carefully trailing down each side of her face.

Aunt Martha stepped back, having fastened two petticoats, each beautifully finished with wide lace bands at the bottom which existed only for beauty because no one would see them. She greeted Lily with a kiss, complimenting her dress and then excused herself in order to supervise the kitchen preparations.

Eva looked into Lily's face and the latter could see the girl's eyes well up with tears. Lily took Eva's shoulders in each hand and gave her a firm look in reply.

"We're not going to have any of this, now," she said. "I'm only twenty minutes late and Will had a very good reason for coming home late with the wagon."

Tears spilled over anyway and Lily wiped them away with her fingers.

Eva's lips were quivering. "You know how I depend on you to be here with me during these occasions. Aunt Martha tries, but I don't feel calm with her fussing about, not the way I do with you."

Lily put her arms around her friend and pulled her close. "I know, dear. But I'm here now and I want to see you in your new party clothes. You've been so secretive about them and I'm dying for a look."

At that, Eva perked up and went to her closet, pulling out a deep crimson velvet shirtwaist and holding it up to herself.

Lily sucked in her breath. It was stunning, especially beside Eva's dark hair. She smiled and nodded.

Eva, her composure entirely regained, handed the waist to Lily, who held it for her to slip into. It buttoned from the back. The sleeves had great puffs at the shoulder, the very height of fashion, which devolved to long, snug cuffs. Lily buttoned the back of the waist, finishing with the three pearl buttons on the high soft collar. Then Eva held out her arms for Lily to fasten the five buttons on each cuff. Lily stood back and admired the front, richly detailed with pintucks from Eva's shoulder to her breast, and then loosely draping to her waist.

"What do you think?" Eva was asking in a hopeful tone.

Lily put a finger to her chin in a thoughtful pose and then observed, "I think it needs a skirt."

Eva giggled and chided Lily, then she retrieved a black taffeta silk skirt. "It has *thirteen* gores," Eva said boastfully, and so it did. Each of the gores was embroidered with silk in a floral design. Like the shirtwaist, it was very fashionable.

Lily helped Eva step into it and buttoned it for her. Then Eva posed, asking her question again with a questioning look.

Lily smiled. "Your highness," and bowed.

Eva beamed and then quickly stepped to her dressing table.

"Not done yet," she said, holding up the earrings Lily had given her for Christmas. "These are the *piece de resistance*."

Lily smiled as she watched Eva put on the earrings. She was thinking of Belle, always tossing a French phrase into conversation.

Then Eva was fussing with Lily's tie.

"What are you doing?" Lily asked. "You told me to tie it four-in-hand and I did."

"I'm just loosening it," Eva said, "so I can see your necklace. We both are adorned with our Christmas gifts."

Lily smiled at her. The little pearl earrings looked exactly as she had imagined they would.

"Why are you smiling?" Eva put her hands on Lily's waist.

"Because you look very royal tonight in your red velvet," Lily said honestly. "And very pretty."

Eva leaned up and they kissed lightly. "As do you, my darling."

They finished getting ready and just as they were about to leave the room, Lily said, "How much planning did it require for you to make sure I bought a green waist after you had bought a red one?"

Eva continued to the door. "I don't know what you mean," she said in an airy tone.

Lily followed her. "You probably picked out the shirtwaist you wanted me to buy before I even arrived in Buffalo. Then you could be sure that your guests would be greeted by Christmas red and green when they come to the door tonight."

Eva turned and flashed her triumphant smile and started downstairs.

THE girls passed through the decorated rooms on the first floor. The library was to be used for coats; pocket doors between the two parlors had been opened and the large rooms brightly lit by chandeliers which made the red and green holiday decor vivid. The dining room was set up for buffet-style service and a sideboard held a large crystal punch bowl and cups. The punch was of claret and fruit juices with lemon and orange slices floating colorfully on the surface. Beside that were bottles of claret and port and also a cut-glass carafe she had not observed at previous parties.

"What's that?" Lily asked, pointing at the amber liquid in the carafe.

"Oh, that's brandy," Eva replied. "Frank likes it."

They stopped in the kitchen to see the Bond's cook slicing a large ham and a temporary hired girl working at a table. Aunt Martha was arranging the Fowler's bonbons in a bowl. She shooed Eva and Lily out of the kitchen and assured the hostess that all was proceeding according to plan.

Almost at 8:30 by the hall clock the doorbell jangled and the first guests arrived. Raymond and Lydia Duttweiler, classmates who had married a month after graduation last year, came in almost apologetically.

"We find that we're always arriving early wherever we go," Ray said with a sheepish laugh. "Now that we are married, there are two of us to keep track of the time."

Lily guided them to the dining room and refreshments and when she returned to the foyer, Eva was greeting a tall man in a flirtatious manner that suggested to Lily that this was Frank Marshall. In the seconds before she was observed, Lily noted that he was an extraordinarily handsome man, with dark hair combed back, a ruddy complexion, thick eyebrows, a good straight nose.

And then Eva saw Lily out of the corner of her eye and beckoned her.

"Lily," Eva said, circling Frank's arm with both of hers, "this is Frank."

Eva looked up at Frank, much taller than she, and gushed, "Sweetheart, this is my Lily."

Lily smiled and offered her hand. Frank stood at attention, clicked his heels together, and bowed from the waist. He took her hand and kissed it.

Lily was a little embarrassed at this chivalrous playacting, but said, "I'm glad to meet you at last, Frank. Eva speaks often of you and your charms."

Frank was repeating the same platitudes to Lily while she was observing his face. The expression in his small, dark brown eyes was inconsistent with his broad smile and it puzzled her. His shoulders were very broad and his neck thick; he gave the impression of being a wrestler and not a banker.

"Oh," Eva was saying, "here are more guests. Lily, take Frank in, will you?"

As Lily led the way down the hall to the dining room, Frank said confidentially, "I hope you're taking me to the refreshments, Lily. I'm parched!"

In the dining room, he made straight for the carafe and poured himself half a glass of the brandy. Lily kept her surprise to herself. Among all their friends, beer and wine were the standard alcoholic beverages, of which almost no one ever drank to excess. She wondered if drinking hard liquor was more prevalent in Connecticut than in the less refined city of Buffalo.

Lily left the dining room and passed into the parlor. Frank was suddenly by her side.

"Oh, don't leave me yet," he was saying with a heartiness that seemed somewhat commanding as opposed to charming, "I've heard about you morning, noon, and night and want to get to know you in the flesh, so to speak."

He was smiling, showing his perfect teeth, but Lily was disconcerted because his voice didn't seem to match his expression.

"Well," Lily replied, uncertain what one might say upon the news that she has been a frequent topic of conversation. "Eva said you were good-looking, but she wasn't entirely accurate."

He tilted his head. "Oh?" he said with some incredulity.

"Yes," Lily assured him, "she didn't say that you are the most handsome man in Buffalo."

Frank threw back his head and laughed loudly. Then she knew he was a man who could be flattered and as a matter of fact enjoyed being flattered.

Fortunately, other guests were coming into the parlor and Lily was able to extricate herself by introducing Frank to them.

When she returned to the foyer, Eva hissed, "What do you think of him?"

Lily smiled and looked toward the door that was now opening again with more guests.

"He is probably the best-looking man I have ever seen," she said honestly.

Eva squeezed her arm. "I know," she said in a stage whisper, "and he's all mine!"

The next guests were Art Lacy and Lulie Hartung, who had been keeping company for over a year and whose engagement was thought to be imminent. The big front door opened again and again, as classmates entered the foyer in a swirl of cold December air. The parlors grew noisy with conversation and laughter, punctuated every now and then with the shrill *tee-hee-hee* of Alice Bradley, whose laugh had always elicited even more laughter from those around her.

And then, almost the last to arrive, was the unknown Roger Hudson. He entered with some tentativeness, but Eva instantly greeted him warmly and insisted that she had been looking for him all evening. He smiled, gratefully it seemed to Lily, and surrendered his Chesterfield coat and hat. Before he could realize that his hands were empty, Eva touched his arm and turned his attention to Lily.

"Mr. Hudson, this is my dearest friend, Lily Kepler," she said to him familiarly.

Lily was very proud of Eva at that moment. Despite her well-deserved image as self-centered, Eva nonetheless was capable of being a gracious and attentive hostess.

Lily gave him her hand, and he shook it with exactly the right amount of pressure.

"Roger, please," he was saying, smiling at them both.

Lily thought he had the saddest eyes she had ever seen. He was not a tall man, but nonetheless several inches taller than she. He had a carefully-trimmed mustache and wore his dark hair very short all over which showed that his hairline was beginning to recede.

"Lily, why don't you take Roger around and introduce him?" Eva said by way of prompting her.

Lily hadn't realized that she had been taking the measure of Roger Hudson, so different from their other male guests. Perhaps it was his reserve, she decided, as she guided him to the dining room where he accepted a glass of punch. Then she introduced him around the big parlor and helped the conversation. When she introduced him to George Tilden, a Cornell student who planned to study law, he and George struck up a conversation and Lily was able to excuse herself.

She found Eva circulating with their latest arrivals, the last on the guest list. The rooms were hopping with conversation which was louder now that so many different conversations were going at the same time. She was making her way across the room to Eva when she saw that Frank was doing the same thing and so she joined a conversation with several girls.

As it happened, Frank Marshall was their topic of interest.

"What do you think, Lily?" Alice said. "Isn't he too good-looking for words?"

Lily nodded. "He certainly is. Leave it to Eva to pick out the best-looking man in town."

The others assented grudgingly.

"But I heard," one said, causing all heads to lean toward her, "that his family won't give him any money and they're supposed to own entire banks in Connecticut."

"Well, that's not such a bad thing," another offered in his defense. "People can make their own money if they work hard and are clever."

"True," the first allowed, "but Jack says he spends money as if he has it." And then she added for emphasis, "He doesn't have it."

"What he does that Ray can't stand is boast," Lydia, the newly-married, said. "He says that, at the club when someone says something, Frank always says that he did that or owns something better than what's being discussed. It drives him crazy."

And then they turned to look at Lily.

"What do you think of him, Lily?"

Lily shrugged. "I only just met him. You know more than I."

"But you're Eva's *bosom* friend," Alice said. "Hasn't she talked about him?"

Lily smiled. "She likes him."

Then she excused herself and circulated. Shortly, she felt a tug at her sleeve and knew instinctively it was Eva.

"Where's Roger?" Eva asked.

"I left him talking with George a few minutes ago. I'm sure he's fine," Lily said. "Where's Frank?"

Eva nodded in the direction of the dining room.

"He's thirsty," she said, then she pulled Lily's arm close. "Do you like him?"

"That might be the question of the hour," Lily said playfully. "I think he's a handsome devil, to be sure. You know how to pick the best."

Eva giggled and they saw Frank appear in the doorway of the parlor, his cheeks flushed and forehead damp. It was indeed warm now in the rooms, but Lily knew that his high color was not from the temperature. She had seen it before.

AFTER some time had passed in general conversation and unorganized merriment, Eva announced the start of the party games. She asked that the assembled make three teams for charades, five to a team; she would serve as moderator. Everyone was skilled at charades, it being the most commonly played game at their parties, and they quickly fell into teams, some members vying to pull in the best-known players for their team.

Eva gave out a card to each team and they huddled to make strategy. The first team had "love sick," and their confusing efforts had the audience shouting out random words before the phrase was finally guessed. The next team communicated "brick layer" somewhat faster, and the third team had no trouble with "bird seed." The party was in full swing.

They played one more round of charades and then Eva announced "Squeak, Piggy, Squeak!" which was a variation on blind man's bluff with an exception. The blindfolded person was given a cushion or pillow and spun around in the center of a circle or, in the case of the assembled at Eva's, a large oval in the joined parlors. The blindfolded person had to approach one of the seated, place the cushion on that person's lap and sit down without touching the person and say, "Squeak, piggy, squeak!" That person had to squeak and if the blindfolded person correctly identified the squeaker, that person became the next "blind man." If the blindfolded person failed to correctly identify the squeaker, he or she had to pay a forfeit, which is how the game achieved its greatest entertainment value.

To be absolutely fair, Eva had given everyone a slip of paper with a number and she drew the first number, which turned out to be chatty Gladys Munger. She was blindfolded, given her cushion and turned round and round at one end of the large group. The party called out encouragements to her as she groped her way to the seated and sat carefully on the cushioned lap of her victim.

"Squeak, piggy, squeak!" she commanded, drawing laughs from everyone.

George Tilden made his best falsetto squeak and Gladys guessed it was Jack Rohmer, possibly wishful thinking because it was common knowledge that she liked him.

Everyone groaned and then laughed as she stood and removed her blindfold. Eva explained her forfeit to the group.

"Everyone should have observed that we have there," Eva said, pointing to the doorway from the parlor to the hall, "a sprig of mistletoe. Gladys, you must stand in the middle where you did before and spell 'opportunity,' after which you should try to reach your chair before some gentleman catches you. If he catches you, he may give you a kiss under the mistletoe."

Gladys blushed and said she hoped she could remember how to spell the word. Upon the last two letters she paused and then threw them out as she hustled to her chair. Rob Bartlett, who had accompanied her to the party, gallantly sprang into action, catching her by the waist just as she was about to collapse into her chair. Everyone cheered and she accompanied him to the mistletoe where he politely kissed her on the cheek.

Eva drew another number, and quiet Clara Richmond stood to face the challenge. This time, however, she was correct in her guess that she was seated on the lap of Frank Marshall. She admitted that she recognized his cologne and not his squeak. Frank was now *it*. He grinned at his fellow party goers as he went into the center of the oval.

Eva assisted him in putting on his blindfold, presented him with his cushion and turned him round and round. The group was somewhat quiet as he stumbled toward the seated. Muffled giggling echoed around the room as he put his cushion on Ray Duttweiler's lap and sat down, giving the command. His guess was incorrect, but it probably was bound to be because he had only just met the assembled. He had to face the men's forfeit.

Eva said, "Your forfeit is to kiss every lady in the room 'Spanish fashion.'"

Frank laughed and rubbed his hands together.

"Please don't misunderstand, dear," Eva said. "Just follow my lead."

She produced a pocket handkerchief and led Frank to the nearest girl. She kissed the girl on the cheek and then wiped Frank's mouth with her handkerchief. Most knew of this forfeit and laughed to see Frank's incredulous look as Eva conducted him around the room repeating the action with each girl. And when she reached Lily, Eva gave her a bold look and then took Lily's face in her hands and kissed her chastely on the lips. As the party howled with laughter, she turned to Frank with her handkerchief, only to have him push her hand away. His eyes were glittering, his smile frozen in place.

As Eva drew another number, Frank left the room by the doorway nearest the dining room. They played a few more rounds and then Eva declared the games at an end. Lily knew preparations for the supper were next and made her way to the dining room.

Frank was still there, eating shelled nuts from the table. Eva had her arm through his and was talking softly to him. Lily glided past them and into the kitchen where Aunt Martha was finishing up a tray of cheeses. Smiling, she accepted Lily's offer to help set up the buffet and together they made several trips, carrying platters of cold sliced ham and turkey, plates of cheeses, and finally a hot pot of Welsh rarebit to pour into the awaiting chafing dish on the table.

As Aunt Martha was placing a basket of toast points beside the chafing dish, its alcohol lamp now lit to keep the rarebit warm, Lily chuckled.

"This item is our entire kitchen at college," she said. "You can't imagine what we are able to cook in a chafing dish. Even fudge!"

Aunt Martha smiled and stood back to look over the buffet. It was a handsome sight, the pile of small white china plates edged with tiny blue flowers, the crisp white linen napkins, the gleaming freshly polished silverware. In the center of the table was a bouquet of deep red roses peeking out from a nest of glossy holly leaves.

"It's lovely, Aunt Martha," Lily said. She had noted during their trips from the kitchen that Frank and Eva were nowhere to be seen and wondered where they had gone.

"Well," Aunt Martha said, "we may as well bring out the dessert. Cook can see to the coffee later."

Aunt Martha carried a very large silver tray covered by a single layer of cream puffs with lemon custard filling. Lily followed her with a devil's food cake on a silver cake stand. It had been sliced in the kitchen but so skillfully that it retained its round shape.

"My work is done, Lily," Aunt Martha said, "and I'll be removing myself. It's past my bed time."

She embraced Lily and passed down the hall greeting partiers as she went to the stairs.

Lily waited a few minutes to see if Aunt Martha had found Eva and then set out to locate her friend. She found Eva and Frank in the library, holding hands. They were standing because the couch and chairs in the room were completely overflowing with coats.

"Excuse me," she said quietly, "but I wondered if you wanted to announce that supper is ready."

Eva's eyes had the telltale shine that told Lily she had been crying. Frank looked at Lily as if he had never seen her before.

"Of course!" Eva said, and pulled on Frank's arm. "Let's go in to our guests. They'll be famished!"

THE supper brought another shift in the sounds of the party, as people sat in small groups eating and talking among themselves. When the fragrant aroma of coffee wafted into the parlors, they went back for cream puffs and cake. Then someone asked Clara if she would play some songs on the piano. As quiet as she was, Clara's personality shone on the piano and she was always invited to parties because of her great repertoire. In the past year she had added ragtime songs and they were always the first requested. Tonight, she began with slower rags as befitted the supper hour.

Lily tarried near the piano, enjoying Clara's music and smiling as she recalled the afternoon of ragtime dancing at Helen's. When she finished, Clara asked if she had a request; Lily asked for "The Easy Winners." Clara nodded and struck the opening chords. In her mind's eye, Lily was dancing with Helen when a light touch on her arm brought her attention back to the present moment. It was Eva.

"How is everything?" Lily asked, leaning close to Eva's ear.

Eva smiled. "Fine," she said nodding reassuringly. Then she leaned close. "I don't see Roger Hudson. Will you look for him? I'm afraid he might need rescuing."

She raised her eyebrows which made Lily raise hers in response. They were both thinking of Gladys Munger who was capable of talking a person into numbness.

Lily set out to survey the rooms and finally ended at the library, where she found Gladys and Roger. Two chairs had been emptied of coats and they were seated, Roger holding an empty plate and smiling politely. Gladys was holding forth, gesturing with her hands for emphasis.

Lily stepped into the room. "There you are, Gladys!" she exclaimed. "Eva has been looking all over for you."

Gladys stopped, hand in mid-air. "Eva? Why ever for?"

Lily shrugged. "I can't say, but she deputized me to hunt for you."

Gladys seemed to hesitate, perhaps reluctant to surrender the sole attention of an eligible man, to answer a call from Eva, who had never been a close friend. But she finally rose and excused herself.

Lily stood before Roger and sighed heavily.

"I don't know what to say, Roger," she said. "People who know Gladys generally try to converse with her in numbers. Please accept my sympathies."

Roger laughed quietly, and then rose from his chair, placing the empty plate on the seat.

"She has a tendency toward loquaciousness, to be sure," he said, nodding. "But it's my fault, I'm afraid. I wandered in here to take a look at Walter's library," he added, taking in the bookcases around them. "I like to see a person's library. One can tell a lot about a person by what books he collects. And here she discovered me, in reverie," he finished, extending his arms.

Lily smiled. He seemed a very polite man, at any rate giving no indication that he had been irritated by Gladys' nattering.

"What can you tell about Uncle Walter from his library?" she asked.

Roger looked at her curiously. "Are you related to him?"

"Oh, no," Lily said, "I call them Aunt and Uncle because I've been around them since I was eight years old, when Eva and I became playmates."

He nodded. "Eva called you her *dearest friend*."

"Yes."

"Would she be your oldest friend?"

Lily smiled and nodded. "Like the sister I never had."

"Did I hear that you are a college girl?" Roger asked

"Yes. It's my first year at Vassar."

He smiled and Lily thought he had a very kind smile, a description she had never before thought to use to describe a man's smile. "How do you like it?"

Lily beamed. "Oh, goodness, how can I say how wonderful it is? Words fail me always when someone asks that. I belong there, that's all I can say."

He nodded. "That's quite sufficient."

"And what is your alma mater?"

"Harvard, and Harvard Law," he said, nodding. "Class of '97."

She quickly calculated that he would be nearly thirty with the years of law school after his undergraduate work. He was a mature man.

"Do you know Frank Marshall?" she impulsively asked.

Roger was idly gazing at the bookshelves. "Not well," he said. "I see him occasionally at the club."

Lily was looking at the bookshelves also. She didn't want to seem too inquisitive about Frank and put Roger on the spot, but wished she could know what someone like Roger thought of him.

"Eva is quite fond of him, " she said and then paused. "Because he's so recently arrived in our fair city, people don't seem to know much about him."

"You sound concerned for your oldest friend," he observed.

"I am, Roger," she said simply.

Eva was suddenly in the doorway.

"Come quick," she called. "We're going to have 'Auld Lang Syne' before people begin to leave."

They followed Eva into the parlors where everyone was standing around the piano. Clara played a few introductory chords and then nodded like a conductor. In voices both hearty and sentimental, the group sang, "should old acquaintance be forgot, and never brought to mind." Lily glanced at Roger, who was singing along in a strong voice, and she thought his eyes looked less sad now than they had a few hours earlier. Or perhaps she just thought so.

After that, people began leaving in twos and fours, with Eva making sure that everyone had picked a walnut favor. Roger found Lily and thanked her.

"For what are you thanking me, sir?" she said. "A life-saving rescue?"

He laughed aloud, which pleased Lily. Then he offered his hand, which she took.

"For the company," he said simply. "I would that we had more time to converse. Perhaps we'll have the opportunity again someday when you're visiting from your Vassar home."

"Yes," Lily replied, smiling. She didn't want to seem too encouraging on the one hand, but talking with him had been very pleasant. He was not like the young men her age, and not just because he was older. He had what her mother would have called *good manners*, the kind that seemed to fall a little more out of favor each year.

And then everyone was gone except Frank. She found him and Eva in the dining room. Frank was just setting down the nearly empty brandy carafe. She looked at Eva who smiled tiredly. Lily saw that she did not belong here and moved toward the hall.

"They weren't a bit soggy," Lily said to Eva, pointing at the nearly empty cream puff tray.

"You leaving too?" Frank called to her. He had one arm around Eva's shoulders.

"Yes," Lily said. "Good night, Frank. I'm glad to meet you."

And then she turned and left the room.

It took some time to undress and take care of her clothes, then to remove the numerous hairpins, brush out her hair and loosely braid it. Then, leaving only one gas jet on very low, she climbed into bed and realized how tired she was from the long day. When she fell asleep, Eva had not yet come upstairs.

LILY was awakened by Eva spooning her, one arm around Lily's waist, her hand gently squeezing Lily's breast. It was morning and daylight lit the room in shafts that escaped the borders of the drapes. Lily sighed into the sensation, the first time anyone had touched her breast, and then she turned onto her back.

Eva's face was close beside hers on the pillow. She was smiling sleepily.

"Isn't this wonderful, waking up together?" she said in a dreamy voice.

Lily wrinkled her brow. "We've waked up together many, many times."

Eva touched Lily's mouth with her fingers. "But we weren't lovers before."

Then she pulled Lily into a kiss that was nothing like the chaste kiss she had planted on Lily's lips at the party. Lily gently broke it off and turned on her side to look at her friend.

"When you kissed me during the game last night, it made Frank angry, didn't it?"

Eva shook her head dismissively. "He was just embarrassed at the forfeit. Because he's a stranger in town, he felt everyone was judging him. He's sensitive like that."

Lily lifted a long curl away from Eva's face. It occurred to her that Frank was not the only stranger at the party and yet their behaviors were quite different.

"What have you told Frank about me?"

"What do you mean?" Eva replied with genuine innocence.

"I mean that Frank Marshall doesn't like me," Lily said, which made Eva shake her head firmly. "No, listen to me, Evie. He said you talked about me 'morning, noon and night,' and that's a quote. Maybe the less you say about me, the better."

Eva was fiddling with the buttons on Lily's nightgown.

"Frank understands that you are my most important friend. He knows that you will always be my most important friend, no matter what. I want you both to get to know one another and care for one another."

She paused, having unbuttoned the placket of Lily's nightgown. "Because I love you both," she said to Lily's exposed neck. "Will you try not to be jealous?" she said, meeting Lily's eyes with her now-playful look.

Lily shook her head incredulously. "I don't think I'm the person to tell that to," she said. She didn't feel jealous, as far as she could tell. Her heart was in Glens Falls.

"I've already told him," Eva said quietly.

"Is that what you two were doing downstairs for so long last night?" Lily said, raising an eyebrow.

"I thought you weren't jealous."

"I'm not."

"Were you worried about my reputation?" Eva asked coyly.

"Should I be?" Lily replied equally coyly.

"Of course not," Eva said smoothly, as she slipped a hand inside Lily's open nightgown. "I know the rules and Frank knows the rules."

She propped herself on one arm and gently pushed Lily onto her back. "But what I like most is that there are no rules that apply to you and me." She smiled when she said it, as if she had discovered the key to the cupboard where the desserts were stored.

They made love under the down comforter in their nightgowns, Eva hiking hers up far enough to allow her to entwine her legs with Lily's. Lily looked up at her friend's face as Eva's desire manifested itself in her expressions that passed by like lantern slides. When Eva's hips began to grind into hers, Lily saw the dark eyes lose focus and mouth slacken. Lily's body began to respond and without conscious decision her hands cupped Eva's bottom and pressed it to her own hips. Just as she was beginning to strain toward Eva, the latter uttered a small cry and her body went rigid on Lily's. Lily embraced her tightly and Eva whimpered into her ear. As Eva grew still, Lily felt her own breathing return to normal and the humming between her legs subside. She saw in her mind's eye her own dream of such a union, and then shut her eyes tight lest Eva see the image of Helen's face in them.

They lay quietly for some time in each other's arms, warm under the covers in the chilly room. Lily had almost drifted back to sleep when Eva spoke, a gentle vibration against her neck.

"Lily?" the voice was soft, vulnerable.

"Hmmm?"

"I will never love anyone as much as I love you," Eva said in a high voice, like a child's.

Lily acknowledged it by tightening her embrace briefly.

"Please remember that when you're back at Vassar among all those smart, rich, pretty girls. I love you best."

Lily was grateful that Eva couldn't see her face because she would instantly know everything in Lily's heart. She felt stricken and confused. Was making love with Lily Eva's substitute for Frank?

"I will," was all she was able to mumble in response.

CHAPTER 15

Sunday morning Will drove Lily to the New York Central Station for her early return to Vassar and Helen. After she had received Helen's letter, Lily had explained to her mother that her Greek tutor was willing to return a day early to help Lily prepare for the exams in January. She explained how important it was for her to do well on those exams before the second semester began. Her mother was skeptical. Lily said it was not unusual. Her mother pointed out that she would be missing church by leaving on Sunday. Lily explained that at Vassar, she went to church every evening and on Sundays. In the end, Lily was victorious. She ran up the stairs to her room filled with joy, fully aware that she had lied to her parents as she had never done before. She had a moment when she wondered what else she might have done for the opportunity to be alone with Helen McIntyre. But it was a brief moment. She fell onto her window seat and drew up her knees, hugging them, suddenly anxious. She had no idea what to do when she met Helen.

The anxiety returned on the drive to the station. Will was talking happily about Mae and Lily was barely paying attention.

"Say," he said, nudging her with his shoulder, "are you listening?"

She jumped. "I'm sorry. What were you saying?"

"I'm going to invite her to the Young People's social at church in two weeks," Will was saying. "What do you think?"

"Oh, my goodness," Lily said, surprised, wondering what else he might have been saying. "Well, that will certainly announce to all parties that you're seeing one another."

"It just seemed to me that it's time to do that," he said, with conviction. "I'm not ashamed of Mae, there's no reason to be secretive about seeing her. I'm quite proud, as a matter of fact, and don't mind showing up with such a pretty, smart girl on my arm."

Lily smiled. "Do you think she'll accept your invitation?"

"That I can't say for sure," he admitted. "But I feel like I'm sitting on my hands, in a manner of speaking."

"In a manner of speaking," Lily repeated, glancing over at him. He was seeming less boyish these days and she wondered if falling in love had wrought that change.

"Should you talk with Papa if she agrees to go to the social?" Lily asked, as a suggestion. "Just to alert him?"

Will nodded. He was pulling up to the station, not overly crowded at this time of a Sunday morning.

He carried her suitcase, satchel and the extra satchel she was bringing back that contained kuchen and some supplies for her larder.

"Brother, why don't you write me and let me know how things turn out?" she said.

He nodded once. "Maybe I will. Wait and see!"

THE train picked up speed quickly once it left the city and the scenery turned uniformly white as they passed fields that had barely a fence line visible in the snow. The car grew chilly and Lily pulled her Vassar muffler closer, warming her cheeks. After a while, the clacking of the wheels on the rails began to sound like "HEL-en, HEL-en, HEL-en," or maybe it was her heart beating in the rhythm of Helen's name. What was she going to do when she met Helen? What could she say after, "Hello?"

She took out a book and ordered herself to concentrate.

At Albany, Lily found herself looking around, as if she might possibly run into Helen there. It wasn't entirely unreasonable because Helen had to take the same railroad, but she felt a bit foolish because Helen could take any one of a number of the Hudson River trains to Poughkeepsie.

Once settled into her seat, Lily took herself firmly in hand, attempting to get a grip on her unruly emotions. She was so unlike the person who traveled these same tracks in September that she made no attempt to continue her reading but sat in dumb wonder the remainder of the trip.

It was late in the afternoon, the winter darkness rapidly overtaking the campus, when Lily finally walked through the Gate Lodge and up the drive to Main. Only one small light was on, over the door under the porte cochere. She tried the door and found it locked, as she expected, but she pulled the bell cord and eventually Peters, the custodian who lived at Main, came to let her in. He brought up the lights in the lobby and helped carry her bags to the elevator. Lily had not often ridden the building's relatively new elevator, it being reserved for seniors as a daily rule. He lit the hallway to her room and helped her with her things. Then he pulled his sweater closer and left her to her chilly room. She mentioned that someone else would be along and he nodded and waved a hand over his shoulder as he stepped into the elevator.

She had not noticed anyone else about, but probably any who might have stayed were upper classmen who lived in Raymond or Strong. Only those who were unable to return home because of the travel distance would have remained at Vassar over break, and those were fewer than a hundred, she had heard. It was very still in the building. But she had no time to be uneasy about being alone in the cavernous structure in the dark of a winter's night when the heat had clearly not been raised to its normal, drafty levels.

Lily unpacked her kuchen, a box of Fowler's chocolates purchased expressly to share with Helen, tinned milk for tea, and a fresh box of tea, then put the satchel with the rest of supplies to one side. She fetched a teapot of water from the sink down the hall and put it under the alcohol lamp so that it would be hot when Helen arrived. She warmed her hands by the heat of the lamp for a minute while thinking of what else she needed to do.

She put the light on in her bedroom and began to unpack, laying out her flannel pajamas and alpaca shawl to wear. At length, everything she brought back was unpacked and put in the proper location. She checked the water and found it boiling, so she put out the flame.

Lily stood in the center of the room and looked around. There was nothing left to do except change out of her travel clothes and put on everything warm that she had. She changed into her flannel pajamas, her felt booties from Bert, and wrapped herself in her alpaca shawl.

Still no Helen. Lily lit the alcohol lamp again and made herself a cup of tea. She unwrapped the kuchen, baked last night just for her, and cut into it, realizing when the fragrance of the cinnamon was released by her knife just how hungry she was. She had eaten the sandwiches her mother packed hours ago somewhere outside Schenectady. She helped herself to a good chunk of the cake and, after finishing the tea, felt a little warmer.

Restless and nervous, she paced around the room and finally ended up in her bedroom looking out the window at the lifeless campus. She wondered what she had been thinking when she came up with this scheme. Helen probably thought it a harebrained idea. Lily pulled back the thick, feather duvet and blankets of her little bed and sat down, hugging her pillow.

And then she heard a small voice, accompanied by a scratching at the door. First her heart leapt to her throat and then she leapt to her feet.

Helen was opening the door when Lily made it to the entry. She pulled open the door wide and said, breathlessly, "Hello!"

Helen smiled broadly in response. "Hello, back! At last!"

Lily stood aside to let Helen enter. The latter was pulling in her suitcase and two satchels.

"I'm an hour later than I had planned. I hope you didn't worry," she was saying as she took off her gloves and unbuttoned her coat.

Lily assured her that she hadn't been worried, almost convincing herself in the effort.

"Well, there was some problem down the line and my train sat in the station at Albany for ages," Helen was saying, putting her coat and gloves on a chair. "It was trying," she said, nodding to indicate it was her final word on the topic.

Lily saw Helen glance at the alcohol lamp and kuchen, and she said, "Would you like some tea and cake? The water is nearly boiling."

Helen rubbed her arms. "I would treasure a cup of tea right now," she said as Lily lit the flame. "The heat is not really on at all, is it?"

Lily grimaced. "I think there's a little, but not much. I hadn't thought about the building not being warm when I had the great idea of coming back a day early."

Helen picked at some crumbs around the kuchen and smiled. "Why wasn't it a great idea?" she asked as she saw Lily escape into her bedroom.

Lily returned a moment later with a flannel robe. She pulled off her alpaca shawl and brought it to Helen.

"Here, put this around your shoulders," she said, wrapping it around Helen's shoulders. "It's wonderfully warm."

Helen smiled in a small, grateful way that touched Lily. "Oh, this is lovely," she was saying. "Was it a Christmas gift?"

"Yes," Lily confessed, pulling on her robe. "I had been complaining of the cold in my bedroom when I study."

The water was quickly hot again and Lily made a pot of tea for them to share. Then she cut the kuchen. They sat under the golden circle made by the drop light at the little table in the middle of the room, each warming her hands on her mug, eating kuchen. Lily asked about Harry's Ping Pong and Helen regaled her with stories. She also passed along her mother's greeting, noting that her mother had taken a liking to Lily. They conversed for a while, and then the teapot was empty, the kuchen half consumed.

Helen leaned forward in her chair, placing her mug on the table. She was looking at Lily with a bemused smile. Lily had to look down at her half-empty mug.

"So, Lily," Helen said slowly. "Dear. You said you had something to show me."

Lily didn't answer. She was having difficulty breathing.

"Was it your new striped pajamas with the cute frog buttons?" Helen's voice was teasing.

Lily had to chuckle at that. "No." She swallowed hard, then looked over at Helen.

To Lily's surprise, Helen looked a little nervous. Her smile seemed to be quivery. But it was the earnest, possibly hopeful look in her eyes that gave Lily encouragement. And resolve.

She rose from her seat and was momentarily taken aback when Helen did as well. Two steps were all that separated them. Lily closed the distance between them and put her arms around Helen; it was the only thing she could think to do to be able to continue standing before the woman she loved.

Helen returned the embrace as naturally as if it was their habit. They stood like that for a while, tightly, actively embracing, without speaking. Lily was aware that she was trembling and that Helen was, as well.

"You're trembling," she said into Helen's ear. "Are you cold?"

Helen laughed softly. "I deserved that, didn't I?"

Lily pulled back to look at Helen. "Yes, you did," she said, smiling.

They smiled at one another and then their smiles slowly faded; Lily's focus was on Helen's lips, closer than she had ever been to them before. She kissed them, briefly.

And then Helen brought Lily's face to hers and kissed her back, not a short or affectionate or puckered-mouth kiss, but a passionate, open-mouthed kiss that went on and on. It was like a kiss that had been in a bank vault, accumulating interest for some time.

Lily's legs began to give way and she broke off the kiss, gasping for air. "I have to sit down," she said.

Helen, her arms around Lily, guided them to the couch. They resumed kissing. Eventually, Helen leaned back from Lily, her breathing labored.

"Is this what you wanted to show me?" she asked, brushing Lily's lips with her fingertips.

Lily looked into Helen's eyes in the dim light around the couch. Now she was afraid and looked down.

"Part of it," she said, very softly, and then looked to see Helen's reaction.

Helen responded by taking Lily's head in both her hands and pressing their foreheads together. They sat like that for a long pause, Helen taking deep breaths as if she were struggling with something.

Then she spoke. "I'm glad, Lily. Scared to death, practically," she grimaced, then continued in a shaky voice, "but so glad it's you."

Then she sat back, gripping Lily's arms. "Now? If you please?"

Lily felt her heart thump palpably. She could barely think what to do next, had never had to think of that. She stood, and Helen stood with her. Slowly, as if underwater, she reached for Helen's hand and led them to her bedroom and closed the door behind them. In the low light of the gas jet, Helen began to unbutton the layers of clothing she had on, pausing only to pull free the belt closing Lily's robe. Lily took the hint and slipped off the robe.

Helen had removed her traveling jacket, skirt and shirtwaist with remarkable speed, and unhooked the front of her corset with one motion, tossing it aside.

Then she took off her petticoats and stockings while Lily was pulling open a dresser drawer.

"I have a nightgown for you, " Lily said.

Helen paused in her chemise and looked blankly at Lily. "Will I need it?"

Lily put it down and sat down on the bed. Before her suddenly stood a completely naked woman, the most wonderful and terrifying sight of her short life. The naked woman was pulling Lily up from the bed and speaking to her.

"You must let go of your flannels, sweetheart," Helen said, deftly unfastening the frogs. Then she found the tie for the bottoms and pulled it, loosening them so that they dropped around Lily's feet.

"Almost there," Helen said, pushing the pajama top off Lily's shoulders and then unbuttoned Lily's drawers, letting them fall and join the pajama bottoms around her ankles.

"Now," Helen said, running her hands along Lily's shoulders and down her arms. She wrapped Lily's arms around her waist and pulled their bodies full against one another. Lily gasped audibly.

"What else did you want to show me?" Helen whispered in Lily's ear.

Shivering, they slipped under the icy bedclothes and pulled them high around their necks. In a bed sized for only one person, and a small one at that, they had to lie on their sides facing one another. But they were oblivious to the snug confines and the heavy covers, kissing and intertwining arms and legs, introducing their bodies to each other. Helen's hands searched Lily's body, racing along her arm, pausing at her shoulder, then firmly enumerating the bumps on her spine, ending in the curve of Lily's bottom.

Lily broke off their kissing to ask, "Why didn't you kiss me the night we exchanged gifts?"

Helen dropped her head onto the pillow, breathing raggedly through her mouth.

"I don't know," she said, sounding surprised at being asked at that moment. "I might have, if Belle hadn't come in. Did you want to be kissed?"

Lily pressed her body against Helen's. "Yes. Oh, yes."

Helen's hand was gently squeezing Lily's bottom. "Then, why didn't you kiss me?"

Lily touched Helen's hair, which was now beginning to come undone. "I didn't know how."

She could see Helen's eyes, suddenly alert, and watched her lips curl into a bemused smile.

"Well," she said, leaning into Lily's face, "you do now."

It wasn't long before Helen shifted their positions, and slid a leg between Lily's. And then everything moved faster - kisses, touching, stroking, squeezing. Lily started to say that she had dreamt of this hour, but Helen rasped, "Lily, talk later!" Lily felt Helen's pulsations, from the blood vessels in her neck to the muscles of her thighs, and her own body fell into rhythm with Helen's.

Lily felt Helen's ecstasy at the same time as she heard Helen utter a falling cry, like that of a great bird, and she circled Helen's body with her arms, lightly at first and then tightly when Helen had collapsed across Lily's body. She had no words in any part of her mind for the experience. Being able to have this effect on Helen was effervescent.

They lay quietly for a long while, their breathing becoming regular again. Lily pulled the covers, which had been pushed aside in the frenzy, over Helen's shoulders. Helen shifted onto her side and gazed at Lily, her beautiful, soft mouth in a lazy half-smile. Lily gently ran a finger along the curve of Helen's bottom lip, smiling.

"So soft," she whispered. "So expressive."

Helen kissed Lily on the lips briefly. "So, who taught you how to kiss and make love over vacation?"

Lily stopped breathing, unable to think of what to say.

"I'll bet it was your friend, the one that was counting the days until you came home," Helen said, squinting. "Her name is..," she added, pausing.

"Eva," Lily said, simply.

"Eva." Helen was grinning. "Didn't you say that she had a beau?"

"She does," Lily said. "They'll be engaged come Valentine's Day."

Helen rested her hand on Lily's shoulder. "I didn't know I had a rival," she said quietly.

Lily looked at her imploringly. "You don't have rival, Helen. If you could look into my heart, you would know."

Helen pulled Lily into an embrace and held her tightly. Gradually it dawned on Lily that there was something fraught in the way Helen clung to her, like a boxer who embraces an opponent to avoid getting more punches. Lily wondered about the stories she'd heard about Helen's broken heart, about Julia Fremont.

"Do you doubt me?" she dared to ask.

When Helen didn't reply, Lily moved away and took Helen's face in both hands, looking earnestly into her eyes.

"You can trust me, Helen," she said in a voice full of promises. "I will show you that you have no rival, that there is no place in my heart for anyone but you."

Helen put her fingertips to Lily's mouth. "Let us enjoy one another in the time we have together."

The moment had passed, like a cloud that moved across the sun. Lily nodded.

Helen slipped a finger between Lily's lips and Lily grasped it immediately, pulling it into her mouth. Helen laughed.

"And I enjoy making love with you, dear Lily." she said, drawing Lily close and kissing her. "We have so much more to discover, do we not?"

Lily smiled now, nodding.

They alternately made love and dozed until dawn edged listlessly into their little room, replacing the gold of the gas jet with silver gray. Lily awoke alone in her bed and immediately started, looking for Helen's clothes. They were all there, on a chair and on the floor. She had been afraid that Helen had gone, and she fell back onto the mattress relieved. And then she felt as if she were being pricked by needles. Rolling over, she discovered that their hairpins carpeted the bed; neither of them had noticed the little wires during their night of joy. She rolled the word around her mind. *Joy*, she thought, *a word I never used before to describe a night.*

And then she heard noises from the parlor and looked around for her robe. It was gone as were her felt slippers. She put on her pajamas and her thickest socks and then she realized that the radiator was warm.

Helen had a pot of water over the alcohol flame and was unwrapping a loaf of something.

"Oh," she said, somewhat disappointed, "I was going to bring you breakfast in bed."

Lily went to her and they kissed. Lily felt intoxicated, or possibly exhausted, she couldn't be certain and didn't care. She was sure only that she loved kissing Helen.

"I requisitioned your robe and slippers," Helen confessed. "They were handy and warm. Say, did you notice the heat is on?"

Lily nodded and headed for the door.

Helen called after her, "By the time you return, your tea and spice cake will be ready!"

Lily looked at her face in the bathroom mirror. Her long hair was tangled and curly and wide. Her eyes were bloodshot. Slowly she began to smile and then shook her head and said aloud, "Joy!"

Helen was slicing into her loaf of Margaret's special spice cake, brought from Glens Falls. Lily sat at the table and poured tea for them both in last night's cups which she noticed Helen had rinsed.

"I feel very special to share your favorite spice cake," Lily said quietly.

Helen pushed the wax paper with the cake and slices closer to Lily.

"And so you are," she said, diffidently, barely glancing at Lily.

They ate without speaking. At length, Lily put her hand on Helen's arm and stroked it gently.

"Do you know what time Bert will be coming in?" Helen asked, offhand.

"I wouldn't think until this afternoon," Lily answered. It wasn't yet nine o'clock in the morning. Fleetingly, Lily thought of her family, having breakfast now, preparatory to getting ready for church.

Helen put her hands in her lap. "There are still more rules to learn, dear freshman."

Lily cocked her head in puzzlement.

"Our VC community, the small town we have here on campus," Helen began, "has certain unwritten but ironclad rules about the behavior of sweethearts."

"Are we sweethearts?" Lily interrupted.

Helen smiled and nodded. "I think we qualify, don't you?"

Lily beamed and sat back in her chair in perfect happiness.

"About the rules now," Helen continued. "As long as we do not remove ourselves from ordinary society by locking ourselves away to be alone together, we will be able to avoid drawing unwanted attention and approbation. If that happens, we may also draw the attention of Mrs. Kendrick, something to be avoided at all costs."

Lily looked at her.

"What that means is that we won't be able to be alone very often," Helen said flatly, shrugging.

"How - often - is *often*?" Lily asked tentatively.

Helen didn't respond immediately and then added, quietly, "Not often."

Lily sighed and pursed her lips. "I will die if I can't kiss you," she said.

Helen took her hand. "Of course you won't die, and neither will I. But we will be constrained to keep our normal associations with our friends and roommates and organizations, etcetera. And," she added significantly, "that means we can continue to meet one another for our walks."

"Our walks," Lily said, longingly.

"Of course," Helen replied, reassuringly. "We are friends, after all! We may associate with one another!"

Lily closed her other hand over Helen's, squeezing it in both of hers, relieved.

"As long as you don't expect that we can spend another night together like last night unless some miracle turns up and one of our roommates goes away for a night," Helen added, grimacing.

Lily sat back and folded her arms. "This is going to be awfully hard," she said in a sad tone.

Helen rose and held out her hands for Lily, who took them in hers and allowed herself to be pulled up and into an embrace.

"It won't be as bad as you think," Helen assured her. "Time passes quickly and opportunities turn up if we're alert to them."

She pushed Lily back and met her eyes with a saucy look. "Besides," she said, raising an eyebrow, "our time together today isn't over yet."

They immediately returned to the bedroom and, brushing the mattress clear of hairpins, climbed under the covers and made love again. And again.

LILY awoke in the late afternoon to footsteps and scraping. Slowly her mind came into focus and she realized that Bert must have come back. She closed her eyes again and pulled the toasty comforter close around her neck, dozing. Then there was scratching on her door and Bert opened it.

"Are you awake?" she asked.

Lily took a deep breath. "Yes, roomie. How was your trip?"

"Oh, fine, fine," Bert said dismissively. "I brought back some swell treats. Some of the gang said they'd come by later for a spread. We'll eat like queens until the good stuff is gone. Will you be up by then?"

Lily noted that Bert had not inquired as to the reason for Lily's sleeping and filed that away for later contemplation.

"Yes, certainly," she said sleepily, "your mother's cooking is wonderful."

"I'll let you finish your nap, then," Bert said. "I'll try to unpack quietly."

"O.K."

"Say," Bert suddenly said, and Lily saw her looking at the floor. "That's a lot of hairpins on your rug. Be careful where you step."

"O.K.," Lily murmured as Bert closed the door. She turned over and remembered that she had rinsed the mugs after Helen left two hours ago, but the parlor probably bore signs of company having been there. She remembered Helen's details about the unwritten rules as she drifted back to sleep.

CHAPTER 16

Lily returned from the library to the fragrance of hot molasses and chocolate wafting down the hall, a sign that someone was trying a variation of chafing dish fudge. She smiled; she was back in her home, embraced by the sociable chattering of a spread, the smell of wet wool, the unearthly clank and hiss of the radiators. And in this home, across the campus, was her beloved. All of it made her almost giddy with happiness.

"What are you grinning about?" Bert was squinting across their parlor from her seat at the table as Lily entered their room. She was surrounded by her Chem book and disheveled piles of paper.

Lily paused, and looked at her roommate. "Nothing in particular," she said in a wistful tone, "I'm just happy."

"Studying makes you happy?" Bert frowned. "In that case, you can feel positively delirious by helping with my Chem. Exams start next week and Chem is first."

"I've already offered to help you with Chem," Lily called over her shoulder on her way to her bedroom.

"Well, I don't want to take any time from your exercise walks," Bert commented.

Lily came back into the parlor and sat down across from Bert.

"You can have my entire Saturday, the day after tomorrow," she said, somberly.

"Oh," Bert said, taken aback. "That would be extremely generous. What about your own studying? You said you were worried about Greek."

"I only walk with Helen three times a week," Lily said in a pleading tone. "That can't be too much."

Bert was staring at her, blinking. "Lil, I was kidding," she said, shrugging. "Honest, I didn't mean anything."

Lily had shrunk into her chair. The stress of following the unwritten rules about sweethearts was always just beneath the surface. She was afraid of losing her friends, especially Bert whom she loved for being the best kind of person.

"You've been kind of touchy since we came back," Bert was saying gently. "Is there something you want to get off your mind?"

Lily pursed her lips, her mind weighing the argument she had been having for nearly three weeks.

"Helen and I are sweethearts," she blurted.

Bert tossed her pencil on the desk and laughed heartily. She had the most cheerful laugh.

"I know that!" she exclaimed. "Alice, Lucy, and Mina - we all know that."

Lily stared at her.

"Did you think we were blind?" Bert was mirthful.

Lily asked, timidly, "Is it alright?"

Bert cocked her head and gave Lily a sympathetic look. "Well, why wouldn't it be?"

Lily sighed as if she had been holding her breath for weeks. "Thanks," she said simply.

Bert picked up her pencil and glanced over her papers. "Of course, it's alright with *us*. I'm sure there are broken-hearted freshmen who don't feel kindly disposed toward you."

Lily smiled and got up to go to her room.

"I'm taking your Saturday, just the same," Bert called after her.

MONDAY, the first day of Mid-years, ended the same as any other Monday, with Chapel. Lily and Helen exchanged smiles as the Juniors passed by at the end of the brief service. When the freshmen emerged into the hallway, Lily was happily surprised to see Helen waiting for her in the crowd of students hashing over the day's exam and nervously chattering predictions of impending doom on the upcoming Trig or History or French lit. exams. She barely heard them as she made her way to the face looking upon hers with a small smile.

"Can you spare half an hour for a walk?" Helen said, and Lily felt a trilling sensation run up her spine.

"I wasn't sure you'd want to, with Mid-years this week," Lily offered.

Helen made a cynical face. "If they can hold Chapel during the week of Mid-years exams when girls hardly need to be reminded to pray, then we can have our exercise. If," she added, "you have the time."

Lily smiled. "I have the time, Miss McIntyre."

Helen smiled almost bashfully and Lily felt they were in a bubble just then, with everyone else separated by a membrane that blurred their faces and dulled their voices to a murmur.

"Well, let's get your walking gear on, then," Helen nudged.

They headed out toward the lake in the darkness. Once across Raymond Avenue, they quickly left the streetlights behind them and had to carefully pick their way on well-worn paths through the snow near the dock where in summer the boats were tied up. Helen led Lily to the board fence that ran protectively along the edge of the lake in this area. They looked over a wide section of the frozen lake that had been cleared of snow, now black in the dim light.

"We haven't skated yet," Lily said. "I brought back my skates, as Belle advised."

Helen put her arm around Lily's shoulder, and the weight of it felt like home to Lily.

"Some girls skate even during mid-year's," she said. "I'll wait until Saturday, and really celebrate the end of exams, and our moment of total freedom from classwork."

"Freedom until next Monday, you mean!" Lily said, noting that they had just two days before the second term began.

"The faculty wouldn't want us to get carried away with too much free time," Helen replied.

Lily leaned her head on Helen's shoulder. "I'd like to get carried away," she said in a dreamy voice.

Helen chuckled. "Yes," she said quietly.

Lily turned to Helen and Helen gently pulled her into a kiss. It was as smooth a movement as if they had choreographed it. Each walk furnished the opportunity for a kiss, an embrace, a chance to exhale from the tension of wanting and not being able to have. These winter kisses found their cheeks and noses cold but their lips quite warm and soft, and minutes after an embrace they may as well have been standing before a roaring fire. They did not talk much during this part of their walk; the spell cast over them required them to speak without words, without even being able to read the other's eyes in the darkness.

Then they heard animated voices of two or three coming across Raymond Avenue toward the lake. Lily and Helen parted and Lily linked arms with Helen as they headed back, calling a cheery greeting to the party as they passed.

"How was Chem today?" Helen asked. The spell was broken now, the mundane reigned again.

"I did myself a good turn, to be honest," Lily replied, "when I only intended to help Bert. I wouldn't have spent much time on Chem if it hadn't been for the day I reviewed with her. It was a good thing as I found out this morning."

"No flunk note coming from Chem," Helen said. "I got one of those freshman year."

"For Chem?" Lily was surprised. "I can't imagine you failing anything. "

"It's not important anymore," Helen said dismissively. "When is Greek?"

"Friday, can you believe it? My last exam. The sword will hang over me all week!"

"Do you need any help reviewing?" Helen offered.

"What? You?" Lily replied, laughing.

Helen was taken aback. "I thought I was a fair tutor. You never complained."

Lily was still laughing. "And you were an excellent tutor. But you're not my tutor anymore. And it would be a waste of time to try."

Helen stopped and looked at Lily, puzzled. Lily took Helen's arm and pulled her close, resuming their walk.

She spoke confidentially. "Picture the scene, dear. You, me, alone in a room, the couch only inches away."

Helen smiled. "You think we would have no self-discipline?"

"I can't speak for you, worldly-wise junior that you are," Lily replied dryly, "but if I were alone in a room with you, I would not be reviewing Greek verbs, no matter how much they might need reviewing."

Helen threw back her head and laughed, happily, Lily thought. "So, poor dear freshman, a self-described stranger to academic failure, as I recall you once said, I can only hope that Saturday doesn't find you with a flunk note from Professor Leach."

"I hope to avoid that fate, as well," Lily said, "especially since Saturday night is Bonfire Night and the skating should be excellent. It sounds like a midwinter night's dream. "

Helen nodded. "It's a fun evening. And we will get to skate together, at least some of the time."

Lily was nodding, grudgingly, and they laughed.

They had entered the pool of light at the entrance to Main, where Lily would go to the stairs and Helen would leave by the door on the other side of the lobby for the walk to Raymond House. The wide room was busy with girls passing to and from the library upstairs, only slightly less socially inclined than other weeks in the term. Lily's fellow freshmen were easy to pick out; they had a harried look, distracted enough to neglect their appearance, darting about as if extra steps were wasted when more facts could be crammed into their minds.

Helen put her hands on her hips and smiled at the sight.

"Why are you smirking at my classmates?" Lily demanded.

Helen sighed. "Because freshmen think Mid-years are a matter of life and death."

Lily looked at her, unamused.

"After freshman year, you realize that only life and death are a matter of life and death."

Lily made no response.

Helen wrinkled her brow. "I meant that to be comforting."

"Thank you," Lily said, the smallest smile curling at the edges of her mouth.

Helen gestured toward the exit. "I'll go study my astronomy now."

Lily nodded, and they locked eyes for a long moment. Then they said as light-hearted a good-night as they could manage.

Lily went upstairs, the glow of their time together still with her.

SATURDAY morning dawned as gray as each day of the preceding week. It was the deep winter of late January when the stingy sun withheld the light that would have made snow sparkle. Across the campus, Vassar students slowly roused themselves on the day after the end of Mid-years, and looked for flunk notes.

Bert and Lily met their friends around the mailroom after breakfast and decided to coordinate their efforts to find out when flunk notes for Chem and Greek were being received by hallmates. They wanted to avoid spending the day on pins and needles if the dreaded faculty notices to failing students had already been delivered and they were not among the recipients.

But it wasn't until after three, the last of the mail deliveries having been completed, that Izzie burst into Bert and Lily's room with the news.

"Marcie Holland got a flunk note in Greek this morning!" she said jubilantly to Lily, who sighed into their couch, smiling with relief.

"And," she continued, looking at Bert somberly, "You didn't receive a flunk note in Chem. I did."

Both Lily and Bert rushed to comfort their friend, offering assurances of help in the next term so she could catch up. Then, after she left, they clasped hands and danced around their parlor positively giddy.

After supper, exams were forgotten as most of the campus bundled up and dug out skates for Bonfire Night on the lake. A stream of revelers crossed Raymond Avenue and bunched up around the few benches to strap on their skates. As Lily and her friends pulled up at the end of the lake and waited their turn for a seat, they observed fires being lit around the lake shore at intervals. The heaps of wood soon grew into blazing sentinels, highlighting the bare trees around the shore and sending long arcs of light onto the lake surface, almost entirely cleared of snow for skating this night. Skaters were already gliding far along onto the finger-shaped lake, small dark shapes of singles, pairs and a couple of short strings of skaters holding hands as they skated in time to the music of a band located somewhere near the street.

Lily thought the scene like something she read from medieval times, a carnival or festival that could only exist in a world without gas lights or electricity, a time out of its time. She smiled slightly, in awe. And she looked for Helen but it was too dark and the large number of skaters on the lake and along the shore made differentiation impossible. She felt Bert pulling her arm; a space on a bench had become available. They fiddled with their skates, having to remove their gloves to match the buckles and straps; it took longer than Lily wanted because her hands were freezing and the leather stiff. And she wanted to find Helen.

They stepped through the snow bank and onto the lake, gingerly at first, getting their skating legs under them. Alice, then Lucy and Izzie emerged from the shore and the group milled around, circling and darting away from the group and then back like bees around a hive. And then Lily spied someone out of the corner of her eye wearing a skating cap with strings hanging down that ended in little balls. She glided away from the group toward Helen who was slowly skating a small continuous circle.

"Hello," Lily called, smiling.

Helen continued circling. "You freshmen are the slowest bunch!"

Lily skated closer. "Oh, really?"

"Really."

"Here now," she said, spreading her arms.

Helen pulled up before Lily, smirking. She sighed, exaggeratedly.

"That's a nice knit cap you have on, Miss McIntyre," Lily commented. "It fits you very well and suits you, if I say so."

Helen took Lily's arm and they skated away from the shore toward the middle of the lake. "Well," she replied, "it was handmade by a pretty, skillful girl."

They were falling into a rhythm now, skating easily in step.

"Did you say, 'pretty, skillful' or 'pretty skillful?'" Lily asked, frowning in feigned puzzlement.

Helen laughed her out loud laugh and shook her head. "There's no fishing to-night, Lily," she said. "The lake's frozen!"

They laughed together joyfully. Helen put an arm around Lily's waist and with her other clasped Lily's hand. Lily copied the gesture and they skated as one person. They were nearly half along the length of the lake now, where skaters were fewer and the moonless dark punctuated only by the bonfires. Lily felt the night embracing them. She had never felt happier.

"Did you get any letters today?" Helen asked.

"None from VC faculty," Lily answered softly. "Thanks to you."

"Oh, pshaw. You're a regular Miss Grind."

"Not when it came to Greek," Lily said earnestly. "Your tutoring really helped me overcome my panic about it."

"And all this time I thought you were just playing dumb to get my attention."

"Now who's trying to fish on a frozen lake?" Lily laughed.

"Oh, see here!" Helen laughed and guided them toward the shore at the far end of the lake where trees dipped their heads toward the surface. She whirled them about in a tight circle, pulling Lily to her. They kissed passionately, out of sight of any who might be passing by in the dim light.

Before emerging from the bower, they embraced for a long moment.

Lily whispered, "Tomorrow will be four weeks since our night."

She felt Helen nod.

"It seems like forever," Lily said, a touch of anguish in her voice.

Helen took Lily's hands and pulled her out onto the expanse of ice.

"Yes," she said, nodding and causing the little balls on her cap's strings to bob up and down.

They entwined their arms again as they began the trip back along the lake.

After a silence, Helen said quietly, "This is what I was explaining, about how things have to be."

"I know, I know," Lily replied quickly. "I just - want more."

She saw Helen nod, and then she leaned close. "I want to make love again."

Helen raised her eyebrows and took a deep breath. Smiling under a wrinkled brow, she said with careful enunciation, "As. Do. I."

And that was the best they could do. Songs were beginning back at the boat dock; the pair picked up their pace. Seniors were singing loudly about the glories of their class, the "Evermore, the Ought-Fours!"

"Better find your classmates," Helen suggested, as they skated free of one another. "It will be class spirit competition now. Time for freshmen to learn the importance of being a class!"

Lily watched Helen skate toward a group and recognized Belle, who waved gaily at her. She turned about, looking for her friends. Eventually, skating from group to group, she located Bert and asked if they had a class song. Bert said the little bunch around her, teammates from hockey and basketball, thought they should do one of their little cheer-songs from games.

"We probably could have used some warning that we were expected to behave as a class," Bert complained, "with class songs and everything."

"We do seem sort of pathetic in the class spirit department. We should find the Strong Hall girls," Lily suggested. "They've always had more *cachet* than we poor Main girls."

The juniors were gathering now into a long string of skaters across the lake. In a moment, they were off, a meandering line skating the length of the lake, holding hands and singing. By the time they returned, their songs were off-key and hoarsely shouted rather than sung, but they were jubilant and proud of their unity.

"You found Helen, then," Bert said as they watched the juniors from the boat dock.

Lily turned to look at her roommate and saw that she was smiling. "Yes, Bert, I found her," Lily replied. "We had a skate."

When it was their turn, the freshmen were indeed led by the Strong Hall girls who had somehow found out about the necessity of class songs and took charge of singing them. Lily thought the songs secondary to the feeling of being part of a long string of classmates holding hands, racing down the lake making noise at the top of their lungs. It was sheer fun and foolishness.

That night, Lily and Bert announced a spread in their rooms where hot chocolate was made, smoked oysters were eaten with hatpins for forks, and the invited participants brought jars of olives and marmalade, boxes of crackers and biscuits. And, being Main girls, no one sang a class song. They did perform admirably the new hit, "Hot Time in the Old Town Tonight," and dared the Strong Hall crowd to top that.

Later, under her feather comforter, Lily reviewed the evening. Helen was right about their following the unwritten rules. She didn't want to alienate her classmates; being part of the class of 1907 was important to her. But she relived their kiss and embrace on the lake and wished very hard that there was a way to be alone together.

THE second term began without ceremony and it felt very much like the first, as well it should. It was a continuation of year-long courses with the same professors and schedules. There was skating only for another week and then the lake was taken over for the harvesting of ice blocks for the college's use in refrigeration. Grumbling rippled across the campus, and then was forgotten about in the February excitement for Valentine's Day and the Colonial Ball that celebrated Washington's Birthday.

Mid-afternoon Valentine's Day found Lily fast asleep in her room. She had stayed up nearly all night catching up on her reading for History, for which she had an exam in the morning. She was sleeping through Chem, the first cut she had made in any class all year. Surrendering to the overwhelming desire to sleep, she had simply pulled off her dress and climbed into bed in her long winter underwear.

She awoke to someone touching her face and gazed sleepily into those beautiful grey eyes framed by dark lashes, very close to hers. She tried to smile.

Helen smiled happily. "Bert invited me in on her way out. She said you broke rules right and left - lights on after ten, cutting Chem. I'm so proud of you, freshman!"

Lily rolled over onto her back, chuckling.

"Happy Valentine's Day," Helen said, quietly cheerful. "I've been looking for you all day."

Lily sighed. "I didn't mean to study all night, but I didn't feel tired until breakfast and by then it was too late to sleep. And then," she raised her arms and let them drop on the bed, "here I am. So happy to see you. Will you be my Valentine?"

Helen smiled and nodded ever so slightly. She presented Lily with a card and small box. Lily drew herself up on one elbow.

"I'm unaccustomed to receiving gifts, you know," she said as she accepted the present.

"Well, that will get easier when you become an upperclassman," Helen said, her voice quiet and sly.

"With crushes, you mean," Lily retorted, shaking her head. "I'm ignoring that and opening my card instead."

It was a cutout Valentine's card with a picture of Cupid offering a bunch of violets to the recipient of the card. The printed sentiment read, "Violets are blue/ but not so true/ as I to you."

Lily looked at Helen, her eyes shining. Even if it was a card sentiment, it was the most Helen had ever communicated of her feelings. Then she opened the little box to find one chocolate heart from Smith Brothers, Vassar's favorite confectionery in Poughkeepsie.

"It's a filled heart," Helen offered.

"With what, may I ask?" Lily asked, coyly.

"You'll have to bite into it to discover that," Helen said with a small smile.

Lily closed the box and lay back down.

"I have your card all ready there on the dresser, but I intended to buy you some violets to go with it."

Helen nodded, still smiling. "I don't need violets. I have a lily," she spoke in a lover's voice.

Lily could only reply, "That you surely do," and reached out her arms to her sweetheart, drawing her into a kiss.

CHAPTER 17

Washington's Birthday, celebrated on his actual birthday to the extent that the administration would allow, was the prelude to one of Vassar's celebrated campus balls held during the year for only the campus community. The girls regarded the event with the same seriousness as if boys had been invited, perhaps even more because they were not. Some dressed in white wigs and a version of historic garb, imitations of Martha Washington or possibly Marie Antoinette. Others dressed in a more masculine manner, with collars and ties; once in a while someone would wear a complete men's dress suit. It was an opportunity for upperclassmen to formally invite an underclassman, provide her with a corsage or other favor and escort her to the ball.

The freshmen learned all of this too late to provide themselves with ball gowns and so they dressed as fine as their wardrobe, and that of such friends who were able to lend them things to wear, would permit. Lily received details from Belle and Helen and confessed that she would have to wear a new shirtwaist and skirt that she had obtained at home over vacation, as it was the best she had. They assured her that she would be appropriately attired.

On the day of the ball, exercises were held honoring Washington, including speeches in the Chapel. Lily could tell from the whispering and giggling that her classmates' attention was truly devoted to the anticipated evening's festivities and not to lectures on taking an example from the Father of Our Country. She felt the same way. Although two of their hallmates had been invited to attend the ball on the arm of an upperclassman, Helen had made no mention or hint to her about such an arrangement. Bert had playfully suggested that Helen might show up in "that smashing dress suit" that she had worn in the play but Lily could only shake her head in ignorance. There would be plenty of dancing that night; Lily wondered how many she might be able to have with Helen. Sometimes rules, written or unwritten, chafed and she was forced to admit to herself as she dressed that she was cross. If there were any occasion at Vassar where sweethearts could attend as a couple, this surely seemed to be it. But Helen had not invited her. She didn't want to be constrained into being passive and just now she wanted to throw open the window in her bedroom and scream.

Standing before the mirror in her bedroom, she fussed with her green shirt-waist's plaid tie, trying it in a bow and then in a four-in-hand, finally pulling it off entirely, flinging it away and sitting down on her bed. She heard someone knock on their door and Bert answer it. Then Bert, still in her wrapper at this late hour, was leaning against her door jamb, grinning.

"What?" Lily said without enthusiasm.

With a flourish, Bert produced a bag from behind her back and presented it to Lily, who tore it open. It was a nosegay of six small deep red roses, nestled amid greens. Bert was chuckling.

"You thought you weren't getting anything from her, didn't you?" she teased.

Lily clutched the bouquet and looked up at Bert with shining eyes. She pursed her lips and said nothing, but she was restored.

Because the ball was held in Main's large dining room, its residents did not have to bother with winter wraps. Taking their time, Lily, Bert and their friends gathered in each other's rooms, admiring each other dressed up for a welcome change, assisting with emergencies or offering accessories that would perfectly finish a look. Then they made their way downstairs as ladies in a promenade, so unlike their normal careless selves that not a hair was out of place in anyone, not a cuff was fastened with a safety pin, not a hem soiled with cinders from the snowy walks. Lily held her nosegay at her waist with one hand; she was bubbling with anticipation.

The great dining room had been transformed and rearranged much as the Raymond House room had been last autumn, with streamers and dance floor space. The freshmen felt more at home than they had in November and were made more gregarious by their finery. Lily's group staked out a table but she didn't sit. Unlike the last time, she wanted to see and be seen, by Helen. Some girls were indeed dressed in ball gowns, expensive affairs with yards of material in the skirts, trains, and sleeves that puffed to their ears. She was dressed much like her fellow freshmen but the nosegay in her hand assured her that she had nothing to feel inferior about.

The band had begun to play and girls were chattering and calling to one another as they tried to secure dances on their cards. Lily promised her first dance to Bert and they stepped onto the dance floor, thereby dodging other dance card requests. Bert offered to lead and Lily readily agreed. They waltzed happily as Bert called out greetings to her fellow athletes every few steps.

And then, through the doors, freed of their winter wraps, some juniors from Raymond entered. She spotted Belle first and caught a glimpse of Helen in the crowd.

"Doesn't Belle look grand?" she said to Bert, admiringly.

Belle was dressed in the latest New York fashion in ball gowns, a royal blue dress with a deep v-cut down to her waist; an ivory silk panel filled the cut, rising to her neck and finishing in a high collar. Silk embroidery decorated the edges of the panel and extended onto her skirt like a tongue. Her sleeves were puffed and her cuffs reached nearly to her elbows. With her dark hair and porcelain complexion, Belle was beautiful. She was smiling and laughing, no doubt accepting compliments as she passed.

"She is the *Belle of the ball*, to be sure," Bert agreed.

"You should dance with her," Lily urged.

"If there's any room on her card by the time I see her!"

The music ended and they milled about, chatting. Lily left Bert talking with her teammates and made her way across the floor. She turned from complimenting a classmate from Chem to find her way blocked. Helen was before her, smiling in what seemed to Lily a hopeful way.

"Miss Kepler," Helen said, bowing her head slightly.

"Miss McIntyre," Lily responded with a small smile, also bowing her head.

"Is your next dance taken?" Helen was saying.

Lily was mesmerized by Helen's beauty. She wore a rose-colored gown of cashmere and lace, the effect one of silky softness that extended to her hair and face. Lily wanted to touch her all over to verify her impression.

"Dance?" Lily realized Helen had spoken. The music had started up again. "Let's dance!"

Helen laughed gently and took her arm, leading them back to the dance floor. Then she expertly began to lead as she had in Glens Falls.

Lily smiled at this and Helen noticed. "Why are you smiling?" she asked, whirling them around.

"Because you look smashing tonight," Lily replied.

"Oh, thank you," Helen said, and then leaned over confidentially. "I bought this over vacation expressly to wear tonight to dance with you."

Lily looked at her in wonder. "How could you know I would dance with you tonight?"

Helen grinned, looking away around the room. She shrugged, still smiling. "I don't know. I just had a feeling."

"And do I have you to thank for my nosegay of roses?" Lily asked innocently.

Helen gave her a startled look. "And who else would be sending you flowers?"

It was Lily's turn to laugh. "They arrived at the very last minute tonight. And I love them so. Thank you."

"I had some trouble deciding what to get for you, not certain what you would be wearing. So, I was a little tardy with my order. I'm glad they arrived in time! Or at all!"

The song ended too soon and Helen accompanied Lily to her table, her arm in Lily's.

"I saw you as soon as I came through the doors," Helen was saying and Lily leaned closer to hear. "You should always wear green, sweetheart. It sets off your hair so well."

Lily forced herself to take a deep breath. Each time she believed she had reached the outer limit of joy, Helen pushed the boundary further.

The table was working again on their dance cards and so Lily and Helen went over theirs together. Helen wrote her name on Lily's card for three more dances; that made four out of the ten slots, counting the dance they just finished. It was more than Lily had dared to hope for. Helen acceded to requests by Izzie, Mina and Lucy, thrilling them by signing their cards for dances. Bert, who hadn't asked for a dance from Helen, dared to ask why Helen hadn't worn her brother's dress suit. That sent the others into a peal of high-pitched laughter which, in life outside an all-girls' college, was normally emitted in the presence of boys. Helen demurred, hinting at not wearing out its appeal by overexposure.

Belle appeared and asked Lily for her dance card, cheerful at finding an open dance. She held out her hand and Lily took it. They stood before one another as the music began and neither went first.

"Would you like to lead, dear?" Belle asked. "Or shall I?"

Lily laughed. "I haven't had a choice all night," she said. "I've been led."

"Then you should lead now," Belle nodded and placed her left hand on Lily's shoulder. "I enjoy following. It gives others the impression that they are in charge!"

Lily laughed and took up her position. It was unfamiliar but Belle helped and they danced very well together. Lily was effusive about Belle's gown and the latter was clearly pleased at the compliments. Belle returned the compliment and Lily apologized again for not knowing about the gowns generally worn for Vassar balls.

"Oh, *Cheri,*" Belle said, shaking her head. "You need not apologize, especially for your beautiful velvet waist. Remember, wear what you have with pride and a head held high, and you will be seen as beautiful and tasteful."

"And if I smile, will I be seen as happy, also?" Lily asked, smiling.

Belle nodded, rolling her eyes upward. "There's a very great deal of happiness around these days. *C'est fou!*"

Lily understood her meaning. "Is that all right with you?" Lily asked.

Belle gave her a look. "But of course! I much prefer a happy household than a grim one."

Lily remembered to lead them in a twirl.

"Besides," Belle was saying, "I saw where things were going. I just watched it grow, like watching buds swell on a tree in the spring and then burst into flower at the right time."

Lily could not respond. She wanted to cry and pressed her lips hard together in a tight smile to stop them from trembling. Belle was smiling, greeting others they passed, seeming oblivious to Lily's reaction.

One of the dances Helen had signed for was the last dance of the evening. Helen offered her hand to Lily, and then led them to the door.

"I'm going to walk you home," Helen said, retrieving her cape and draping it over her arm. With her other arm, she guided a surprised Lily down the hall to the main lobby and stairs.

"It's very—gallant—of you," Lily stammered. They were alone for a moment, with the promise of a few more moments to come.

Helen smiled and slipped her arm more closely in Lily's. They began the climb to Lily's floor.

"Why didn't you invite me to be your date tonight?" Lily asked, wanting to know.

They walked in silence to the second floor and turned down Lily's hall, strolling slowly it seemed to Lily.

"I hope there was no need for a formal invitation," Helen answered quietly. "Did you require one?"

They had reached Lily's door. She turned and replied equally quietly. "One always wants to know another's intentions."

Helen gave her a look of apology. "Will you invite me inside?"

Lily opened the door and pulled Helen inside by the hand. They immediately embraced, exhaling at the same time, and stood in each other's arms for a long while. Then they kissed and kissed again.

"How could you not know my intentions by now?" Helen said, rushing her words in between kisses.

"Because you've never shared them with me," Lily responded before resuming a kiss.

And then they stopped trying to converse, falling onto the couch and into each other's desire. They were well aware that in minutes the hall would fill with returning partiers and they would have to let go of each other, unrequited passions pushed down again. But they seized the moment, in their beautiful clothes, to communicate without words. Lily ran her hands over Helen's dress; it was indeed as soft as it seemed and the sensation of the cashmere created an indelible, tingling memory. Helen's hands on Lily's face and throat spoke to Lily of Helen's intentions; her touch was tender and almost worshipful.

"I become tongue-tied with you, at times like these," Helen whispered.

Lily touched Helen's lips. They were full and warm from kissing. "Why? Are you afraid?" she asked gently.

Helen smiled a little at the phrase that had become their private joke. "Possibly that."

They heard voices coming along the hall from the stairs. Her fellow freshmen were returning from the ball. Helen would have to leave. Lily sat up and Helen followed.

"Trust me," Helen hissed.

Lily saw Helen's beseeching eyes and at that moment she felt the stronger of them. She rose and held out her hand to Helen, pulling her up. Pressed by the knowledge that Bert would be coming in at any moment, she retrieved Helen's cape and gloves and watched her prepare to leave.

"You needn't worry about my trusting you," Lily said, handing Helen her gloves. "To use a figure of speech, all of my eggs are in your basket, my love."

They kissed quickly in goodbye and Lily opened the door.

"Soon," Helen said into Lily's eyes.

"Soon," Lily replied into Helen's.

And Helen was off down the hall, her cape billowing as she returned greetings called out as she passed.

Later, in bed under her down comforter, curled tight while she warmed the bed, Lily contemplated this woman she loved. She thought that she might have selected a better analogy in replying to Helen's request to trust her. Lily was on the circus trapeze and was flying without a net to keep her from crashing if she fell. And she knew that she was powerless to alter her feelings for Helen in any way. She wouldn't have chosen to do so even if she could.

CHAPTER 18

It was the end of the day at the end of the first week in March. Lily was attending a meeting of the Settlement Club for the first time at the suggestion of Helen who had been a member since her freshman year. From her description, the club seemed interesting to Lily. But mostly it was also the opportunity to spend a little time with Helen.

She was early, out of habit, and watched other attendees enter singly and in groups. How different Vassar girls were from her classmates at Central High. Here it was infrequent to run into a silly girl only interested in gossip or fashion and, while nearly everyone here loved to talk about boys and eagerly followed the athletic contests among the Ivy League schools, they nevertheless were serious about their studies. Lily understood how they could do both, it seemed perfectly natural to her. But it wouldn't have seemed so to Eva, or to most of her friends in Buffalo. Or to her mother.

At the starting time for the meeting, Helen blew in and slid onto the seat beside Lily, out of breath. "Physics lab!" she said, unbuttoning her coat. "A long hustle from here!"

Lily smiled. Helen noted the open notebook and pencil at the ready.

"Are you taking notes?" she asked.

Lily glanced around and then quietly closed her notebook. "Force of habit," she said sheepishly.

Helen smiled into her eyes, and whispered, "Hello, you."

Lily nudged her with an elbow, looking pleased. "Hello, back."

Someone had taken up a position behind the professor's podium and was speaking. Helen said it was the Settlement Club's Elector, or president.

"Alright, everyone," said a short, spectacled girl in a brown shirtwaist. She wore her hair in a bun on top of her head and spoke authoritatively. She was looking around the room.

"I can see that our regular members have responded to the call for recruits," she was saying. "We have a number of new faces here tonight and that's good. First, let's review minutes from the last meeting and do the treasurer's report - which I understand is a good one - and then my job will be to introduce our club in such a way as to not scare away potential new members. "

Lily sent Helen a skeptical look. Helen looked back inquiringly.

"New recruit?" Lily whispered.

Helen shrugged, then smiled.

The business part of the meeting went by relatively quickly, and then the Elector stepped from behind the podium, her smile an attempt at warmth. Lily realized that the girl was nervous and admired her suddenly for making the time to be Elector of the Settlement Club.

"I would like to explain some of what our club does. And if any of our members want to interject their own reasons for joining, I hope they'll do so."

There were a few quips and some chuckles before she went on.

"When people hear the word 'Settlement' or 'Settlement worker,'" she said, "right away they think of a do-gooder or somebody interfering in the lives of poor or immigrant people, imposing our ideas and ideals on unfortunates. We want to do good work, of course, but settlement workers don't tell people what to do. We don't make decisions for the people we work with. What we do, in a nutshell, is live in neighborhoods where there is great poverty and suffering, where people live in tenements without water or sanitary facilities or heat. And we get to know them, we ask them what they need, and then we help them succeed in getting what they need to improve their lives.

"The College Settlement was established at 95 Rivington Street in New York in 1889. I'm sorry to say that it was Smith College graduates that founded it and not Vassar girls, but we have been members of the College Settlement from the start. And, for those of us who want to work in settlements for a year, or two years, that's where we go. We live together at 95, eat together, teach, organize, canvas, lobby - all from our Settlement House. Some who have lived there say the camaraderie reminds them of their college days."

"But without the grocery store at Main," a sardonic voice called out. There was laughter.

"Well, that's so," replied the Elector. "The food isn't quite as good as here at VC -" she added, rolling her eyes. Much laughter followed because almost no one praised Vassar food.

"And sometimes, the situation of people who come to us for help breaks one's heart because we have to try to work with the inadequate city and charitable services available to new immigrants. Those agencies often fail people who need help the most. So, you need to keep in mind that you will be much involved in the lives of strangers if you decide to move from fundraising here to a year at 95."

"Tell them about the graduate programs," someone called out.

"Yes, good point," the Elector said, raising a finger. "For those who truly love taking courses," she paused and peered over her glasses for effect, "New York University has a graduate program in Sociology that is an excellent way to continue with settlement work without so much daily interaction. Plus," she added, "you don't have to live at 95 in that case!"

Someone rose from the first row. It was one of the club officers.

"Phoebe, let me add something at this point about the field of settlement work," she said.

"Of course, Eleanor, " the elector said, smiling warmly, and stepped back.

"We in 1904 think we're pretty modern, especially at places like Vassar and Smith," said the slender girl with intense brown eyes. "But this is the beginning of a new century and the seeds of great change have been sown. Think of a world without college courses in Sociology, or even Psychology. That was the world into which we were born. And if that's the way the world was twenty years ago, just imagine what these disciplines will be like twenty years hence.

"My point is, not too briefly, to be sure," she said with a self-deprecating smile, "that more than any other kind of work that Vassar graduates can do, settlement work is the vanguard of some entirely new way that society will create to help the poor and the newly arrived immigrant so that they may secure a way of life that we take for granted. It's purely radical!"

Some of her club mates in the first two rows applauded. She bowed and sat down.

When the meeting ended, Helen leaned over and said, "Walk with me. I have something to tell you."

"And I have a question," Lily said. "As a potential new member," she added in a voice intended to evoke a smile. It succeeded.

They left the building and Helen guided them to walking paths that wouldn't take them so far away that they would miss supper.

"What's your question?" Helen asked, snugging her arm through Lily's.

"Do you think you will do a stint at the settlement house after graduation?"

Helen looked into the distance. "To be honest," she said, "I don't know. It's too far away. But," she added, "I wouldn't be surprised if I do."

"Why?"

Helen shrugged. "I think I could do some good. Maybe I could teach dramatic skills to Hungarians!" she enthused. Then she added, more seriously, "And I think I would learn a lot from the experience."

"I have another question," Lily asked, carefully.

Helen looked over at her, eyebrows raised.

"Are settlement workers Socialists?" Such philosophies were anathema to her family, her social class of small business owners.

Helen didn't seem surprised at the question. "Some are," she nodded once. "Not me," she reassured Lily, smiling.

"More questions?" she asked. Lily shook her head and squeezed Helen's arm.

"Alright then, I have news, " Helen announced.

Lily nodded attentively.

"Belle's Aunt Cornelia, her favorite aunt from New York who kindly looks after Belle when her parents are off gallivanting in Europe—which is so often—is traveling to Cleveland this weekend."

Lily nodded once.

"And, the trip being so long, Aunt Nell likes to stop for the night. You may think that Albany is the most logical place for said overnight stop. But, as it happens, she refuses to set foot in any Albany hotel and has been firm on that for years and years."

Helen glanced at Lily. "But, as it also happens, Aunt Nell very much likes the Nelson House in Poughkeepsie."

"Oh," Lily said. She had heard the Nelson House was a first-rate hotel, where visiting parents most often stayed.

"And," Helen paused for effect, "she is arriving Saturday afternoon from Grand Central and niece Belle will meet her and spend the afternoon and evening with her."

Lily was beginning to see the point to the story. "Yes?"

"Yes," Helen agreed, "Belle took pains to explain to me that she will be away from our room from 3 p.m. until 9:30 p.m. at the latest."

Lily looked at her. Helen grinned.

"Would you skip supper Saturday evening?"

"How could we make sure we're alone?" Lily asked in a hushed voice.

"I'll pin up a *sleeping* note on the door - it's the only note people respect - and we'll keep the lights off," Helen replied, confidently.

"Belle did this for us?" Lily asked wonderingly.

"Well, she's terribly fond of Aunt Nell and looks forward to having tea and supper with her. But, yes, she saw this as a happy confluence of events," Helen said, nodding.

"*Opportunity*," Lily enunciated, recalling what Helen had said so long ago in January.

"Yes, indeed," Helen said happily.

Lily involuntarily took a deep breath and felt the tension leave her as she exhaled. She tried to laugh. They were nearing Main now.

"I want to cry," Lily said, helplessly.

"Oh, please don't," Helen said encouragingly. "Just say you don't mind skipping supper on Saturday."

Lily shook her head. "Three o'clock?" she said in a trembling voice.

Helen laughed happily. "Be on time!"

As soon as Lily scratched at the partially open door, it was opened by Belle. It was three o'clock on Saturday and Belle was just putting on her hat.

"Right on time, Rutie," she said cheerfully, as she adjusted the tilt of her felt cap that featured a large feather curling up and over. The hat gave the impression that its wearer was racing downhill at breakneck speed. It was a good image for Belle just now.

"I'm late, no surprise there!" Belle laughed at herself. "Make yourself at home. Helen is hunting up a piece of paper. Why is it that we, who live and die in an ocean of paper at VC, can so rarely find a clean piece? Not even an entire sheet, just a bit?"

Lily laughed easily, and took off her coat. Belle gasped and stood back, hand on her breast in mock horror.

"What is that?" she said, breathlessly.

Lily looked down at her attire. "It's a turtleneck sweater," she said, "that I borrowed from Bert. It's her athletic sweater, and so comfortable and warm. It's pretty raw outdoors this afternoon."

Belle was not mollified. "And does the giant *W* across the front stand for *woeful?*" she said, dramatically.

"Worcester High," Lily corrected her. "It's actually an honor to have one of these because only star athletes may acquire one."

Belle was putting on her gloves. "You have no idea what a relief it is to hear you say that. Now I may be sure that I will never have to wear one!"

Helen emerged from her bedroom, scrap of paper in hand, wearing a colorful silk kimono over what seemed to be long underwear. She made for the table and found a pencil.

Belle had her hand on the door. "Good heavens," she said, looking from one to the other. "How fortunate the two of you found each other. One wears athletic garb voluntarily and the other thinks a kimono will hide long johns!"

Lily laughed while Helen frowned as she gave the scrap of paper to her roommate.

"Will you pin this on the door block? And don't let the door strike you on your way out," she said with droll sarcasm.

Belle took her leave and Helen sighed heavily. Lily retrieved a paper package she had brought and put it on the table.

"I stopped at the grocery on my way," she said quietly.

"Oh," Helen crooned, "that was good thinking. What did you - " then she stopped herself and finished, "ignore that last part. Let me greet you."

She spread her arms and Lily melted into them, exhaling. They kissed; Helen broke off laughing.

"This is a bulky sweater, thick as anything," she marveled.

"Well," Lily stood back, lifting the long kimono arms, "you have single-handedly demolished the intended effect of this silk gown!"

They laughed at themselves.

"I had planned to remove my woolens before you arrived and wear only the kimono, so as to appear seductively attractive, " Helen offered, shaking her head, "but it's so cold in my room that I left them on. And then I couldn't find a piece of paper on which to write 'sleeping.' Then you were here. And here I am!"

"Well," Lily responded confidentially, "I will show you why I wore Bert's sweater."

She placed Helen's hands under the waistband of the sweater and watched the latter's expression change to surprise.

"Lily Kepler," she said, feigning shock, "where is your corset?"

Lily smiled. "That's the secret of these heavy athletic turtlenecks. Girls can't play basketball wearing corsets. And," she added coyly, "you have more than once complained about how slow freshmen are. I thought one less garment might give me an advantage."

Helen looked at her with mouth half open, in surprise and awe. "I believe you are a bit of a rebel."

Lily stepped toward Helen's bedroom. "And," she added over her shoulder, "I think I will have a definite advantage because you have all that long underwear to unbutton."

Helen gave a little shout and raced past Lily into her room. Lily laughed and followed her.

Helen's bedroom was a small slice of space with a window and a tiny closet whose door was open because there apparently wasn't sufficient room for her clothes and shoes. Her little bed was pushed up against the outside wall. The desk was piled with books and papers, leaving no writing surface at all. On her dresser, placed over a hat stand, was the skating cap Lily had given her. A few unframed illustrations were pinned to the wall.

The moments Lily spent observing Helen's room for the first time were not wasted on Helen who called, "ta-da!" from her location under the covers. Her shoulders were bare and she was grinning.

"Still slow," she said smugly, teasing.

Lily responded with a small smile and began to undress. She no longer felt shy about being naked with Helen, even in the wan late winter daylight from the window. When she slipped under the covers and into Helen's arms, neither of them was smiling. All of their suppressed desire, the passion left over from stolen kisses during their evening walks and the skating party, the accumulated heat of their too-short minutes alone after the Colonial Ball, surged to the surface. They became intertwined so tightly that they moved as one person.

When they grew calm, still in each other's arms, Lily felt amazement. And delight. And she felt powerful. She lay her head on Helen's shoulder, her mouth against Helen's neck. The feeling of Helen's pulse tickling her lips was overwhelming.

"I love you so very much, Helen," she said with feeling. She had not dared to speak her love before but could not have stopped herself from confessing it now.

Helen seemed to take a deep breath, but said nothing in reply. She tightened her arms around Lily and then relaxed her embrace. They lay like that for a while, Helen on her back facing the ceiling, Lily facing Helen, thinking.

"Are there others on campus like us?" Lily asked, tracing Helen's collarbone with her fingers.

Helen nodded. "I know two sets of sweethearts in my class alone."

"Do they ever spend time with each other, the two sets? You know, have a spread just for themselves?"

Helen shrugged. "I wouldn't know. Why do you ask?"

"I just think it would be nice to do something, like go for a tramp, with other sweethearts. Girls who know how we feel."

"Maybe you could start a club!"

"And what would Mrs. Kendrick have to say about that, I wonder!"

They laughed, and Helen added, seriously, "I know that there are people involved in settlement work at Rivington Street who work with sweethearts that they have been with since college. They work side by side with other sweethearts."

"After college."

"Uh-huh. And you know the professors who live together in the houses on Raymond Avenue."

Lily nodded.

"I'm sure they have little dinner parties and teas with their colleagues."

Lily nodded again.

"What are you thinking?" Helen wanted to know.

Lily hesitated, then said, "I'm happier than I've ever been in my life. And I'm so proud to be your sweetheart. I only wish there were some way to share all of this with others."

After a minute, Helen shook her head. "It would be easier if one of us were a man, wouldn't it?"

Lily thought about that. "But how could you be a man and still be you? I love you because you are a woman."

Suddenly, Helen propped herself on one elbow, her eyes bright with an idea. "I can wear my brother's suit!"

Lily sat up. "You should not wear your brother's suit," she warned.

"Why not? I have heard I wear it well," Helen protested.

"You wear it too well," Lily replied, climbing out of bed. "Do you have a robe? Not the kimono. I need to go down the hall."

Helen got up and pulled out a chenille robe, holding out for Lily to put on, then wrapped the robe and her arms around Lily from behind.

"What does 'wear it too well' mean, exactly?" she teased into Lily's ear.

Lily released herself from the embrace and drew the waist sash snugly.

"You know very well the effect you have on VC girls when you wear that suit," she said in a tone of mild scolding. "With the slightest encouragement, any one of them would tear it from your body."

Helen cocked her head and grinned. "And what effect do I have on you when I wear it?"

Lily started for the door to the parlor and turned back.

"I'm a VC girl," she said, raising an eyebrow.

Helen laughed delightedly.

"Make me some tea, will you?" Lily asked. "I have to admit I'm getting hungry. And I brought edibles."

When she got back, Helen had dressed in her kimono, *sans* the long underwear, and had the kettle over the spirit lamp. It was the supper hour and the hallways were empty. Lily opened the packet and revealed that she had purchased cheese, slices of bread, and some biscuits for dessert. Helen proudly produced two apples for their repast. They used the wrapping paper as a tray and carried their meal into her bedroom where they set up a picnic on her bed. Leaning against the wall, the lovers shared bites of the apple and, giggling, nibbled the same piece of cheese until they reached each other's lips.

Helen went to make a pot of tea, and Lily pulled a chair close to the bed to use as a tea table. Helen returned with two unmatched cups, a tin of milk and then went back to bring the pot of steeping tea. She sat at the edge of the bed, her hands hovering around the warmth of the pot, seemingly lost in thought.

Then she abruptly sat up and poured them a cup of tea. "What do you hear from your friend Eva?" she said in a casual tone, as if she had just thought of it.

Lily added milk to her cup and handed the tin to Helen. "Well, I told you she was engaged on Valentine's Day."

"Oh, yes, you did," Helen replied. "Have you heard from her since?"

"Yes, I had a letter last week. She had lots of news about engagement celebrations. Her aunt and uncle gave her a small dinner party to honor the happy couple. She invited most of the people who were at her Christmas party."

"I'm sure you were missed," Helen interjected.

Lily looked over her cup at her lover, but did not reply to that. "She was writing me from Hartford, she said, because she and Frank had traveled to Connecticut to announce their engagement and introduce her to his family."

"Have you told her about me? About us?" she finally asked in a small voice in a neutral tone.

Lily understood now why Helen had asked about Eva. "In every letter. I tell her what you said, that we went skating, or walking after chapel, that we danced at the Colonial Ball. She can't miss the importance of you in my life."

"Have you told her that we're sweethearts?" Helen gently pressed.

Lily pursed her lips. She had not done that. "I want to tell her in person rather than in a letter," Lily explained, knowing that it was only partly true, that she didn't know how to tell Eva this hurtful thing. "But she will know it before I tell her, believe me."

"How will she know it if you don't tell her?"

Lily pulled the robe closer around her chest, as if she felt exposed. "Because she knows me better than any other living soul. She will know. She probably knows it now."

Helen drank her tea in silence. The room was becoming quite dark now. "Will I know you better than anyone?" came her voice, wistful.

Lily leaned over and put her arms around Helen. "Oh, my darling," she whispered gently, "I want you to. And I want to know you better than anyone. Even better than Belle knows you."

There was enough light left to see that Helen smiled at that.

They cuddled under the covers and shortly found themselves making love again, this time with great tenderness, as if a barrier in their path had been removed and they wanted to leisurely explore what lay beyond it.

They had lain peacefully motionless for a long time, the noises of the hall a distant murmur, when Helen broke their reverie.

"Lily?"

"Hmmm?" Lily responded. She felt weightless in her relaxed state, as warm beside Helen as she would have been on a beach in July.

"Remember when I asked you to come home with me Thanksgiving? And how you hesitated but it turned out fine?"

"Uh-hmmm," Lily assented.

"Well, I have another proposition along those lines," Helen said confidentially.

Lily became completely alert.

"You know that in two weeks we will begin our two-week spring vacation," Helen went on. "I was thinking how excellent it would be if we went to New York and stayed at the St. Denis, where lots of VC girls go on weekends."

"For the whole vacation?" Lily was astounded.

"Well, for a week, probably," the other responded. "It would get pretty expensive. But we could go to Glens Falls for a few days. I know Mother would enjoy seeing you again. She has asked about you in letters."

"She has?"

"Oh, yes," Helen said earnestly, "you made quite an impression on her."

"She likes me because you like me," Lily explained. "And she likes you to be happy."

"Nicely summed!" Helen observed. "So, how much persuasion will I be required to exert this time in order to secure your agreement? Imagine it, Lily, a week in our own hotel room, with all of New York's museums, theater, lectures, opera, just outside our door - for those hours we *choose* to leave our room," she added wickedly.

Lily had misgivings about this plan. "Your plan is a dream come true, but," she paused, "I know my family is expecting me to go home. This is a long vacation and I won't be going home again until June. I can't say that I will be free to do it."

Lily could feel Helen's body sag.

"But wait until I write them and explain the opportunity I have to see things in the big city. My parents used to travel there together every year to buy furniture. I'm not sure they would agree to my going there unchaperoned."

"Oh, Lily, you can persuade them, I know it," Helen pleaded. "You persuaded them to let you come to Vassar."

"Why don't you come to Buffalo with me?" The idea suddenly came to Lily. "We could visit my family for a few days, then visit your family for a few days, and then spend the rest in New York. Provided I can convince my parents that these days proper girls can do that."

CHAPTER 19

Lily's face was turned toward the swiftly passing scene on her left as the New York Central train gathered speed out of Albany in the early afternoon. She saw the scene, but she did not register it. Her mind was not on the late March rain outside the car, rendering still more dreary the browns and blacks and greys of winter laid bare by the melting snow. It could have been glorious May outside if her mood were any indication.

She turned her gaze from the window to the figure seated beside her, book in hand, head bent slightly to one side in concentration. A thrill went through Lily as she realized anew that Helen was beside her as she traveled westward to Buffalo. This action was one she had repeated four or five times already since they left Poughkeepsie. The thrill was invariably accompanied by shallow breathing that eventually forced her to sigh deeply. As she did so this time, Helen looked up from her reading. They smiled into one another's eyes.

"Are you actually reading that?" Lily asked dubiously.

Helen nodded, holding up the slim volume. "It's Mrs. Browning," she said, displaying the title, *Sonnets from the Portuguese*. "From the library. I've kept it out ever so long that I know I'll find a slip in my box any day demanding that I show it."

She put the book in her lap and caressed its worn cover. "To be honest, I think I like Elizabeth Barrett Browning more than her husband, the touted Robert."

Lily leaned back in her seat, then turned her head toward Helen. "'Because thou hast the power and own'st the grace / To look through and behind this mask of me...,'" she recited.

Helen smiled, opening the book to Sonnet 29, whose first lines Lily had spoken. "I thought your poetic heroine was Emily Dickinson," she said.

"Women who write poetry are my heroines," Lily replied.

They became aware that a large middle-aged man sitting across from them scowled in their direction from time to time. Helen found a small piece of paper and, after writing briefly on it, folded it in four and passed it to Lily.

Lily frowned in puzzlement, but blushed when she opened it and read, "I'm kissing you right now."

Smiling, comprehending that Helen was playing to their scowling audience a few feet away, Lily took out her pencil and wrote, "Kissing you back."

Helen sighed and shook her head when she read it and quickly handed back a reply.

"Is that ALL???" made Lily laugh out loud. She wrote, "What do you think?" and elicited a pursed-lips smile and raised eyebrow in response.

At Utica, the man got off and Helen immediately took the seat opposite Lily. The train followed the sinuous course of the Mohawk River, now running wide and brown in the spring melt. Lily could feel Helen's gaze and met it with her own. Helen's face was openly happy, her grey eyes unguarded and unwavering as they locked onto Lily's. Lily understood the intimacy of this moment and she allowed Helen to see behind her mask of academic grind to the romantic who reveled in this transporting, soul-embracing love.

She surprised herself when she was the one to break the moment by looking at her hands in her lap. She caught her breath and realized that she was becoming anxious. The conductor had just announced their approach to Syracuse; the train was relentlessly carrying them to Buffalo.

Helen immediately resumed her seat beside Lily. "What is it?" she asked, leaning close to Lily and touching her arm.

Lily smiled wryly. "Aren't you the slightest bit nervous about meeting my family?"

Helen cocked her head with a start. "Why, no. Should I be?"

Lily shook her head. "Well, I am."

Helen looked serious. "Don't you think they'll like me?" she asked earnestly. "I'm neat, have good manners, am kind to animals."

Lily smiled and shook her head. "And your mother is responsible for our victory in getting permission for me to go to New York. My mother's awe at your mother's persuasive powers may have worn off by the time we arrive."

Helen took her hand and patted it reassuringly. "Things will work out. I know they will," she said cheerfully, adding, "and I will make a good impression on your parents. I promise!"

Lily smiled in spite of herself. "When my family is in the room, will you try not to look at me the way you just did?"

Helen smiled and nodded. Then she leaned close to Lily's ear. "I'm especially looking forward to meeting your friend, Eva," she said, "and offering my congratulations on her engagement."

Lily looked at her out of the corner of her eye and saw Helen's devilish grin. "Please be - diplomatic," Lily pleaded. "I have no idea what to expect from her when you meet."

And that was a concern Lily had carried for the week since she wrote to Eva to say that she was coming home for a short stay and bringing Helen as her guest. Eva had not replied to her letter, in which she also suggested that Eva come to tea.

Before long, the train left the Rochester station on its final leg of the journey across the state. The daylight was beginning to fade and the passing landscape outside the car receded into shapeless forms, forcing one's attention to the dimly lit interior of the car. It was nearly full now; Lily could hear several conversations around them. Beside her, Helen napped, her hat in her lap and her head on Lily's shoulder. In this setting, Lily suddenly felt very protective of Helen, so vulnerable in her slumber. She determined that she would not allow Eva to behave rudely toward Helen. She would be on guard against slights from any quarter to the person she loved most in the world.

SOMEHOW, in the dark Exchange Street station, crowded with passengers flowing to and from the trains, Will found them right away. Lily, tired and overwrought, was so happy to see him that she hugged him. Startled, he laughed and then looked at Helen, lifting his hat with a big grin. Lily introduced them and Will guided them outside.

"I hit the jackpot today," he called over his shoulder to them, a suitcase in each hand. "We're right close by, over here."

Will loaded their suitcases into the wagon and, as Lily handed him their satchels, he whispered, "Wow, she's *pretty*!" Lily nodded and patted his arm.

Helen sat in the middle as Will drove them home.

"Excuse the delivery wagon," Lily said.

"Goodness, no!" Helen exclaimed. "It comes with a very good-looking driver. I think it's just perfect. And it's decorated with the family name. If my brother saw this, he'd want one just like it!"

Lily looked over to see her brother make a bashful face, something she hadn't seen in years. Helen had plainly won the affections of her brother.

"How are things with your Mae?" Lily asked as they waited at a congested intersection. "You never did write me as you said you would."

"Didn't Mama write you? After the dance at church, Mae came to dinner to meet Mama. She made a good impression, let's say. Papa helped because he already knew her from the store."

"Things are going well, then," Lily summarized.

"Oh, yes, you can say that," he laughed. "And she's going to come to dinner while you're here so you can meet her, too. She really wants to meet you, my-sister-the-college-girl, and all."

"Lily," Helen interjected, "perhaps we can persuade her to join us at Vassar next year!"

Will protested. "No, wait just a minute now!" But the girls laughed loudly and he shook his head, laughing with them.

AT the house, Will helped with their suitcases and then left to return the wagon and accompany their father home from the store. As they took off their wraps, Mama Kepler emerged from the kitchen dressed much finer than usual. Lily detected a desire to make a good impression on Helen. She thought that tentatively a good sign.

Lily gave her mother a hug and introduced Helen.

Helen took Mama Kepler's hand. "I'm so glad to finally be able to meet you, Mrs. Kepler," Helen said quietly but with great sincerity. "Lily talks about her family often and fondly."

Mama Kepler was abashed with pleasure. "Oh, we're just hardworking, plain people, dear," she managed to reply.

Lily stared at her mother, from whose lips such phrases had never passed. The expensive dress and pearls she wore made her comment ludicrous, but Helen was serene in her grace.

"And quite special people, too, if Lily is any indication," she said smoothly.

"Well," Mama Kepler said, apparently out of platitudes for the time being, "why don't you girls go upstairs and get settled. Can you manage your bags?"

Lily assured her they could and Mama rustled down the hall to the kitchen again in her taffeta as they climbed the stairs. Lily saw that Helen was smiling broadly.

"Well, this is my room," Lily said, pushing open the door. She stepped in ahead of Helen to light the gas jet. She motioned Helen to come in and closed the door behind them.

Helen stood with her suitcase in her hand. She was staring at the double bed.

"We will have to stay in my room together," Lily said, sounding apologetic. "We no longer have a guest room. Mama took it over as her office."

Helen turned to look at Lily, a bemused expression flitting across her face. "So," she said slowly, mildly, "we'll be sharing that bed for our four nights here."

Lily caught Helen's tone and nodded regretfully. "Yes, I hope you won't mind."

Helen dropped her suitcase and burst out laughing. Lily giggled and they fell into one another's arms.

"You never mentioned this little detail!" Helen said in a loud whisper.

A voice called from the top of the stairs. "Girls," Mama Kepler was saying, "will you come down in half an hour? Papa will be home by then and we'll eat right away."

"Yes, Mama," Lily replied through the closed door. She held up a finger to Helen, indicating that she should wait.

"Half an hour. Don't be late," Mama repeated.

Lily nodded to Helen, eyebrows raised. "The last word."

"Will she enter without knocking?" Helen whispered.

Lily shook her head. "Not now, not with our honored guest in here."

"I can't imagine what my mother wrote that so impressed your mother," Helen said. She stepped close to Lily and pulled her into an embrace. "But I don't mind," she smiled and kissed Lily.

They kissed a good deal, making up for the hours lost on the train when they were side by side or gazing deeply into each other's eyes.

Lily broke off their embrace and rested her hands on Helen's shoulders. "My big bed is a double-sided sword, I'm afraid," she warned gently. "We will be able to sleep together, but I can't make love with you in my family's house. Please, sweetheart, understand and help me."

Helen sighed, drooping her head and shoulders in exaggerated disappointment; then she brightened. "How wonderful it will be to have our own room in New York where nobody will disturb us or care what we do when we are alone together!"

Lily and Helen descended the stairs half an hour later, dressed for dinner and refreshed from their journey. Helen presented Mama Kepler with a small gift. The latter was abashed and delighted, holding it before her until Lily prompted her to open it.

"Oh," Mama said in an awed voice as she unwrapped a box of stationery. "Crane's Linen Lawn," she recited as she ran her fingers over the surface of the letter size paper.

"My mother gave me specific instructions about what to get for you," Helen said. "This is one of her favorite papers."

Mama Kepler blushed. "Thank you very much, Helen."

Lily introduced Helen to her father and saw in the exchange that Papa was charmed by Helen's warmth. She was outgoing in the way that Lily's family was not. She offered her hand and a wide smile to Mr. Kepler, and he beamed in response.

Their supper had more dishes than their usual lighter evening fare and Lily noted that the roast beef was not left over from the noonday meal. By these indications, her mother had declared this first supper with their guest as a special occasion and she was grateful. Lily realized that she was seeing everything in her family's home through Helen's eyes and tried not to make comparisons to what she had seen at Helen's. Her mother always put her best foot forward in situations like this; she had the means and the restraint to make a tasteful presentation. Lily knew that and was proud of her mother in this.

After supper, Will left for a club meeting and the others settled into more comfortable chairs in the family parlor, where they had tea. Mama took up her crocheting, Papa perused the *Buffalo Evening News* but they engaged Lily and Helen in conversation for an hour or so.

"Mama," Lily said in what she hoped was a nearly indifferent tone, "do you still have the letter from Mrs. McIntyre?"

Mama Kepler looked up from her needlework and gazed into the distance. "I'm trying to think where I put it," she replied. "I know I answered it. Why don't you look in the slot in the desk with all the opened mail?"

Lily did but it wasn't there. Other locations were suggested and she checked to no avail. Then Helen, seated across from Mama Kepler at a table with a bright lamp, picked up an envelope amidst other papers on the table.

"Oh, that's right!" Mama Kepler exclaimed. "I didn't put it away, thinking you might want to read it."

Helen removed the letter from the envelope and read through the two pages quickly. Lily was scanning Helen's face but it gave no clue to her reaction to the contents. Then Helen passed it to her.

Lily viewed it as her mother would have. The ivory vellum stationery was engraved, both envelope and letter paper; that would have assigned gravity to whatever message was contained. Mrs. McIntyre, in a beautiful hand, opened the letter by addressing Mama as a social equal - no, more as a friend. "My dear Mrs. Kepler," she said in greeting. She spoke of the weather, how pleased she was that her Helen had found such a fine friend in Lily. The Keplers must be so proud of her achievements and graces. With the smoothest transition, she broached the subject of the five-day trip to New York. She ran through all of the reasons why Mrs. Kepler would reasonably object, and then she removed each obstacle by explanation and precedent. Surely, she concluded, the Keplers could see that she and Mr. McIntyre were confident that their daughter's safety and reputation would be secure if she were to travel to the St. Denis, a fine establishment where they themselves stayed while in the city. The opportunities for museums and opera in that metropolis were second to none and she hoped the Keplers agreed that the experience would be invaluable and also fun for two studious girls like theirs.

Lily carefully folded the letter and returned it to its envelope. She slipped it back onto the table and said nothing. Then she stood and stretched. "I think I'll go up and finish unpacking and then go to bed."

Helen stood up immediately and said, "That's a good idea."

Everyone said goodnight all around and the girls ascended the stairs to Lily's room. Once inside, Lily turned to Helen. "Your mother should be a diplomat or a lawyer!"

Helen chuckled. "Why do you say that?"

Lily held out her arms. "She treated my mother as her social equal. You can't imagine what powerful magic that surely was." She was shaking her head in admiration. "My mother knows your family's standing in Glens Falls. I told them all about it over Christmas. Keplers and McIntyres aren't social equals."

"I can't think it was such a big thing as that," Helen said, shrugging.

"But Mama left the letter out on the table deliberately so anyone could see it. It was proof that your mother's tone persuaded my parents to let me go with you to New York."

Lily sat down on the edge of the bed and began to unbutton her cuffs. "Your mother is a master."

Helen laughed as she sat down beside Lily. "Well, you may tell her that when we get to my house!"

They were settled into Lily's double bed when Helen suddenly sat up in the darkness.

"What is it?" Lily asked, lying on her back.

"The light in the window," Helen replied. "Is that the moon?"

"I think so. When there are no leaves it's very bright in here when the moon is full."

Helen lay back down on her side, facing Lily. "Of all the ancients, I always fancied myself most like Artemis. The huntress."

"What would you hunt?" Lily said sleepily.

"Deer," she said. "Pretty girls," she added in a whisper.

"I heard that," Lily said. "Time to surrender your bow and arrow."

Helen leaned very close to Lily's face. "And why would I do that?"

"Well," Lily sighed, "because, hopefully, your hunting days are over."

When Helen didn't respond, she added, "Kiss me goodnight, sweetheart. I must sleep now."

Helen kissed her lightly several times, then gently, warmly, for a long time. Lily smiled and turned onto her side. Helen spooned her, one arm circling Lily's waist and cradling a breast. Both were asleep in minutes.

LILY awoke first the next morning. The low tones of men's voices in the hall startled her into consciousness and she needed a minute to register that she was not in her room at Vassar but in her own bed in Buffalo. Having grasped this, she turned to confirm that Helen was in bed beside her. Helen was facing away from Lily, sleeping soundly with long inhalations and quick exhalations.

The more awake she became, the more thoughts and feelings crowded to the forefront of her mind. Being here in this most familiar place, surrounded by high school memories pinned to the walls and stuffed into her bookcase. Being here beside her beloved who, barely two months ago, seemed only a longing, a dream, probably a crush, though she'd never admit to the last. Mama and Papa's permission to travel to New York unchaperoned, a permission that still puzzled her despite having read the letter from Helen's mother that won their case. Eva, invited to come to tea this afternoon, but still unaccounted for. Helen, now shifting her position and stretching, accidentally touched Lily with her hip, sending a rush of sensation through Lily.

She got out of bed as stealthily as possible, put on her robe, and looked out of her door to confirm that the bathroom was available. When she returned, Lily sat on her window seat and brushed her hair. Humboldt Parkway was wet but the day seemed to have the potential to clear up later. Little scraps of blue peeked through the clouds, now rapidly being blown in an easterly direction. Lily knew this meant the wind was coming off frozen Lake Erie; all winds off the lake would be cold ones until June. Over the decades, Buffalonians had learned to be patient with their spring weather because their compensation was autumn, long and gentle, with affectionate breezes late into October from the warm lake waters.

Lily turned from the window to see Helen lying on her side facing Lily. She was smiling. Lily smiled in response.

"I was thinking how pretty you look, brushing your beautiful auburn hair in the morning light," Helen murmured sleepily.

Lily's eyes shone with emotion and she made no reply. She wanted to wake up every morning for the rest of her life and repeat this moment.

Helen stretched and yawned and gradually brought her body to a sitting position. She blinked, squinting into the distance as if to think about something. Then she raised a finger. "Robe," she said. "That's the word I'm looking for. What did I do with my robe?"

Lily chuckled and pointed to it draped over the back of a chair. "Did you sleep well?" Lily asked.

Helen was working at tying the sash on her robe. "I did," she replied, locating a fugitive sash end. "I did sleep well. That's a long trip from Poughkeepsie," she said, shuffling to the door.

"Yes," said Lily, "but it's much shorter on the return trip, I've found."

Helen turned back and grinned sleepily, then left for the bathroom.

THEY were kissing good morning, except that Helen and Lily were in her bed again and their kissing was becoming more heated.

"You're not helping very much," Lily said weakly between open-mouthed kisses. They were no longer exhausted from their trip, but rested and full of desire.

Helen pushed herself up on her hands to look at Lily. With a half-smile, she pressed her hips into Lily's. Lily gasped then closed her mouth to prevent noise.

Helen leaned her face close to Lily's. "Shall I stop?"

"Girls!" Mama's voice was outside in the hall.

Helen and Lily flew apart and stared at the door.

"Yes, Mama," Lily called back, trying not to sound afraid.

"It's 9:30," Mama said through the door. "You might want to get up now. Eva called and said she can come to tea this afternoon around 1:30."

"Alright," Lily said, "we'll get up now." Then she added, "Thank you."

"Alright then," her mother said, "Trude's holding breakfast for you."

Lily was dressed before her heartbeat slowed to normal. Helen seemed chastised. Lily kissed her chastely on the lips before they left the room. "Welcome to the Land of Oz," she said in a conspirator's tone.

Helen smiled at the reference to the recent bestseller. "We're not in Kansas anymore," Helen added as she followed Lily downstairs.

LILY and Helen were hunched over a picture puzzle at the table in the family parlor. The box had no picture of the final image and the 200 pieces didn't interlock, which made the assembly of the puzzle a test of concentration. Lily was unable to keep her focus on the task and when the hall clock chimed 1:45, she put down the wooden piece in her hand with a snap. Helen looked up inquiringly.

Lily shook her head slightly so as not to garner too much attention from her mother, who sat reading on the settee in front of the family parlor window. "Eva has always lived in her own time zone," she said quietly, raising an eyebrow. "There's really no telling what time she'll be here."

She didn't add that she was feeling more anxious by the minute. What kind of mood would Eva bring with her? How would she treat Helen?

"No matter," Helen replied smoothly. "We're enjoying ourselves, aren't we?"

Lily tried to smile in response. But the waiting was torturous for her. She drew a deep breath and tried again to find a match for her puzzle piece.

At five after two, the doorbell rang. Lily looked up at Helen, who smiled encouragingly.

"Are you getting the door, dear?" Mama Kepler asked at the same time.

"Yes, Mama," Lily said, rising stiffly from her chair.

Eva started talking the moment Lily opened the front door. "Oh, my goodness, it is so blustery out! Am I very late?" she chattered, handing Lily her umbrella and unbuttoning her coat. "You know how the trolleys are on any day. I think on Saturdays people buy everything for the week and pile into the trolleys without any consideration for who might get injured from their parcels."

She paused as she handed Lily her coat to hang up, then took off her hat, placing it on the hall chair. When Lily turned back to face her, Eva was smiling happily, her arms open to embrace Lily.

Lily smiled as cheerfully as she was able, which was not much and which she was sure didn't escape Eva's notice. She embraced Eva, and was surprised to find her friend clinging to her. Lily broke it off, taking Eva by the shoulders and looking into her eyes.

"How are you, dear?" she asked Eva, in a confidential tone.

Eva tilted her head as if to deflect the inquiry. "I'm glad to see you, that's how I am," she said declaratively, and then smiled.

Lily looked at her for a moment, then took her by the hand. "And I to see you," she said sincerely, then added, "You look lovely in your new dress."

"Oh, this old thing," Eva said teasingly. "But I'll accept the compliment."

"How old is *old*? Two weeks?" Lily was leading Eva along the hall toward the family parlor.

Eva nodded, then laughed. "One week," she admitted. "But I've already worn it twice."

They passed into the parlor, warmer than the hall with the heat from the glowing coal grate. Mama had closed her book and was looking up in cheerful greeting. Helen was standing, her fingertips resting on the table before her, a tentative, if hopeful, smile frozen on her lips. Lily felt all eyes on her.

"Helen," she said, guiding Eva to the table, "this is my friend, Eva, of whom I have spoken so highly." She was looking into Helen's eyes, trying to communicate what she could not with words.

"Eva, this is my friend Helen, who used to tutor me in Greek," she said, letting go of Eva's hand.

Eva did not step toward Helen and so Helen quickly moved around the table to face Eva, her hand extended.

"Eva," Helen said graciously, "I'm glad to finally be able to meet you in person."

Eva had lost any advantage she might have hoped for with her reticence because now she was receiving cordial treatment by someone towering over her.

"And I'm glad, too," she responded, shaking hands limply.

Then she moved to the settee and gave Mama Kepler a kiss on the cheek.

"How lovely your dress is, Eva," Mama Kepler was saying. "I don't think a color exists that doesn't look grand on you."

Eva demurred and settled herself on the settee beside Mama Kepler. Lily looked at Helen and they sat down.

"Oh," Lily said suddenly, "our tea. I'll get it."

"No, no," Mama Kepler said dismissively, "I'll go. You young people have things to talk about."

She left the room and it seemed like some of the energy left with her. For a minute, no one said anything.

"When are you leaving?" Eva asked.

"Tuesday morning," Lily replied. "We're going to Glens Falls to stay with Helen's family for several days before we go on to New York."

"Well, that sounds like an exciting trip, New York City," Eva said honestly. Then she added, "Your mother was very disappointed that she wouldn't be able to see you longer."

There was an awkward silence, broken by Helen.

"Lily, why don't you invite your mother to come to Glens Falls with us?" Helen said cheerfully. "That way she could see you longer. I know my mother would welcome a visit from her Buffalo friend."

Lily chuckled until she laughed along with Helen, and then she looked over at Eva, who was not laughing.

Mama Kepler burst into the room with a big tray of tea things. Lily moved the little table on which they usually served tea so that Mama could serve from the settee. Eventually everyone had tea and molasses ginger biscuits and the conviviality of the room improved.

Mama Kepler brought up the news about some of Lily's Central High classmates and that occupied some minutes. Then Lily addressed Eva.

"When you last wrote, you were trying to decide on a design for your wedding dress," she said, interested. "Have you narrowed it down much?"

"A little," Eva responded, in a reserved tone. "My father wrote to say that I have only to tell him how much my dress will cost, and he will send the money."

Lily leaned forward. "It's wonderful that you and your father are in communication! Will he give you away?"

"Well," Eva moved in her seat as if uncomfortable, "I believe I will ask Uncle and Father both to do it. If they're agreeable."

Lily smiled, pleased. "How wonderful, Eva!"

When Eva did not continue the strand, Lily forged ahead. "Have you picked out my dress yet?" she said, slightly teasing.

Eva shook her head.

"I'm sure it will be beautiful, whatever it is," Lily said, trying to move the conversation forward.

She looked at Helen. "Eva has excellent taste. She picked out my green velvet dress at Christmas that I wore to the Colonial Ball."

Helen smiled at Eva. "Then you do indeed have excellent taste because it was beautiful."

"Eva tells me that this ball was for the students at Vassar only," Mama Kepler interjected.

"That's true, Mama," Lily said, certain she had written her mother about the ball.

"Why would Vassar have a ball where no boys are invited and girls are left to dance with girls?" Mama's voice had some irritation in it.

Lily was trying to understand her mother's tone. Helen stepped in.

"You see, Mrs. Kepler," she said reasonably, "we have a few entertainments during the year to give girls a chance to, well, be girls, and dress up and play at being sophisticated. It's really just practice for life after college, when we go out into the world and find husbands."

"I don't know why girls have to wait to find husbands," Mama Kepler said, stubbornly. "If there were dances with boys at Vassar, girls might find husbands at any time."

Lily stole a glance at Helen, who was thoughtfully studying Mama Kepler.

"Well," Helen said in a neutral tone, "the purpose of college is the education," slowly speaking the last word.

Mama Kepler put her cup and saucer down with a small but distinct clink. "Well, you'll need your education, dear Lily," she said, smoothing her skirt and enunciating *education* as Helen had, "if you're going to refuse to marry."

Lily's eyes flew to Eva, who was looking down, folding and refolding her napkin. She instantly understood the communication that must have passed between Eva and her mother. What confounded her was the reason why Eva had betrayed her. Blood was rushing to her head and interfering with her thinking, she who was so good at thinking fast.

Slowly she looked at Helen who looked back with sympathy. Helen couldn't step into the conversation now, Lily knew that. But looking into Helen's eyes helped her concentrate on deflecting her mother's words.

"I have never said that I refuse to marry," Lily said with quiet firmness. "And I can't imagine saying those words. I don't know what the future will bring." Then she added, "You and Papa have been happy all these years. Who wouldn't want a marriage like yours?"

She later had no memory of what was said after that. Her thoughts were of lying, again, to her mother, of the screen she was erecting between her and her loved ones, the dichotomy between the person she was becoming and the person they wanted her to be.

When Eva rose to leave, Lily accompanied her to the door and waited silently, her hand on the doorknob, while Eva put on her coat and hat. Eva did not speak or look at Lily.

Lily opened the door and said, grimly, "I'm paying you a visit on Monday."

CHAPTER 20

That night when Lily turned down the light in her room, Helen was visible in the moonlight, sitting up in their bed.

"The moon must be nearly full," Helen said quietly, almost wistfully. "It draws me so. I do believe I am a child of the goddess of the moon."

Lily climbed in beside her and lay on her back. "I'm sorry to be such a poor hostess," she murmured.

Helen lay down on her side facing Lily. "You're very worried, aren't you?" she said.

"I'm very angry," Lily replied.

"But you're also worried. Won't you tell me why?"

Lily closed her eyes and sighed. It felt good to be alone with Helen, to trust in Helen. In their solitude, some of the tension was leaving her body.

"The way you heard Mama speak of Vassar today was the way she spoke of the idea of college a year ago," Lily confessed. "I had forgotten how narrowly I succeeded in getting to Vassar."

Helen put her hand over Lily's. "You are also making a success of being a college student. And you still have your ally in your father. I can tell that he's proud of you."

Lily smiled wanly. "Eva doesn't understand that I have so much more in common with you than I do with her."

"Oh, *contraire*, as Belle would say," Helen said quickly. "I think she understands that very well. I heard her talking away in the hall when she first came and then when you introduced us, her demeanor had completely changed."

"Well, she obviously had things to hide, didn't she?" Lily replied tersely. "In all the years we've known one another, we never repeated our conversations to anyone. I can't - grasp - why she did it."

They lay in silence for a long while. Then Helen kissed Lily on the cheek and turned away from her. Shortly, Lily heard Helen's steady breathing and knew she had fallen asleep. Lily turned on her side and closed her eyes, but she didn't sleep. She was worried about the conversation Eva had with Mama. She was frightened for her future at Vassar, and she intended to keep that fear to herself.

THE Sunday morning sunshine that greeted the Keplers and their guest as they walked to church suggested spring, and spirits were lighter all around. Helen slipped her arm through Lily's and smiled into her eyes. Lily pulled Helen's arm close and returned the smile, remembering anew that they were going to be together day and night for another eight days. Later, when they sat in their pew, Lily sent up a sincere prayer of thanksgiving.

Their Sunday dinner included Lily's brother Alfred and wife Gertrude, now getting round in the face and belly in her incipient motherhood. Lily thought Gertrude looked alternately pleased and bewildered at the changes being wrought upon her. The mother-to-be was basking in the attentions and approving noises of Mama Kepler, who made sure to point out to all present how beautiful a woman in Gertrude's condition was, performing the primary function for which women were made. Lily glanced over at Helen across the table and saw the raised eyebrow and the tiniest of smiles; she smiled and then directed it in Gertrude's direction. She looked at her brother Will and saw that he had observed their exchange of glances; he was grinning as he spooned some more potatoes on his plate.

Even Alfred seemed a bit off center now that his life and wife were progressing into a future not entirely predictable or controllable. Will teased his brother about the temperament of the baby, suggesting that he or she might not turn out to be as tidy as his or her parents. Alfred laughed nervously and promised it wouldn't matter what kind of temperament their first-born had. As if an outsider, Lily observed the changes that had rapidly occurred in her family.

But the Kepler Sunday afternoon habits had not changed. After Alfred and Gertrude left, Lily and Helen helped Mama with the kitchen tasks. By the time they were done, Will had gone out and Papa was napping in his chair. Mama went to her room to take a nap, also.

"Let's go for a walk," Helen nudged Lily as they stood alone in the kitchen. "We haven't had our daily exercise in a couple of days. Don't your feet just itch to tramp?"

Lily looked at Helen, who was smirking cheerfully at Lily with hands on her hips. She assented and they dressed to go out. The gray cloud cover had returned in the afternoon and with it the hint of warmth had dissipated. It was March again, the month that is never spring in Buffalo.

They walked along Humboldt Parkway for a dozen blocks; the sandstone sidewalks on the new street were high and therefore dry, giving an excellent surface for a brisk pace. As they turned around to retrace their steps, both slowed their steps at the same time.

"See that?" Helen observed, "we are so accustomed to walking together that we automatically adjust our rate. It's—"

"Communion," Lily interjected, a reference to the Palm Sunday services of that morning. They both laughed and then walked in silence.

"Are you feeling a little better about things?" Helen asked quietly.

Lily shook her head. "I am concentrating on our time together, on how happy it makes me."

Helen smiled. "Really? Oh," she said, putting a hand to her breast, "I'm glad to know that."

Lily looked at her, puzzled. "But you know how I feel."

Helen put her arm through Lily's as they slowed to a stroll. "Yes, of course," she said. "It's only that I've felt a bit awkward at times since we arrived. I'm glad my being here with you is a good thing."

"Your being here is what gives me reason to be hopeful," Lily explained. "Imagine my enduring the Sunday dinner-in-praise-of-motherhood without you. Or Eva's treachery yesterday and Mama's anti-college comments." She squeezed Helen's arm. "You are Hope itself, sweetheart."

"And what have you against motherhood?" Helen asked ironically.

"Absolutely nothing," Lily replied, "so long as someone else is the mother."

Helen leaned over and gave Lily a look. "Heretic," she commented in a low voice.

"I'm serious," Lily replied. "It's not a snap decision."

"Are you also serious about not marrying?" Helen's voice seemed thoughtful.

Lily shook her head. "I've tried and tried, but I can't imagine it."

They were approaching the Kepler house.

"Especially not now," Lily added as they turned up the front sidewalk.

THAT evening, after a light supper, Will pulled Papa Kepler, Lily and Helen into a game of gin rummy. Mama sat in her chair with her crocheting. Lily watched with pleasure as Helen charmed her father and brother with her demure wit and subtle flattery. She loved Helen the more for drawing out her father's warm personality. Even Mama smiled from time to time.

As the evening ended and everyone prepared to go up to bed, Will made Lily and Helen promise to play euchre the next evening when Mae came to dinner.

Lily was in bed by the time Helen returned from the bathroom, the covers pulled snug around her neck. Helen slipped in beside her and put an arm around Lily, kissing her lightly.

"Hmm," Lily responded, "So tired." Her eyes were closed; she was slipping into unconsciousness.

"I just have one question," Helen said.

"Hmmm?" came the slow response.

"This afternoon, when we were talking about you not getting married," Helen explained. "What did you mean when you said, *especially not now*?"

Lily blinked several times sleepily, then sighed. "Because of you," she mumbled, and fell asleep.

IT was raining the next afternoon when Lily rode the trolleys to the Bond's Franklin Street house. Lily thought it took a long time for anyone to answer her ring, but eventually there was Virgie, shrinking behind the door for protection from the precipitation. Lily quickly stepped inside.

Virgie stood placidly while Lily removed her mother's mackintosh and handed it to her. The girl took the dripping garment reluctantly.

"Is she in her room?" Lily asked, pulling off her galoshes.

Virgie nodded, then added indifferently, "I don't think she wants company."

Lily pushed stray wet strands away from her face. "I'm sure she doesn't," she replied, and climbed the stairs.

She let herself into Eva's room and closed the door. Eva was across the room, sitting on the settee, surrounded by catalogs and magazines. She pretended not to notice Lily until the latter stood before her.

"Oh," Eva said, sounding cheerful but not meeting Lily's eyes, "it's you."

Lily didn't reply, but simply stood looking at her.

Eva gestured to the items around her. "I'm trying to decide on my wedding dress design. I have it down to about six different -"

"Eva," Lily interrupted in a tone which visibly startled Eva, who put down the catalog in her hands and sat still, avoiding looking at Lily.

"I hardly know what to say to you," Lily said quietly, "despite having two days to think about your betrayal. How could you tell Mama what I said about marriage?"

Eva's chest began to heave. "It wasn't my fault," she said in a shaky voice. "Besides, you come here to talk about betrayal. I say that cuts both ways, wouldn't you?"

"I have never betrayed your confidence," Lily said heavily.

"But you have betrayed me, Lily Kepler, and you know it," Eva said stubbornly.

"I have not betrayed you," Lily said, confirming what she had suspected about Eva's reaction to her letters. "I am the same friend to you that I have been all these years."

Eva looked at her savagely now. "You broke my heart. We were sweethearts and you found yourself another one at Vassar."

Lily met her eyes with her own intensity. "We were never sweethearts."

Eva's jaw dropped. "What about our lovemaking?" she spat, pointing at her double bed.

When Lily didn't reply quick enough, Eva seized the silence, tears beginning to brim over her lashes. "Yes, what was that, Lily?"

"We never spoke about being sweethearts," Lily said quietly and in a steady voice.

Eva's tears were flowing freely now and she pushed the catalogs from the settee to the floor in a furious motion. Papers fluttered around Lily's feet.

"I gave you my passion, Lily," she said, her voice full of grievance, "I gave you my body, bared my deepest desires. How did that not make us sweethearts? Tell me that!"

"It didn't," Lily said simply. Then she added, "Your sweetheart is Frank, Eva."

Eva cut her off. "Don't tell me who my sweetheart is," she said, pausing only to dab at her running nose. "I know Frank is my sweetheart. I'm not talking about Frank. When you left here in January, we were sweethearts."

Lily gestured with her hands in frustration. "Eva, I don't understand you. You are going to marry Frank in a few months and start life in his house."

"I know that!" Eva was shouting. "That has nothing to do with us."

"It has everything to do with us," Lily replied, equally loudly. "You can't have both a husband and a wife, or a husband and a mistress."

Eva looked at her with eyes that were slits. Then her face crumpled and she began to weep anew. "You are mean to say that," she sobbed.

Lily sighed and picked her way through the mess of catalogs and sat down beside the audibly sobbing Eva. She waited a few minutes for Eva to calm and, when the latter didn't, Lily frowned and put an arm around Eva. With the slowness of a glacier calving, Eva leaned into Lily's arms and cried less noisily. Eventually, she was reduced to sniffling.

It occurred to Lily as she sat waiting for Eva to be restored to conversation that she had come in from the rain and now was in the midst of indoor rainfall. She realized this would be an observation best kept to herself. She had long been immune to the effects of Eva's tears.

Eva sat up and tried to find a dry spot on her handkerchief. Lily retrieved her own and passed it to her oldest friend.

"You always have a clean handkerchief," Eva said in a shaky voice as she dabbed at her eyes.

"It's one of the things you have most liked about me," Lily replied, dryly.

Eva nodded and started to chuckle, then threatened to weep some more. "I don't want to lose you," she said to the handkerchief.

When she looked at Lily, her eyes swimming, Lily knew that was the truest thing Eva could say. "You can't lose me," she said softly, wiping fresh tears from Eva's cheeks with her thumbs. "We're sisters."

"Really?" Eva was whispering.

Lily nodded. "Yes, we are. Sweethearts come and go, but sisters remain constant."

Eva threw her arms around Lily's neck and cried some more. When she finally recovered herself, Eva sat back on the settee and sighed.

"Look at this mess," she said, as if seeing it for the first time. "I don't know how I'm ever to decide on a dress. Will you help me?"

Lily shook her head. "No. I still want to know how you came to repeat our conversation to Mama."

Eva looked worried. "It wasn't my fault."

"Eva," Lily admonished.

"Okay," Eva admitted. "But I think she tricked me. She asked me to come to tea and - "

"When was that?" Lily interrupted.

Eva sighed. "I think it was last week, or maybe the week before."

"So, you went to tea," Lily prompted.

"Yes, I was surprised when she telephoned," Eva continued. "I wore that marine blue dress with the ruffled front that you like."

Lily sent her a baleful look which ended that tangent.

"She asked me if I had heard from you," Eva said, raising her eyebrows. "Of course, I had received your letter just the day before where you said you were hoping to come home for a few days with your friend Helen and then go to New York City with her."

They were silent for a minute.

"I knew then," Eva said in a flat tone. "You had dropped little hints about her since you went back in January, but I knew when I got that letter that you were sweethearts."

Lily brought the conversation back to the subject. "Did you tell her that you had heard from me?"

"Yes, I said I had got a letter just recently."

"And?"

"Well, she just said that she didn't know if it was proper for two young girls to travel to New York City unchaperoned. And she asked me if I knew any girls who had made those kinds of trips unchaperoned. I think she wanted to know if she was being old-fashioned."

"What did you say?"

"I said that I didn't know of any, but then not many Buffalo girls go to college, either. Well, that sent her into her lamentations about things changing - you know that speech."

Lily nodded, smiling grimly.

"And then she said how happy she was for me that I had found someone as handsome and from a good family and with good prospects as my Frank. She worried that all your education would scare away men that might be a good match for you."

"And?" Lily knew what was coming.

"I just said that maybe you wouldn't get married."

Lily covered her face with her hands.

"It just came out," Eva rushed to add.

"Would it *have just come* out if you hadn't just received my letter?" Lily asked pointedly.

There was no response for a long time.

"I don't know," Eva said, weakly. "But she asked me why you might not marry, and I told her what you said, about the women professors on campus and having a profession."

Lily had a cold feeling deep inside about that revelation to her mother. After a pause, she asked, in a voice that was almost pleading, "Do you love me, Eva?"

Eva clasped Lily's hand with both hers. "Of course!"

"Truly love me?" Lily's eyes were also pleading.

"Yes!" Eva emphasized. "Why?"

Lily put her hand around Eva's so that both their hands were clasping. "Please understand that Vassar is the most important thing in my life," she said in a voice not entirely steady. "I'm not talking about Helen or any of my friends. I'm talking about the experience of learning at Vassar that is so precious to me."

Eva nodded earnestly. "Yes, I know."

"Mama was against my going, as you remember," Lily said and Eva nodded. "I don't want her to find reasons for me not to go back to college in September. Do you understand what I'm getting at?"

"Yes," Eva nodded. "I mean, no. What can I do?"

Lily sighed. It might already be too late. "Whatever you can do to encourage her to think that my prospects of making a superior marriage are improved by my education at Vassar and my association with girls from excellent families."

Eva nodded several times. "If she asks you to tea again," Lily added.

They both smiled at one another.

LILY returned home late in the afternoon, feeling the exhaustion that follows emotional exertions such as her meeting with Eva had required. The house was quiet and, not finding Helen in the family parlor, she went up to her room. Helen was sitting on the window seat as if it were hers. Lily never ceased to be surprised and a little envious with the way Helen was at ease in any environment.

"Did you see me wave to you?" Helen asked brightly. "I waved as you came up the walk."

Lily joined her on the seat which spanned a double window. She began to remove her shoes.

"No," she replied. "The branches from the tree, even in winter, obscure the view into this window."

Helen looked thoughtful, and then smiled like the Cheshire Cat. "Good!"

Lily gave her a puzzled look. Helen leaned over and kissed her on the mouth. Then she sat back and smiled. "*Very* good!" she said.

Lily faced Helen on the seat, extending her legs. Helen lifted one of Lily's stockinged feet and began massaging it.

"How does that feel?" she asked.

Lily moaned and looked at her languidly. "Sheer torture," she murmured. "Please stop."

They laughed, then Helen peered at her. "How was your visit?" she asked in a quiet, casual tone.

Lily leaned back against the window frame, closing her eyes. "The air is cleared, to put it neatly," she said finally.

"Did she say why she told your mother what you said?"

Lily nodded. "It was what came to mind at the time."

Helen furrowed her brow.

"This is how her mind works, Helen. She's not a mean-spirited person. But she is not terribly introspective. Or imaginative. Will you also be torturing my other foot sometime soon?"

Helen smiled and began to massage Lily's other foot. "And do you feel better after talking with her?"

Lily nodded once. "At least about my friendship with Eva. It matters."

"Yes," Helen said quickly. "And it matters to me also that your friendship is repaired."

Lily looked into those eyes, pale green now behind very dark lashes. How she loved this woman!

Mama Kepler, Lily and Helen were waiting in the family parlor, perusing the evening papers. It was nearly six-thirty; they had set the table, dished the pickled beets and set out the large basket of Trude's fresh biscuits. All that remained was the beef stew, quietly waiting on the warm stove. That and the arrival of the other three diners.

Noises from the front hall announced them, a woman's laugh and Will's hearty chuckle. And then Papa, Will and his Mae filled the quiet parlor like a gust of March wind.

"Here we are at last!" Will announced, his arms wide in presentation. "Did you think we were never coming?"

The women rose to greet the newcomers. Mae stepped directly to Mama Kepler and greeted her first. Lily was taking in this girl who had captured her carefree brother. Mae was only a bit shorter than Lily, and fine-boned. Her hair was a warm sandy blond, her nose enviably small.

As she turned toward Lily, Will stepped close.

"Mae, this is my number one sister," Will said. "Lily, this is Mae."

Lily smiled broadly as they shook hands, an expression that mirrored Mae's. The girl's wide eyes were smiling, as well. Lily felt long, slender fingers clasping hers firmly.

"I congratulate you on your forbearance, Mae," she said light-heartedly. "*Number one sister!*"

They laughed.

"I am glad to meet you at last, Mae," Lily continued. "Will has spoken of you often."

Mae still held Lily's hand in hers. "And I am glad to finally meet you, Lily," she said sincerely. "I can only imagine what college must be like."

At that Lily and Helen both laughed, recalling their conversation with Will on the way from the station.

"And this is Helen, Lily's friend from college," Will gestured toward Helen.

Mae held out her hand to Helen, who took it in both of hers.

"I'm pleased to meet you, Mae," Helen said, "and want to let you know that Vassar has authorized me to recruit new applicants for this fall's freshman class. We can talk later."

Will stepped between them, to general laughter, and took Mae's hand from Helen. "No, no, no, no," he intoned, shaking his head.

The evening was off to a festive beginning. The newcomers freshened up for dinner and Mama Kepler, Lily and Helen made the final preparations for their table. Lily and Helen sat facing Will and Mae. Lily looked at her father and saw him smile broadly.

"Isn't this a happy sight, Mama?" Papa called to his wife at the other end of the table. "Young people, laughing and fooling, around our dinner table. And this fine stew!"

He reached for Helen's rimmed soup bowl and began to serve the table from the large tureen before him.

Lily glanced at her mother and observed that her smile seemed polite and no more.

Lily asked Mae what her job entailed.

"I'm a bookkeeper. There are three, and I have the least seniority as the one hired most recent," Mae replied.

"But she makes a big contribution," Will interjected, raising his eyebrows and grinning at Mae.

"I think you mean a big impression," Lily cracked, "on you!"

Mae joined in the laughter at this. Lily glanced sideways at her mother and saw that her polite smile seemed frozen; she seemed to be focused on making sure the food was being passed.

Helen shook her head. "Lily, I believe Harry and Will could be brothers."

"I believe you're right, Helen," Lily replied, sending Will a squint-eyed look.

Will replied with a puzzled expression. "What does that mean?"

"It means that you would probably enjoy Ping-Pong immensely," Helen said sadly.

"What's Ping-Pong?" Will asked, interested.

"Oh, no," Lily groaned. "You had to bring it up."

"It's a game," Mae said. "I've seen it played in my parish hall."

Will's eyes lighted up.

"And I'm afraid you will indeed enjoy it," Mae said regretfully. "You like every sport ever invented."

"How is it played?" Papa asked Helen, who described it briefly.

"I think we have the room to play Ping-Pong, don't you Mama? I think old people might play it, too," Papa said.

Mama simply looked at him in reply, causing the young people to giggle.

Mae asked what college was like.

"Well, we go to classes and when we're not in class, we study most of the time," Lily replied.

"*Lily* studies most of the time," Helen interjected, leaning toward Mae.

Lily ignored her and continued. "We have lectures scheduled every Friday evening with interesting speakers."

She paused to look over at Helen to see if a comment was coming. Helen was occupied with a biscuit and merely raised her eyebrows.

"But on Saturday nights, we may socialize with our classmates or attend a play put on by one of the Phil clubs. That's the organization for dramatics. And - " she paused only to glance at Helen, "Helen here is the star in plays for her Phil club."

"Oh," Mae said, looking over at Helen with enthusiasm, "I love to act in plays! Have you done *Seven-Twenty-Eight* or *Good as Gold*? I was Dorothy in that one. I wasn't very good but I enjoyed dressing up and pretending to be someone else. Don't you?"

Lily smiled at Helen who sent her a sideways glance.

"Yes, I do enjoy the costumes and the putting on. My high school did *Good as Gold*. My mother's afraid I'll go on the stage one day and have a career as an actress like Maxine Elliot," Helen said. "But I do it simply for fun."

"Are you planning a career with your Vassar degree?" It was Mama asking.

"Oh, I can't say, Mrs. Kepler," Helen said smoothly, not missing a beat. "I could marry soon after I graduate and my children would be my career, wouldn't they?

And they would receive the benefit of my education. I sincerely believe that a mother can't have too much education, for the sake of her children."

"I agree with you, Helen," Mae said emphatically. "I am studying every evening to improve myself so I can be a better person and someday a better mother."

Mama Kepler adjusted a spoon beside her plate. "That's very admirable," she said to no one in particular.

"I think even Will has been giving some thought to enrolling in courses at Bryant and Stratton to improve himself," Mae added.

Everyone looked at Will, who seemed somewhat ill at ease. "That's so," he admitted. "I have given it some thought."

Lily laughed at him. "How much more thought would you say it needs?"

Mae nudged him.

"I didn't want to say anything until I had made up my mind to do something for sure, but," he said, addressing his father, "I'm starting to look down the road at ideas on how to keep up to date with our business. And I think it would help if I knew some modern practices so I could talk them over with you, Papa."

Papa sat back in his chair. "That sounds like a fine idea," he said, nodding, a small smile peeking from beneath his mustache.

Will smiled. "I mean, one day I'm going to want to have a family of my own and I don't want to still be in charge of deliveries."

"Well," Mama Kepler said declaratively, her voice slicing into the conversation, "you have plenty of time to think about having a family. You're young and free of entanglements."

Lily scanned the table. Papa looked at his wife thoughtfully but said nothing. Mae was looking at her plate. And Will, faced with Mama's dismissal of his sweetheart, pursed his lips as if to keep from answering. She put her napkin beside her plate and slowly rose. "Mama, let's bring in dessert now," she said in what she intended to be a neutral tone of voice.

They enjoyed apple pie and sharp cheese with conversation that was pleasant but sparse.

"Mama, let's leave the young people to enjoy themselves," Papa said when they had finished and the table cleared. "We parents are sinkers to a good time."

She reluctantly followed, taking care to say a polite good-night to Mae, who thanked her sincerely for her hospitality.

Once they were gone, Will led them to the family parlor and said, "Euchre!"

They sat around the table in the parlor, partners across from one another. After the first hand, Helen looked taken aback.

"My goodness, Lily," she said, fanning herself, "do all Buffalonians play cards this furiously?"

The others laughed.

"We have lots of winter evenings to practice," Will said, shuffling the cards.

Helen gestured from Will to Mae. "Are you exchanging signals about your cards?"

Mae beamed. "I'm afraid so. We've played together for a few months now."

Helen shrugged in Lily's direction. "We are obviously handicapped, Lily. We have no signals!"

Lily laughed at her. "It's a game, Helen."

"It's only a game if you're winning," Helen countered. "We're simply lambs to the slaughter!"

She joined in the general laughter in response to her comments.

Will finished dealing, set the kitty in the middle of the table and turned to Lily at his left. She ordered the card up and they began another hand. There was no chance for conversation which Lily found somewhat frustrating because she wanted to get to know Mae.

After Lily and Helen lost the second hand, Lily collected the cards and, instead of shuffling them, suggested a cup of tea.

"I think we'll cheerfully concede this game to you both, won't we Helen?"

"Indubitably!" the latter replied cheerfully. "But we request a future rematch when we've had the chance to develop our own secret communication."

Will asked Mae if she had the time for a cup of tea. She looked at the clock in the parlor.

"If the water is hot, I have time before I have to catch the trolley," she said.

As they moved toward the door to the kitchen, Will put an arm around Mae. "Time before *we* catch the trolley," he was saying affectionately.

She tried to argue the point, but he shook his head. "I'm seeing you home properly."

There was sufficient hot water in the kettle for a pot of tea and they all sat around the kitchen table, relaxed in a way they had not been at supper.

"How many times have you visited our home?" Lily asked Mae.

"Just the once before," Mae replied.

Lily looked at Will. "Was Mama any nicer the first time?"

Will made a face and tried to chuckle. "She was polite, according to her definition of the word."

"Ah," Lily said, eyebrows raised. "Frosty."

Mae smiled. "Can't blame her, really. I'm not the girl she was hoping for. My *Da* is the same way about Will."

"What you said tonight about studying to improve yourself - Mama should recognize herself in Mae, Will," Lily said, looking now to her brother, who rested his hand on Mae's arm as they sat side by side. "Mama came from plain beginnings and worked her way up over the years to -"

"Snobbery!" Will said quickly.

Lily ignored him and touched Mae's hand. "If you can find a way to help Mama see what you have in common, that you are both strivers, it might help persuade her not to obstruct you."

Mae looked thoughtful. Helen poured Lily a little more tea and leaned closer to her as she did so. Lily smiled at this, then saw that Will was watching. When their eyes met, he smiled, and Lily smiled back.

"I don't think I ever told you this, Will," Mae said, glancing at him, "but I picked Kepler's on purpose when I was applying for jobs. I didn't apply to any businesses in South Buffalo because I was afraid I'd never leave. My classmates who aren't married to boys they've known all their lives think they are doing fine wrapping soap at Larkin's. Whenever I didn't think I could take the freezing trolley all the way downtown to Bryant and Stratton one more evening after a full day of working, with not even a kind word of encouragement from my family - and no warm gloves! - I pictured myself filling little boxes of oatmeal at the H-O six days a week for the rest of my life. That gave me the stubbornness to persevere."

They were silent for a while, Mae's intensity radiating over their little group.

"I admire you immensely," Helen said simply. "I haven't had to work for anything my whole life."

Lily smiled. "Speaking for myself, Mae, I'm awfully glad you agreed to keep company with my brother here."

At that, Mae beamed and looked affectionately at Will who smiled back. Lily knew for certain they were in love.

"He needs a bit of work, to be sure," Mae said, and Will laughed harder than the rest.

"Well, you're the girl to do it," Will answered, looking at his girl with unabashed pride.

Then he stood. "And this girl needs to catch a trolley or she'll oversleep tomorrow."

When they said goodnight at the front door, Lily embraced Mae and said simply, "I'm so glad."

Mae nodded, her pretty eyes smiling into Lily's.

HELEN and Lily were changing into their nightgowns. Their suitcases were mostly packed for the trip to Glens Falls in the morning. Lily pulled hairpins from her hair as she sat at her little dressing table. With Will gone to accompany Mae home and her parents in bed, the house was quiet.

"What a day this has been," she said in a voice that was almost a whisper.

Helen was already in her nightgown, brushing her hair. Lily could see her sweetheart's reflection in her mirror. Helen was smiling at her.

"Certainly, for you," Helen whispered back.

"I like Mae very much."

Helen put down her brush and pulled on her dressing gown. "I like her, too," she replied. "She would like Vassar, though I know she'll never see it."

"Perhaps her daughters will one day," Lily said thoughtfully.

Helen left the room and when she returned, Lily took her turn in the bathroom. When she came back, she was surprised to find that Helen had turned down the gas jet. The room was dark except for the moonlight flooding through the window. She turned toward the bed, pulling off her robe and then for some reason looked back at the window seat. There, reclining full length on the tufted cushion, was Helen, completely naked, her arms folded across her body.

Lily walked slowly toward the vision of Helen, her beautiful body like alabaster in the moonlight, each fleshy curve and angular bone accented with shadow as if lovingly shaped by a master sculptor. She stood at Helen's feet and met her beloved's gaze.

Helen smiled and spoke softly.

"She walks in beauty, like the night
Of cloudless climes and starry skies;
And all that's best of dark and bright
Meet in her aspect and her eyes."

Lily swallowed. She gave not a thought to her earlier refusal to make love with Helen in her family's home.

"Cover me," Helen said breathlessly, her arm extended to guide Lily into her embrace.

With a single motion, Lily pulled her nightgown over her head, and leaned into the moonlight and those alabaster arms. Their lovemaking was silent but greedy.

CHAPTER 21

The rattle of the alarm awoke Lily from a deep sleep and, for a moment, she had no idea where she was. She turned over and felt Helen beside her, and then she remembered. Her body remembered the night previous, also. She felt exhausted, and exultant.

Helen stirred and threw a limp arm across Lily's waist.

"Mmmm," Helen sounded.

Lily took a deep breath. "We must get up, sweetheart," she said, not moving, trying to will herself to stay awake.

"Mmmm," was the reply.

"Up," Lily said, her voice stronger, "and at 'em."

Helen rolled over onto her back. "Let 'em be, whoever they are."

Lily smiled. *This is happiness*, she thought.

Half an hour later, reasonably presentable, they descended to join the family for breakfast. Lily's father was at the dining room table, reading the *Buffalo Morning Express*. The girls served themselves scrambled eggs and ham from the sideboard. Mama came into the room with a pot of coffee and fresh toast.

"Good morning, girls," Mama Kepler said brightly as she poured coffee and set the plate of toast on the table.

"Will has gone for the wagon to take you to the station," she said, stirring her coffee. Then, for the first time, she looked at Helen and Lily, who were moving in low gear by comparison.

"Did you sleep all right?" she asked. "You look tired."

"Wonderfully, Mrs. Kepler," Helen replied with surprising heartiness.

Lily looked at Helen's plate instead of Helen. "I think I was awake for a bit. All the excitement of last evening and the trip today," she said, trailing off.

"Well," Mama said, "it is a lot of hubbub, to be sure."

Lily noted that her mother had dropped her cheerful attitude of a moment before.

Papa Kepler rattled his paper, folding it neatly in half.

"Young people enjoy hubbub, Mama," he said agreeably. "You remember how much energy we used to have."

Mama smirked. "All our youthful energy was spent in that little storefront, trying to build up a business."

"And didn't we succeed?" Papa replied, smiling at his wife. "And now we have children who don't have to do that and can have a happy youth."

"That's so," she admitted in a voice that suggested she had no interest in the thread of the conversation. A few minutes later, she left the table.

Lily ate a large breakfast as she always did when she was especially tired. Helen had only coffee with toast and jam. When they had finished, Papa put down his paper and rose.

"I'm going to say good-bye now, girls," he said.

They rose from their seats. Helen extended her hand and he covered it with both of his large hands.

"I'm glad to have met such a fine friend of our Lily's," he said, his eyes crinkling with kindness. "I hope you will have happy and safe adventures in New York's other big city."

Helen assured him they would and thanked him warmly for the hospitality. Papa tilted his head toward Lily, who stepped into his embrace.

"Thank you, Papa, for everything," she said, kissing him on the cheek.

"I don't know that I did anything," he replied. "Your mother should get your thanks."

He stepped back from her and craned his neck toward the door to the kitchen. Then he pulled a folded bill from his pocket and closed Lily's hand around it. It was five dollars.

"Just a little spending money," he said in a stage whisper, "for New York. You have a good time, now."

Lily threw her arms around him and thanked him again. He patted her on the back and then took his leave.

The girls went upstairs to do up their hair and put on their traveling clothes. As Lily carried her suitcase to the door of her room, Helen took her arm to stop her.

"Look," she said, nodding toward the window seat, now in shadow. She looked back at Lily, who smiled to show that she understood Helen's meaning.

"Our altar of love," Helen said into Lily's eyes. They kissed in remembrance.

By the time they put down their suitcases in the entry hall, they could see Will pulling up in front of the house. Mama joined them to say good-bye. She seemed ill at ease.

"Lily, I put a little gift for Mrs. McIntyre in your suitcase, in case you didn't see it, " Mama said. "They're lavender sachets. Don't forget to give it to her with my greetings."

Lily glanced at her suitcase, wondering how she could have missed the scent of lavender when she closed her bag.

"I won't, Mama," she said.

"And I put in some new handkerchiefs for you," Mama added. "The ones you brought home had ink stains on them."

Lily was touched by her mother's thoughtfulness. As Will opened the door, Lily stepped over to her mother and gave her a big hug.

"Thank you, Mama," she said, nodding once, "for everything you've done to make our stay lovely."

Mama Kepler smiled wanly. Will was picking up their suitcases. "Be careful, now," she said somewhat sternly.

"I will, Mama," Lily said. "Please don't worry. We'll be safe and very proper."

"I'll look after her, Mrs. Kepler," Helen said. "She's in good hands."

Mrs. Kepler made no reply and did not attempt to smile. Calling out final good-byes, Lily and Helen followed Will down the sidewalk to the wagon.

HELEN led the way as they stepped off the train at the new Fort Edward station, a short ride from Glens Falls. Although it was the same ornate structure with the pyramid cupola they had passed through in November, Lily had little recollection of it. As she looked around, she wondered what she could have been thinking about those months ago.

She caught up to Helen, who was greeting an elderly man in work clothes. He had removed his hat.

"*Bonjour, Monsieur* Jondreau," Helen said, smiling in respectful greeting.

The slight figure nodded once; Lily thought it a courtly gesture.

"Your mama has sent me to bring you and your friend home," he was saying. "Let me take your bags."

The girls surrendered their suitcases and the diminutive man carried them under some strain. They followed obediently, exchanging sympathetic glances, as he led them to a carriage.

The day was clear and dry, which made their half-hour ride to Warren Street in the open carriage pleasant although brisk. Their route eventually took them close by the Hudson River on their left, moving rapidly over uneven riverbed here; it was turgid, caramel and frothy with the snow melt. River Street became Warren Street, with a number of factories on either side. And then the street became residential as it approached the center of town.

Mr. Jondreau gallantly lugged the suitcases up the steps to the front door, then nodded, perspiring, for Helen to open the door, or perhaps to open it quickly, which she did. He smiled, relieved of his burden, and took off his hat to wipe his brow. Helen asked after his fare; he assured her that Mrs. McIntyre had made all the arrangements. She gave him a tip which, when he seemed reluctant to accept the gratuity, she followed by declaring that his presence at the station had been such a comfort, not to mention his superhuman work with their heavy bags, that he must do her the kindness to accept a small appreciation. In that case, he allowed, he would accept.

When he left, Helen closed the door, sent a merry look to Lily, and they both laughed.

"He has always been ancient," Helen said, sliding an arm around Lily's waist. "Since the time I was small. I used to practice my French on him. His people came from Quebec to work in the paper mills."

Then she looked around. "Where is everyone?" she asked, puzzled.

"Hello?" she called to the empty stairway. Then she shrugged. "Oh, well, let's go up and settle in. Eventually someone will turn up."

Lily opened the door to the same guest room which had been hers in November and put her suitcase down. As she was looking around, Helen came in and closed the door.

"What am I to do, with three nights in my little bed all by myself?" she pouted, pulling Lily close.

"Exercise your memory," Lily replied coyly.

They smiled and then kissed.

"Do you know what I would really like to do right this minute?" Lily asked, frowning.

Helen shook her head.

"Sleep."

"Capital idea, that," Helen agreed. "When you're changed, come across the hall. We can *nap* together, anyway," she added.

In a few minutes, Lily entered Helen's room wearing her robe and slippers. Helen was already reclined on her bed, in a pretty dressing gown, smiling sleepily at her. Lily lay down beside her and sighed.

"Helen," she said, drawing out the name by way of beginning an inquiry.

"Mmmm?"

"When I was here last November," Lily began, "and you were in your bed, did you think about me?"

"Why don't you ask if I thought about you over Christmas when you weren't here?"

"Okay. Did you think of me then?"

"All the time." Helen settled into her pillow and sighed. "Give me your hand. I want to fall asleep holding your hand."

Lily slid her hand into Helen's and quickly fell asleep, a faint smile on her lips.

THEY awoke with a start at a knock on the open door of Helen's room. It was Agnes, the McIntyre's young maid.

"Sorry to wake you, Miss McIntyre," she said apologetically, her knocking hand still hovering beside the door. "Mrs. McIntyre asked me to wake you and your friend to join her for tea in her room."

"In her room?" Helen mumbled, propped up on her elbows.

"Yes, ma'am," Agnes confirmed. "She says to come as you are."

Helen tried to smile through her sleepiness. "Thank you, Agnes. Please tell her we'll be along shortly."

"Yes, ma'am," the young girl replied. "And welcome home to you both."

After she left, Helen lay back and looked at Lily, who was squinting back at her.

"Did you hear that?" Helen whispered. "She said 'welcome home to *you both*.'" She pushed herself into a sitting position. "Goodness, it's 4:30."

In a few minutes, over Lily's protests that she needed to repair her hair before being seen, Helen took her by the arm and they padded down the long upstairs hall to the room at the end. She knocked and then entered. Lily followed and found herself in Mrs. McIntyre's spacious bedroom and sitting room.

Mrs. McIntyre was seated before a big window furnished cozily with a small settee with two stuffed club chairs and a low table between. On the table was a large tea tray. She rose, smiling, her head tilted just as Lily had observed Helen do.

"Here are my sleeping beauties!" she said, stepping to embrace them. She was wearing a handsome quilted brocade dressing gown which, although expensive-looking, gave the impression that she was shorter and wider than Lily recalled.

Helen greeted her mother and gave her a big hug. Then Mrs. McIntyre turned to greet Lily.

"I am so happy to see you again, Lily," she said, holding open her arms. Lily timidly stepped into a hearty embrace and felt the sincerity of the welcome.

Mrs. McIntyre gestured for them to sit. She resumed her seat on the settee and began to pour tea.

"How was your trip up from Buffalo? Were the cars crowded?" she asked. "Two lumps, Helen," she added, handing a cup and saucer to her daughter.

"No, not too bad, especially from Albany," Helen replied, looking at Lily, who nodded in agreement.

"Lily, you are milk and no sugar, yes?" Mrs. McIntyre asked, pausing in her pouring.

"Yes, thank you," Lily replied, surprised at her remembering. Helen grinned at her.

"We do enjoy traveling to and from Albany this time of year, Lily," Mrs. McIntyre said, handing her Lily her tea, "because in summer the racing crowds make the train from Albany nearly unbearable. Saratoga, you know."

"Oh, of course," Lily replied, having heard of the fashionable horse racing resort town.

"Now, girls, eat," Helen's mother urged them, nudging a tray of tea sandwiches and several kinds of biscuits. "I asked Margaret for a nice spread for your homecoming."

Lily and Helen helped themselves, not having eaten much since breakfast. Lily sank back into her chair upon realizing that she was eating a cucumber sandwich, the summery fresh flavor of it melting in her mouth. She wondered how expensive cucumbers were in March.

"When did you come home?" Helen asked her mother, helping herself to another sandwich.

Her mother looked at Helen thoughtfully. "A little after three, I think. I stopped by your room and saw you sleeping so peacefully that I decided to have a little nap myself. Just a few minutes, to refresh myself."

Lily took a sip of her tea and imagined Helen's mother in the doorway of the bedroom, watching them sleep as they held hands.

"And what club or committee did you have today?" Helen asked, giving her mother her full attention.

"Oh, today was my book club," her mother said happily. "It is my favorite afternoon because I'm in the company of my favorite friends and we have such a jolly time," she laughed. "We always remark how young we feel after we've finished!"

Lily smiled to see Mrs. McIntyre's delight. "Does your group discuss books?" she asked, curious.

Mrs. McIntyre looked at Lily with merry eyes. "Yes, we manage to squeeze in some discussion! But we are less structured than many groups. We don't assign a member to write up a presentation on the book or author. We just read the book and talk about it."

She paused to freshen the girls' tea cups.

"We just discussed a brand-new book that I daresay even you modern college girls haven't read. It's called *Green Mansions* and is about Rima the Bird Girl and the man who falls in love with her. It's awfully moving."

"Did it make you weep, Mother?" Helen asked, with mock sympathy.

"As a matter of fact, it did," she replied, "and so it will you when you read it. It's a story about a love that endures for a lifetime in spite of the absence of the loved one."

"If you will lend it, I would like to read it," Helen said, nodding once.

"It's downstairs in the parlor," Mrs. McIntyre replied, then turned to Lily. "How did you find things at home in Buffalo, Lily? I'm sure your mother was glad to see you."

Lily replied affirmatively and then expressed her thanks for helping persuade the Keplers to permit their daughter to travel to New York with Helen.

"Oh," Helen's mother said, "I was glad to be able to help. You know, we mothers worry so about our children, boys and girls both. But we especially worry about our daughters because we want them to have a good reputation out in the world, where every action is recorded and judged. And that world is a lot smaller than we realize."

"A good reputation in order to marry *well*," Helen added in a conspiratorial tone.

"Yes, dear," her mother replied patiently, "but also to open doors among polite people. You enjoy being invited to a party as much as any of your friends."

Helen picked up another biscuit, peering at it closely. "I do enjoy parties. I enjoy them so much that I could eschew the brass ring of marriage in favor of using my good reputation to attend more parties."

Mrs. McIntyre folded her hands and chuckled. Lily saw that she did not seem distressed to hear Helen speak against marriage. Then she sighed and looked out of the window for a moment.

"I know how you feel about marrying, my beautiful daughter," she said, turning back to look at her daughter affectionately. "I recall having exactly the same feelings at your age. And there were some who thought me far gone when I turned up with your father, a rich boy from a tiny town north of Albany, an area they equated with unmapped wilderness. My relatives thought I was tweaking their noses with my insistence on marrying someone outside their milieu."

She paused, then her face took on a softness. "But it turned out that I wasn't against marriage at all. Your father's charms won me over."

Helen and Lily smiled at the story.

"You know my Unitarian streak is too deep to have been erased by the local Presbyterians over these many years. I won't struggle with you about your marrying or not marrying. But I hope you will understand the costs of being married and compare them with the cost of remaining single."

She leaned forward and opened her hand, fingers extended.

"First," she said, touching her forefinger, "if you marry, you will be expected to produce one or more children, but because you will marry your equal, you will have household staff to take care of the children and the house. That will free you to devote your time to whatever else you want to do. I have been useful in all manner of good causes since I married your father. I have also thoroughly enjoyed my days. Once you are able to find and keep a good cook, everything else is a snap!"

She laughed and they did, as well.

"Consider your life as a single woman," Mrs. McIntyre continued, pointing to another finger. "Your brother will inherit half of our estate, and he will combine that with whatever he earns. I'm optimistically assuming here that he will become a useful citizen whenever Yale is finished with him!"

They all laughed.

"So, a single daughter will be an extra relative, to put it gently. If you continue to make your home here after Vassar, eventually we will die and you will be left with your portion of the estate and whatever your brother gives you. Possibly this house."

"But I plan to have a career, Mother," Helen protested. "I've told you that."

"Yes, you have," her mother agreed. "Let's look at that path."

She touched another finger. "For the sake of argument, let's say you decide to teach. Just as an example. I know that Vassar discourages its young women from that particular career path. So, you work for the rest of your life for very small wages and when you can no longer climb the steps to the schoolhouse, what do you have? A small pension? My concerns for your remaining single revolve entirely around economic security, Helen, please believe me."

They were silent for a while. Helen was nodding.

"Your reasons are very sound," Lily said, in quiet admiration of Helen's mother.

Helen turned to look at Lily balefully. "Whose side are you on?"

Mrs. McIntyre stood, smiling. "We don't have sides, except in argument, you know that, Helen. Now, we should see about getting dressed or risk being less than our beautiful selves at supper!"

THAT night, when they went up to bed, Helen asked Lily to come to her room to take down her hair. When she had changed into her nightgown, Lily quickly tiptoed across the hall.

Helen had already changed her clothes and was seated at her dressing table, pulling out hairpins. She smiled and gestured for Lily to pull up a chair beside her at the mirror.

"You're so much faster than I," Lily confessed.

"What have I been telling you?" Helen teased. She began brushing her hair briskly.

Lily was dropping hairpins into her little box. "Your mother is so - reasonable," she said, trying for the word she meant, "so patient with you."

Helen put down her brush and looked over at Lily for a few moments. Then she rose and moved her chair behind Lily. "Let me brush your hair," she said, her hand out for Lily's brush.

Lily surrendered her brush. She sighed with pleasure when Helen began to brush her long hair in slow strokes.

"I think your hair is one of your best attributes, my dear," Helen said softly. "I certainly enjoy it!"

Lily smiled into the mirror's reflection of Helen's face.

"You know," Helen continued, "you mustn't be distracted by my mother's tactics regarding marriage. Make no mistake about it, she conveys the same message as your mother: *we must marry*. College is but a detour on that road."

Lily had no reply. She watched Helen gather her hair and pull it together, smoothing it with her palms. Then Helen leaned her chin on Lily's shoulder.

"Her example of the impoverished spinster teacher dragging her aged self up the schoolhouse steps is her favorite cautionary specter. But there are more careers available to a single woman than that."

Helen was looking at Lily in the mirror with an expression Lily had not seen before.

"And there are even more opportunities for two women who - join forces."

Lily saw her own reflection in the mirror. She was blinking, taking in what Helen said and wondering if it meant what she thought it might mean. And then she saw Helen's smile grow until she was grinning at Lily.

"Every now and then, I render you speechless, don't I?" Helen said, impishly. She sighed, caressing Lily's arm. "How can I say good-night and send you to your room?"

Lily rose. "I think you must."

Helen stood and drew Lily close. "Two more nights and then - New York!" she said. "And freedom! We never have to leave our room if we don't want to."

Lily nodded happily and Helen raised her eyebrows in reply. They kissed and then kissed some more until they drew apart with great reluctance. As Lily stepped toward the door, Helen pressed her lips together and nodded for her to leave.

Lily fell asleep thinking about the possibilities of joining forces with Helen.

HELEN and Lily were enjoying a late breakfast the next morning when Helen's mother joined them.

"Good morning girls," she said cheerfully as she poured herself a cup of tea and settled into her accustomed seat at the end of the table. Lily observed again how Mrs. McIntyre's eyes often were crinkled with merriment.

"Good morning," Lily and Helen replied almost in unison, then looked at each other across the table and laughed.

"I hope that you slept well," Mrs. McIntyre nodded, stirring her cup.

They agreed that they had.

"I was just about to start my correspondence and thought I would come down to see what you had scheduled today. Do you have plans?"

Helen nodded. "I thought we would walk downtown and look into the shops."

"Shopping," her mother repeated, "excellent idea!"

Lily smiled at Mrs. McIntyre's tone of relish.

"Why don't you buy some pretty things to wear in the city?" she was saying. "Fowler's has all their spring things in now. And the light fabrics and sunny colors did my heart good last week when I stopped in. I don't like winter," she said to Lily. "Less and less as I get older."

"That sounds bully, Mother," Helen declared. "We will be sure to look into Fowler's."

"And I want to be plain in my suggestion," her mother continued. "Both of you should pick out nice outfits and have them put on my account."

Lily sat back in her chair, unable to think of some reply to this generosity. Helen was grinning at Lily and at her mother. Then Helen rose from her chair and put her arms around her mother who had to quickly put her cup down to keep from spilling her tea.

"Mother, you're the best!" Helen said.

Taken aback but pleased, her mother laughed and patted her daughter's arm.

"You're very kind, Mrs. McIntyre," Lily said with feeling.

Helen stood beside her mother, an arm affectionately around her shoulder, beaming at Lily.

"Lily, it gives me great pleasure to be able to do it," Mrs. McIntyre said. "Especially for two such pretty girls!"

Helen and Lily went directly into Fowler's after they stepped off the streetcar. They wanted to make the most of what was left of their morning as they had promised to be home at 12:30 for dinner with Helen's parents. Lily noticed that the tasteful interior of the store and the quality of the merchandise closely resembled Flint & Kent's back in Buffalo. She felt at home as she followed Helen to the ladies' dress department.

They kept a saleslady bustling in and out of their dressing room for half an hour, bringing skirts and jackets and shirtwaists. Helen made her decisions first, choosing a fawn-colored serge two-piece suit and an emerald green shirtwaist. Then she and the saleslady shuttled armloads in and out until Lily pleaded with them to stop.

"This, I think," was how she hesitantly stated her choice. She was wearing a silver gray five gore golf skirt, with a matching bolero style jacket. The jacket was trimmed with matching silver-grey cord sewn into leafy designs along the front placket.

Helen, seated, head propped lazily on her hand, was smiling.

Lily looked at her. "Ever since we arrived in Glens Falls, all you have done is smile," she said, with a little smile.

Helen sighed. "Who wouldn't?" she shrugged, still smiling. "I'm in my home town, on vacation, shopping," she paused for effect then continued, "with my sweetheart." She raised an eyebrow for emphasis.

The saleslady appeared in the door and Lily blushed. Helen chuckled to see it. She gestured to the things the woman could take away and they were alone again.

"And you like making me blush, I think," Lily said.

"Almost as much as I like rendering you speechless," Helen said, smirking.

Dressed in her new clothes, Lily turned to face Helen. "What do you think of this?"

Helen was nodding. "That color really shows off your hair," she murmured. "And I think it is the same silver gray of our alma mater colors."

Lily turned to see herself from behind.

"If we got you a rose waist, you could be our mascot for Field Day," Helen cracked.

Lily sent her a baleful look.

"I'm joking, " Helen said quickly. "But you could wear a pink waist under that jacket to beautiful effect."

Lily shook her head and began undressing. "This suit will be more than enough added to your mother's account. I have shirtwaists to wear."

Helen sighed and got to her feet. "Oh, all right," she said, "be frugal. But I assure you this is not an abuse of my family's largesse. Give me your suit."

Lily handed the items to her and Helen left to finish the transaction. After dressing, she found Helen in the midst of a cloud of white summer dresses.

"Our purchases will be delivered this afternoon," Helen said quietly. She held up a white lawn dress with translucent sleeves and a yoke covered with tucks. "This is what I shall wear next year at graduation," she said, admiring it. "All the graduates wear white. The exercises look like this," she laughed, waving her arm around the display racks. "An ocean of white, but noisy like a flock of seagulls!"

As they neared the exit, a floorwalker rushed to open the doors and the girls stepped into a sunny spring morning. They strolled along the street, pausing to window-shop.

"Are you aware of the graduation daisy chain tradition?" Helen asked as they gazed at shoes in Walkup's window.

Lily nodded. "It's where some sophomores make a big chain from daisies and carry it to graduation."

"Yes," said Helen, "and the seniors get to choose which sophomores to honor with the privilege."

Lily looked at her to see if Helen was being sarcastic, but she seemed earnest.

"You'll be a sophomore next year," Helen continued. "Would you like to carry the daisy chain to my graduation exercises? It is truly an honor, honest."

"I hadn't thought of that," Lily said, thinking of it now. "If I were selected, I would be able to stay on after exams so I could come to your graduation."

Helen smiled, nodding. Lily smiled and nodded.

AFTER dinner, Helen and Lily relaxed with Mrs. McIntyre in the family parlor, reporting on their morning of shopping. Somewhere a telephone rang and shortly Agnes appeared in the doorway.

"It's Mrs. Highland calling for Miss McIntyre," she announced.

Helen sent her mother a puzzled look.

"It's Daisy, dear," her mother clarified. "Now Mrs. Harold Highland. Remember? You were her maid of honor last July."

Helen laughed as she rose and followed Agnes out of the room.

Mrs. McIntyre turned to Lily, shaking her head. "And people your age say that people *my* age are senile!"

They both laughed. Lily was aware of feeling at home here.

When she returned, Helen sat down and said to Lily, "Daisy's asked us to pay her a call tomorrow. She's in her confinement now and is dying for company."

"How is she feeling?" Mrs. McIntyre asked. "When I last spoke with her mother, she said Daisy was spending more time in bed."

"She said she was feeling fine," Helen said, then nodded to Lily, "but as you will see, Daisy is the epitome of optimism."

"Well, her mother will see that she's taken care of," Mrs. McIntyre said. "I'm sure we don't need to worry."

"In fact," Helen continued, "Daisy called because her mother saw us downtown this morning and reported that to Daisy."

THEIR final full day in Glens Falls was a beautiful one. The sun warmed Lily's arms when she and Helen set out to call on Helen's high school friend Daisy. They had decided to walk to their destination on Glen Street as part of their exercise regime.

"We're going to Daisy's family home," Helen said. "The honeymoon had its effect immediately, if you follow," she said, leaning confidentially toward Lily. "So, they have had no chance to set up housekeeping on their own, which I think suits her mother very well. Daisy is their only girl and she was spoiled far more than I over the years."

Lily made a face. "Your Spartan life."

Helen sent her a sidelong glance. "Well, there's having, and then there's having *more*. Daisy had more clothes in high school that any three of her classmates put together. But don't get me wrong - she's the nicest person and not a bit affected by having her mother heap things on her."

"Was she your best friend?" Lily asked, thinking of Eva.

"Just about," Helen said. "I didn't really have a best friend. I had friends who had specialties. One friend was in theatrics, another was my bicycling pal."

"What was Daisy's specialty?"

"I'm going to let Daisy tell you that," Helen said with a small smile.

They strolled along beautiful Glen Street now, its large homes set back from the street, framed by mature trees that, in a few more weeks, would leaf out and provide deep shade over the street in summer. Lily took it in appreciatively. They were signs that Glens Falls had quite a number of well-to-do citizens.

"No sweetheart?" Lily asked.

Helen shook her head. "No sweetheart. I was so carefree - and innocent of such terrors," she chuckled. "That was all in the dark future."

Lily said nothing, but suspected they had neared Julia Fremont territory and she let it go, pretending to study the passing front porches.

Before long, Helen turned them up a wide sandstone sidewalk toward an enormous three-story home, with many peaks and a turret, clad in shingles as were so many homes in this lumber-rich town.

The maid who answered the door was expecting them and led them upstairs to a bright sitting room where a young woman reclined on a chaise, a pretty crocheted lap rug across her legs. Her protruding abdomen was the first thing one noticed about her. But when she saw the girls enter, Lily saw her face transform into what she later would recall as human sunshine.

"Finally - welcome company!" Daisy declared in as hearty a voice as could be managed from her reclining position. "Give me a hug, stranger!"

Helen bent to embrace Daisy and then introduced Lily. Daisy directed them to pull chairs close to her.

"I am allowed to get up only when necessary," she said, then added, her head tilted toward them, "and these days it is necessary to get up often!"

She laughed at her condition and the girls laughed along with her.

"I was so pleased to learn that you were home," Daisy said to Helen. "We only had the one visit at Christmas and then had to share our time with Betty." She looked at Lily, eyebrows raised. "Betty is a talker, doesn't have lots of friends. You know the type."

Lily smiled and nodded. Daisy was vivacious for someone in her condition.

"You're looking at my walrus belly, aren't you?" Daisy said to Lily, who had in fact glanced at it furtively. "I always wondered how a human baby could find room inside a woman's body. Oh, goodness, now I know firsthand. He just took all the room he wanted and pushed the rest of me up against my spine. Then when he finished that, he started expanding my skin. Isn't this breathtaking?"

She ran her hands over the great mound and laughed cheerfully. Lily couldn't help but smile.

"How are you feeling?" Helen asked.

"Better than I look, actually," she replied. "I began to puff up at around 24 weeks, and had to give up wearing any jewelry at all, even my wedding band," she said, holding out her hands. "But the doctor says that hypertension is not unusual and Mother oversees my diet to keep the salt out. So don't you worry. But," she added, with a mischievous look, "on your way home, will you tell Lily how svelte I was, how slender my neck, how long and artistic my fingers used to be?"

Helen smiled at her. "And you will be again. In how long?"

Daisy sighed. "Less than four weeks now. And we both, baby and I, will be only too glad to live separately. It's been fun, but he's getting bored in there, aren't you, my boy?" she said, patting herself.

"Will it be a boy?" Lily asked, ignorant of anything having to do with babies.

Daisy smiled at her, and Lily thought she had very kind eyes. "I think so. Others have told me stories about boys kicking more, causing indigestion more often. You wouldn't believe some of the advice I've been given by people who thought they were being helpful! It's a good thing I don't scare easily." And she laughed again.

Helen touched Lily's arm. "And she doesn't scare easily. I can attest to that."

Daisy raised her eyebrows and seemed ready to speak, when her mother came into the room with a tea tray.

"Mother, how kind of you to bring up the tea yourself," Daisy said as they watched her mother place the tray on a small table nearby.

Helen rose and greeted Daisy's mother and introduced Lily. The woman picked up a tea cup and saucer.

"Now, Mother," Daisy said, "Helen will pour. Thank you so much."

Her mother stood over the tray, hands clasped. "You won't overdo, will you, dear?" she said, meekly.

Daisy assured her that she would not overdo, and her mother reluctantly left the girls alone again.

They delved into their refreshments and Helen poured a glass of water for Daisy. The sunshine gleamed Daisy's fair hair and created a kind of halo around her head. Lily thought of an engraving of the Madonna that she had seen once.

"So, Lily, how long have you and Helen been friends?" Daisy was asking, bringing Lily back from her reverie.

"Well, she was my Greek tutor last fall," Lily replied, "and we got to know one another."

Daisy was smiling at her in a way that Lily couldn't discern. "She's a handful, isn't she?" Daisy said confidentially, and laughed.

"Pardon me," Helen said from the tea table, "but I'm in the room, you know."

Lily looked over at Helen, grinning. "Yes, Daisy, she is most definitely a handful."

"Did she tell you about how she turned me into a hooligan in the tenth grade?"

Helen rushed back to her chair. "How can you say that? It was your idea!" she said, with exaggerated offence.

Daisy threw back her head and laughed out loud. "You were always such a good actress, Helen! Lily, she made me carry it out."

"We need the facts here," Helen said. "Lily should understand who did what."

She turned to Lily. "Daisy said one day in the tenth grade, 'What would the teachers do if they filled up the blackboard and couldn't erase it because they had no erasers?'"

"It was an *idle* question," Daisy protested.

"And I said, 'Why don't we find out?'" Helen continued. "So, we removed all the erasers from all the classrooms on the second floor."

"My nerves were shot, Lily," Daisy said. "She made me hold a sack in the hallway while she broke into the classrooms and brought out all the erasers. I was so afraid someone would come along and there I would be, all alone with an old flour sack full of blackboard erasers."

"I wouldn't have let you get all the blame if you were caught," Helen said in a wounded tone. "But we didn't get caught, did we? Never."

Daisy smiled and shook her head. "It was so much funnier than we imagined. First our teacher, Mr. McKivigan, having searched high and low for an eraser, sent someone next door to borrow an eraser. The student came back empty-handed and before you knew it, all the teachers were standing in the hall telling each other that they had no erasers."

"Our classmates began to giggle and we could hear the other classes breaking up, too," Helen added.

"There wasn't much learning that afternoon," Daisy said. "Someone found a sack of erasers in the janitor's closet later that day. But no one ever found out who played that trick."

Helen smiled at her friend. "It was our finest hour."

"If we were delinquents, I would agree," Daisy said. "You're simply fire-proof, Helen McIntyre."

In a little while, Helen said they should be going. "If we don't leave soon, your mother will be back to see that you get your rest," she added.

She kissed Daisy on the cheek and stood holding her hand.

"You're not allowed to worry about me," Daisy said seriously. "Women have babies every day. There's no reason to be concerned."

Helen sighed, gave her hand a squeeze, and let go.

"There is one thing you can put on your calendar for June, when you come home for the summer," Daisy called as they were near the doorway.

"What's that?" Helen asked.

"I haven't been allowed to have chocolate for three months," Daisy complained. "Would you bring me a box of Huyler's?"

Helen agreed that she would.

THEIR last evening in Glens Falls was spent in the cozy McIntyre parlor with Helen's parents. They discussed possible itineraries for the girls' stay in, as they called it, *the city*. Mrs. McIntyre strongly recommended visiting the Metropolitan Museum of Art because the new East Wing might be open now and she was eager for a report.

Later, while Lily was packing, Helen slipped into her room and closed the door.

"My father has given us a present for our trip," she said, and unfolded a twenty-dollar bill.

Lily gasped. "Twenty!"

Helen giggled. "Yes, he has just about paid for our whole trip in one swoop."

Lily sat on the edge of her bed, shaking her head. "Does your mother know?"

Helen frowned at her and sat down beside Lily, folding the bill.

"I'm sure she does. This isn't grocery money, Lily. My parents can afford it. Still," she added, "it was terribly kind of father and the way he gave it to me was very sweet. He said that he wanted me to promise that we would take cabs from the station to the hotel and vice versa. He didn't want to think of us trying to manage on streetcars with our suitcases."

She put her arm around Lily and they grinned at one another.

"Tomorrow!" Helen whispered.

"Yes!" Lily whispered back.

They kissed goodnight for a good while.

Chapter 22

The train entered a tunnel and it seemed ages to Lily before it emerged into the midmorning light of the city. Wide-eyed, she gazed out of the window, ready to be amazed, ready to believe anything about this almost mythical place that was the other urban bookend to New York State. The approach to Grand Central station was a construction zone, with cavernous excavations like great gouges all along the last half-mile.

"The Central is putting all the rail lines underground," Helen said, leaning close to look outside, as well. "One day, if it's ever finished, it's supposed to be much nicer. And they'll get a new station, too."

The train, devoid of its locomotive now, slowly crawled into the train shed. When they stepped onto the platform, Lily's jaw dropped. She had never seen any structure so large. The wrought iron and glass shed had enough tracks for eight trains at a time. And it seemed to her that every train in the state had arrived with them. The sound of human voices rising in the vast space seemed like a collective *ahh*, punctuated by metal couplers striking each other and the high-pitched squeal of wheels on rails, all merging into a stunning, cacophonous din.

Helen had her arm and was tugging it. "Stay close to me. Look for a redcap," she said loudly, as passengers pushed past them, jostling Lily's suitcase.

And then, suddenly, a young Black man in a smudged uniform and cap appeared before them, smiling and nodding.

"Take your bags, ladies?" he said, already extending both arms in the direction of their suitcases.

Helen spoke for them in the affirmative and the slender redcap picked up the bags as if they were empty. The girls followed him as he cleared a path through the throng and eventually led them into the only slightly quieter station building.

"A cab for you, ladies, today?" he said, pausing briefly, bags firmly in hand.

Helen said, "Please," and he grinned, leading the way across the bustling expanse of the main floor.

Lily watched the redcap stand on the edge of the broad sidewalk outside the terminal, barely nodding his head toward the line of horse-drawn hansom cabs along 42nd street to their left. In moments, a cab drew up before them. Helen tipped the redcap, who was effusive in his thanks and, touching his hat, turned quickly toward the doors to the station.

"The redcaps have no salary, you know," Helen said as they climbed into the cab and arranged their skirts close around their feet. "Their income derives entirely from pleasing passengers by being indispensable. They are also walking encyclopedias about the trains and the city, too. My mother taught me to tip them well."

Lily smiled in response. Such a lesson from Mrs. McIntyre didn't surprise her at all.

She relaxed in the cab, its progress uneven along the congested streets. The city was quieter than the station, but not quiet. Streetcars, carriages, construction noises, the tweeting of police whistles at intersections, and people talking, or rather shouting, everywhere. Lily had thought she lived in a city, but this city of several *million* souls was not the same as her own of only several hundred thousand.

The trip south on Park Avenue to their destination at Eleventh and Broadway took nearly an hour. When the cab pulled up at the St. Denis Hotel, Lily calculated that they had been traveling by various means since before eight o'clock that morning. It was now nearly one-thirty. She looked at Helen, who had been smiling radiantly since they crossed the city line and didn't seem as tired or hungry as Lily felt.

"We're here!" Helen said cheerfully.

The St. Denis was a typical six-story brick building with ornamentation only over the windows. They paid the driver and turned to find a bellboy with pants too short for his legs picking up their suitcases. He didn't wait for them, but went to the door and through it. Lily looked at Helen in surprise, but the latter shrugged.

"He may not speak English," Helen whispered as they followed. "Foreigners are half the population of the city. Imagine!"

The first floor spread out openly, with palms and stuffed chairs arrayed in groups. To the right was a restaurant entrance, Colonial Room stenciled on the closed glass doors. Helen was making her way across the room to the front desk, a long counter behind which smartly dressed young men were waiting on guests, their movements and smiles smooth, as if to suggest that they were both servants to and equals of their guests.

Helen interacted with a clerk who looked about their age. Lily watched him work. His long, smooth fingers lightly held a pen and when he finished writing he passed it with a flourish to Helen for her use. Unlike some of her male peers in Buffalo, this pale young man with pomaded hair wore his dark suit as if he had dressed like this every day of his life. She knew he surely had risen to this position from a more modest beginning, perhaps even as a bellboy. She wondered if he was ambitious, if he had looked around his city and picked a lofty goal for himself.

She realized that Helen was looking at her with a quizzical expression and came back to the present. The bellboy had reappeared with their bags and was prepared to see them to their room.

"The clerk gave us a room facing Eleventh, away from the traffic on Broadway," Helen said in the elevator as it lurched upward toward the third floor. "He also said we have plenty of time for dinner at the grille downstairs."

Lily nodded. "Food." She nodded again. "Good."

Helen laughed and hooked an arm through Lily's.

"Are you very tired?" Helen asked, sympathetically, after the bellboy had left them alone in room 304. She was removing her hat.

Lily stood in the center of the small room and gazed tiredly around. "I've never been in a hotel room," she said.

"Really and truly?" Helen said with genuine surprise. She was opening her suitcase.

Lily shook her head and, pulling the hatpin from her hat, took it off. "My parents came to New York to buy furniture, but never brought us. We would have been in the way of the business. And we had school, which always came first."

The room was large enough for a double bed, a bedside table, a dresser, a small table with two chairs, and one window. There was an electric chandelier and an electric sconce beside the bed. Lily put her hat on the dresser.

"Come and see our bathroom," Helen called. "The clerk said that only forty rooms have a bath. I think he was impressed that we had reserved one of them."

Lily stepped into the bright white bathroom, white marble tiles on the floor and walls, white fixtures, white towels. It was very modern.

"Our own bath," she said quietly. "Our own private bath," she said with more vigor. "

" For a dollar more per day. And worth every penny," Helen said, with a firm nod.

Lily drifted out of the room and opened her suitcase. Helen came up behind her and encircled Lily's waist with her arms.

"We can do that later," she said, nuzzling Lily's ear. "I think we had better get you something to eat before you faint dead away."

Lily turned around and smiled, nodding.

"First things," Helen said, raising her eyebrows.

"First things," Lily replied, understanding. They kissed.

"Our first kiss in our own hotel room," Lily said, looking around with a small smile.

"Dear Lily," Helen said, her head tilted, "you will lose count of the kisses to come in 'our own hotel room.'"

They laughed and Helen took her by the hand. "To the Ladies and Gentlemen's English Grille!"

The girls ordered the plate lunch special for thirty-five cents, deciding that it was the less complicated selection given their need for nourishment. The Grille's location below the ground floor was made more intimate by the attractive decor. The walls were trimmed with dark wood strips laid out to look like lattice frames, and painted within to suggest trailing vines. The walls in between were hung with small tasteful prints. Tables were draped with long white cloths and the waiters were stiff and attentive.

"You just keep smiling," Lily commented when they had finished. She was feeling refreshed from their meal and relaxing with her second cup of tea.

Helen leaned over her place, fingering her spoon. She looked up at Lily with her eyes, now green amidst the painted foliage.

"And why wouldn't I smile? Why wouldn't any sensible person smile in my place?" she asked in a confidential voice. "I'm having a meal with a beautiful girl in the greatest city in the country!"

Lily rested her chin on her fist and felt a blush start. Helen had never called her beautiful before.

"Now I've rendered you speechless again," Helen said with mock sympathy. "Unless you don't agree that - " here she paused dramatically, "New York is the greatest city in the country."

Lily laughed, and gazed at Helen with pleasure and love. "I don't know much about New York to know if that's true, but it does seem to be in great part under construction!"

Helen nodded. "Can't you just feel the energy in the air? It's almost palpable. And I want to show it to you, or what little we can see in the brief time we have now."

Lily leaned close. "I thought you said that we might not leave our hotel room."

Helen sent her a sly look. "Did I say that?"

Lily nodded.

"Well, then, what are we doing sitting around here?"

LILY had removed her new gray suit from her suitcase and was smoothing it over a chair. She felt Helen's hand on her back and turned to find herself in Helen's arms.

"You do that like a woman of experience," Lily teased. "Just take me into your arms so smoothly."

Helen simply looked at her with shining eyes. "What would you like to do right now?" she whispered.

Lily sighed. "I would like to take off these traveling clothes and get under the covers with you."

"Bully!" Helen declared, and began unfastening the buttons on her shirtwaist cuffs.

In moments, it seemed, Helen was reduced to her chemise, and jumped into bed.

"Please hurry, poky, the bedclothes are very chilly!" she called plaintively.

Lily laughed and shook her head. In a minute, she joined Helen and they embraced, shivering.

"We haven't taken our hair down," Lily said between kisses.

"Careless girls," Helen murmured. "Death by hairpins again."

Lily's chuckle was cut short when Helen began kissing her neck. They made love through their weariness, warming their bed, discarding their remnants of clothing. And then they fell asleep.

The daylight was receding when Lily awoke. She lay on her side and watched Helen sleep. Her sweetheart's face was full of innocence, like a child's. With her eyes closed, Helen's essence was hidden. Plato's phrase, "The eyes are the windows of the soul," came to her and she understood what he had meant. And she appreciated how much she was able to read in Helen's eyes, perhaps more than Helen knew.

Helen stirred and opened her eyes to find Lily gazing at her. She took a deep breath and stretched her arms, letting them fall limply onto the covers. Then she smiled into Lily's eyes with what seemed so much like love that Lily was encouraged.

She whispered, "I love you so very much."

Helen replied, "And I love you," her eyes a bit more serious.

Lily's face must have registered surprise, because Helen quickly said, "But surely you've known how I feel."

Lily touched her cheek tenderly. "Some things must be said, darling."

Helen turned onto her back. "It's a hard business," she said, looking at Lily.

Lily shook her head. "What's hard?"

"Being in love." She looked at Lily, who had no reply.

"It puts one at such a disadvantage, don't you see? Being in love. It's the most naked condition of all."

"How?" was all Lily could ask.

Helen was frowning now. "All your most tender feelings, your happiness, your sanity even, are entirely exposed to be crushed. Being in love is like lying down in the street just waiting for a wagon to run over you."

Lily felt they had reached the point where her next question was inevitable. "The way Julia Fremont did?"

They were silent for a while.

"Won't you tell me what happened?" Lily asked softly, touching Helen's arm.

After a pause, Helen said simply, "She left Vassar in the afternoon after her last examination."

Lily waited without moving.

"She told me that she was not coming back the day before my last exam. Chemistry."

Lily remained silent.

"I didn't take the final exam and flunked Chem."

Lily's imagination filled in the blanks.

"I was supposed to do the 'flunk re' over the summer but I refused. I didn't plan to return to VC."

Lily was still silent, unmoving. This was the story she'd waited for.

"What do you want to know?" Helen asked.

"Why she left."

"Because she had gotten engaged over spring vacation and was to be married in October. She had no real interest in a college degree."

Helen paused, then added, her voice hushed with remembered pain. "Only love could make one so blind. I had no idea, saw no sign in her. She came back from vacation and never told me."

Lily made no reply.

"By March that year, we had no friends left. We had become consumed with each other and put off even our roommates. When she told me her *news*, I had no one to confide in."

Her voice was matter-of-fact. "We broke those unwritten rules I explained to you in January. Never considered the consequences of turning our backs on VC."

"But you came back in the fall."

"You can thank my mother for that. She understood that I'd had a heartbreak of some kind and never pressed for more details. But in July she began a quiet campaign to get me to see that I must continue. She made sure to point out the day they paid my tuition in August and that was it. I had to go back."

There was a pause.

"Plus, I began to remember what VC had been like in the first months that I was there, before Julia. And I remembered how much I had loved it and felt at home there."

Lily nodded, smiling.

"So, I did my Chem 'flunk re' in the fall, in addition to my other courses. It occupied my time since I had no close friends."

"What about Belle?"

"Our Mirabelle, I called her 'Miracle Belle' once, picked me out at Phil when we were planning to put on the fall play. She fancied that I would look smart in a dress suit, which is how I came to possess Harry's. She made me laugh. And then I began to have friends again, because of her. I owe her a great deal, Lily."

Lily smiled. It simply confirmed her opinion of Belle.

Helen raised an eyebrow. "She knew we would become sweethearts, way back in October."

"But I didn't know then!"

"Neither did I. But she is very astute about human nature. And you can see how correct she was!"

They lay quietly, each with her own thoughts about the history just revealed.

Then Lily said firmly, "I could never choose any man over you. Julia Fremont's a stupid girl."

Helen smiled, then grinned.

Later, after wishing for a Vassar chafing dish supper in the privacy of their room, Helen and Lily nonetheless repaired their hair and dressed for dinner in the hotel's more formal restaurant, the Colonial Room. And then they retired for the evening, to undress again and embrace in their bed. That night, when glancing into the bathroom mirror, Lily saw herself smiling. And she began to see that these days together, entirely alone for the first time, were a great exhalation for them.

LILY stood at their window looking out at the morning; the light streaming into their room indicated they were facing east. It was past eight, the day before Easter, that odd Saturday between the mournful Good Friday service and the jubilant Sunday to come. When she was little, she used to wonder if she should feel sorrowful on this day because Jesus was still dead or excited because the next day he would arise from the dead. She smiled to herself at the memory of that Lily, so far removed from the worldly young woman she was today. "Light years" removed, Helen's astronomy Professor Stone might say.

She turned to see if Helen was still asleep, and found her lover lying on her side, hand under her head, gazing sleepily at her. Lily smiled and sat on the edge of the bed beside her.

"You're overdressed, " Helen murmured, sliding her hand along Lily's robe-covered thigh to the tie at her waist.

"What shall we do today?" Lily asked. When their eyes locked, she saw that they both were remembering the night just past in this room which the city did not permit to become entirely dark or silent.

Then Helen's mouth slowly curled into a smile as her fingers pulled the tie loose. "You mean after we make love?" she said in a seductive tone, her hand finding Lily's breast.

Lily smiled in response and sighed into Helen's arms, forgetting how hungry she was.

SOME time later, they went down for breakfast in the English Grille. The waiter brought them each a roll and a soft-boiled egg in a little cup, and almost in unison they picked up their knives and began to crack the shells.

"So would you like to visit the settlement?" Helen asked. While they were getting dressed earlier, she had suggested going to the College Settlement on Rivington Street as a morning destination.

Lily nodded, scooping out some perfectly cooked egg with her spoon and closing her lips around it. She squeezed her eyes shut from the pleasure, prompting a chuckle from Helen.

"Why are you laughing?" Lily asked, pulling off a corner of her roll.

"Because you're happy," Helen replied. "Because eating a soft-boiled egg makes you happy."

Lily thought about that as she chewed. She stirred her coffee and lifted it to her lips.

"It never used to," she replied quietly, peering over her coffee cup at her beloved.

Helen met her look and then looked away to focus on breaking her roll.

"You know," Helen said with a small smirk as she pulled a bit from her roll and popped it into her mouth, "there is now one career path that is closed to you."

"And that is?" Lily recognized Helen's sardonic tone.

"Vestal Virgin," Helen replied matter-of-factly, pulling off another bit of roll.

Lily pressed her lips together and put down her coffee cup. She could feel her face growing hot as the memory of ways of lovemaking she had learned the night before flashed over her. She was trying not to smile.

"Oh, now I've done it again," Helen said in mock sympathy. "This time, not only rendering you speechless but also making you blush. Do you think me very wicked?" she added coyly.

The waiter appeared beside their table with a pot of coffee, asking if they wanted more.

"Yes," Lily said, looking at the waiter, and then sent Helen a look, saying, "Yes," again.

Helen laughed with delight that sounded like that of a child's pleasure in operating a new toy.

Back in their room, they put on their coats and hats and prepared to leave for the day. Lily turned from the mirror to see Helen buttoning her coat.

"Your collar," Lily said as she straightened Helen's coat collar. She left her hands lightly on Helen's shoulders.

"Do you mind that I tease you?" Helen asked softly, seriously.

"I'm easy to tease, I guess," Lily replied, unsure if she did mind it.

"It's just that I don't know how to be out in the world without touching you or kissing you or saying what I feel," Helen stammered, frowning. "I think that's why I teased you downstairs."

Lily looked at Helen, whose face was somewhat contrite now. "*Vestal Virgin?*" Lily reminded her.

She turned to get her gloves and bag, but Helen swept her up and held her tight.

"Lily," was all she said in Lily's ear, like an exhalation.

Lily put her arms around Helen's neck and returned the embrace. At length, she replied, "Yes," with feeling.

THEY got off the Third Avenue Elevated to find fewer people about than they had seen uptown. When they reached Rivington Street they encountered almost no one along the sidewalks. Shops whose signs were in both Hebrew and English were shuttered, their awnings of striped canvas or brown with scalloped edges folded back against the buildings. The street seemed closed in on itself; they walked past blocks that were solidly built up of six-story buildings, some with little wrought iron balconies that would give residents a view of activity on the street below. It seemed eerie to Lily that all around them was evidence of people, even to the spoiled apple in the gutter, as if everyone had evacuated just before they arrived. It was the first almost-quiet location they had encountered in New York.

After a few blocks, Helen took Lily's arm, turning them to a three-story town-house in the middle of a block. It was an old brick townhouse that looked about the same age as the Bond house on Franklin Street. The brick walls were darkened with decades of soot, but the door had a coat of bright red paint and the windows were clean. Someone had attached a small sign beside the door: College Settlement, 95 Rivington. Helen smiled at Lily and rang the bell.

They waited some time for the door to be answered, but at last the red door opened. A woman in her mid-thirties stood in the opening.

"Hello," she said, and Lily noted the kind tone in her voice.

Helen explained the nature of their call. "We belong to our Settlement Club at school and thought we would stop to pay our respects," she said, smiling.

The woman stood back to let them into the front hall. Then she held out her hand.

"I'm so glad to meet you," she said, her smile matching the warmth in her voice. "I'm Elizabeth Williams, our head resident."

Helen and Lily introduced themselves.

"And are you Smith girls?" Miss Williams asked.

"Vassar," Helen answered. "Class of '05."

Lily added, "Class of '07."

The woman gestured for them to follow her into one of the rooms off the hall. "We have two Vassar alumnae with us now," she offered, "out of a total of twelve residents. Perhaps you know them."

Helen agreed that their names sounded familiar.

"I'm afraid I can give you only an abbreviated tour of our house," she said apologetically, "because we're going to have our dinner soon. Would you like to join us?"

Helen and Lily exchanged glances and Helen replied for both of them. "No, but we thank you. We've just had our breakfast a short while ago."

"Oh," Miss Williams said pleasantly, and then started. "Oh," she said with more inflection, with a curious look at them.

Lily pursed her lips to keep from smiling. It was plain that the head worker was surprised that anyone would have breakfast so near to the dinner hour.

Miss Williams then began to describe the purpose of the room in which they were now standing. It was a lending library with a few shelves of books and tables on which were well-read newspapers. Lily's attention, however, was on Miss Williams who seemed the essence of a sparrow. She was petite and very thin, which made her arms, tightly encased in her black shirtwaist, seem especially long. Her dark hair was drawn tightly back over her round head and wound into a bun in the back, giving her nose a more prominent appearance. But it was her movements, quickly stepping to a place and then darting away to another, that fascinated Lily. She was not a person who could be still.

They were now in a room in the back of the townhouse. Miss Williams was gesturing out of the window toward the back lot.

"On any other day of the week, you would find our playground teeming with noisy children," she was saying, "but as I mentioned, today is the Hebrew Sabbath, and our day of rest, also. We teach them exercise, singing, dancing. They learn English so quickly!"

"We have programs for mothers to help with their English, or cooking, or budgeting," she was saying as she hurried them to another room. "We help our neighbors form groups they run themselves so that they can continue to operate with minimal participation from us. That's really the heart of what we want to do, to help our immigrant neighbors make the transition to becoming Americans."

"Do either of you speak German?" Miss Williams asked suddenly. They were on their way to another room, this one with many mismatched wooden chairs in rough semblance of rows.

Lily offered that she did.

Miss Williams paused, and touched Lily's arm. "Oh, my dear, we could certainly use you. Most of our residents come to us speaking nothing except French or Italian, and neither of those fluently. And our neighbors are largely German Jews. They come here right off the ships and need assistance in obtaining such services in the city as there are for new arrivals. It would be such a help to have another person who can speak to them in their own language. Do you think you could join us this summer? Our summer program is a great deal of fun and some of it is at our beautiful Mount Ivy up in Rockland County."

When Miss Williams paused for breath, Lily replied.

"I don't think I would be able to do that," she stammered, having been surprised to be the recipient of an ardent invitation to work. "My family will want me at home this summer. I'm just a freshman," she added needlessly.

Miss Williams looked disappointed. "Oh, of course. You must excuse me. I'm always looking for resources and fresh hands!" She laughed to show that it was all right. "Where is home for you?"

"Buffalo," Lily nodded.

Miss Williams grasped Lily's hand. "But so am I from Buffalo!" she exclaimed. "Might our families be acquainted? My brother Frank is a lawyer. His family lives on Irving Place."

They exchanged names of families with whom they socialized and found that they had no social intersections. But Miss Williams seemed heartened to find a fellow Buffalonian.

The girls found themselves back in the hallway.

"Are you sure you can't stay to dinner? There is always plenty and we have a fine cook."

Helen and Lily thanked her for the invitation and declined it again. At the door, Miss Williams stopped them.

"Will we see you this afternoon at the Carnegie Lyceum? Do you know about the lecture?" she asked.

They didn't.

"I'm not surprised as it hasn't been well publicized," she said. "But Dr. Anna Shaw is stopping in New York on her way back to Washington to give a few words of encouragement about the suffrage question."

"Really? Dr. Shaw here this afternoon?" Helen was awed. She turned to Lily. "What an opportunity, to see her, to hear her," Helen said. "We must go!"

Lily wasn't certain who Dr. Anna Shaw was but readily agreed.

"What time?" Helen demanded of Miss Williams.

"Two o'clock," the woman nodded.

They took their leave of Miss Williams, thanking her for the tour and saying they would look for her and the others at the Carnegie Lyceum.

All the way back to the hotel, Helen waxed about Dr. Shaw, her magnetism, speaking ability, and how she skillfully defeated all the points against a woman's right to vote with humor and deft sarcasm. And then she admitted she had not ever seen the vice-president of the National American Woman Suffrage Association, but she wanted to very much. Lily was intrigued.

As they strolled the final block from the Elevated, Lily's attention was drawn to the large Gothic church spire looming into view on their left, down a block from the St. Denis. At the corner, she took Helen's arm and led them along the front of the church to the sign. It was Grace Episcopal Church.

"Tomorrow's Easter," Lily said. "Let's come here."

Helen raised her eyebrows. "Ten a.m. is kind of early," she said in a grim tone.

Lily smiled and squeezed Helen's arm in hers. "'It is a good thing to give thanks to the Lord,'" she said.

Helen turned them around and into the direction of their hotel. "Psalm 92," she said, nodding at Lily.

That afternoon they took the handy Sixth Avenue Elevated up to 59th Street; Lily felt as if she had a bird's eye view of the city that seemed bursting with energy both kinetic and potential. Around her were strangers whose faces seemed variously intent, or tired, or impatient, or possibly all three simultaneously. Outside the greasy windows passed blocks of stores, a Huyler's store, the ornate New York Herald Building, Macy's department store, a Child's Restaurant. As they walked the final blocks to the Carnegie Hall, Helen took Lily's arm in hers and shivered. Lily laughed to see her excitement.

"People say she's the most extraordinary speaker in the country. A couple of VC girls saw her and their faces were incandescent when they tried to describe the experience."

Looming up on their right was the great brick structure of Carnegie Hall, two stories of arches over the entrance, the phrase "Music Hall Presented by Andrew Carnegie" carved in stone across the lintel. Helen led them to the Lyceum, the complex's middle-sized auditorium seating around 600 people. They were almost forty-five minutes early and already others were taking seats. The long, narrow hall had no balcony or boxes, the aisles were along either side. Helen wanted to be as close to the front as possible but they had to settle for seats a dozen or so rows from the stage.

For what seemed a long time, they sat facing the stage on which were two potted parlor palms at either side, two chairs, and a lectern. And then two women came onto the stage. An older, white-haired woman sat down. The other, much younger, stood half-facing her.

"That's Dr. Shaw, sitting," Helen said, leaning close to Lily to be heard in the din of the milling crowd of mostly women.

"Who is the other woman?" Lily asked.

"I don't know."

Lily was observing the standing woman. She was of medium height and seemed athletic, like Bert, shifting as she stood as if she would rather be running in a field than having to restrain her pent-up energy. When she smiled at something the seated woman said, she turned her head in a self-conscious way that made Lily think of her brother, Will.

When the younger woman approached the lectern, Lily looked around. The room seemed two-thirds full. They were becoming quiet now, their faces turned up toward the stage. She thought many of them could be her peers. They exuded a fresh-faced optimism, smiling in expectation.

The woman gripped the edges of the lectern and spoke. "Good afternoon, ladies," she said in a strong voice, then added, "- and gentlemen."

Everyone fell silent.

"My name is Frances Kellor. I belong to a new organization called the Women's Trade Union League of New York. Our mission is to work for unionization of women workers - particularly those in the garment factories - and to work for suffrage. We are looking for members and will be available after today's lecture to sign you up and answer questions."

She paused and looked back at the seated woman. "Dr. Shaw said I could advertise," she said lightheartedly.

The audience laughed and a few applauded.

The speaker took a deep breath. "I have a great honor today. We have the privilege of hearing Dr. Anna Howard Shaw talk to us because she was kind enough to interrupt her journey from Boston to Washington today to share her thoughts on the state of suffrage. As most of you know, Dr. Shaw is vice-president-at-large of the National American Woman Suffrage Association. She has spent more than fifteen years traveling the country, to every state and territory, speaking on suffrage for women. Her achievements - she's an ordained minister, a medical doctor - her successes, her qualifications, frankly, leave me tongue-tied!"

Dr. Shaw had risen from her seat. Frances Kellor looked back and shrugged.

"I present Dr. Anna Howard Shaw," she said, gesturing and stepping away from the lectern.

The room erupted in applause as the woman stepped into the center of the stage. She stood, smiling broadly, her cheeks deeply dimpled, and accepted the acclaim. Short and stout, Dr. Shaw had a round face and a firm jaw, straight nose ending softly, brown eyes under a strong brow. Her white hair was drawn up in a bun, but strands had escaped here and there, possibly evidence of her day of travel. Her creased traveling suit was dark and appropriate for an older woman, but not particularly fashionable.

She stepped to the lectern, but instead of standing behind it, she stood beside it, one hand on the edge. The audience became quiet.

"It does my heart good to see so many young people here today!" she said, speaking without notes in a voice strong and pleasing. "People like Frances Kellor, who does not merely *belong to*," she glanced at the younger woman now seated, "but is a *founding member* of the Women's Trade Union League of New York, are the leaders of the twentieth century. And just in time, too, for those of us who have labored in the fields of women's rights are getting tired!" She patted her white hair and laughed, inviting the audience to laugh with her.

Lily and Helen looked at one another, grinning.

"These days it is common to read in the press and magazines that our movement for suffrage is *becalmed*," the speaker continued, emphasizing the word, "like a ship whose sails cannot find a favorable breeze.

"Let us look back for a moment over the pathway along which we have toiled since this movement took definite form in a little obscure church - a few hours away- in Seneca Falls, New York, less than three score years ago. Let us compare, if we can, the position occupied by women in the home, in the church, in education, in industry, in law, and in the government, with that which they hold today. Then we shall be able to comprehend something of the struggle and the marvelous successes which have marked the progress of the greatest moral, social and economic revolution the world has ever known.

"The demands made by the first suffrage convention included the right of a woman to personal freedom, to acquire an education, to make a living, to claim her wages, to own property, to make contracts, to bring suit, to testify in court, to obtain a divorce for just cause, to have a fair share of the accumulations during marriage, to make a will, to have a voice in government, all of which were denied when the Declaration of Sentiments was framed. Today all of them are granted in some states, and in no state are they all denied. In less than sixty years, these demands are answered by the fact that the number of women graduates from our colleges and universities increased at a ratio of over one hundred and fifty-nine percent from 1889 to 1900."

The audience interrupted her with applause. She was speaking faster now.

"That in 1901 forty-two thousand girls were graduated in the public high schools; that five millions of women are engaged in gainful occupations and professions."

They interrupted again, and she held up a hand.

"Recently I was asked my opinion of the greatest need of American women and I replied, *Self-Respect*. The assumption that women, as women, have neither discernment nor judgment, and that any man is superior in all qualities that make for strength, stability and sanity in human character, to any woman, simply because he is a man and she is a woman, is still altogether too common and universal.

"The time has come when women must question themselves to learn how far they are personally responsible for this almost universal disrespect, and then to set about changing it. They should refuse to submit to being referred to as unthinking, irrational and hysterical beings, petty and uncontrolled by reason and common sense. They should cease to be content to be talked down to, as if incapable of comprehending the everyday affairs of life, upon which they are often much better informed and better capable of giving sound and correct judgments than those who lecture them. They should seek information in every possible direction, study the problems of life which face them, draw their own conclusions, and adhere to them unless they are proved false."

She drew them in and alternated humorous anecdotes from her travels with exhortations like those of a stump preacher. After forty minutes, she moved to her conclusions.

"I could stand here and talk for hours, truly, because there is so much to be said about the work to be done to grow our membership and win more states, but if I were to do so, I would miss my train, you would miss your suppers. So, I will endeavor to sum up what I wish you to carry away with you this very cold spring afternoon, especially those of you from the College Equal Suffrage Leagues.

"There is a retrograde movement, sometimes loud and aggressive, but for the most part silent and insidious, against the progressive development of women. If it has reached such proportions as to attract the attention of those who are not continually watching the ebb and flow of women's progress, it is time we recognized its existence and united to meet and oppose it. It is unquestionably true that there is a marked tendency toward a reactionary movement against women's economic independence. When women first entered the world's market of labor, men looked on indulgently, believing it but a passing phase which would soon wear off; that women lacked the qualities of initiative, perseverance and consecutive action necessary to industrial success, and that they would soon learn that they were unfitted for the practical business of life. But when women began to prove themselves in many cases not only equal but sometimes superior to men in the fields of activity which they had formerly relegated to themselves, and gradually more and more lucrative positions began to open to women in technical and professional lines of service, then the reaction began. Then the opposition began to manifest itself, not because women work, but because they have proved themselves worthy to occupy lucrative positions of honor and trust. Men do not cry out against inventive genius and machinery which have usurped women's work and taken it out from the home to the factory and the workshop; but the cry is ever against *women*, who are simply following their work where changed industrial conditions have taken it."

She paused, put her hands on her hips, and glared at the audience.

"A *dead* movement does not arouse the antagonism of great sensational magazines, nor would it pay to employ expensive writers to impede its progress. A *decaying* cause does not demand redoubled energies to stop its onward movement," she said, her voice rising. "The movement which calls forth such frenzied opposition is not dead; it is not even *sleeping!*"

The entire room arose as one body and cheered. The speaker grinned happily, her eyes twinkling, waiting for them to fall quiet again.

"If you think our organization worthwhile, come and help us make it worthwhile. If you believe the ideal of self-government is a good one; if freedom is worth having; if work for the public good is worth doing; if the problems of human development are worth solving; if it is worthwhile to be one with the infinite in bringing to pass order and peace and justice in human governments, then our ideal should be our life; the very breath of our body."

Lily stood frozen by the experience, her hands clasped together exactly as they were when the applause finally stopped. Helen finally put an arm around her and Lily blinked several times.

"What did I say?" Helen said, squeezing Lily.

"I've never heard anyone speak like that," was all Lily could utter.

"Let's speak to her," Helen said, tugging at Lily's arm. "There's a receiving line of sorts."

It was quite a long line, but Dr. Shaw shook hands and spoke to everyone who waited. When it was their turn, she looked from one to the other with what seemed to Lily an approving look.

"And what college do you girls attend?"

"Vassar," Helen said, shaking the speaker's hand.

Dr. Shaw gave her a sympathetic grimace. "Your Dr. Taylor doesn't allow a suffrage club, does he?"

"I'm afraid not."

The white-haired woman, shorter than both Lily and Helen, leaned closer and said in a confidential tone, "Why don't you form a club off-campus, quietly? You could meet at Smith Brothers!"

They both laughed that this famous woman knew the student hangout in Poughkeepsie. Then Dr. Shaw turned her attention to Lily, taking her hand.

"One of my tricks in speaking to large audiences is to pick out people here and there and address them during my talk," the white-haired woman said with a warm smile, "and I picked you out easily because of your beautiful red hair."

Lily blushed, and stammered, "I wondered if you were speaking to me."

"I was," the latter said, closing her other hand over Lily's in a clasp and looking into Lily's eyes.

"We shouldn't hold up the line," Helen said, and both looked at her.

"Of course," Dr. Anna Shaw replied, "it's too bad I'm not staying in the city overnight. We - three - could have dinner and talk about how to start a clandestine suffrage club at Vassar!"

When they were fastening their coats in the outer lobby, Lily saw that Helen's face was clouded.

"What's wrong?" Lily asked, surprised that anything could be.

Helen pulled on her gloves, shaking her head. When they were outside in the blustery afternoon, she spoke.

"She was flirting with you!" Helen sputtered. They were rapidly walking toward the streetcar stop on Broadway.

"No, she wasn't," Lily said.

"Oh, yes, she was," Helen insisted. "You didn't notice? She held your hand in both hers, she flattered you, she had that look of someone who wants to—"

"What?" Lily was thunderstruck.

"Have you for dessert!"

Lily looked at her beloved and began to laugh.

"It's not funny," Helen muttered, as Lily's laughter grew. "She's one of my heroines."

They waited among crowds for the next trolley. Lily slipped her arm through Helen's, grinning.

"Do you see now that she was flirting with you?"

Lily looked at her with love and delight. "I see that you are jealous," she replied, "and I find that irresistibly delightful and most pleasing."

By the time they reached the St. Denis, daylight was fading and they were famished. They went immediately to the English Grille and ordered the plate special.

"You know," Helen said as they waited for their meal, "we haven't spent much money on meals or entertainment thus far."

Lily was glad to see that her sweetheart had recovered from the flirtation incident on the jostling streetcar return trip.

"We did just arrive only yesterday," Lily observed.

"True, but what I'm getting at is that perhaps tomorrow we could choose a restaurant on purpose and eat away from the hotel."

The waiter arrived with their plates.

"You have someplace in mind, I think," Lily said, scanning the food before her.

"Yes," Helen replied, pausing until the waiter had retreated. "Let's go to Luchow's. It's not far away and you can enjoy some of your German food. They specialize in that."

"But I know Luchow's! My family went to the Luchow's at the German village during the Pan-American Exposition three years ago," Lily exclaimed. "How interesting to be able to visit the home restaurant, as it were."

They cleaned their plates and asked for dessert as compensation for having missed their dinner earlier.

"Tell me your thoughts about the things Dr. Shaw said," Lily inquired as they ate their pie.

"What kind of thoughts do you mean?"

"Well, you are more advanced than I in thinking about taking action for causes. She called for action. Do you think you will do something?'

"You mean like setting up a secret suffrage society?" Helen smirked.

Lily shrugged.

"I don't know about that idea," Helen said. "But I want to make a contribution after school. I don't know if it will be in settlement work or suffrage, but something. I don't imagine myself devoted to club or church committee work like our mothers until I'm too infirm to do anything else!"

Lily chuckled and agreed.

"What about you—after Vassar?" Helen prodded her.

Lily stirred her coffee. "I don't know, honestly. Listening to Dr. Shaw today, I was ready to follow her and ask how I could help the cause."

Helen sent her a look.

"Not for the reason you're thinking!" Lily admonished, and Helen grinned. "Oh, you're teasing again!

"My point is," she continued, "I want to volunteer for suffrage after I graduate, but my family is quite pragmatic, I'm afraid. I wouldn't even ask them for money to live at the Rivington Street Settlement; they would neither understand nor sympathize with the notion of paying to have their daughter work for penniless immigrants at no salary."

Helen nodded. "Your mother wants you to marry as soon as possible, never mind pragmatism."

Lily sighed and closed her eyes. "Oh, yes, she does that."

Then she added, "But I want my life to be meaningful, Helen. I think becoming educated obliges us to find ways to make a difference."

Helen smiled and nodded.

"I just don't know yet how to make that happen."

They got up and made their way to the elevator in the lobby.

"I'm very proud to be your sweetheart," Helen murmured as they waited for the car.

Lily was surprised and touched.

"And I know what would be a perfect ending to a wonderful day in the city," Helen added, watching the elevator doors open. "I'll show you."

In their room, Helen pulled a small wrapped package from her suitcase and held it out for Lily to see.

Lily was taking off her hat and had to step closer to see what it was.

"*Cashmere Bouquet*?" Lily read on the package of soap. "You brought it from your house?"

"Yes," Helen nodded, tearing open the package and wafting the perfumed bar of soap under Lily's nose. "Wasn't that foresighted of me?"

"And your idea for a perfect ending is?" Lily asked, standing very near Helen.

"Well," Helen replied, addressing the bar of soap, "we might enjoy a hot bath with this luxurious soap and then retire early, tomorrow being a long and busy day."

She looked up at Lily with a little smile, eyebrows raised in question.

"Do you think there will be sufficient hot water?" Lily asked coyly.

"To ensure that, we should probably bathe at the same time," Helen replied, placing the soap on the table and removing her hat.

Lily began to chuckle and then to laugh.

"And why do you laugh?" Helen was undressing.

"Because I find your premeditation so romantic," Lily said, smiling into Helen's eyes.

Helen was now stepping out of her skirt. "That's very nice, I'm sure," she said, folding her skirt over a chair, "but once again you lag far behind in clothing removal."

She stepped close to Lily and began unbuttoning her suit jacket. "I think we are going to have to invest some time in remedial lessons on that."

Helen had drawn a hot bath and was stretched out in the tub when Lily came into the bathroom. Steam was rising from the water into the stark white room. Helen drew up her feet to make room for Lily to sit opposite her. The warmth infused her and soothed her thoughts, evaporating all but this moment.

"I could see your face transform as you stepped into the water," Helen said, smiling languidly. "You have the smile that Buddha wears on those little statues."

Lily nodded, perfectly content.

They used a good part of the bar of the popular beauty soap on each other, taking care to keep their hair dry. When they were done, Helen got out first and wrapped a towel around her wet body so that she could help Lily out and dry her. Lily returned the favor. Then Helen took her hand and led them to their bed and to lovemaking.

CHAPTER 23

Lily opened her eyes to find Helen awake, lying on her side facing Lily. She had never seen Helen's expression as soft and her eyes as trusting. This morning they were more green than gray, spring green. She felt herself being drawn into them, letting go all that made her soul distinct and separate.

"Resurrection Day," Helen murmured, smiling.

Lily blinked and nodded slightly. "What time is it?"

"A little after nine. Probably too late for Grace Church."

Lily took a deep breath and smiled a little. "Yes," she agreed. "I don't really want to leave this bed right now."

Helen stroked Lily's arm. "Do you mind very much—not getting to church?"

"Not really," Lily confessed, "but it would have been nice to say we went to services on Easter when I write my parents about our trip."

"Well, we're going to the Metropolitan Museum of Art today," Helen said. "Do you think they'll be impressed by that?"

Lily chuckled. "I very much doubt it."

"Lily," Helen breathed, resting her hand on Lily's shoulder.

Lily smiled. "I love the way you say my name. The way you pronounce it makes it sound musical." She gently pushed Helen's hair back from her cheek. "Or maybe it's just that it sounds like love the way you say it," she said softly.

They kissed gently, free just now of desire's tension, indifferent to the clock or ceremony or obligations. The city was an ocean, their little room an island paradise.

WHEN they stepped onto Broadway after one o'clock wearing their new suits, the weather was breezy and damp, undecided between rain and snow. Helen took Lily's arm and led them across the street. When they reached the entrance to Grace Church, Lily frowned, puzzled, and looked at Helen.

"Just come along," Helen said, leading them up the stairs.

She pulled open one of the great doors and they stepped inside. The monumental sanctuary yawned before them, its Gothic arches crossing the ceiling far overhead like outstretched fingers. Helen guided them to a pew where they sat down. A few people were here and there, but the immensity of the space created a silence that insulated them like cotton wool.

It was the largest church Lily had ever entered, many times more ornate than St. Peter's at home. Each detail of a doorway, pew, and pulpit was not simple turned wood or cast plaster, but a layer of detail over a detail that was finished with another embellishment. She decided if the church building was intended to awe, then it had been successful with her.

She turned from her observation to find Helen gazing at her.

"You are beautiful," Helen whispered, smiling.

Lily touched her new pink shirtwaist, peeking from beneath her coat and suit jacket. "Thanks to you and your legerdemain," she whispered back.

When Lily had emerged from the bathroom earlier to get dressed in her new gray suit, she found that the white shirtwaist she had laid out was gone and replaced with a pink shirtwaist with high tucked neck and tucked trim along the front. While Lily was in the dressing room at Fowler's in Glens Falls, Helen had picked it out and added it to their purchases. And she was as gleeful as a child on Christmas morning when Lily made the discovery.

Helen took Lily's hand and they sat quietly, their attention drawn to the stained-glass window over the high altar, gleaming in its vibrant colors despite the cloudy skies outside. Lily sent up a prayer of thanks, and another prayer.

Then they rose and exited as quietly as they had entered, and made the now-familiar walk to the Elevated. They could see their breath on the platform while they waited for the cars.

"Now, when you write to your parents," Helen said dryly, "you can tell them that you went to church on Easter."

Lily shook her head, trying not to smile.

They stepped off the Elevated and descended onto Columbus Avenue, crossing Central Park to their destination, the Metropolitan Museum of Art. Inside, among the Sunday crowds, Lily leaned back to take in the arches of the Great Hall to the domed ceiling. She felt dwarfed.

"Everything is so large in New York," she whispered to Helen.

"This way," Helen nodded, reaching for Lily's elbow.

They spent an hour gazing at paintings by Thomas Cole and Frederick Church, Lily's favorites. Helen called her attention to Vermeer and Rubens, which were her favorites. They both liked the Rembrandt. Then they admired the tapestries, armor, and Japanese pottery until Lily sat down on a bench.

"Tired?" Helen asked, sitting beside her.

Lily shook her head. "My mind is swirling. It's more than I can take in."

"I can understand that," Helen said. "I felt that way the first time I visited, and there was much less to see than there is now."

"How many times have you been here?"

"At least half a dozen. Most often with my parents. My mother loves art and is an excellent guide to all of this," Helen gestured with an arm.

"Wonderful," Lily said dreamily, thinking of what it would be like to be guided by Helen's mother.

"Would you like her to give you a tour sometime?" Helen was smiling.

Lily nodded eagerly, and Helen laughed, putting an arm around her.

"She *is* a good old girl, even if she is my mother!" she said, giving Lily a squeeze.

They agreed that they had seen enough for one visit, and exited back into Central Park. Helen suggested an exercise walk and Lily readily agreed. They had to walk somewhat briskly in any case because the air now seemed colder than earlier.

Helen seemed to know where she wanted to go, and eventually they came to a large stone terrace with wide stone stairs leading down to a plaza in the center of which was an enormous fountain in a shallow pool. It was not operating this time of year, but Lily could tell that it must look grand when it was flowing. Nearly three stories tall, in two tiers, the fountain was topped by a larger-than-life-sized bronze statue of an angel, her wings spread wide. She seemed to have been captured by the sculptor in mid-stride, one arm reaching out toward the ground, her robes fluttering with her movement. Pigeons landed briefly along the leading edges of her wings and then lifted away, making room for others who landed and left in a kind of choreography.

"Isn't she grand?" Helen said proudly, as if she had created it.

"Oh, my, yes," Lily said, breathless. "Imagine creating something like that."

"And a woman did it, too!" Helen nodded. "They call this the Bethesda Fountain. She is the Angel of the Waters. See, she's holding out her hand to bless the water flowing from the fountain. Well, that part you have to imagine, but I've seen it in summer."

"I want to," Lily said without thinking.

"Then you shall!" declared Helen, laughing happily.

They walked along the shore of a small body of water until they came to a gracefully arching cast iron bridge, painted white. At the center of the long span, they stopped. Lily scanned the dormant landscape and turned to Helen.

"The only green in Central Park is right here," she said, slipping her arm through Helen's.

Helen smiled but her look was questioning.

"The green in your eyes," Lily explained.

The emotion Lily felt was rapidly bringing tears to her eyes and she blinked, looking out over the water. And then she realized they were being snowed upon.

They laughed at the sudden, thickly falling snow shower and Lily, who had brought her umbrella over Helen's objections, put it up to shield them from the large, fluffy flakes. Other visitors hurried past them, crying out and laughing. But they remained in the middle of the Bow Bridge, enveloped by the gently swirling white.

"Isn't this bully, and it supposedly spring, too?" Helen said, incredulous. "And we're here in the middle of it!"

Lily squeezed Helen's arm, and the latter looked at her. "Will you marry me?" Lily said, firmly.

Helen laughed, then saw Lily's earnest expression. "But no one would marry us, silly," she said sensibly, still smiling.

Lily looked at her steadily. "It's a yes or no question," she said.

Helen's smile vanished. She searched Lily's eyes.

"Helen McIntyre, will you marry me?" she asked again.

Helen swallowed. "Yes," she said, nodding. "Yes."

Lily put her free arm around Helen's neck and they embraced. Then Lily drew back and kissed Helen soundly on the lips. They kissed much longer than they would have had it not been snowing on them in Central Park on Easter Sunday.

Then the snow stopped as suddenly as it began. As Lily was shaking the snow off the umbrella, Helen leaned toward her.

"You have tears," she said in a tender voice.

"No," Lily replied, collapsing the umbrella. "Snow."

"Yes, tears," Helen said, her gloved hand beneath Lily's chin.

Lily pressed her lips together to keep them from giving away her surging emotions. Helen gently put her arms around Lily and embraced her. They stood like that for a while. Lily surrendered to her tears and then pulled away and made a show of fishing her handkerchief from her pocket.

When she thought she was calm, she looked across the gray waters without seeing them.

"I will remember this day if I live to be a hundred," she said, then looked at Helen.

Helen nodded.

"May we go to Luchow's now?" Lily suggested.

Helen agreed and turned them toward a path that led out of the park.

"I'm thinking of a poem," she said, "but I can only remember the first part." And then she recited, quietly, her arm in Lily's, "'Come live with me, and be my love, and we will some new pleasures prove.'"

Lily and Helen entered Luchow's, only three blocks from the St. Denis and immediately were immersed in a dim but boisterous space. Dozens of conversations, punctuated by laughter, rose into the vaulted ceilings and spilled back onto the diners. They stood in a small mahogany-paneled area near the door for a minute, until a round man who seemed to be the *maitre d'* approached them, his starched shirt front fairly gleaming at them in the low light.

"*Gut* evening, ladies," he said formally, but with a little smile, in a strong German accent.

Helen said that they would like to be seated. The man frowned and shook his head.

"We are completely filled now," he said, gesturing broadly. "I am very sorry."

"*Entschuldigen Sie,*" Lily said humbly in German, addressing him formally.

He was transformed by this simple "excuse me" in his native tongue, and tilted his head sympathetically toward her.

She continued in German. "I can certainly understand that you have no room for us. But I am sorry that we won't be able to enjoy Luchow's fine food again. I live in Buffalo and my family often visited Luchow's during the Pan-American in 1901."

Helen stepped back at the man's reaction. He threw his hands up and cried, "*Ach!*"

"I was in Buffalo the whole month of July that year," he said excitedly in German. "I was trying to train waiters for the Luchow's restaurant at the Alt Nurnberg. What a time I had with them dumbheads!"

Lily laughed and nodded with understanding. "But you must have succeeded in your mission," she said, smiling, "because my family was very pleased with the service we received in August and September."

He clasped his hands together with pleasure. And then he held up a fat finger. "You wait here a minute," he ordered them, and then hustled away.

Helen leaned close to Lily. "What are you two talking about?" she said.

Lily said confidentially, "How hard it is to get good help these days."

Helen looked at her, puzzled. Lily smiled back.

In a few minutes, the man returned, beaming. "*Komm mit mir,*" he said, nodding.

They followed him around tables and through rooms with stuffed animal heads on the walls and shelves of beer steins, up two stairs to an enormous room with a vaulted ceiling. Also paneled with dark wood, the room was divided by decorative carved arches that broke the space into more intimate dining areas. Along the walls were paintings. Their guide brought them to a corner, to the only empty table. He pulled out a chair for Lily with a bow, and she sat. He did the same for Helen.

"This," he said conspiratorially, "is Mr. Luchow's own table. We always keep it free for him. He sits here when he wants to keep an eye on things. But," he interrupted himself, holding up that finger again, "he won't be using it tonight. And so," he finished, opening his arms, "it is yours!"

"We are in your debt and thank you most kindly," Lily said, bowing her head.

But the man shook his finger. "No—no—no," he said, "In Buffalo, people were very good to me. They invited me to their homes when I was away from my family for so long. I have a good opinion of Buffalo. This," he gestured at the table, "is what I can do to pay back the kindness."

With that, he nodded his head in a curt bow, and then located the nearest waiter, giving instructions they could not hear but concluded from his gesturing that they were to be treated well. The waiter hurried over to them with menus.

"What just happened?" Helen said, bewildered.

"Well, he has fond memories of Buffalo," Lily replied, smiling, "so we were seated and at Mr. Luchow's own table."

She laughed to see Helen shaking her head in wonder.

"I thought you might have promised him your hand in marriage, the way he was behaving!" Helen said.

Lily opened her menu, smiling. "I couldn't do that, of course." Looking over the top of her menu, she added coyly, "I'm already engaged. Or have you forgotten?"

Helen shook her head and Lily thought she blushed, but perhaps it was just the hazy light of the gas jet.

In another room, a string quartet started up with a waltz, adding another layer of animation to the scene. They smiled at one another happily. Before they had the chance to go over the menu, their waiter brought them a bottle of Reisling, compliments of the house. He quickly offered to bring seidels of their Wurzburger beer if they preferred, but they gladly accepted the wine.

"Aren't you glad our host was well-treated in my home town?" Lily said, lifting her glass to Helen.

They clinked glasses in a toast, grinning into each other's eyes.

"I confess that I don't understand much of this menu," Helen said. "What should I order?"

"Do you want roast beef or roast pork?" Lily asked.

"Oh, that's so much simpler!" she replied.

They decided on the beef ragout and were soon presented with rimmed plates of meat, potatoes, carrots, and turnips, covered in a delicious sauce. The heat of the wine, and the convivial atmosphere of the popular restaurant seemed to Lily a perfect ending to the most perfect day of her life.

THEY strolled their way back to the St. Denis, indifferent to the cold night. At the desk when they retrieved their key, the desk man also handed them a note.

Helen opened it and gasped happily. "It's Belle!" she exclaimed. "'Everyone gone. Call me a.s.a.p.,'" she read aloud.

"Telephones!" she said excitedly, and led Lily around a corner to a wall on which were mounted half a dozen big oak-cased telephones. Helen gave the number and, in a minute, her face broke into a grin.

"What do you mean, *everyone gone*? You of the thousand and one knights?" she said, then laughed loudly at the reply.

They spoke for a minute or two, while Lily sat in a chair across the hall and enjoyed watching her beloved in her new fawn serge suit, her fingers idly tracing the outline of the telephone mouthpiece in front of her. She was beautiful, and so desirable, Lily thought frankly and without blushing at the thought. Perhaps it was the wine.

Helen finished the call and held out her hand, pulling Lily out of her seat. They headed for the elevators, Helen relating her conversation all the while.

"Well, she's had a dreadful vacation, as she tells it," she said. "Her preferred beau was a complete bust once she had the chance to get to know him, so she sent him away. But there was no one else on the bench to send into the game this week, so to speak, and she was reduced to socializing with Lydia Harbridge. Do you know her? Very dull. And then her aunt left this morning, leaving our poor social butterfly alone in that great apartment at the Waldorf. So, she called us on the chance that we have some time free tomorrow afternoon. I said we did. Was that all right?"

The elevator came and they stepped on. Lily agreed that it sounded like fun.

"I do want to shop tomorrow morning," Lily said.

"Capital idea!" Helen said, rubbing her hands together. "What shall we buy?"

"Something I have in mind," Lily said, reserved because of the presence of the elevator operator.

"A mystery," Helen said, in a low voice.

They both laughed.

LILY was the first to finish undressing this night. She stood in the bathroom doorway, naked, her nightgown in one hand, watching Helen, whose back was toward her. When Helen had undressed and picked up her nightgown, Lily dropped hers, stood behind Helen and took the nightgown from her, tossing it on the bed. Then she encircled Helen from behind, pulling her close, feeling the warmth of Helen's body. Helen covered Lily's arms with her own in an embrace, and sighed against Lily's body.

It was a long while before they lay still in each other's arms.

"'Come live with me and be my love,'" Lily whispered.

Helen, her head nestled in Lily's neck, kissed Lily's throat. "Yes," she murmured sleepily. "Yes."

THE Sixth Avenue Elevated carried Lily and Helen directly to Herald Square, where Broadway intersected Sixth Avenue at Thirty-Fourth Street and where the great new R.H. Macy and Company store dominated the landscape. Surrounded by theaters, the New York Herald building, rooftop advertisements and other businesses shoulder to shoulder, Macy's stood eight stories tall, full of pride in cream stone and brick. The top floor Palladian windows, surmounted by a balustrade like a crown, were the boldest element. The building fairly dared any other entrepreneur to surpass it in mercantile glory.

Lily thought of her city's elegant Flint & Kent department store that opened its new building just a few years earlier, and pictured its four stories swallowed entirely by the Macy's store. It would take someone a while to adjust to this city where everything was Brobdingnagian.

The store was as oversized within as without. The high ceilings stretched back along the Thirty-fourth Street side with no end visible. Departments placed along either side of the great escalator were islands floating in an ocean of marble floors. Conversations between customer and salesgirls, if they could be heard at all, were muffled by the expanses. The very air smelled prosperous.

Lily approached a floorwalker and asked, "Ladies Jewelry?"

The man smiled with a small bow and extended his arm. "Just the other side of the escalator, madam."

As she began to lead the way, Helen took her arm. "Whatever are you looking for?" she asked with curiosity. "You seem on a mission!"

Lily stopped and looked into Helen's cheerful eyes. "I am," she confessed. "I still have the money my father gave me. I want to buy you a ring."

"A ring?" Helen said, surprised.

Lily nodded. "I proposed, you accepted, and I want to give you a ring."

The smile left Helen's face; she took a deep breath, blinking a bit.

"Come on," Lily nodded, taking Helen by the elbow and leading her to the little crystal island that was ladies' jewelry. Behind glass cases of every size and shape were arrayed necklaces, brooches, rings, earrings, all glinting enticingly against black velvet. They paused at a large display of rings beneath the glass counter.

"I love emeralds," Lily said, pointing at a ring with a large square stone and little decoration. "But I want you to have a ruby ring, because your birthday is in July. What do you think?"

Helen was abashed and opened her mouth twice to speak, but failed and shook her head.

"It is all right that I give you a ring, yes?" Lily asked, her brow wrinkled.

Helen nodded, and they both laughed.

"I can't believe that I've actually made you speechless, Helen McIntyre!"

They resumed looking at the rings, and then Lily turned to Helen.

"But I don't understand," she said emphatically. "You've received countless gifts from admirers and crushes at school. You're accustomed to them."

Helen tilted her head at Lily and sent her a look. "This is—different," she said, quietly. "I've never been in this—position—before."

Lily looked at her beloved, taking that in. "Is this *position* one you want?"

Helen smiled immediately, radiantly, and nodded firmly.

"Ruby, then?" Lily asked with a small smile.

Helen nodded. A salesgirl showed them a number of rings with rubies. One caught their attention. In the latest style that would come to be called Edwardian, it was a pierced filigree design with a small ruby set on a dome built up in gold scroll work. The salesgirl had one in Helen's size and handed it to her to try. Helen looked at Lily while she slid it on the ring finger of her left hand. Lily took Helen's hand and held it so they could both look at it. On her finger, the ring looked very modern, light and youthful, but elegant. It had none of the ponderous shape or excess detail of the jewelry of their parents' generation. This was a ring for the twentieth century girls. And it was an expensive $4.75. Lily bought it. The saleslady offered a jewelry box, but Helen declined to remove it.

As they left ladies jewelry, Lily leaned close to Helen. "That was almost the most fun I've had since we came to New York!" she whispered, giggling.

"And what was the most fun you've had since we came here?" Helen replied with feigned innocence in her voice.

"You'll have to guess," Lily replied coyly, looking around the store, then turning back and grinning.

Helen stopped and raised a finger. "You know, the Waldorf-Astoria is down the street," she said. "We are practically at Belle's. I'm hungry and she'd give us a substantial tea, I'm sure!"

Lily smiled at the thought of seeing Belle again.

"We passed a Huyler's on the Elevated," Lily said. "Why don't we get your friend Daisy her candy and send it to her now? She seemed to long for it. Perhaps it will cheer her to know it is at hand to consume as soon as she is able."

That is what they did. The store handled the sending of the box of candy for them, and they bought a decorative tin of chocolates to take back with them.

"I want to have our photograph taken in Poughkeepsie," Lily said as they strolled along Thirty-Fourth Street toward the Waldorf-Astoria. "Don't you think that's a good idea?"

Helen smiled, looking into the distance. Lily wondered if she was thinking about the photograph taken with Julia Fremont.

"Yes, I do," Helen said firmly.

Lily liked that reply very much.

THE Waldorf-Astoria, two hotels joined together, loomed thirteen and seventeen stories respectively at the corner of Fifth Avenue and Thirty-Third Street. It was furnished with the very latest electrical technology and private bathrooms and could accommodate 1,000 guests. A substantial number of those guests called the hotel their permanent home. Belle's aunt Nell was among them.

After Macy's, Lily had finally become inured to splendor and smiled as she took in the coffered ceiling of the lobby supported by marble Corinthian columns, the ornate elevator doors, the tessellated floors spread with oriental rugs, the tapestries. They stepped into the elevator and Helen confidently provided the floor they desired, as if they belonged there.

A maid opened the door for them, took their coats and hats, and invited them into the small foyer, while she went to announce them to Belle. In a couple of minutes, Belle herself came rushing to greet them, her hair unpinned, wearing an expensive dressing gown and an enormous grin.

"*Mon cheries, mon amis!*" she cried, embracing them in turn.

Amid much laughter, Belle took each in an arm and guided them into a spacious but densely furnished parlor. They all sat down without ceremony, as if they were back at school except in more handsomely decorated surroundings.

"I cannot tell you how happy I am to see you," Belle said emphatically, "even if you are an hour early. As you can see, I am not put together, but you have seen me much worse!"

She laughed, and the others joined her, nodding affirmatively. The maid appeared and Belle asked her to prepare tea for them. Then she sat back and smiled at both of them across from her perch on the other settee.

"You have saved me from *mortel ennui*," Belle said gratefully. "I shall be in your debt at least until the end of the week."

Helen said, "You didn't entirely explain on the telephone why you were left alone with only your schoolwork. Poor dear," she added with false sympathy, "did you get much reading done?"

Belle gave her a prim look. "I actually did do a good bit of reading. And," she nodded, "I have part of a paper written."

"Well done," Lily said, smiling.

Belle gestured to her. "You see, Helen, someone appreciates good study habits. How much have you got done these two weeks, hmmm?"

Helen and Lily looked at one another, grimacing.

"Not as much as you," Lily confessed.

"I could have guessed as much," Belle commented, "by the beamish looks you bring to my lonely abode today."

"All right, now," Helen said, bringing the subject back to Belle, "what happened to your parade of beaus this week?"

Belle sighed and began her tale. "I made a major miscalculation, or should I say, misjudgment of character," she said sadly. "Mr. Willard Berkey and I have corresponded since Christmas when we were introduced. As you may imagine, he is a fine physical specimen, which must surely have clouded my usually discerning observations. Rendered me blind as a proverbial bat, I think! Lawk!"

She laughed along with Helen and Lily. The details of her attraction unfolded and she explained that she had refused engagements with other of her gentlemen acquaintances during the spring recess so she could devote her evenings to Mr. Berkey and a mutual friend with whom he was staying.

The maid wheeled in a cart containing tea sandwiches, biscuits, and fancy breads. Helen and Lily confessed their hunger and fell upon the food while Belle poured tea.

"Well, you may eat all you wish, but I hope you have made no plans for supper, because you will be my guests tonight. *Monsieur* Henri has a table reserved for us in the Palm Garden."

"Are we dressed well enough?" Lily asked, between bites of her little deviled ham sandwich.

"*Mais oui bien sur*," Belle assured her and then looked at them critically. "Are those suits new?"

Helen explained their shopping treat at Glens Falls.

"I think your pink waist shows off your coloring perfectly," she said approvingly to Lily.

"I picked it out," Helen said, proudly.

"And I taught you what you know of *la mode*," Belle quipped.

"All right, now," Helen interrupted, "you were saying that Mr. Berkey began to show his true colors..."

Belle held up a hand, picking up the thread of her story. "I think he must have had some classmate write those letters to me from Princeton," she said, "because the person I sat with for four evenings was not one and the same."

She sighed again. "He is from Grand Rapids, Michigan. His family owns a furniture company. They are quite wealthy, new money. He said that his family *sent* him east—said in a tone as to suggest being exiled to Elba—to get a fancy education. But that he would like nothing better than to be at home, *outdoors*. What is *outdoors*? Wolves? Mosquitoes? Central Park is *outdoors* to me, and I told him so. He just laughed loudly. *At me*."

Lily chuckled at the urban girl across from them.

"Willard said that he has no interest in going to Europe, that all the people who matter have already moved to America, or want to."

Helen pursed her lips. "Oh, my, I'm almost afraid to ask how you responded to that."

Belle opened her arms. "What can one say to such a Yahoo? I perhaps became a bit cold at that point and explained that my parents are at this moment in Europe, that half of my family resides in Europe—with no intent or desire to emigrate to America. And I think I added for good measure that I love Europe, have gone there almost every summer of my life, and can't wait to go again!"

After the laughter had subsided, Helen added, "You should have told him what Oliver Wendell Holmes said!"

Belle yelped. "Yes!" She turned to Lily and quoted, "'Good Americans, when they die, go to Paris!'"

They laughed again and then Belle said, "That was our last meeting. I told him that it was clear that we hadn't enough interests in common to develop further. He seemed to take it well, or perhaps he was relieved to be released from such *foreign* attitudes."

Helen and Lily commiserated with Belle, but commended her on sending Mr. Berkey away.

"Well, any sensible person would put a strong door between a Mr. Berkey and herself, wouldn't she? He who likes the *outdoors* might own an ax or Bowie knife, kept close at hand in case of a sudden encounter with Europeans!"

She poured more tea and they all relaxed, suit jackets removed, legs drawn up, as if they were in Helen and Belle's room at Raymond.

"You know that Mr. Berkey isn't all that unusual in my experience," Belle said sadly. "He's the most extreme example of the uncultured I've encountered, but American college boys I meet are mostly interested in making money. They don't care a fig for painting, or music, poetry, even architecture. Men make money in architecture, for heaven's sake, but where are they?"

"Or they're interested in sports," Helen added.

Belle rolled her eyes. "Don't start me on that!" She raised a warning finger. "I have developed a few test questions to gauge a boy's interest in sports. If he runs with the ball, figuratively speaking, he is not invited to call on me."

She pulled at her gown. "I think I may not find an American with whom I have enough in common to want to marry. I may have to cast my net across the Atlantic."

The day was beginning to dim outdoors as they gossiped about VC friends that Belle had heard from or met at parties.

"What have you been doing since you arrived?" Belle asked, turning attention to her guests.

Helen and Lily were silent, then Lily offered, "We went to the Metropolitan Museum of Art and Central Park."

Belle looked at her, eyebrows raised in amusement. "And was it *outdoors*, as I said?"

"Exactly as you said!" Lily laughed.

"What else?" Belle asked, looking from one to the other.

"We went to a lecture at the Carnegie Lyceum, given by Dr. Anna Shaw," Helen said.

"And we ate at Luchow's," Lily offered.

Belle was taken aback. "With the crowds there?"

Helen added, with satisfaction in her voice, "Lily and the *maitre d'* share a common love of Buffalo. We were treated very well."

"What else?" Belle demanded.

Helen and Lily hesitated. "We only arrived Friday afternoon," Helen added, frowning.

Belle looked at her, open-mouthed. "Have you not been to a single theatrical performance? A concert?" She held out her hand and ticked off the evenings. "Friday, Saturday, Sunday? Before she left, Aunt Nell and I saw *The Wizard of Oz* at the Majestic, *Piff! Paff! Pouff!* at the Casino, and the extraordinary Richard Mansfield in *Dr. Jekyll and Mr Hyde* at Daly's. You missed them all?"

Lily finally offered, "We were tired at the end of the day."

Belle looked away and then at Helen. Lily could tell that some sort of communication passed between them, but she couldn't decipher it.

"Well," Belle said finally, quietly and kindly, "perhaps on your next trip to the city you can get to a matinee or two." Eyebrows raised, she held out her left hand and waggled her ring finger. "Something new?"

Helen held out her hand. They all looked at her ring. "Yes," she said. "Isn't it beautiful?"

Belle leaned back again. "It is," she said, looking from Helen to Lily. "Perhaps a gift?"

"Yes," Lily responded without hesitation. She wanted someone to know.

Belle nodded slowly, and smiled. "It's plain that your vacation was infinitely more enjoyable than mine. I'm very glad of that."

She rose. "Friends, I'm going to get ready for our supper now," Belle said, excusing herself. "You can entertain yourselves for a while, can't you?"

They agreed that they could.

The Palm Garden was an enormous domed room, ringed by small round electric bulbs. They gently lit the profusion of large palms and ferns so that the effect of the whole was a twilight fairyland. Or, as Lily thought when they entered, it was the kind of *outdoors* that Belle preferred. Their hostess was greeted by name and they were shown to a table off to one side where they could look out on the scene.

When their waiter arrived, Belle ordered a bottle of champagne.

Lily said, "I've never had champagne. What does it taste like?"

Belle's eyes twinkled in the low light. "What does it taste like? What do you think, Helen?"

Helen shrugged. "You are better at describing such pleasures than I."

"It tastes like," Belle hesitated, tapping a finger to her lips, "it tastes like the Fourth of July in your mouth!"

With their first glass, Belle held hers up for a toast. "To spring recess!" she declared, and they laughingly clinked glasses.

Belle was right about the taste of champagne. Lily loved the little explosions of the bubbles on her palate. And she also enjoyed the way it made her feel after her first glass.

They ate beautifully prepared courses, served on dishes with gold trim that glinted in the lights far above them. When they finished the bottle of champagne, Belle signaled for another.

Lily held up her refilled glass. "To *frisson*!" she said cheerfully.

Belle laughed delightedly. "To *amour ardent*!" she added, with a shake of her head.

They looked at Helen, who looked panicked, and then said firmly, "God bless us every one!"

They laughed almost hysterically, more than perhaps was seemly in the Palm Garden. But they didn't care about anything except the enjoyment of each other's company.

Helen and Lily returned to Belle's suite to retrieve their coats and their tin of Huyler's. Belle called the concierge to arrange for a cab to take them back to their hotel. Then she walked them to the elevator.

"Remember, I'm coming to the St. Denis tomorrow at noon so we can return to Poughkeepsie together. You remember that, don't you?" she said emphatically.

"Noon tomorrow," Helen said. "You will have a cab outside."

"Lily, help her remember!" Belle said, her words somewhat slurred.

"I do," Lily said, "I mean, I will. I have it mem-mem-" she paused, bewildered at having lost the rest of the word.

"*Memorized*," Helen said.

Lily pointed at her and nodded.

The elevator doors were opening. Belle shook her head at both. "Tell the cab driver you want to go to the St. Denis, girls!" she admonished them.

In the chill of the night, Lily's mind cleared. They held hands tightly in the cab as they rode back through brightly lit streets.

"Champagne is very interesting," Lily offered.

Helen laughed a tipsy laugh.

Lily looked at Helen, so close beside her. "Do you think Belle figured out how we spent our evenings?"

Helen nodded. "Belle knows." She turned toward Lily added dramatically. "Belle knows everything about everything there is."

And then she kissed Lily, in a cab on Broadway. They kissed passionately all the way to the St. Denis.

THE next morning, Lily awoke in a state of wonderment. She lay on her back, blinking at the ceiling for some time, remembering dinner at the Waldorf-Astoria and the champagne. Then she sat up and immediately winced at the sudden headache dashing across her forehead. Touching her temples, she gingerly put her feet on the floor, sighing. There she saw bits of clothing strewn on a path from the door to her feet.

She swallowed. "Goodness," she said, feeling like the wreckage she observed.

Helen stood in the doorway to the bathroom, chuckling, freshly bathed and dressed in her robe. "Is that what you think last night was?" she said with a lascivious grin.

Lily was remembering now. Replaying moments of such abandon made her blush.

"Does your head hurt?"

Lily nodded gingerly.

"You have a champagne headache, dearest," Helen said solicitously. "I have had a restorative bath and am running you one now, nice and hot. You'll feel much better after and then we can go down and have some coffee to continue our recovery."

"We have to pack," Lily said, slowly rising from the bed, the sheet falling away from her naked body, leaving her shivering.

Helen put an arm around her. "First, a hot bath. You will be surprised how quickly a suitcase can be packed when time is of the essence."

Lily slowly sank into the tub, feeling it was even better than champagne just then. She smiled languidly at Helen, hovering over her. "Are you making sure I won't drown?" Lily asked.

Helen bent and gave Lily a kiss that lingered so gently that Lily felt herself melting into the water.

"How can I go back to Vassar and not wake up with you beside me every morning?" Lily whined.

"It won't be so bad," Helen assured her, pushing Lily's hair away from the water. "We'll still have our daily walks. And maybe opportunity will knock."

"I don't think I can study," Lily said seriously. "I'm demolished as a student, Helen. All I want to do is be with you, make love, sleep, eat, repeat!"

Helen smiled into Lily's eyes. "Don't worry. It will all come back to you. And I'll still be here."

Two hours later, they had dressed and put up their hair, breakfasted, and packed their suitcases. Helen put her bag into the hall, and turned back to find Lily standing in the center of their room, looking around. She slipped her arm around Lily's waist.

"I will always remember this, Helen," Lily said with quiet intensity.

She looked at Helen and they shared one last kiss before leaving their own little world.

At ten minutes after noon a driver entered the lobby of the St. Denis and located Helen and Lily. He carried their suitcases to the awaiting cab just outside the hotel entrance. Belle was waiting for them inside.

"*Boujour les amoureux!*" Belle greeted them sunnily.

Lily blushed at being called *lovers* as she smiled at Belle in greeting. The girls squeezed into the small cab across from Belle, who had a large covered basket beside her.

Belle was smiling happily at them. "I always return to VC alone and it makes me sad, but today we have a party going up the river, in a manner of speaking, and I'm enthused!"

"You'll be glad we don't have a fourth here with us," she added, patting the basket.

Helen said to Lily, "Belle orders up food to bring back to college, something always looked forward to by our hall-mates because it's prepared by the chefs of the Waldorf-Astoria. But, dear roommate, this is a rather large basket you have today."

"Yes!" Belle acknowledged. "I gave the concierge a larger order than usual because we three can have a last good meal tonight before we have to go back to rolled goat and tombstone pudding," she added with a grimace that made the others chuckle affirmatively.

"But how will we keep our dinner to ourselves tonight?" Helen asked. "You know people on our floor are alert your arrival with The Basket."

"Well," she replied, leaning closer, "first I am arriving hours earlier than usual. That element of surprise will serve us just as it did Hannibal when he crossed the Alps to invade Italy. Then you'll go on ahead and make sure the way is clear. Finally, once we've got our treasure safely in the room, we won't turn on the light. We'll eat in your bedroom with the door closed."

Helen and Lily laughed at her premeditation. Lily checked her purse one more time for her train ticket.

Belle waved at that. "You won't need that. I had the concierge arrange for us to have a compartment. It just seemed the right touch for our return to the academic grind."

Lily was taken aback. They were traveling the hour to Poughkeepsie first class. "You don't really think about money, do you?" she asked, wonderingly.

"You don't need to, do you, dear?" Helen replied to Belle. "Lily," she added, turning to her sweetheart, "your family is well-to-do. My family is wealthy. But Belle's family is as rich as Croesus."

Belle gave Helen a little smile. Then she addressed Lily.

"*C'est vrai, cherie.* I don't think about money. I have never needed to. But I would like to think that my family raised me to appreciate money. And I try not to be ostentatious," she paused at the look Helen sent her. "But I do! There are other girls with as many clothes as I!"

"Besides," she added, tilting her head at the basket, "I like to put money to good use for the enjoyment of my friends."

"And we appreciate it," Helen agreed with a nod.

"Yes," Lily added, "thank you."

Belle smiled warmly into Lily's eyes.

At the station, Belle waved to a redcap who brought a handcart and loaded up their suitcases. They breezed through the crowds to their train behind the efficient young man who stowed their bags on the overhead racks without a wasted movement. When he left with his generous tip, he gently closed the door to their compartment which instantly reduced the station noise to a faraway din. Lily felt like royalty as she sat down and loosened her coat.

When a vendor came by with hot tea to sell, Belle ordered three mugs. "It's not like home," she said as they cradled their warm vessels, "but it will warm us."

She pulled the cloth off the basket and poked through the paper-wrapped packages. Then she handed her mug to Helen sitting across from her.

"Here," she said with satisfaction as she pulled out a wax paper package, "lemon snaps."

She offered them around with pride as if she had baked them herself. "I always ask for lemon snaps for the basket, don't I, roommate?" she said as she nibbled.

"Every time," Helen said, returning Belle's tea mug.

They relaxed and waited for the train to begin its journey north. Lily was grateful her headache had abated, though she still felt a certain dullness of mind. She leaned back in her seat and observed Belle chattering animatedly with Helen about something or other, content to be passive.

Later, as the train vibrated beneath their seats, gently swaying every now and then, their conversation quieted. And then Belle surprised Lily, as she so often did when Lily had drawn conclusions about her.

"I thought about the two of you going off together last night," Belle said, looking with some wistfulness at Helen and Lily across from her. "And I think I envied you. Please forgive me."

"Why did you envy us?" Lily replied.

"*Pourquoi pas?*" Belle shrugged. "I could see a serene happiness surrounding you both when you came to see me yesterday. It made me sorry that I'm not looking for a VC sweetheart."

Helen and Lily started.

"Oh, Belle," Lily exclaimed, "what a line you would have outside your door if you gave the slightest encouragement!"

Belle raised her eyebrows. "You think so? I have always viewed myself as too aloof to be attractive to my classmates."

Lily started to reply, but Helen put a hand on her arm. "Don't bother to contradict her. She is well aware of her beauty, aren't you?" she said. "Besides, the only sweethearts you are interested in are of the male variety," Helen declared.

Belle agreed that was true. "But I've had such rotten luck meeting a compatible young man that it makes me think."

After a pause, she added, "And I've been thinking about the two of you."

"How interesting to be thought about," Helen replied, bemused. "Will you tell us?"

"*Certaiment*," she nodded. "I see two paths for our futures. When I marry, I will have a big church wedding, all the acknowledgment and gifts a happy society can give my husband and me. We'll have big houses in several climes. I will have many servants to supervise and give grand parties several times a year. I will have one, possibly two, children—no more! And I will have time to do as I please."

She paused, then looked at the others directly. "If you decide to make a life together, you will have no wedding, no public celebration. You will have to work to live, without children of your own. When you die, you may become invisible, leaving no record at all except as the unmarried women in your families."

Helen frowned and leaned toward Lily. "She doesn't resemble either of our mothers and yet..."

"There is a similarity in the theme," Lily finished, nodding.

Belle held up an interrupting hand. "But, to my point now. What you will have for your 'compensation,' as Mr. Emerson might say, is love. And I? I might easily have everything but."

She looked at the lovers, her brow wrinkled. "Who will be the more fortunate?"

Helen smiled encouragingly. "Did you have too much champagne last night, or too little?"

"Are you going to play devil's advocate?" Belle challenged her.

"No," Helen shook her head, "these choices are extreme ends of the possibilities. And you must confess that you are the mistress of your fate and can decline all offers of marriage until you find a qualified man to love and who will love you."

"Probably a penniless Count!" Belle exclaimed, laughing.

"And I'll do my best to live so as not to become invisible after I die," Lily said, frowning.

Helen grinned. "That's the spirit, now. We're twentieth century girls! What is there we can't do if we try?"

"LILY, water," Belle said, handing her a teapot.

Lily understood and left Helen and Belle's room to fill the pot. They had dropped her suitcase in the lobby of Main and continued to Raymond. Lily lugged the heavy basket up the stairs behind them. They had wanted to avoid the elevator and the classmates that might see them.

When Lily returned with the water, Belle put the teapot on their illegal gas burner, then they joined Helen in her little bedroom. She had been unloading her bed which the maid, in order to clean the floor, had piled with all of Helen's scattered things.

"The picnic ground is ready!" she said cheerfully, gesturing to her bed. "Bring a chair, someone."

They packed into her small space and unloaded the basket, untying the small butcher paper packets to reveal thin-sliced ham, roast beef, sliced bread, crackers, a chunk of cheese. Beneath these were little jars of mustard, jams, pickles. There were half a dozen large oranges and bananas, and small tins of tea and coffee. Belle put aside the remaining lemon snaps. Lily was amazed that one could simply telephone and have such a basket assembled.

"Well, let's eat!" Belle said, and they did.

Every now and then they could hear talking in the hallway very close to the door; they fell silent until the voices faded.

"We will certainly welcome our floor mates later," Belle said to Lily. "The perishables must be eaten, after all. But," she added, retrieving a pickle from the jar with a hat pin, "first, we feast!"

Lily, sitting on one end of the bed, leaned against the wall.

"Are you tired, dear?" Helen asked from her seat the across the picnic on the other end of her bed.

Lily nodded, trying to smile. "I'm also thinking about classes tomorrow. Are we allotted a day to return our minds to academic discipline?"

Belle waived a hand airily. "Or two or three, whatever you need."

"Remember that the faculty have also been away for two weeks," Helen added.

"*Tout sera bien,*" Belle nodded. Then she sat up in her chair. "The water," she said and left the room to check the status of the teapot.

Lily looked over at her beloved who was peeling an orange. "How shall I be able to sleep without you beside me?" she said wearily.

Helen sent her a wry smile. "I think you could sleep right now with or without me."

"Need a hand out here," Belle called in to them.

Lily sat up. "I'll go."

Helen held up an orange segment and Lily bent over and took it in her mouth. Then Lily leaned close and kissed Helen firmly on the lips.

Helen grinned, licking her lips. "Sweetest kiss I've ever had," she said. "Go!"

They had tea without milk because there was none, but Helen passed around their tin of Huyler's chocolates and the milk wasn't missed. It was getting dark outside by the time they finished their tea and Lily prepared to leave.

"Take fruit with you," Belle urged.

"I'll take an orange for Bert," Lily agreed, putting on her coat.

Belle pressed a banana into Lily's coat pocket. "And something for you, too."

Impulsively, Lily hugged Belle, who laughed with delighted surprise.

"Thank you, Belle," she said. "You will meet a wonderful man, I know it."

Belle nodded, smiling. "*Tout sera bien,*" she repeated.

Then Belle looked at Helen, who was standing in the door to her bedroom.

"I will remove the leftovers from your bed so we can throw open our door to the scavengers," she said. "Say good night to Lily."

Helen touched Belle's arm affectionately as the latter passed into the bedroom, then she strolled across the sitting room to stand before Lily. They looked into one another's eyes for a long minute and Lily suddenly felt like weeping. Helen seemed to sense it and pulled her into an embrace. Lily held on for dear life.

"I hope it wasn't a dream," Lily said into Helen's neck. "I'm afraid I'll wake up to find that this happiness wasn't real, that we didn't go to New York."

Helen pulled back and held up her left hand, the ruby ring visible even in the dim light. "You see? It was real. Why would you doubt it?"

Lily pressed her lips together to stop their trembling.

Helen glanced toward her bedroom, then took Lily's face in her hands. "Kiss me goodnight," she softly commanded, and they kissed, gently, poignantly.

"See you tomorrow?" Lily asked.

Helen smiled brightly. "Same time, same place."

Lily gratefully dropped her suitcase inside the door to their room. Bert wasn't there but signs were everywhere that Bert had been there. Their room smelled faintly like leather; Lily spied a basketball and athletic shoes on the floor that must have come back with Bert. She looked around at their meager furnishings and felt comfortable, as if she had put on an old but favorite sweater. Her texts and notebooks were stacked on their table just as she had left them over two weeks earlier.

Dragging her suitcase into her bedroom, she unpacked just enough essentials to allow her to get ready for bed. In a few minutes, she turned down the gas and slipped under the covers. No sooner had she done that when their door opened and Bert rushed in.

"Lily? You here?" she called, and Lily answered affirmatively.

Bert came into Lily's bedroom; Lily told her to turn up the gas so they could see.

"Mina said she saw you in the hall just now," Bert was saying, somewhat out of breath. "I was way down in Alice and Winnie's room. They had a great spread! But I had to hurry back to see if it really was you." She paused and grinned. "It is you! How was New York?"

Lily patted her bed and Bert immediately parked herself expectantly. "New York was wonderful," she replied, stretching out the last word. "I had champagne last night. I think I was intoxicated. I had such a headache this morning!"

They laughed together.

"I came back today with Helen and Belle. Belle had a huge basket of food made up for us to have for supper. It was also a great spread."

She patted Bert's hand. "Before I fall asleep, which I have to warn you could be momentarily, tell me about your vacation. Did you get to spend much time with Karl?"

Bert sighed happily. "Yes, we had lots of time together, with our families and also alone."

She raised her eyebrows and Lily sent her a wide-eyed look.

"We talked about getting married after next year," she said shyly. "He'll be finished with Yale then. Both of us don't want to wait any longer than we have to."

Lily looked at her, feeling sad. "You would quit VC after two years?"

"I would do it, Lily," Bert replied in a serious voice, nodding. "Can you understand?"

Lily nodded slowly. "A month ago, I wouldn't have, but now I do," she added, allowing Bert to look into her eyes and see her love for Helen.

Bert studied Lily's face for a moment and then her grin slowly returned.

"Good!" she announced, and Lily felt that Bert had comprehended.

They said good night, Bert turned the gas down and closed Lily's door. Lily lay on her back listening to the familiar sounds of her roommate moving about. Tomorrow classes would begin and life resume its structured pace. After her first class, she would write a long letter to her parents, detailing her time in New York. She had only sent them a postcard from the city to say they had arrived safely.

Then she turned onto her side and fell asleep remembering Helen's kisses.

Chapter 24

Professor Wylie stood at the head of the Lily's English class waiting for the chattering girls to settle down. Her head was tilted, her smile almost a smirk, her expression that of a teacher who had seen it all before. She was in her early thirties, and her status as a Vassar professor had remodeled what once almost certainly had been delicate features and a soft smile. Once in a while during the year Lily thought she had glimpsed in Laura Wylie someone once like herself, young and open to new things.

"There are," she began, pausing to let all eyes focus on her, "twenty-one class hours until final examinations."

The class groaned; Professor Wylie smiled with satisfaction.

"Today, we will begin with Mr. Wordsworth," she said, picking up a slender volume from her desk and opening it to a bookmarked page.

"'Stern Daughter of the Voice of God! O Duty!'" she intoned, and vacation was officially over.

Lily returned to her room after the first hour class and wrote to her parents, telling them with enthusiasm of the Metropolitan Museum of Art, with excitement of their dinner at Luchow's, of hearing an inspiring speech by a renowned speaker. She also mentioned having dinner at the Waldorf-Astoria, a name she knew her parents would recognize. She wrote, "We visited Grace Church on Easter Sunday," carefully conveying the truth. And she added how much she appreciated the trust Mama and Papa placed in her so that she could take what had been such a wonderful trip to New York City.

On Friday evening after chapel, Helen and Lily took their evening exercise walk. In the two weeks they were away, winter had surrendered and the campus landscape seemed poised between seasons. One warm day might tilt everything into a riot of spring. It wasn't warm that evening, but the pervasive damp cold of March was absent.

They crossed the little footbridge and headed up toward Sunset Hill. By now, even Lily knew the way in the darkness; she recognized the many details that defined their path and could tell where they were by how the campus lights appeared as she climbed. At the top, they stepped gingerly off the path to avoid sinking into the spongy turf and stood in a clearing, looking out over the scene below. It was the same spot where Helen had described the constellations back in November. The evening's moonlight highlighted the lake across Raymond Avenue.

"Will the boats be put into the lake very soon?" Lily asked, as Helen put an arm around her waist affectionately. "Last fall I saw girls out on the water and wanted to go out."

"The first of May, I think," Helen murmured into Lily's hair. "Shall I row or will you?"

Lily smiled and pulled Helen's arm tighter. "We can take turns, don't you think?"

Helen's lips touched Lily's cheek and Lily immediately turned her head to meet them with her own. A charge went through her body and she pressed her body into Helen's, caring nothing for the moonlight or boating. They kissed again and again.

Breaking off, her chest heaving, Lily breathed, "You make me wanton," into Helen's ear.

Helen squeezed her and then pulled back, chuckling. She smoothed Lily's hair back several times, shaking her head.

Then they both heard a sucking sound and giggled. Their boots were sinking into the earth. Helen led them down from the hill and along a path they seldom took that ended in the dark, looming shape of the nearly completed chapel that would open in June. The entrance from the campus sidewalk was framed in a cloister, with stone pillars open to the campus. They stepped onto the tile floor and could almost hear their breathing in the high arches surrounding them.

"Next fall, we will hike over here every evening for chapel," Helen whispered. "No more creaking floors and benches upstairs in Main."

But Lily cared nothing for the grand new edifice at that moment. She pulled Helen by the coat collar into a passionate kiss, pressing her against the wall of the chapel.

"Yes?" Helen finally said, weakly, out of breath. "Do you have a plan this evening?"

Lily stepped back and made fists of her hands in frustration. "No," she squeaked.

Then she backed away from Helen until she felt one of the pillars behind her. Through the darkness, she stared hard at Helen. "I need to kiss you like I need to breathe," she said at length, with ferocity.

They remained still, Lily's words reverberating through the space. Then Helen slowly walked to Lily and took her face in both hands.

"I love you," she whispered, and Lily understood for the first time how far those words had traveled to reach Helen's lips. It was sufficient. The fire of her desire, overwhelming a minute ago, was banked again.

Helen seemed to sense the change and offered her arm. Lily took it and they headed back toward Main. "I'll come by your room tomorrow morning at 9:30," Helen said easily, "and we'll be off to E. L. Wolven, Photographer, for our photograph."

"I'm wearing my new gray suit, with the pink waist," Lily said, "even though no one will be able to appreciate how nicely I wear those colors."

Helen replied, "But we will remember when we see the photos. I will also wear my new fawn suit."

Lily squeezed her beloved's arm in excitement. She could hardly wait to possess a photograph of them together. To anyone else, it would appear a photo of classmates, chums, perky college girls. But, just as only they would be able to recognize the colors of their suits, so only they would know that the two girls in the photo were sweethearts and lovers. And, she smiled, betrothed.

HELEN and Lily climbed the stairs to the Wolven Studio above City Drug on Main Street in Poughkeepsie. The enterprising owner had secured the business of the Vassarion yearbook staff in recent years and, by so doing, he had become well-known on campus to those interested in having photographs taken. He advertised the latest in "browntone platinums."

A slender young man with precisely parted hair, glossy with brilliantine, greeted them, identifying himself as Mr. Wolven's assistant. He had them wait while he disappeared behind a curtain. A faint odor of chemicals reached the waiting room they occupied. Along the walls were examples of the photographer's art which they studied until Mr. Wolven himself appeared, removing an apron as he entered.

He was a young man with a long face and dreamy or possibly distracted expression. His appearance was not as tidy that of his assistant.

"How do you do?" he said hastily, thrusting out the hand not clutching the bunched apron. He shook hands with each of them in turn.

Helen explained that they wanted to have a photograph taken together. Edmund Wolven observed that they looked like Vassar girls, a comment that Lily thought was foolishly restating the obvious because Vassar girls were instantly recognizable everywhere in town by their dress, their jaunty attitude and the simple fact that they were strangers to the locals. But he was making conversation, she decided, to put them all at ease.

The photographer suggested that he take several poses and provide them with the opportunity to select one or all for printing. He outlined his prices for the session, the proofs, and copies of the images they selected. The girls looked at one another and nodded in agreement. They had both received their April allowances from home.

With the business part settled, the photographer pulled back the curtain and ushered them into the studio proper where, he said, "the magic" happened. His assistant was already there, readying plates for the camera.

"I'm thinking of a pose where one of you is seated and the other stands beside her," Wolven said, pulling a chair into the center of a clear space with a painted backdrop on a moveable wall.

The girls agreed that would be fine. He suggested using a bench for another pose. They agreed to that, as well.

"Very good," he continued. "Let's start with the bench. Now we must select a backdrop for this pose. Otis, pull out the clouds."

The assistant rolled out a backdrop panel that featured painted gray smoke-like clouds. Helen and Lily looked at one another and shrugged.

"We might use this for a close-in pose," he said, encouragingly. "That would show both of you from your shoulders up."

They liked that idea. He posed them, went to the camera and checked their placement, adjusted them several times, and finally said they were ready.

"May we smile?" Lily asked, not moving.

"Oh," the photographer said, surprised, "certainly, if you want. Ready, then?"

They smiled, and the plate was exposed.

They got out of the way while Otis and Wolven rearranged the room, moving in a large backdrop with a Tuscan villa scene containing a pillar covered in vines and hills in the distance. He had Lily sit and Helen stand beside her, then stepped back to examine the scene.

"The palm!" he hissed at Otis, who scampered to fetch a large potted palm and place it behind Lily.

They smiled again for this image, genuinely amused at the interactions between Wolven and Otis.

For the last exposure, the photographer arranged them standing, Helen slightly behind Lily's shoulder. Lily held her forearm across her waist and, without hesitation, Helen covered it with her own. They looked directly into the camera lens without smiling this time.

And then the session was finished. They paid a deposit and were promised proofs delivered to campus by the following Wednesday.

WEDNESDAY before supper Lily burst into Helen and Belle's room, envelope in hand. Only Belle was there, chatting with a girl Lily recognized but did not know.

"What's up, Rutie?" Belle greeted her cheerfully. "Do you know Ida Crandall?" Lily introduced herself. Belle noticed the envelope.

"I don't know where herself is, but she hasn't anywhere else to be this time of day," Belle commented. "I do know a Wolven envelope when I see one, however. Don't you want to share your photos with us?"

Lily smiled sheepishly and opened the envelope, pulling out one proof, the pose that focused on their faces. Belle examined it, then passed it to Ida as she sent a smile to Lily.

"Very nice, dear," she said, nodding like a proud parent. "Why not show us the rest?"

Lily sent her an alarmed look, which made Belle chuckle.

"You can't imagine that Ida or anyone we know is in the dark about the two of you," she said. "So, pull out the rest now. Helen said you had several poses taken."

Just then Helen entered the room. "Don't listen to her!" Helen declared dramatically. "What did you say?" she directed at Belle, which made Lily laugh.

"The proofs came back," Lily said, handing her the envelope.

"Oh, swell!" Helen said, enthused.

She pulled out the other two poses, then Belle handed her the third. She quickly looked them over and looked at Lily, beaming.

Belle had her hand out. "Our turn."

Helen handed them over and everyone examined them. "Oh, Lily," Belle said, "you moved in this one. Your face is blurry."

It was the pose where Helen stood beside a seated Lily. Lily nodded but didn't say that she was secretly glad that if one pose had to be rejected, it was this one. When she first looked at it, she was immediately reminded of the photo she had seen in Glens Falls of Julia Fremont. She didn't want Helen to think of that, too, every time she looked at it.

Helen was shaking her head. "But these other two are excellent, don't you think?" she said to Lily.

Lily nodded. "I can't decide which I prefer more."

Helen held out her arms expansively. "We will have both printed up!" Then she looked at Belle and Ida. "Would you like copies? Signed?"

Everyone laughed. Ida stood and stretched. "None for me, thanks. I'm going to get ready for supper," she said, and left the three of them.

Helen sat at the table where she had tutored Lily nearly eight months ago and spread out the proofs, gazing at each in turn. Then she looked at Belle.

"Are they stuck on each other?" she quizzed her roommate, with a nod toward the images.

"Plain as the nose on your face," Belle declared. "But quite lovely, just the same. I'm going to get dressed for supper now," she added airily over her shoulder as she headed for her room.

Lily sat beside Helen as they admired themselves in the photos. "So, do we really look like sweethearts?" Lily said, needlessly because she had seen it, too, the moment she opened the envelope. It was the unguarded way their eyes looked into the camera, the identical little smiles in the close photo. It was the way Helen's arm lay over Lily's as they stood, as if it belonged there. And it was the way she stood just *that* much closer to Lily, a small but significant intimacy that would have been absent from a photograph of chums.

Helen smiled at her. "Stunningly handsome sweethearts, I should say."

Abashed, Lily reluctantly nodded in agreement. They decided to order copies of the two poses.

On Friday evening, Lily couldn't find Helen at chapel or in the hall afterward. Finally, she spotted Belle who rushed up to her with an anxious expression. Pulling Lily to one side, she said in an anguished tone, "She's been in her room since she opened her mail before dinner. Oh, Lily, she's been crying without ceasing."

Lily clutched Belle's arm. "What has happened? I have to go to her," and she headed for the stairs.

Belle had no choice but to follow because Lily still gripped her arm. "She had a letter from home," Belle said, hurrying to keep up with her. "I think something happened to a friend, but I couldn't get anything sensible from her."

Lily stopped, blinking, trying to think of what could be wrong. Just then, Bert caught up with her and asked what was the matter.

"Daisy," Lily said to Bert, realizing.

"Yes—that's what she kept repeating," Belle said. "Daisy!"

Lily looked at Bert. "Don't worry about me tonight, all right?"

Bert nodded and Lily flew down the stairs with Belle hurrying behind.

When they reached Raymond House, Lily had learned nothing more. Belle turned up the gas in their parlor and Lily observed that the door to Helen's room was closed tight. Suddenly, she was apprehensive.

"I don't know what I can do," she whispered to Belle, "if it's the worst."

Belle touched Lily's arm in sympathy. "There may be no comfort for her now," she said. "But if anyone here can help, it's you. She trusts you."

Lily looked at Belle, surprised. Later she would wonder if she was surprised that Helen trusted her, surprised that Belle knew Helen trusted her, or surprised that she herself had not understood that.

But now, thus encouraged by Belle, she went to Helen's door and let herself in, closing it behind her. In the dim light of the gas jet she saw Helen lying on her bed, turned toward the wall; she was unmoving. Lily quietly stepped to the bed. When she sat on the edge, she inadvertently sat on a piece of paper, which she retrieved. It was a small, letter-sized paper.

Helen inhaled raggedly and Lily gently put a hand on her shoulder.

"Sweetheart," was all she said, softly.

Helen didn't turn around, but began to cry with choking sounds, the kind that seem to begin deep inside a freshly broken heart. Lily felt extraneous and, casting about for some purposeful act, she focused on the paper in her hand. She decided to see if it was the letter Belle referred to. Stepping to the gas jet, she turned it up and saw Mrs. McIntyre's beautiful handwriting.

It was a brief note, only a page and a half. It dwelt entirely on Daisy's death after the birth of her daughter, who was to be named Rose. Daisy had seemed to come through the birth successfully but the doctor was called back later that day when her bleeding would not stop. She died around nine p.m. on the first day of her daughter's life.

Lily leaned against the wall under the light, trying unsuccessfully to comprehend that the young woman, whose voice she could still hear teasing Helen and whose laughter was full of good cheer, was gone forever. She had not known Daisy except for the day they visited her in Glens Falls, but it seemed so wrong that she should be dead, just like that. And Daisy had told them not to worry about her being confined for high blood pressure. "Women have babies every day," she had said reassuringly. And, irrelevantly, she wondered if Daisy had enjoyed the Huyler's they had sent from New York. It seemed particularly cruel that Daisy might have eschewed the chocolate, the only thing she said she longed for.

She turned toward Helen, who was sobbing more quietly now, then sat on Helen's chair and untied her boots. She eased herself onto the small bed, spooning her beloved, without speaking. They lay like that for a while and then Lily found herself silently weeping.

As if she could feel Lily's sorrow, Helen stirred and turned to face her. "Daisy's gone," she said in a strangled voice.

"I know," Lily said, weeping more openly now.

They embraced one another and cried without inhibition until they were exhausted from it.

"Stay with me tonight," Helen whispered into Lily's hair, now coming loose from its hairpins.

"I will," Lily replied and held her more tightly. "I will."

"What time is it?" Helen asked, as if she had been away for days.

"After nine, I think," Lily answered.

Helen slowly sat up and Lily did, as well.

"You missed supper," Lily observed.

Helen shook her head. "Not hungry."

Lily leaned over and untied Helen's boots. "Let's get ready for bed now," she said softly as one would to a tired child.

Helen let Lily undress her, then Lily also undressed to her camisole and drawers. She gently removed Helen's hairpins and used her fingers to smooth her beloved's hair. She pulled back the covers and Helen obediently got under them. Then she lay beside Helen and drew up the covers against the April chill in the room.

They were warm under the covers but Helen shivered often as if from a fresh icy blast. When she wept anew, Lily dabbed at Helen's wet cheeks with the sheet and stroked her arm. Then she would quiet for a while. Lily began to feel sleepy during the lulls but would be brought back to the present when Helen's grief came back like a spasm. Evening became night and all campus sounds outdoors and in the halls faded to silence. They were alone, except for their sorrow.

Lily had dozed lying on her back, an arm around Helen as she lay nestled in Lily's shoulder. Then she was awakened by Helen speaking softly.

"I kissed her," she was saying as Lily awoke. "She was the first person I ever kissed."

Lily took in a lungful of air to help her think. "You said she wasn't your sweetheart," she said sleepily.

"She wasn't," Helen replied, "but I told her one day in our senior year that I wanted to kiss her, and what did she think about that?"

"And?"

"She thought about it for a minute and then said that we ought to have some practice for the real thing, so kissing each other seemed like a reasonable thing to do."

Lily chuckled silently.

"So, we agreed and I leaned over very slowly and our lips met. It was a surprise and we drew apart for a moment. But then we both leaned together and truly kissed."

Lily didn't speak, letting Helen savor the memory.

Helen sighed. "It was the best moment of my life—up to that point. I knew then that I wanted to do it again."

"How did she feel about kissing you?"

"I think she was a little surprised that she liked it. She was born to kiss boys, and I think that our friendship changed a little after that. She was a little more careful around me. Maybe she could tell that I wanted to kiss girls. And her."

"Were you in love with her?" Lily asked, referring to the one whose name couldn't be spoken because it was too sharp a sound this night.

"I don't think so, and I didn't think so then," Helen replied. "But I was ready to be in love with somebody."

Then Helen began to tremble again. "But I can still feel her lips, Lily," she said through sobs, "I can still feel them."

LILY awoke when the morning sun had reached the windows, but she was not wide awake. Her eyes felt puffy and scratchy and the arm under Helen's neck was numb. She felt as though she had not slept at all. Helen seemed to be soundly asleep, for which Lily was grateful. Helen certainly needed the "sleep that knits the raveled sleeve of care," she thought as she gently extricated her arm. Carefully, she got out of bed, located Helen's chenille robe and ventured out to use the bathroom down the hall. No one was awake yet, Saturday mornings being the one time VC students had no schedule. Even breakfast was served at 8:00 on Saturdays, an official imprimatur on sleeping in.

She returned to Helen's bed and lay quietly but not comfortably on the very slender bit of mattress left to her. Nonetheless, she fell asleep.

The minutes of the morning ticked by, measured by the progress of the sun on the wall of Helen's room. Eventually even Belle, whom Lily knew was a legendary late riser, began to stir in the parlor. She thought it time to join the world of the living.

"Sweetheart," she said, holding Helen's face in her hands, "I'm going to see about getting us some tea. What do you say?"

Helen released her embrace of Lily but didn't otherwise move. Lily rose and put on Helen's robe again and a pair of socks from Helen's clean laundry pile. She pulled a brush through her hair, freeing some stray hairpins. Then she went into the parlor to find Belle heating water. Belle looked up, smiled in her beatific way, and put her arms around Lily, kissing her on each cheek.

"I went down to breakfast and brought back rolls for you both," she whispered. "Is she awake?"

"Kind of," Lily said, pulling the robe closer. She felt hungry, and chilled now that she wasn't in Helen's arms. "I'm quite hungry, I think. Thank you for bringing rolls."

"And," Belle said softly, "from our New York basket I held back a jam when the others feasted on our leftovers. So," she proudly presented the little jar, "you have *framboise* for your bun."

Lily smiled, but sadly, and Belle's smile reflected hers. It was not a happy morning.

Lily sank into a corner of the sofa and watched Belle moving about. When the water boiled, Belle made a pot of tea and placed it on the table to steep. Then she went into Helen's room. Lily heard her say, "Get up now. Tea is ready." Then she returned and poured cups for herself and Lily. Lily sat at the table and pulled off a bit of her roll and ate it.

Helen appeared unsteadily in the doorway, pulling her kimono over her underwear, her hair unbrushed. She sat down silently, her gaze unfocused. Belle poured her a cup of tea and put it in front of her.

"That's good and strong, just the way you like it," Belle said in a mother's gentle tone. "And here is a roll with jam," she added.

Belle sat down and sipped her own tea. When Helen made no move to eat, Belle broke the roll and spread jam on part of it.

"We who live must eat to live," she said declaratively.

Helen nodded and took a small bite. Despite her exhaustion, Lily observed Belle's influence over Helen with interest. She decided to think about it later after she had some rest.

In a few minutes, Lily had finished her roll and tea and excused herself to get dressed. Helen paid no attention until Lily emerged fully dressed and ready to leave. Then she seemed alarmed. Lily confessed that she had to go back to Main to get some sleep. Helen nodded but she seemed so small in her grief and weariness that Lily felt anguished about leaving her. Belle rose from her seat and took Lily by the arm.

"My turn," she said reassuringly, leading her to the door. "Get some sleep and don't worry. She'll sleep, too."

Lily nodded and left them. When she climbed the stairs to her room, Bert was just coming down the hall wearing her navy-blue gym uniform. She was on her way to basketball practice but turned around and accompanied Lily to their room.

"A friend of Helen's died giving birth," Lily said in response to Bert's questions. "They were very close in school. I met her a few weeks ago."

She paused, at a loss for words. "It's a terrible thing. She was so sweet," and she stopped because she didn't want to conjure up the image of Daisy again with all the attendant sadness. She only wanted to sleep.

Bert pinned an "Asleep" note on their door block and left Lily alone to rest. She slept soundly until late afternoon.

At Sunday services Lily looked for Helen, but she was not in the chapel. That was her second consecutive cut, and students were only allowed three per semester. Lily thought this serious, as all freshmen did, and didn't hear a word of the sermon by visiting Dr. Reverend Patterson of Bridgeport, Connecticut.

After the dinner hour, Lily knew she had to study for a math exam the next day, read several chapters for English, and research for a history paper due on Thursday. But all she could think of was Helen's unknown state of mind, so she went to Raymond instead of the library. She found neither Helen nor Belle and pinned a note to say that she had stopped by.

Bert had friends in their room when she got back, so Lily went to the library. She almost didn't see Belle, alone at a table surrounded by open texts. Lily had never seen her there.

"Hello," Lily whispered, standing beside Belle's table. Her expression was questioning and Belle smiled in response.

"You see, I do study sometimes," Belle said, gesturing around the table.

Lily nodded, and Belle leaned closer. "She's much better," she whispered. "Don't worry."

"Where is she?" Lily asked, as a couple of others looked up from their work.

Belle noticed them. "She's alone," she replied, then took Lily's hand. "She wants to be away from all of us today."

She nodded, then Lily nodded, as well.

It was easier after that to concentrate on her work. Later she considered going for a walk, but her heart wasn't in it, and she settled down with her shawl and her reading. As she got ready for bed, Lily realized that she couldn't imagine walking without Helen beside her. She wondered about that and then fell asleep hoping to see Helen the next evening for their walk.

Lily carried her coat to chapel the next evening as she usually did, and was pleased to see Helen waiting in the hall in her regular place.

"I have time for a short walk," Helen said, with a smile that said she was glad to see Lily but her eyes lacked the luminance Lily loved. "How about you?"

Lily agreed that she did and Helen helped her on with her coat. Once outdoors, Helen suggested a route around the main buildings and to the Gate Lodge and back. She looped her arm through Lily's and they set off.

"How are you?" Lily asked as they briskly strode the well-lighted paths.

"I'm all right," Helen said quietly, nodding. "I have a physics exam Wednesday for which I had intended to study over the weekend. So now I have to bear down to be ready."

Lily commiserated with her on the workloads just now. "And to make matters worse, after the history paper I will have a quiz in Greek on Friday," she complained. "I'm afraid that's not going to turn out well."

"Well, don't embarrass your tutor," Helen quipped, still in that subdued tone. "I wouldn't want to ruin my reputation in case I need to make money next year."

They chuckled at that and then fell silent, their boots crunching rhythmically on the stone path to the Gate Lodge. Lily could feel that Helen was not her old self. She closed her hand over Helen's arm and gave it a squeeze. She glanced over and saw Helen smile in response.

"Thank you," Helen said, and then looked at Lily, "for coming to me this weekend."

Lily was surprised to be thanked. "What else would I do?" she said.

They had reached the shadow of the old brick Gate Lodge through which Lily had passed for the first time in September. Here they would turn around and walk the several hundred feet back to Main. Helen pulled Lily into her arms and in their long embrace Lily felt some of Helen's lingering sorrow. Then they kissed briefly and began to retrace their steps.

"I believe I saw crocus shoots today, around the Rockefeller steps," Lily commented. "I can't wait for spring."

Helen nodded, smiling. "It's worth waiting for here. We have crocus and daffodils and narcissus springing up in the most surprising places." She warmed to the subject. "And then we have forsythia blooming all around the buildings. Over by Sunset Hill the orchard in blossom is a like a cloud hovering close to the ground."

She gave Lily's arm a squeeze. "You will love it. We can love it together."

Lily exhaled, relieved to hear her beloved's voice again.

FRIDAY afternoon after her Greek exam, her last class of the day, Lily emerged from Rockefeller to find that the continuous drizzle of the last several days had ended. The air didn't feel damp so much as humid. It took her a minute to realize the difference and then she grinned. Spring had arrived.

She unbuttoned her winter coat and let it swing freely as she walked to Main. Along the sidewalks her VC fellows passed with a happy bounce in their step, chattering and laughing as if on holiday. Everyone felt the change in season.

Near the rear entrance to Main she saw Henry, the college's gardener, raking last fall's leaves from a corner. Lily stopped to watch and saw him delicately extricate leaves covering the green shoots of spring bulbs. These she recognized from home; they would be daffodil blooms in a few weeks.

She was still smiling when she entered her room and found the Wolven Photography envelope on the table. It was the photograph prints they had ordered from the proofs. Lily tossed her books onto the couch and ripped open the envelope. She carried the card-mounted photographs to the window and gazed at them. In the seated pose, Helen was beautiful, her smile open and confident or maybe serene. Lily could feel Helen's arm over hers in the pose where they stood side by side. Taking a deep breath, Lily smiled all over.

Storing her two photos, she stuffed the rest into the envelope and rushed through the late afternoon to Raymond to give Helen her copies. Helen wasn't in yet, but Belle was.

"*Bonjour*, Rutie," she greeted Lily with a twinkling smile. "Are you filled with *joie de vivre* because it's spring at last?"

"Partly that, to be sure," Lily replied, breathless from hurrying up the stairs. "But the photographs are back from Wolven's," she added, opening the envelope.

"Oh!" Belle enthused, moving quickly to her side. "Let's see!"

"This is yours, if you'd like it," Lily said, handing Belle a copy of the photo taken of her and Helen seated. "I know you liked this pose best when we looked at the proofs."

Belle held the photo in her hands as if it were precious. "You are a thoughtful girl," Belle said warmly, "and I am very glad to have this. *Merci beaucoup, cheri.*"

She put her hand on Lily's cheek just as the door opened and Helen came in. "What's up?" she said by way of greeting.

"Lily has brought photographs," Belle said, "and she has given me one."

Helen took the envelope from Lily hastily and pulled out the photos. "You didn't give her one of mine, did you?" she asked.

"Of course not," Lily said with a chuckle. "I had an extra one printed of us seated. I thought she might like it."

"And so I do, Helen," Belle said primly. "You never gave me a photograph. And last year I gave you one of me."

Helen looked puzzled. "But I didn't have any photographs of myself to give." She looked from Belle to Lily, both of whom were looking at her. "What? Was I supposed to go and have my picture taken in case someone would like a copy?" she said, defensively. "I just didn't have any. Didn't want any."

"Well, thanks to Lily, I have one now," Belle said, holding up her photograph. "And it's a handsome thing. You look very happy, both of you."

Helen was admiring her copies. "And I wouldn't have looked as handsome last year if I had a photograph made. So, there you are. Good things come to those who wait," she said, nodding decisively.

They laughed at Helen's evasion.

Belle put her photo in her room and emerged with her little change purse. "I am going to the store before it closes. Do you want anything?" she asked Helen.

Helen had flopped onto their couch. She frowned at Belle. "Are you getting milk?" she asked.

"But of course," was the reply.

"Get me something like—those little sugar biscuits, or maybe cinnamon hard candy," Helen said, staring at the ceiling.

She looked over to see Belle looking dubiously at her. "I'll pay you when you get back," Helen said sighing. "I'm too lazy to get my money now."

Belle shook her head, sent Lily a look, and then took her leave, closing the door behind her. Helen immediately rose from the couch and carried her photos into her room, nodding to Lily to follow. They stood before the windows gazing at their likeness in black and white.

"I'm glad you suggested having our picture taken," Helen said, nodding at the photos.

Lily slipped her arm through Helen's. "I'm glad, too," she said quietly.

Helen stepped away from the window and put down her photographs. Then she held out her hand and pulled Lily toward her into a kiss.

"How was your Greek quiz?" she asked between kisses.

"I probably passed," Lily said before being kissed again.

"Good," Helen said, kissing Lily's neck.

"And your physics?" Lily was finding it hard to breathe.

"I can't remember," Helen said, her hands holding Lily's face close to hers.

"How much time do we have?" Lily asked, her voice husky with desire.

Helen shook her head. "None at all," she breathed.

Lily closed her eyes and Helen kissed her again. They grasped and pressed against one another on the verge of recklessness. Voices in the hall parted them and they locked eyes, holding each other at arm's length, clutching each other's arms.

"This is cruel," Lily whispered.

Helen nodded several times. "Yes."

They heard the door open and heard Belle call out a greeting. Lily left Helen's room first, Helen following.

"Oh, you are here," Belle said cheerfully, putting down her little packages. "The vultures saw me pass by in the hall and want to know if we're planning a spread this weekend."

She gestured to the small pile and said to Lily, " Does this look sufficient for a spread?"

Lily smiled and shook her head.

Belle pulled out a small white paper bag and tossed it at Helen. "You owe me a nickel," she said.

Helen opened the bag and pulled out a cinnamon hard candy. She offered it to Lily, who took it, and then popped one in her own mouth.

"I looked around the store," Belle said casually, "and saw these. I thought, *red, hot and spicy*. These describe you both perfectly." She tilted her head and smiled in an amused way.

The next morning Bert asked if Lily wanted to go into town with her. She would be shopping for a gift for Karl's birthday. Lily readily agreed and when on Main Street, she stepped into Ambler's Books, News & Stationery. There she found what she was looking for: a volume of Mrs. Browning's *Sonnets from the Portuguese*. The day before she had noticed that Helen still had the college library's forlorn copy of the book. She bought it to keep for Helen's birthday in July.

CHAPTER 25

O n Mondays, it was Lily's habit to return to her room after the first hour class. This day, she stopped by the mail slots to check the morning mail. One letter awaited her. She recognized her mother's handwriting on the beautiful Crane stationery which Helen had given her mother in Buffalo. Letters from her mother usually arrived on Wednesday or Thursday; this would be last week's letter, Lily realized. She had no reason to think its irregular arrival suggested anything momentous. About this, she was wrong.

On the first page, Mama reported that Will had become engaged to "the Irish girl," as she put it. She wrote as if reporting on a death in the family. Lily frowned with worry for Will and Mae as she read between the lines. Her mother was truly agitated about the event. She could almost hear her voice. "He says he agreed to take classes from the priest and raise their children as Catholics." She knew Will didn't care about the religion of his children; neither did she, but she understood that it was probably an expectation of Mae's family and likely smoothed the way for approval of at least one of the families involved. Mama strongly suggested that Papa was as unhappy about the engagement as she, which Lily doubted.

By the time she turned the page, she was dispirited, and completely caught unawares by what her mother had to say next. "Your papa and I have discussed your being so far away and have decided that one year at that school is enough. With the upset of your brother, I want you to come home when your exams are finished and stay with me and your papa. We don't have money to throw away on Vassar College."

Lily stopped breathing, reading the paragraph over and over to make sure she understood it. Then she gasped for air, panicked. Here she was, in her room, surrounded by everything familiar, needing to prepare for her next class, and yet she was sitting on her couch filled with the knowledge that this life would be extinguished in a month. It was impossible to reconcile the two realities.

She wished Bert would come in. She would rather see Bert just now than Helen. What would Helen say? Lily had promised that she was not like Julia Fremont who left after her freshman year.

It was too much to grasp and she suddenly felt the urge to flee. Stuffing the letter in her pocket, Lily rushed out of the room without her notebook for her next class, and headed toward Sunset Hill. Halfway across campus, she realized that she couldn't bear that idyllic setting just now, and instead hurried to the trolley stop at the Gate Lodge. She went into Poughkeepsie and walked the streets aimlessly. A church bell tolled the noon hour and she stopped on the sidewalk, looking around to find her bearings. Not far from Smith Brothers, she went there and had a cup of tea and a sandwich, eating only because she was trembling from hunger.

Back on the streets again, Lily was vaguely aware of warmth on her face. She looked up at the blue sky as if it were a dream. *Spring*, she thought, dazed. *The sun is warm. But not for me.* Walking again, she soon rounded a corner and found herself on Academy Street, facing a large, park-like area, at the end of which was an enormous sandstone church. Without deciding to, she walked to the entrance of Christ Episcopal Church and found one of the heavy wooden doors open to the spring warmth. She entered and sat in a pew in the darkest corner she could find. The sanctuary was very large and empty. Off to one side votive candles flickered on a pricket stand.

Eventually, Lily pulled out the crumpled letter and reread the paragraph in the dim light. Then she smoothed the letter, folded it and put it away. She looked with hard eyes at the cross in the chancel.

"This is not right," she whispered bitterly and, in so doing, felt tears well up and spill down her cheeks. "Not right."

Lily surrendered to her tears and cried as silently as she could. She remained for much of the afternoon, the reality of her future gradually coming into focus between her sobs. Then she decided that she should return to campus, having cut her classes for the second time all year. Her handkerchief was wet and as she fiddled with it, a white square appeared before her. She looked up to find a priest standing beside her pew, offering her his clean handkerchief.

He smiled at her so sympathetically that Lily almost began to cry again.

"Please," he said, offering the handkerchief again. "Take it."

Reluctantly, but in need of it, Lily accepted it, blew her nose and dried her face. She stood.

"Thank you," she said in a tremulous voice. "I'm not Episcopalian," she added needlessly.

The priest, a thick man of medium height and crinkly eyes, smiled broadly. "You are welcome here, no strings attached," he assured her.

"I'll return this," Lily said, holding up the handkerchief.

"You don't need to."

He stepped back to let her step out into the aisle. She looked at him with a resentful face.

"Does God hate happiness?" she said in a challenging tone.

The priest raised his eyebrows and opened his hands. "Be patient with Him?" he suggested kindly.

Lily returned to campus at four-thirty and decided to go to Raymond and speak to Helen before supper. She found Belle just returning to their room.

"*Bonjour!*" Belle greeted her, then stopped when she saw Lily's grave expression.

Lily stood just inside the doorway, unable to greet Belle, who immediately stepped toward her.

"Your eyes—have you been crying, *cheri*?" Belle asked, frowning with concern.

Lily began gasping and the tears began to flow again. Belle quickly closed the door and enfolded Lily in her arms.

"Can you tell me what's the matter?" Belle said at length, pushing stray hairs from Lily's wet face. "Come, sit down and tell me."

Lily sat beside her on the couch with its tasteful throw and matching throw pillows that had so impressed her last fall. She blew her nose on the priest's handkerchief and calmed herself. Then she pulled out the letter and handed it to Belle.

"It's from my mother," she said. "Read that paragraph," she added, pointing.

Belle scanned the paper and then sighed, putting it down on a little table beside the couch. She squeezed Lily's hand.

"*C'est fou!*" she finally said, quietly but emphatically. "Just crazy, that's all. Of all people."

Lily twisted the handkerchief without being aware of it. "I don't know how to tell Helen," she said glumly.

As if on cue, the door opened and Helen strode in.

"Hey—" she began, then took in the scene on the couch. "What's happened?" she asked, coming toward them.

Belle stood. "Lily has had some bad news, roommate."

Helen quickly sat beside Lily and took her hands in both her own. They had sat like this in December after opening their Christmas gifts.

"Tell me," Helen urged her.

Lily looked over at Belle, now seated at the table where Helen tutored Lily, her look asking how to tell her sweetheart such news. Belle smiled sympathetically.

"My mother has written," Lily said, trying to hold her voice steady, "to say that I cannot return to Vassar next fall."

She held her breath and squeezed Helen's hands, waiting for the reaction. Helen didn't move. They sat as if players in a *tableau* for a long moment. Finally, Belle broke the silence.

"Isn't it ridiculous?" she said, matter-of-factly. "One of the brightest freshmen, a credit to VC."

Helen searched Lily's puffy eyes. "Are you sure that's what she said?"

Lily handed her the letter and pointed out the paragraph. Helen read it and then tossed it onto the table where Belle was seated.

"Well, we have to change her mind, that's all there is to it," Helen said. "You must come back."

"I don't think it can be done," Lily replied, slowly shaking her head. "Will has become engaged to Mae and that has caused upset in the family, at least for my mother. She can be intractable in these situations."

Belle pulled the letter close with one finger and reread the paragraph. "She says that they 'don't have money to throw away on Vassar College,'" Belle began slowly. "But Vassar College has money for students."

Helen sat up. "If you got a scholarship, you could come back at no financial sacrifice to your parents," she said, warming to the idea.

Lily looked from one to the other, doubtful that money was her mother's motivating factor. "I don't know," she began, but Helen cut her off.

"Tomorrow, go to Mrs. Kendrick and see about it," she urged. "She'll know how to proceed."

Helen was now squeezing Lily's hands. Lily felt somewhat encouraged and agreed to do that. She left soon after to return to her room, break the news again, this time to Bert, and get ready for supper.

After chapel, Helen waited for her in the hall as usual. Lily felt exhausted by the day. Helen took her arm and pulled her aside.

"We can skip our walk tonight, dear," she said confidentially. "Why not get some rest now? You look rather wretched, you know," she added with a little smile.

Lily nodded. "I skipped my classes today. I should find out the assignments."

Helen touched a finger to Lily's lips, looking into her eyes with love. "There's time enough tomorrow after you've had the chance to restore your strength."

Lily was forced to agree that she could barely stand upright. Helen gently led her down the stairs to her room and said good-night. Lily told Bert her plans and in five minutes was in bed and asleep.

Mrs. Kendrick, Vassar's Lady Principal, was the administrator on campus available to all students. With the advent of the Student Association in recent years, the position had become more like that of a dean of students, someone mostly on the students' side. Her apartment was in one of the wings of Main; she had office hours from noon to two weekdays. Lily was available one of those hours and, when she reported to Mrs. Kendrick's, she fortunately found no other girls waiting in the hall. Like all other freshmen, she had heard things about the powers of the

Lady Principal; after the way the upperclassmen had described her, the freshmen thought her like the witch in *Hansel and Gretel*. Timidly, she knocked and was invited in.

Lily thought Mrs. Kendrick's parlor very homey, with various kinds of chairs scattered, a divan covered with brocade fabric, a very large potted palm, and framed artwork on the walls. She especially liked a miniature statue of the god Mercury in the corner.

Mrs. Kendrick, a middle-aged woman on the path to becoming stout, greeted her apologetically.

"You are a freshman," she began, gesturing for Lily to take a seat, "but I'm afraid I don't yet know all the names of our class of '07."

Lily sat, and Mrs. Kendrick selected the high-back wooden chair with arms that loosely resembled a throne. Irrelevantly, the thought raced across Lily's mind that it would make a good prop for a Phil play.

"I'm Lily Kepler," Lily said.

Mrs. Kendrick smiled kindly and Lily felt somewhat more at ease. "And how are your classes coming along, Miss Kepler?" she asked.

"They're fine, thank you," Lily replied, thinking of the work missed in the last two weeks with the bad news from Glens Falls and Buffalo.

Mrs. Kendricks waited, her fingers loosely intertwined in her lap.

"The reason I've come to see you," Lily began, "is to ask about the possibility of my becoming a scholarship student in the fall."

Mrs. Kendrick looked puzzled. "Has your family had some trouble that you think makes this necessary?"

Lily had anticipated a request for explanation and, during her morning class, jotted down several possible replies. After eliminating the ones that would require her to fabricate some scenario, she was left only with the truth. So, Lily explained her situation.

"I thought if I could show them that I was a good enough student to be awarded a scholarship," she finished, "they might be convinced that I could stay. And they would not have to spend their savings on me."

Mrs. Kendrick looked intently at Lily for some time; uncomfortable in her gaze, Lily looked down at her hands. She didn't feel her case was good enough. After all, her parents had paid her tuition for this year.

"Have you come to care so much about Vassar?" the Lady Principal asked gently.

Lily was not expecting such a question. She felt her throat constrict and willed herself not to cry. "Yes, ma'am," she said, nodding. "Going to school here has been like a dream for me. My professors are wonderful. My classmates are very smart."

Mrs. Kendrick smiled. "And you've made good friends, too?"

Lily blushed and nodded, remembering Helen's warning about sweethearts and hoping Mrs. Kendricks was only asking in general.

"Well, dear girl," the latter said with a small smile and a sigh, "if your parents have made up their minds to prevent you from continuing with your career at Vassar, there is little we can do to change their minds."

Lily nodded. Mrs. Kendricks had accurately grasped Lily's situation.

"But," she continued, pausing after the *but*, "why don't we test the waters, so to speak? I will speak to your teachers and look into what financial assistance might become available for the next year. What do you say to that?"

She stood, and so Lily stood. "I'd be awfully grateful to you, Mrs. Kendricks," Lily said warmly.

Mrs. Kendricks led the way to her door. "Give me a week, and I'll let you know what I find," she said with a reassuring nod.

Walking back to her room, Lily felt a great weight had been lifted from her shoulders. It still hovered overhead like a dark cloud, but she felt the respite gratefully.

Lily's walk with Helen that evening was a pleasant one, aided by the rapidly greening lawns and the dabs of lime green at the ends of tree branches that would soon unfurl. The warm air had opened the pores of the earth and from them rose the perfume of the soil, wet and welcoming to all the seeds that had waited patiently through the cold. Lily had been spending every available moment in the library the last two days in an effort to make up work and this evening was her first attention to the world outdoors. As she strolled with Helen through the pines that bordered the campus, she tried very hard to live in the moment and not to permit thoughts of a future without Helen beside her, without Vassar.

A note was on the table when Lily returned to the room the next Monday to get ready for dinner. Bert was in her room. "You have a note on the table," she called out.

"I see it," Lily said, opening the folded paper.

It was a note from Mrs. Kendrick, asking Lily to see her during office hours. Bert was standing in the doorway to her room when Lily looked up and raised her eyebrows in question.

Lily waved it. "It's from Mrs. Kendrick." She folded it again. "Maybe it's something to do with a scholarship."

Bert was buttoning the cuffs on her shirtwaist. "You don't seem all that excited. I'd be chomping at the bit to find out what's up."

Lily gave her a small smile. "Can't find out, until two o'clock, at least."

Bert threw an arm around Lily's shoulders and gave them a squeeze.

"It's the second day of May, and a fine spring day it is, so I'm voting for good news from our Mrs. Kendrick!"

She guided a chuckling Lily out of their room and down to the dining hall.

"Miss Kepler," Mrs. Kendrick smiled when Lily entered. She gestured for Lily to sit.

"I have spoken with your professors," she said, "and was pleased to hear that they think very well of your academic talent and achievements."

Lily could hardly imagine Professor Leach having a good opinion of her achievements in Greek.

Mrs. Kendrick continued, "And I have good news for you on the scholarship front. After graduation next month, a scholarship tailor-made for you will become available," she explained. "As with nearly all of our scholarships, it is for half of the tuition."

"Two hundred dollars?" Lily asked.

Mrs. Kendrick nodded. "Yes, you will need to secure additional funds. But I have been in communication with one of our recent alumnae from Buffalo. She and some fellow alumnae are beginning to establish a Buffalo Vassar Club, like those in Rochester and other cities. These clubs are invaluable aids for young women like you wishing to attend Vassar. Do you know the Bragdon family?"

Lily shook her head.

"Well, if they are able to come together in the next couple of months, you could ask them for a loan of the $200. The Vassar Clubs don't give scholarships, but rather loan the money which the student will repay after graduation."

"I see," Lily said, nodding.

Mrs. Kendrick paused and smiled kindly. "Do you think this will help your case with your family?"

Lily tried to smile. "I hope so." Then, remembering the effort taken on her behalf, she added, "I am very grateful for what you have done for me in this."

Mrs. Kendrick rose from her chair. Their meeting was ending. "My dear, this is what I do every day, and what makes my job so satisfying."

She walked with Lily to the door. "I know you girls call me 'the warden,' and you think I'm a real spoilsport, an old fogey, and whatnot."

"Oh, no, that's not true," Lily protested.

Mrs. Kendrick looked at her, surprised. Then she leaned over and said, "I don't mind at all. I remember how I felt about rules when I was your age!"

Then she laughed and Lily smiled to think of this authoritative woman as a nineteen-year-old. She thanked Mrs. Kendrick again.

In her afternoon class, Lily found her mind wandering repeatedly as she turned over what to say in her letter to her parents about the scholarship. She kept wrenching her attention back to the professor because this class was one where students who appeared inattentive were often called upon deliberately and embarrassed if they were unable to reply appropriately. As a result, she focused on neither her thoughts nor the class and, at the end of the hour, wandered out of the building in a fog.

Bert bounded up beside her as she made her way to the Vassar Brothers Laboratory for her Chemistry lab hour.

"What's the news?" Bert demanded, breathless.

Lily smiled. Bert's optimism had made the year much more cheerful than it might have been.

"I can have a scholarship for $200," she said.

"I knew you would get it!" Bert exclaimed with a little jump. "What about the rest?"

Lily shrugged. "I'll have to see about that," she said. "I don't know how my parents will receive the news."

Bert clapped her on the shoulder, encouragingly. "I have to get to practice now," she said. "Field Day's in three weeks and we're aiming to be upset champions in basketball! See you later!"

AFTER chapel, Lily spotted Helen in the hall where she usually waited. In the crowd exiting the chapel doors, Helen had not yet seen her. Lily watched as Helen greeted girls she knew, grinning as she exchanged quips. *What a beautiful smile she has*, Lily thought. *I don't want her ever to be sad.* She felt that dark cloud near, like a mantle around her shoulders now. Then Helen looked her way as if she could feel Lily's gaze as she approached. Helen smiled on Lily and it felt like a balm that soothed her worries.

"Which way shall we tramp tonight?" Helen asked when they had made their way outdoors.

The evening was mild, the hour too early for the damp chill that soon would accompany the spring night.

"Let's go up to Sunset Hill," Lily declared. "We haven't been up there in a while."

Helen linked her arm through Lily's. "Sunset Hill it is!"

As they walked, Lily explained her meeting with Mrs. Kendrick. Helen smiled and nodded, relief evident in her shoulders and her easy stride.

"I knew there was a way!" she said, punctuating the air with a swing of her arm.

Lily hesitated. "You know that my parents have to approve this," she warned.

"Well, sure, but why wouldn't they?"

Lily could sense that Helen couldn't or wouldn't see the situation as she did. "You read my mother's letter," Lily said haltingly. "You know that she wants me to quit Vassar."

Helen was shaking her head. "Yes, but now you have the imprimatur of a scholarship," Helen said, pulling her arm from Lily's. "You are a scholar. Who wouldn't be proud of a daughter who achieved that?" she said loudly, gesturing with both arms.

Lily pursed her lips. "Your mother respects scholarship," she said at last, sighing. "My mother does not."

They walked in silence for a time, climbing the path through the pines.

"Your mother doesn't respect *you*," Helen said finally.

Lily had no reply to that. They were silent until they reached the top of Sunset Hill and stepped between the evergreens into a clearing that had become their special spot since that night last November when they viewed the constellations.

"If I can't come back," Lily said gently, but Helen interrupted her.

"You must come back," she said emphatically. "You have to make them see how important it is for you to come back."

Lily nodded. "Yes, I will do my best to persuade them," she assured Helen. "But if I cannot come back," she continued, which prompted Helen to turn away.

"Please, listen to me," Lily pleaded. "We can make contingency plans. You will graduate in a year." She was speaking faster. "If I can't come back, I'll get a job and save my money so we can be together."

Helen didn't turn back to address her. "If you don't come back, I'll never see you again," she said in a wooden tone.

Lily took Helen's arm and turned her to face Lily. "Do you think you can get rid of me that easily?" she asked, incredulous.

Helen didn't meet her look, but a corner of her mouth curled.

"Remember this, Helen McIntyre, you would find it very difficult to get rid of me, if you tried," Lily continued. "In fact, I think it would be impossible."

Helen smirked and looked at Lily sideways. Lily softened in the gaze of those grey eyes. She rested her hand on Helen's cheek.

"*J'adore*," Lily said simply, shaking her head.

Helen pressed her head into Lily's hand in reply. Then they embraced, standing still as the trees around them, each with her own thoughts and fears.

The small circle of light from Lily's student lamp reflected brightly off the surface of the stationery on her desk. She had been staring at the paper for some time, trying to think of how to begin to respond to her mother's letter of last week, only seven days ago. Time had fallen out of its rhythm during that week since, speeding up or slowing down depending on her mood. As she picked up her pen for the umpteenth time, she heard Helen's words again: *Your mother doesn't respect you.* It was a strange thing to hear; parents were not supposed to respect their children. All her life, Lily had been taught to respect adults in all matters. It occurred to her that her parents respected Alfred; wasn't he one of their children the same as she? At what point in her life should she be accorded respect? Why not now? Was she a child, or an adult?

These were inconvenient thoughts to be in the forefront of her mind when she needed to write to the people in control of her future. It would take over an hour and several discarded drafts to complete a reply to her mother and father that she believed was respectful and yet passionate. She sealed the letter and fell into bed, as exhausted as a marathon runner.

"So, do you want to play hooky this afternoon?" Helen asked teasingly over her shoulder.

It was Sunday afternoon, the warm spring sunshine caressing Helen's hair so that little sunbeams gleamed at Lily following behind her. The days since Lily had mailed the letter to her parents were accompanied by an increasing suspense each day as the mail was delivered. She had received no reply so far and today was Sunday, the day on which there was no mail service. Lily felt that steel bands had been removed from her chest. To celebrate her respite, she had hunted up Helen who was more than willing to forgo her physics text for a ramble.

"Your junior class philosophy of not studying too hard must be rubbing off on me," Lily replied, catching up to her.

They headed out on a circuit of the campus, turning into the path running along Raymond Avenue to College View Avenue. The trees on either side of their path were mostly pine, shading them from the welcome warmth of the sun. They walked briskly, talking little.

As they neared the Athletic Circle, where the Field Day would be held in two weeks, the two stepped into the sunlight and cut across the great lawn, passing some girls practicing basketball on the outdoor courts. Already, the tender grass beneath the baskets had been worn thin by rubber-soled canvas athletic shoes.

They were walking toward the east side of the campus past the observatory and along paths that eventually would take them near the lawns where girls played golf. Helen was striding confidently along familiar routes. Because they seldom had time or daylight for such long circuits, Lily was taking in the landscape as a tourist would.

The click of golf balls drew them to observe the golfers for a few minutes. Then Helen turned them west toward Sunset Hill, and guided them parallel to the hill until they reached an apple orchard. Lily stopped and clasped her hands, gasping in delight. It was in full bloom this day, nearly blinding in the bright sun.

"I didn't even know this was here," she cried. "Oh, Helen, isn't it beautiful?"

She looked at Helen, who was grinning at her.

"But I knew it was here," Helen said. "I try to remember to come by and see it at this time each year."

They stepped into the orchard and were quickly enfolded by the trees. The tiny white blossoms, tinged with the palest pink, crowding along the bare, sharp-angled branches, gave the illusion of softness.

"It's like being inside a cloud, isn't it?" Lily exclaimed, looking around.

Helen laughed at her delight. Lily tipped back her head and turned round and round, letting her arms trail freely. When she stumbled, Helen caught her in an embrace. They smiled into each other's eyes with a joy not expressed since the infamous letter had arrived. A fleeting thought pushed into Lily's consciousness, *How can this happiness not last forever?* But she pushed it back into the darkness and focused only on Helen's face.

Lily took Helen's hand and led them to a spot beneath one of the trees. She sat down and Helen sat beside her. Lily lay back, her head in Helen's lap, gazing up at the face of her beloved framed by blossoms and bits of blue sky beyond. Helen looked indulgently down on her and then leaned over and kissed her on the lips. Lily reached up and pulled Helen into a more passionate kiss. When they broke it off, Lily noted with satisfaction that Helen's nostrils were quivering.

Without a moment's hesitation, Lily said, "Wouldn't it be lovely to make love right here, in the midst of this beauty?"

Helen stroked Lily's forehead gently and nodded, smiling. "You've become so much more daring than the freshman who was afraid to speak to a junior last fall," she replied.

Lily gave her a look. "I was afraid to speak to you in particular, not because you were a junior."

"Why was that?" Helen frowned.

Lily smiled. "Because you were so beautiful and I liked the way you laughed with your friends."

"You had a crush on me," Helen smirked.

"I did not!" Lily protested.

Helen laughed. "Yes, you did! You may deny it 'til the foot of Main Street, but why not simply admit it and get it over with?"

Lily sat up. "Well, if it was a crush," she said, picking bits of grass from her skirt, "and I'm not saying it was, it certainly was not the drooling, gift-giving, poetry-writing mashy kind."

"No, it wasn't," Helen agreed matter-of-factly. "You shrewdly accomplished your goal by hiring me to be your tutor."

Lily stared at Helen open-mouthed. Then she got up. "I'm not even going to dignify that with an answer," she muttered.

Helen rose and stood before Lily, smiling with her head tilted in the way that Lily found so disarming. Then she slid an arm around Lily and pulled her close.

"You're awfully easy to tease," Helen murmured into Lily's ear.

Lily pursed her lips and said nothing.

"I'm awfully glad you needed a tutor, Lily Kepler," Helen said softly.

Slowly, Lily put her arms around Helen's neck and buried her face in it. She inhaled the perfume of Helen's skin and pressed her lips against it.

She whispered into Helen's ear, "I want so much to make love."

Helen embraced her tightly and then released her, taking Lily by the shoulders.

"My May allowance has arrived," Helen said. "When we hear back from your parents that they now approve their daughter's return to VC, why don't we celebrate with a night at the Nelson House?"

Lily searched Helen's face and then nodded in agreement. They strolled arm in arm through the orchard as if in a slow procession and then emerged on the other side onto the fields surrounding Sunset Hill. Lily was thinking about the way Helen qualified a night together by linking it to good news from Lily's parents. As they approached the campus buildings, she felt the dark cloud return to hover over her head.

CHAPTER 26

The letter arrived on Wednesday, a warm, windless sunny day that portended no calamity. The weather was almost summery and girls strolled about in their light cotton shirtwaists as if they had no obligations.

The envelope was on the sitting room table when she returned to her room in the late afternoon. It was very slender, likely containing no more than one page. That was a bad sign, indicating that her mother had nothing to say that was not related to Lily's letter describing the scholarship. She sat on the edge of her bed holding the sealed envelope loosely in both hands, slowly realizing how the future really can change in a moment. She had not understood that when the first letter had arrived, the one where her mother took back the permission her parents had granted for Lily to attend Vassar. But she understood now, looking at what was surely a coda to Mama's previous message. And she understood that, despite the autonomy she had become accustomed to at college, she in fact had no control over her life in any meaningful way.

Full of dread and reluctance, Lily opened the envelope and took out the page, written on both sides in Mama's tidy handwriting. Nothing in her experience prepared her for the vehement, angry tone of the letter.

> "...I received a call from Louise Bragdon who said she graduated from Vassar in '01. She said she had been contacted by the school regarding the possibility of a scholarship loan for you. She said that these were made to girls whose families might have difficulty paying the tuition. I told her we most certainly did not need her scholarship money and sent her on her way. How could you humiliate your father and me in this way? The suggestion that we may have financial difficulties, which we do not, could have repercussions for the business. I don't know who this Bragdon girl

may have told, but I was ashamed to go to church on Sunday and look people in the face. After all the years we have worked to make a good name in our community and you throw it in the gutter with your selfishness.

"...My letter made very clear that your father and I have decided that one year of college is sufficient to get notions of 'higher education' out of your head. Your place is here with me and your father, preparing for your future..."

Mama saved her best lines for last.

"We have much work to do to see you married well. Do not consider yourself too good for young men in Buffalo. With your bookish ways and careless appearance, you will be lucky if an eligible man with a good living will look at you twice."

LILY sat staring vacantly, the air around her filled with her mother's spite. She had no thoughts at all in reaction to the letter. She sat like that for a while, until voices in the hall brought her back to the present. Stuffing the letter in her pocket, she left the building quickly, her head down, to avoid running into her hall mates.

Wanting to get away from others, she walked to the lake on the other side of Raymond Avenue. The boats were in the water now, tied at the little dock, waiting for boaters who were now getting ready for supper. The sight of the little rowboats gently bobbing made Lily's heart sink. How long ago was it that Helen had agreed to go rowing together in May? Was there no place on the campus or in town that she could go and not be reminded of her happiness here?

Lily walked past the construction site of what would be the new library, something she would not see completed because she would not be here. Had anyone passed her now, the stranger would have guessed from Lily's expression that she was grieving the death of a family member.

There was only one bright spot left in her life and she turned toward Raymond Hall, to Helen. The halls were empty, everyone having gone in to supper. Lily went upstairs anyway and scratched on Helen's door. When there was no answer, she let herself in and went into Helen's bedroom. Taking off her shoes, she lay down on Helen's bed and pressed her face into her beloved's pillow and quietly wept.

When supper was over, she heard singing through the open window. Groups of girls had been gathering on the steps of their halls after supper, before chapel, now that the weather was mild. Strong girls sang to Raymond now, she surmised. They were singing "Sweet Adeline."

"In the evening as I sit alone a-dreaming
Of days gone by, love, to me so dear,
There's a picture that in fancy oft' appearing,
 Brings back the time, love when you were near."

Raymond girls answered with "Beautiful Dreamer," their high voices drawing out the words:

"Beautiful dreamer, wake unto me,
 Starlight and dewdrops are waiting for thee."

It was Belle who discovered Lily.

"Why Rutie," she said, "It's you. I heard a sound and couldn't think what it was." She sat on the edge of Helen's bed and put a gentle hand on Lily's shoulders.

"What is it, dear?" she asked softly. "You know that your sweetheart is looking for you since you weren't at chapel."

Lily turned over to face Belle and the latter frowned to see Lily's puffy eyes and tear-streaked face.

"Have you heard from your parents then?"

Lily nodded. She gave Belle the letter, unable to speak. As Belle read the letter, Lily could see her blink repeatedly, her eyes growing large. As she turned the page over to continue, the paper snapped loudly. When she was finished, Belle sighed as she put the letter on the bed. She sat for a minute without speaking, pursing her lips and frowning.

"Lily," she finally said quietly, "if I am proud about anything in myself, it's my ability to get along with almost anyone. To be able to find something good in other people."

She shook her head several times. "But I must confess that—I do not like your mother."

Lily nodded slightly.

"I'm sorry to have to admit it," Belle added. "I'm sure she has redeeming qualities, but I simply don't want to know them."

Lily touched her arm in thanks.

"And I do not find your appearance to be *careless* in any way," Belle declared, making Lily smile. "If anyone can speak of *appearance* with authority, it is I!"

She looked down at Lily on the bed with sympathy, which caused Lily to lose what composure she had regained. Belle put her arms around the weeping girl and rocked her gently.

They heard the door open and Helen's footsteps, and then she was there with them.

"I looked all over for you," she said, kneeling beside her bed. "Even Bert hadn't seen you for supper."

Belle rose and let Helen sit beside Lily who was sobbing now that Helen was there. Helen looked up at Belle who retrieved the letter and handed it to her. After reading the first side, Helen abruptly stood up to read the second side. She tossed the letter away from her as if it were diseased and walked back and forth in the little room, agitated. Lily had stopped crying and was holding her breath to see Helen's reaction.

"How can anyone talk to her daughter like that?" Helen cried, opening her arms in Belle's direction. "Did your mother ever say such things to you?" she demanded.

Belle shook her head slightly and looked at Lily, sitting up on the bed now, clasping her hands to her throat.

"She's cruel!" Helen exclaimed to Lily, making her jump.

Helen leaned toward her and pointed a finger at Lily. "And she wants you to come home so she can marry you off," she said angrily. "She'll have you married in a year," she spat.

Lily shook her head. "That won't happen. I wouldn't consent. You know that."

Helen shook her head. "It doesn't seem to matter what you want, don't you see that?"

She turned away and then abruptly back to face Lily almost accusingly. "If you don't come back in the fall, she will have you married within the year," she said, her eyes the color of cold steel now.

"No, Helen," Lily began.

"She *will*," Helen retorted.

"Helen," Belle said quietly, with emphasis.

"What?" Helen demanded of her.

Belle turned and stepped out of the bedroom. Helen seemed to become aware of her tone and went to the open window where the evening air sent a warm breeze into the troubled room. Lily didn't move, hadn't strength even to speak. They were a *tableau* in the growing twilight.

Then suddenly Helen sat on the bed beside Lily and took her by the shoulders. "You must write to your father," she said urgently. "Can you write to him privately at his office?"

"Sweetheart," Lily pleaded.

"No, listen to me," Helen interrupted. "You said yourself that he was the one who supported your going to college. And when I came to Buffalo to stay with you, I could tell that he loves you and wants you to be happy."

"He won't contradict my mother," Lily said softly.

"But you must try! You can persuade him, I'm sure of it," Helen said passionately. "Promise me that you'll try!"

Lily nodded several times. "Yes," was all she said.

On Friday she wrote to her father, with a trembling hand that made her already-difficult handwriting even more challenging to decipher. She found it very hard to plead with her father because she had always been careful not to take advantage of his kindness which seemed to flow from a bottomless spring within his spirit. Now she was pressing her case, *selfishly* as her mother would put it, and she felt guilty.

After giving the letter to the mail girl downstairs, she stopped at the store and bought a package of biscuits and a tin of milk. She was nearly out of spending money, not yet having received her May allowance, but she had not been eating much and felt hungry now that the letter was mailed.

There were two weeks left until final exams. Papers were coming due, which caused all manner of anxiety in her hall when needed library books went missing, giving freshmen yet another lesson in cutthroat academics. Bert was trying to find time to cram for her weakest subject, Chem, and also to practice for Field Day which was Saturday. Lily tried to keep up with Greek and finally had to let it go completely because she could not concentrate long enough on the subject. Instead, she devoted her energies to completing papers and reading for her other classes. Fleetingly, she wondered why she was bothering with any class work at all, she who had no future in higher education. But she didn't know what else to do.

Belle fell into step beside her as she walked to the Vassar Brothers Laboratory for her Chem lab.

"I've been looking for you this week," Belle said, somewhat out of breath. "How are you?"

"Going to Chem lab," Lily replied without feeling. "I live from one class to another."

"Oh," Belle replied, nodding empathetically. "I wanted to tell you an idea that came to me the other day."

Lily looked at her in question.

"I've been thinking of creating a private scholarship," Belle said, slipping her arm through Lily's. "I would decide the recipient and award it myself."

Lily pursed her lips, suspecting what was coming.

"If you can find a way to return, I would be honored to award you the scholarship."

They were walking slowly now. Lily looked at the sidewalk as Belle glanced over at her.

"Thank you, Belle," Lily said softly.

"Well, I fell to thinking that I have access to ready money, essentially for the asking," Belle said brightly. "Rather than spend it on more clothes, which we know

I have no room for, I thought I could do a good deed for a talented student. As a loan, of course."

Lily nodded and smiled at Belle. "I wish I could accept it," she said.

"Of course, you know that you could run away and live with my aunt in New York."

Lily almost grinned at that. "I wish I could run away," she admitted.

"I know," Belle said after a moment.

They had reached the lab building. Belle freed Lily's arm.

"It was a good idea," Belle said hopefully.

Lily agreed. "You are a wonderful human being. Helen is lucky to have you," she said with feeling.

"But *you* have me, too!" Belle called to her as Lily moved toward the steps. "And the offer doesn't expire!"

The tenth annual Vassar Field Day enjoyed glorious weather. The Athletic Circle was dry, the winds light, the sun very warm. And, because sports were taken seriously at Vassar, nearly the entire student body was involved, either as athletes or enthusiastic spectators. Early in the morning, girls were dragging mattresses from their rooms to spread out in choice shady spots under the elm trees in the Circle. From there, cliques would hold court, enjoying spreads, singing class songs lustily in competition with other classes, cheering with a boisterousness bordering on rowdiness that belied their upbringing. For good reason, attendance at Field Day was restricted to women only, excepting such men as were necessary for the judging and, of course, the men on the faculty who were accustomed to the high spirits of VC girls.

A formal march to the Athletic Circle was held before the events began where each class assembled behind its class banner and passed through a natural arch made by tall yews which surrounded the Circle. They processed around the cinder track bordering the inside of the Circle singing loudly and getting the day off to a rousing start.

Lily didn't look for Helen among the juniors because she was not participating as an athlete. That much she had learned on their walks during the week that were short in distance and long on silences. Lily couldn't blame Helen entirely for that; she, too, had not known what to say. Weeks ago, Helen had closed off the discussion of how they would get through the separation of the next year, Helen's senior year, if Lily couldn't return. And Helen had been so angry the week before when she read Mama's second letter that Lily was at a loss about what they could safely discuss. At night she lay awake turning over Helen's actions and words, trying to decipher them, to understand if Helen was remembering Julia Fremont's departure.

Then she heard singing from somewhere closer to the Circle. It was the senior class athletes, setting off on their march into the Circle, lustily crowing a class song. "Ought-four, ought-four, nobody better! We're tip of the tops, true red letter!" they sang.

When they passed under the yew arch and into the great, green-ringed Circle, Lily felt a shiver at the grand spectacle. Girls were waving streamers with their class colors, and cheering madly. She spotted a large contingent of freshmen, waving their red streamers. Searching for the yellow colors of the junior class spectators, she saw them in several clots and made a note to look for Helen among them when she could.

When the events finished, the crowds began to dissipate with some heading for their rooms, mattresses in tow, and other assembling around the basketball court for the final event of Field Day. Lily knew that Bert's team would play the second game and took the opportunity to look for Helen. She eventually located some of Helen's clique who kindly said she hadn't been out all day. And then she spotted Belle, forehead damp from the heat, but radiant nonetheless beneath her parasol.

"Did Helen turn up today?" she asked.

Belle shook her head. "I think she is spending the day in the library," she replied.

Lily nodded and they parted ways when Belle took the sidewalk to Raymond. Lily went to her room and changed into her summer white lawn skirt and shirtwaist with sleeves so soft they barely registered on her arms. Then she went downstairs to the library, entering the addition to Main that everyone called "Uncle Fred's Nose" for its benefactor. She needed to see Helen, without whose presence the campus seemed colorless and her very life without meaning.

The library was a stark contrast to the noisy world she had left outdoors. Very few students were at the tables, the true grinds, mostly, with no interest in sports and likely no place among the cliques that made spectating at Field Day a social activity. Lily found Helen on the top floor at a table alongside one of the tall arched windows that overlooked the lawns. She was resting her chin in a hand, gazing outdoors, her pencil poised over her notebook. Unseen, Lily stopped still and took in the sight of her beloved. Helen was wearing a cool summer waist and skirt in fabric whose smooth drape told Lily it was expensive. Lily's eyes followed the line of Helen's shoulders down her back, just as her hands had traced those same planes in their private world in New York. Helen's fair hair was drawn up in its soft pompadour, her slender neck exposed above her collar. Lily longed to cross the short distance between them, impulsively enfold Helen in a smothering embrace, and assure her that things would work out for them, and in so doing persuade both of them that it was true.

Helen suddenly turned and, startled, discovered Lily, who smiled in response. Helen sat back in her chair and Lily pulled out the chair beside her. Sitting across from her would have been too far away.

"Are the games over?" Helen whispered.

Lily thought Helen seemed very tired, or sad, she couldn't tell.

"The basketball games are starting," Lily replied, wanting to touch Helen's arm. Helen nodded and rested her hands in her lap.

"Why don't you come out with me to watch the basketball game?" Lily urged.

Helen shook her head. "You go ahead," Helen whispered, not meeting her eyes. "I need to finish this."

Lily gingerly extended her hand and covered Helen's, squeezing firmly. Helen looked down at her lap and slowly covered Lily's with her other hand. She nodded very slightly.

"You go on," Helen repeated. "Give Bert a cheer for me."

She looked up but not at Lily. Lily thought Helen's eyes were filling with tears and she hesitated between embracing her or leaving which she felt was what Helen wanted. Taking a deep breath, she stood up and quietly returned her chair to the table as it had been.

"I'll see you tonight, then," Lily said in a forced cheery whisper.

As she left to return to the Circle, it was Lily who was near to tears.

When she returned to the Athletic Circle, Lily found her class's basketball team on the sidelines of the game in progress between the juniors and seniors, singing "There'll Be a Hot Time" at the top of their lungs. The rollicking nature of the popular song had rendered it a veritable anthem, the music of Field Day, 1904, and Lily had heard it half a dozen times already. Bert spotted her and pulled her into the crowd happily. Lily let the boisterous cheer wash over her like an afternoon shower; she didn't join in the spirit, but it was a change of mood.

When the games were over and the freshmen, who lost to the sophomores by four points, were going back to Main, one of her classmates caught up to Lily, clapped her on the shoulder and said, enthusiastically, "Next year, first place!" and jogged away. Lily watched her go, a girl sure of a *next year* at Vassar. And it occurred to her that a year from now, that girl wouldn't even remember that Lily had been in the class of '07.

CHAPTER 27

The new week brought a change in the weather. Monday's overcast morning also carried a breeze that smelled like rain. Lily, as was her habit, stopped at Main's mailroom after her first class. There were already four or five girls crowded around the half-door, asking about mail. From where she stood behind them, she could see the mail slot for her room. There were two letters in it. She looked at them for a long minute and then turned away and went upstairs to her room. One letter would likely be from Karl; he often wrote on Friday nights and Bert received it Monday. The other was likely addressed to Lily.

She put her books down and stood with a finger resting on the table in their sitting room. The hallway was quiet this time of the morning with everyone out around campus. She was contemplating what to do about the mail waiting downstairs. It seemed that this moment was, figuratively, like the calm before a storm. Sighing, Lily decided to go for a long walk and observe her campus as the outsider she would soon become.

Heading out to the Gate Lodge, she crossed Raymond Avenue to the lake. A well-trod path was laid around it and she walked it without haste, remembering when it was frozen and recalling how each class skated the length singing class songs lustily. She remembered skating with Helen, too.

She crossed the street again and struck out on the pine walk that ran along Raymond and extended into the long circular path around the campus. She passed the Athletic Circle, now empty of players but showing signs of the recent Field Day in the worn places in the grass. Benches carried from other parts of campus were still scattered about the running track and broad jump areas.

She passed the observatory with its signature dome. Out to the golf lawns she tramped; they were silent now that classes were in session. She had been retracing the path she and Helen had taken so recently, a fact realized when she turned toward the orchard behind Sunset Hill. As she stepped into the still-blossoming rows of trees, she felt a gusty swirling breeze come up. The petals began to quiver and then to flutter around her like snow. She held out her hand and petals lighted briefly on it and then were whisked away again. The ground around her became speckled with white dots as she slowly walked through the shower of petals. The wind that would bring rain was increasing by the time she exited the orchard and she looked back to see branches swaying briskly as if trying to shake off the blossoms. Already the orchard was reverting to another ordinary stand of trees, like Cinderella had reverted to a servant the minute after midnight. Lily turned her back on it and climbed Sunset Hill, winding her way back to the heart of the campus.

She felt a kind of numbness when she entered Main and went again to the mail window. It was nearly dinner time and the crowd around the window was thick. When she got closer, she saw that their mail slot was empty; Bert had picked up the mail. With unaccustomed lethargy, she climbed the stairs to their room. There on the table was an envelope imprinted with "Kepler's Fine Home Furnishings." She took it into her bedroom and sat down. As she looked at her father's angular handwriting, she thought with sadness, *Oh, Papa.* Then she opened it. Her allowance fell out of the envelope and extra money for her train ticket home. She put it back in the envelope and opened the letter.

It was not a long letter, that was not her father's style. He said he had received her letter and understood how much she liked attending Vassar. And then he said, as she had predicted, that the decision about her returning in the fall was done and would not be changed. He added, "Your mama is afraid if you stay on at college that you will think yourself too good to marry a local boy. But you are a good girl, and a smart girl, already too good to marry some shopkeeper."

As her mother's spiteful words had driven her to tears just ten days earlier, so her father's loving words cut through her defenses now. She wept quietly, less sorrowful for herself than about how Helen would take the news that the last desperate attempt to continue at VC had failed. She dreaded telling her.

Late in the afternoon, when she knew Helen would be in her room, Lily put the letter in her pocket and went to Raymond. The door was ajar indicating that a resident didn't mind having visitors. She scratched on it and stepped inside. As Helen emerged from her bedroom, Lily was closing the door to the hall. Helen's face fell when she saw that.

"I've heard from my father," Lily began, taking the letter from her pocket and offering it to Helen.

Helen looked at the letter and then at Lily, silently. She didn't move to take the letter.

Lily took a deep breath, trying to maintain her composure. "He said no," was all she could say.

Helen returned her gaze to the letter still in Lily's hand. She had a fierce expression.

"You didn't try hard enough," she said through gritted teeth.

Lily stared at her. "Helen, of course I did."

Helen made no reply.

"I told you that he wouldn't contradict my mother," Lily said gently, hoping her tone would help bring back the Helen she knew.

Helen shook her head repeatedly. "You have to go now," she blurted, pointing to the door.

Lily was taken aback. "Sweetheart, we can make plans to be together when you grad—"

But Helen cut her off.

"Go now," she said, looking into Lily's eyes with a ferocity the latter had never imagined Helen possessed. "And don't come back."

Lily began to gasp for air, her eyes welling up.

"Helen, please, I'm not Julia Fremont," she pleaded, and immediately realized her mistake in saying it.

Helen stomped to the door and opened it. "Get out," she said, pausing between each word for effect, "and don't come back!"

Lily was trembling now, choking with tears. She could not think at all and blindly obeyed Helen's order, rushing out of the room and almost knocking down Belle in the hall.

"Rutie!" Belle exclaimed, as Lily rushed past her toward the stairs. In a moment Belle's voice emerged from within the room she shared with Helen.

"What have you done?" she was asking in an accusing tone.

A light rain had begun but its effect was intensified by gusts of wind that pushed the drops like little needles. Girls were hurrying along the sidewalk as Lily raced past them. Someone called out, *"Festina lente!"* in jest as Lily jostled someone's arm, mimicking Latin Professor Moore who was forever calling after scurrying students in the hall to "hurry slowly!"

She had no idea where she was going and recognized no one around her. Her only impulse was to get away, to escape from the razor edge of the new truth that she would have neither Vassar nor Helen in her future. It was impossible to grasp. She ran until she ran out of sidewalks and then ran along paths that were becoming muddy and slippery. When she finally stopped, out of breath, she found that she was near the new Chapel. It was an entirely deserted part of campus except for the immense Gothic edifice that would have its first services in three weeks. Today, it was empty.

The rain suddenly changed to big, drenching drops and then poured in sheets. Lily ran to the big wooden doors and pulled. The Chapel was not secured and she slipped inside. When her eyes became accustomed to the darkness, she saw that the pews were installed and much of the chancel finished. The sounds of the pounding rain high overhead were muffled by the slate roof.

She sat down, heedless of her wet clothes, the dustiness of the pew, of everything except the silence that surrounded and engulfed her. Her future was no longer bleak, it was dark as a starless night, without compass or anchor or even a toehold. Eventually, she lay down on the pew curled into herself, weeping until she had no more tears, finally sliding into a dreamless sleep. And that is how a workman found her the next day at dinner time when he looked for a spot to eat his sandwich.

The man tried to rouse Lily, but failing that went away. From somewhere far away, Lily was aware of some disturbance and was glad when it stopped. Then it began again and more voices hovered around her. They, too, stopped, and then new voices came up, someone touched her, and then she was lifted up and carried in strong, hard arms. She felt rain on her face and knew that she was outside. And then she was inside again, and the smell seemed familiar. She had been here before, but she had no curiosity about where she was.

A woman was undressing her as if Lily were a rag doll. When she was alone again, she gradually absorbed her surroundings. She was in bed, a white bed with white sheets and blanket, in a white room. The infirmary. It didn't matter. Lily turned her face to the wall.

Eventually, a man came in and touched her, looking into her eyes, pushing a thermometer into her mouth. Lily felt like an observer, as if she were perched on the light in the ceiling and looking down. She couldn't make out what he said. It was not important. Left alone again, she fell back asleep.

Lily awoke to a woman's voice speaking in loud, hearty tones. She was opening the curtains, making the room almost too bright for Lily's eyes.

"And how are you this morning?" the nurse asked, but didn't wait for a reply. "You've had a long sleep and must be very hungry. Yes?"

Lily didn't respond but followed the woman with her eyes. She didn't know if she was hungry. The nurse pulled up a metal chair beside the bed, scraping it loudly, causing Lily to wince at the sound.

"I have here," she was saying as she leaned over the table beside the bed, "the very best meat broth you have ever tasted. None of that tinned stuff or bouillon cubes, but the real McCoy made from roasted beef and bones. Wait until you taste it."

She looked at Lily who hadn't moved or made any expression. Then she bent over Lily and, putting her hands under Lily's armpits, hoisted Lily up into a half-sitting position. Lily felt like a formless mass of gelatin.

"There now, you take some nourishment," the nurse declared and prepared a spoon of broth from a steaming bowl.

Lily looked at her and something in her expression seemed to soften the nurse's authoritarian manner.

"Why not try just this little bit?" she coaxed. "It's been a while since you've eaten and you need some nourishment."

She held the spoon to Lily's lips and Lily obediently opened her mouth. A little dribbled from the side of her mouth and, with tenderness, the nurse dabbed at it with a napkin. This small gesture brought Lily into the moment and she began to weep, weakly, her shoulders shaking. The nurse put the spoon beside the bowl and took Lily's hand in both hers. She sat, her head tilted sympathetically, while Lily cried, which wasn't long because Lily hadn't the strength for it. When she subsided, the nurse dabbed her eyes just as she would have dabbed at a skinned knee.

"Now then," she said, once again in charge of the patient, "shall we try some more broth?"

And they did try, and Lily did receive the spoonfuls of broth. When they were finished, the nurse helped Lily get comfortable under the covers and then stood beside the bed, her hands crossed in front of her very white, starched apron.

"I want you to know something, young lady," she said. "I have had lots of Vassar girls in here who were heartsick from one thing or another."

Lily looked at her.

"I haven't lost one patient yet to that affliction," she nodded, "and I don't intend that you should be the first. So, you just make up your mind to live."

That evening another nurse came in and spooned more broth into Lily. All she really wanted to do was sleep. No matter that she had slept for hours already, she felt so tired. The next morning the nurse who had taken care of her the day before was back, carrying porridge. Lily recognized it as the standard breakfast fare in Main's dining hall. The nurse helped her sit up and watched as she fed herself. Lily was too indifferent to be embarrassed at the scene, eating so that she would be left alone again as soon as she was finished with the food. A short time later, the doctor came in. He appeared to be disinterested in any but the most perfunctory exam and left only the smell of cigar smoke behind when he hurried out of the room. Lily turned toward the wall and curled into a ball, drifting again into the cocoon of sleep.

The shadows in the room were growing long when Bert came to see her. Lily hadn't been sleeping but rather drifting unfocused, but she wondered why the nurse had admitted Bert without checking to see if Lily was awake. The nurse had done that for Bert last fall when she was in the infirmary. Bert pulled up the chair and sat down beside the bed.

Lily looked at her roommate without expression. Bert, on the other hand, looked exceptionally anxious.

"Boy, you sure gave everybody a scare," she was saying in her enthusiastic way.

"When you didn't come back for supper Monday, I was a little worried. But when you didn't come back for the night, I went over to Raymond to see if you were there. You weren't. I didn't sleep a wink."

Bert was shaking her head, reliving those hours. "I couldn't think where you could have gone with the rain so bad, but I held off until the next morning before I went to Mrs. Kendrick."

She looked at Lily beseechingly. "Don't be mad at me for that. You weren't to be found anywhere. I didn't know what else to do."

Lily frowned and spoke for the first time in two days. "I'm sorry," she said through cracked lips, her voice hoarse from disuse.

Bert impulsively clutched Lily's forearm firmly. "You're o.k. now, that's the thing," she said, nodding. "That's the main thing."

She seemed ready to cry. Lily had never seen her cry. She put her hand over Bert's to comfort her, Bert who had always been stalwart and cheerful, even about Chemistry which was a torture for her.

"I'm sorry," Lily repeated.

Bert pursed her lips and looked down. "Belle told me," she said very quietly, delicately, as if she feared setting off a scene.

They sat silently, there being nothing to say about what Belle told Bert.

Finally, Bert cleared her throat. "The nurse said that you aren't physically sick, that you could leave whenever you want."

Lily pulled back her hand and turned her head so she didn't meet Bert's eyes.

"Finals begin Monday," Bert was saying. "That's four days from now."

Lily didn't respond.

"You should see everybody on the floor, running around, trying to copy notes, hunting for someone to cram with," Bert continued in her jocular voice. "It's pure panic!"

Lily was silent.

"You're going to be out in time for finals, right?"

Lily shrugged one shoulder indifferently. "Why would I bother?" she said in a flat voice.

Bert let go of Lily's arm and sat up. After an awkward moment, she stood and returned her chair to its place.

Standing beside the bed, she said, "Tonight it's ice cream for dessert. They probably don't serve it here, do they?"

Lily shook her head. "Thanks for coming," she said tiredly.

Bert nodded a couple of times. "Well, I'd better be going," she said, waving an arm toward the door. She looked again as if she might cry.

Lily nodded, then Bert was gone and she was alone again. She hadn't given a thought to her courses, but now decided her comment had been right. Why should she take final exams? Her college career was over whether she took them or not.

The evening nurse brought her two poached eggs and two pieces of toast, plus a pot of tea. She left Lily alone to eat.

IN the morning the doctor stood beside her bed, looking down at her propped up by pillows. He looked as if he had just consumed a distasteful dish.

"Miss Kepler," he began sternly, "there is nothing physically wrong with you that can be found. If I were you, I would think about returning to your regular routine."

And then he was gone. Lily noted that he hadn't said that she had to leave, only that she should think about it. She had no idea how to begin thinking about it. When she wasn't sleeping, she stared at the wall, watching the sunlight move across it as the hours passed.

At 7 p.m., when chapel services were beginning, Lily was surprised to see Belle enter the room. The latter smiled broadly as she crossed to Lily's bed and pulled up the chair along the side of the bed so that she was facing Lily.

"You skipped chapel," Lily murmured.

Belle chuckled and made herself comfortable. "The senior vacation has begun," she said in a chatty tone, "and they are on their *howl*, as it is called, which causes everything on campus to be off its center. As Hamlet said, 'The time is out of joint.' I will hardly be missed at chapel."

Lily smiled a small smile, because Belle always found whatever joy could be wrung out of a moment.

Belle took Lily's hand and squeezed it. "And how are you, dear Rutie?" she asked, still smiling, but with serious eyes.

Lily couldn't reply. Her lip trembled and tears welled up in her eyes. Belle nodded in understanding.

"I must speak to Helen," Lily managed before dissolving completely. "Please help me."

Belle sat on the edge of the bed and took Lily in her arms, rocking her while she cried. After a time, Belle gently released her and gave her a handkerchief. Lily took deep breaths to calm herself.

"Dearest Lily," Belle said carefully, "I am here for two reasons. First, Bert came to see me to tell me that you were here. I did not know it. She asked if I would visit you, but she needn't have done so. I would have come anyway, because I am your friend."

Lily looked into Belle's eyes and saw that it was true. It helped. Belle smoothed Lily's hand with her own and frowned.

"I cannot be a go-between in this," she said haltingly. "I am here as your friend. Do you understand what I mean?"

Lily understood. There was no hope at all.

Belle held Lily's hand tightly. "If you only remember one thing from all that has happened in the past month, remember this: there is *more* than this dark day."

Lily looked away.

"You don't believe me," Belle said. "You think my life is pretty clothes, plenty of spending money, parties, beaus. Is that what you think? That I have never had my heart broken? That things have never been hopeless for me?"

Something in her tone, a defensiveness Lily had never heard in Belle, made her turn to meet Belle's gaze.

Belle hesitated, and they looked at one another. Then she nodded and spoke to Lily's hand. "I was sixteen, staying with my aunt in New York when, at one of her parties, I met the most handsome man I had ever seen. He was twenty-four, with curly hair and bright blue eyes, and his evening clothes showed off his perfect, trim body. He liked me right away. I fell madly in love with him and we began to see one another at dinners and parties that season, then he paid me calls and met my aunt. She tried to counsel me to be cautious, reminding me of my age and his, urging me to write my parents about him. But I was deliriously happy and thought her hopelessly old-fashioned. He took me to museums, even to the Bronx Zoological Park on a lark to see the sea lions."

She looked into Lily's eyes. "And then one afternoon when he called for me to go to a matinee, he suggested that we might spend the afternoon there instead. My aunt was out and not expected back for several hours."

Belle pressed her lips together before going on.

"Well, Lily, I was a fool. He—simply put, he took advantage of me," she said softly. "I had brushed aside all the protections society sets up to prevent a young, naive girl from being alone with a sophisticated—seducer—and I now had no chance at all. Once he started to make love to me, he would not be stopped by polite request, entreaty, or even cries of pain. And when he was finished, he simply left me sobbing, lying on my aunt's sitting room rug, my underthings torn."

She stopped, the memory reflected in her face. Lily was transfixed, recalling that sitting room floor.

"I was so ashamed," Belle was shaking her head, "that I never told anyone after it happened. My aunt would have been distraught, thinking that she had failed me and my parents. I was terrified that he would talk about me, but apparently he wasn't interested in bragging or ruining my reputation. I avoided going out for fear I would see him, but one evening when my aunt persuaded me to go to the opera with her, he was there. As we passed on the stairs, he bowed his head and he smirked, just enough so that I could see it."

Belle looked at Lily hard. "I loved him with all of my being, Lily. When he achieved his goal and left me, I felt less than nothing. And I thought I had lost my chance to marry a man of my class, because who would want me after that? I was raised to be wanted by an upstanding man. I was sixteen, and finished."

She leaned toward Lily. "That's what I thought then. It was *my* darkest day, Lily," she said. "And then other days passed, also dark, until the days became ordinary."

Leaning back in her chair, she raised an eyebrow. "You are only the second person who knows this."

Lily knew immediately who the other person was.

"I am telling you so that you will know that I understand what I'm talking about when I tell you that there is more than this dark day."

And then Lily understood why Belle had told Helen. It was to help Helen move on from her broken heart. Belle was looking at her expectantly.

"Thank you," Lily said. "Thank you for telling me."

Belle sighed as if relieved, and smiled. "It's time to leave this place, don't you think? They're billing your parents $1.50 a day, you know."

Lily didn't know. She would be asked to explain that bill. "I think they want me to leave," she said honestly.

"And there are final exams to prepare for," Belle added.

Lily shook her head. "I don't see any reason to take them."

Belle frowned deeply. "Such a bright girl with so little foresight," she said disapprovingly. "If you don't take your finals, then you have no grades for the year. Did you know that?"

Lily didn't know that.

"And if you have no grades for all the work that you've invested this year, isn't that simply confirming to your parents that they shouldn't have sent you here?"

Lily felt browbeaten.

"If that means nothing to you, then think about your future education. You may wish to return to college, if not here then elsewhere, and completing your year would mean records that could be appended or forwarded to another college."

Lily looked at Belle who had a tiny smile forming at the edges of her mouth.

"Such a lot to think about, isn't there? It would make anyone want to leap out of the infirmary and take care of business."

With that, she stood, then leaned over and kissed Lily on the cheek. "Wherever we are in the world, you shall always be my friend, Rutie," Belle said. "I want you to be the brave girl I know you to be. You don't think I know that about you, but I do. If I can do it, you can."

And then she was gone. It was as if the light in the room had been switched off. For a few minutes, Lily had not been consumed by her grief. Now it was back, as if it simply had been hiding behind Belle.

THE next morning, Lily left the infirmary. When she returned to her room, morning classes were in session and she was alone on the floor. Things looked very much as they did when she was last here. Even her text was on the table where she had put it down five days earlier. She stood in the doorway of her bedroom for a long time. It looked tidy; her bed was made, the floor was clean. The maid must have been a little surprised to find no work to do after Monday, she thought. Then she looked down and saw the dried mud on the hem of her skirt. She was wearing clothes she had worn on Monday. She decided to take advantage of the solitude to take a bath. The bathtubs were always in high demand evenings and weekends, but not during classes.

The water was lovely hot and she filled the tub so that when she climbed in, she could immerse up to her chin. There she sat, letting the warmth penetrate her pores and loosen her joints so that she felt weightless. Eventually, when the water began to cool, she reluctantly finished her bath and returned to her room.

Lily sat on her bedroom window's wide sill and brushed her hair, gazing idly out at the green lawns now dappled in sunlight through the towering elms. She became aware of two strong conflicting impulses, the first to leave the campus at once and avoid running into everyone she knew including Helen; and the other to cling desperately to every detail she held dear about Vassar even though it meant that she would see Helen, so recently the source of her greatest happiness. Without choosing to, she was suspended between the two, detached from volition and numb to deep feeling.

And then Bert was there, in the doorway to her bedroom. Lily turned and saw her roommate's glad expression; she tried to smile in response.

"Bully!" Bert said heartily as she crossed the room and put an arm around Lily's shoulders, giving them a good squeeze. "I'm so glad to see you here!"

It was this touch, a friendly human touch, that shattered Lily's false calm. Her lip trembled and she sank into tears at once. Bert, flummoxed at this reaction, gently patted Lily on the back.

"Oh, say now," she said hoarsely, "please don't cry, Lil. Please."

Lily moved away from Bert and retrieved a fresh handkerchief from a drawer. She regained her composure shortly and sat on the edge of her bed.

"Crying seems to be my specialty," Lily admitted.

Bert stood by the window where Lily left her. "It's almost time for the dinner gong," she said. "Will you go down with me?"

Lily took a deep breath. She knew this return to campus routine was inevitable. She nodded. "I will have to get dressed."

"I'll wait for you," Bert replied, with a loyal nod.

Lily stayed close behind Bert as they entered the dining room. She tried not to look at faces but felt she was being watched, observed. How many knew she had been in the infirmary? How many knew of her heartbreak? She didn't want to know. The classmates at their regular table were quieter than usual, despite today's status as the last day of classes. With exams beginning Monday, this was the last chance for them to be exuberant before the grind of studying began. Lily kept to herself and was grateful that no one engaged her in conversation.

"The people at our table know, don't they?" she asked Bert when they returned to their room.

Bert stood in the doorway of her room, looking uncomfortable. She nodded. "They knew you were in the infirmary, that couldn't stay secret," she admitted. "Then Lucy and Izzie theorized about the cause—you know how they get—and guessed that it was something to do with Helen." She hesitated, then finished, "So, yes, our table knows."

Lily felt exhausted and headed for her bedroom. "It doesn't matter if they know," she shrugged.

The next day, Saturday, passed quietly for Lily, as she spent her day lying on her bed when she was not being reminded by Bert to dress for a meal. Later, the only thought she could recall having from the entire day was that in a week she would be on a train home to Buffalo. Seven days.

Sunday was summer all over Vassar. Lily indifferently followed Bert as they went to breakfast and then to Sunday services in the chapel. The big room at the top floor of Main was becoming too stuffy now, collecting warmth rising from all the open windows and doors on the floors below. In a week the Baccalaureate service would be held as part of the graduation rituals; nearly all of the student body would be gone except for the seniors and the sophomores who would make and carry the daisy chain on Commencement day.

But this day was an ordinary Sunday, except for a musical piece that Ruth Potter, a senior, had been selected to perform; it was a solo from Mendelssohn's oratorio, *Elijah*. Lily had barely paid attention to the service thus far, but the rich mezzo-soprano tones of Ruth's voice penetrated Lily's cotton-wool numbness and she let her guard down. "'Oh rest in the Lord,'" she began softly, soothingly, "'wait patiently for Him, and He shall give thee thy heart's desire.'"

The words were repeated over and over again in the solo until Lily could bear up no longer. Tears rolled down her cheeks as she sat perfectly still amid the music that she had let in. Later, during the sermon that seemed to her mere droning sounds, she felt within her a rising ferocity whose source had no explanation. By the time the service ended and she watched the upper classes leave the chapel first, no Helen in sight, she had decided two things. First, it was important that she let nothing and no one touch her, if she was to remain functional. And second, she would take her final exams.

That afternoon, she looked over her schedule. Chemistry was first on Monday. She didn't need to worry about it; the course had basically been the same as her college preparatory course at Central and she had tutored Bert all year. Greek was Wednesday; nothing could be done for that. The only question she had about the others was History, so she hunted up Alice and asked what had been said about the exam. In the end, she didn't study for any exam, but reported for each, opened the blue book, and began writing.

By mid-week, she felt the need to go for a walk, having conquered her fear of running into people. She was still unsure of whether she wanted to run into Helen but she seemed to want to, the way one cannot resist touching a fresh wound despite the pain. The lilacs were in bloom now, the usually nondescript bushes bursting in lavender panicles. The slightest breeze wafted their seductive perfume across her path. She walked and walked, observing groups of seniors on their "senior vacation" before graduation, idly lounging under the trees singing to the accompaniment of ukuleles, or playing tennis or golf. When she went into town to buy her train ticket home, she found them strolling down Market street three abreast, arms linked, laughing as they entered Smith Brothers to order sweet treats. She observed them, but they didn't touch her. She felt no envy of their four years at Vassar, or self-pity for herself. She felt nothing, not even the heat of the sun.

Bert reminded her that they needed to tell Peters to bring up their trunks from the catacombs so that, between exams, they could begin packing to go home. Big steamer trunks had begun appearing along the hall like harbingers of the big shift in the rhythm of Vassar. Thursday night, with one exam yet to go, Lily began packing her trunk. And that is when she found the book of Elizabeth Barrett Browning's sonnets that she had purchased for Helen's upcoming birthday in July. She had planned to give it to Helen before they parted for what, when she purchased it, had seemed a duration of only the fourteen weeks of summer vacation. The little book trembled in her hand and she stared at it for a long time. Then she hunted up a piece of brown paper and string, sat down at her desk and took her pen in hand. In the flyleaf, she wrote in as firm a hand as she could, "To Helen McIntyre, Happy Birthday 1904, Lily Kepler." She could not permit herself any more. When the ink dried, she wrapped the book and addressed the package to Helen, then walked to Raymond. The mail room there was closed at this time of day, so one more time she climbed the stairs she knew so well. Fortunately, the door to Helen and Belle's room was closed. She placed the package on the floor outside the door, illuminated by the slender shaft of light coming from within.

On the way back to her room in the darkness, Lily was aware that she was crying again. She took deep breaths and promised herself that she would not feel any more pain, that the worst was past.

Lily had purposely purchased a ticket to Buffalo on the 10:30 a.m. train on Saturday. That would give her time to finish packing, watch for any flunk notes from her professors which were to be delivered that morning, and get to the station. It would also mean that she would arrive in Buffalo in the evening after supper, a family gathering she wanted to avoid this day. She sent her trunk on Friday to the railway express, and gave all of their room's furniture and decorations to Bert, who was dumbfounded at the extravagance.

"You can always sell it," she assured Bert, there being a tidy business at this time of year in such trade.

Mina stopped in to see Lily Friday afternoon when she was alone in the room, packing her suitcase and satchel. She stood in the doorway, looking pained.

"Mina," Lily said.

Mina opened her mouth to speak, but nothing came out. She tried to smile.

"Good-bye, Mina," Lily said, understanding, trying to smile.

"I wish you were coming back," the latter stammered.

Lily grimaced. "Then it's unanimous."

Mina looked as if she could cry. Lily interceded and crossed the room to pat her shoulder. The girl nodded several times, putting on a brave face.

"I'll write to you, if you'll write back," Mina offered.

Lily nodded. "Of course we'll write. You can tell me the mischief our little band gets into next year as sophisticated sophomores."

Mina looked around the room. "What about Bert?"

Lily smiled. "I hope you will look after her, Mina. Remind her that she cannot wear her gym suit anywhere but the gym. And make her remove her muddy hockey boots at the door. And laugh at her jokes, please."

Mina chuckled. They stood silent for a long moment, then she quickly embraced Lily and left.

On Saturday morning, Lily prepared to leave. Bert, who was not leaving until the afternoon, had nonetheless arisen when Lily did and they breakfasted together with the few remaining members of their table. Back at the room, Bert wanted to go down with Lily to the Gate Lodge where she would catch the trolley, but Lily shook her head. They stood in the middle of their little parlor, they who had always talked so easily, with nothing to say now.

Lily spoke first. "If you have the time, you could write. I would like to hear from you, about your hockey and volleyball and basketball and whatever other sports you discover."

Bert tried to smile.

"And tell me about Karl, and your plans."

Bert nodded. Her composure was beginning to crumble. Lily picked up her satchel and suitcase.

"No tears," she said to Bert, firmly.

Bert pursed her lips, nodding several times.

They embraced briefly because that was all Lily would allow, keeping her promise to herself not to be touched emotionally. And then she left, taking the stairs because the hall around the elevator was crowded with chattering girls and their belongings.

She reached the lobby and turned toward the doors when she heard, "Kepler!" Turning, she spotted the mail girl leaning out her half-door, waving an envelope.

Lily put down her suitcase and went to retrieve what was surely a flunk-note from Professor Leach confirming what she already had accepted in her mind, a failure in Greek.

"I told her you might already have gone, but she insisted I take it," the mail girl was saying as Lily stepped to the window. She handed Lily an envelope, which Lily accepted and then quickly turned away, shoving it into her little drawstring purse. Her heart in her throat, she snatched up her suitcase and hurried out the doors and along the path to the Gate Lodge, as if she could outrun yet more pain.

Standing at the trolley stop, she desperately tried to keep from breaking down. The handwriting on the envelope was Helen's. The envelope contained some object. When she pressed it with her fingers as she accepted it from the mail girl, she immediately knew what it was. And then she knew that she had been wrong when she promised herself that the worst was past.

WHEN she changed trains at Albany, Lily went to the ladies' lounge and shut herself in a water closet so she could be alone when she opened the letter. She was hoping that a note would be enclosed, but when she carefully tore open one end of the envelope, there was none, only the beautiful ruby ring. She rolled the envelope carefully and replaced it in her purse, then she leaned against the wall and gave herself up to grief.

As her train raced westward into the sun, Lily sat by the window, oblivious to the verdant New York landscape passing by, crossing streams that sparkled in the sunlight and fields showing neat lines of bright green shoots. Everything was growing abundantly after the long winter; the harvests would surely be excellent this year. Lily felt out of time, unsynchronized with the season. She had been most alive in winter and now her spirit was sere as the fields of last November.

It was nearly seven in the evening when the train pulled into the Exchange Street station. Lily had not notified her family of her schedule and, as a result, no one was there to meet her. She stepped onto the platform and put her bags down, looking around for a cabbie. In a minute, a middle-aged man in everyday clothes, somewhat worse for wear, stepped up to her and touched his hat, on which was pinned his metal hack license badge.

"Pardon, ma'am," he said in a lilting Irish accent. "Will you be needing a lift? My cab is just outside."

She nodded and he picked up her suitcase. His cab was indeed near the entrance and he held out a rough hand to help her inside. She gave him her address.

"I'll have you home in a wink," he grinned, nodding.

He was true to his word, skillfully maneuvering through the crowded streets until they reached Humboldt Parkway, where he let the horse trot easily on the wide thoroughfare. Lily took a deep breath. She wasn't looking forward to being at home, having no kind feelings toward her parents, particularly her mother. But she was not looking for conflict, and hoped that she would be left alone.

The cabbie kindly carried her suitcase to the door. Lily paid him and then she was alone on the porch, facing the door and what was behind it. She opened it to find her father coming from the parlor. He immediately smiled happily and held out his arms as he approached her.

Lily put down her suitcase and satchel and received her father's embrace.

"Hello, Papa," she said quietly.

"Welcome home, Lily!" he said, heartily.

Lily nodded. Her mother was coming down the hallway from the kitchen, wiping her hands on her apron.

"We didn't know when you were coming," she was saying in a kind of scolding tone, "or we would have had Will meet you."

She gave Lily a quick embrace. "We weren't even sure you were coming home today. You didn't write last week."

"I had exams, Mama," Lily said, not meeting her eyes.

"Or the week before, either," Mama added.

Lily nodded and said nothing about her stay in the infirmary.

"Ach, but you're home now, that's what counts," Papa interjected heartily. "You must be tired from your trip, too."

"I am, yes," Lily said.

"I'll bet you didn't have any supper," Mama said. "There's ham and scalloped potatoes and some cabbage salad. Come and have something. You can unpack later."

She held out an arm to emphasize her desire that Lily follow her to the kitchen.

"When will your trunk come?" Papa asked, which brought Lily's attention back to him.

"I think Monday or Tuesday," she said, having difficulty focusing on two conversations.

"Come along, now," her mother was saying, and Lily followed obediently.

"I don't want much," she said as her mother retrieved a ham from the icebox and cut two large slabs. "Really, I'm not very hungry."

Her mother scoffed at that. "You have lost weight, daughter, and probably had no dinner today with your train ride. You must be starved."

She was now scooping a large portion of scalloped potatoes onto the plate with the ham. Placing it on the table before Lily, she quickly retrieved a knife and fork and put those on the table. Lily had not eaten anything since breakfast and the aroma of ham and scalloped potatoes was powerfully persuasive. She ate, tentatively at first, then steadily. Mama poured Lily some milk, and she drank it. They did not speak and her mother did not sit at the table with her.

When she finished and declined cake for dessert, Lily said she was going to bed. As she passed the parlor, she said good-night to her father.

"I put your things in your room," he said.

"Where is Will?" she asked.

"He's in South Buffalo," Papa answered. "The wedding is in two weeks, you know, there's lots to do, I guess."

"That's soon," Lily said.

"Yah," Papa acknowledged. "He didn't used to move quickly for anything. You remember?"

Lily nodded. She felt as if she were moving underwater. "He's lucky to have Mae. She will be a good influence on him, Papa, I know it."

He nodded. "I think so, too."

"He'll make you proud," she added.

Papa looked at her directly; she felt his gaze and met his eyes for the first time since she came home. It was hard to do.

"I am proud of each of my children," he said with a slow, firm nod. "Each one."

Lily couldn't respond and turned away to go upstairs.

Her suitcase, satchel and little purse were in her room when she entered. The scene could have been last September when they sat in the room just like this, packed and ready to go to Vassar with her. On her bed a clean nightgown was laid out. Lily undressed and got ready for bed. The sheets were smooth and cool, the feel of the bed so familiar. As she turned to fall asleep, she said to herself with some defiance, *It was not a dream. I am not the same person I was in September.*

CHAPTER 28

Monday afternoon found Lily sitting in the Keplers' backyard under the great elm tree. Some years earlier Papa had constructed a circular wooden bench that surrounded the tree. Lily had often sat there during summers in high school, reading for hours.

Today she was not reading, but seated on the side facing the rear of the property. A casual observer looking from the house would not have seen her, and that was her intention. Since her return home to Buffalo, she had gone through the motions of a family member, saying little to anyone. But when she was free of obligations, she sought places to be alone, and tried to avoid being seen lest her mother ask something of her or, worse, voice some pointed comment that would hurt her. She still had the numbness that she had brought with her from Vassar, but she was not in any way immune to further hurt. So, she sought refuge in the shadows, like a wounded animal hides away under bushes to lick its wounds.

A rustle told her someone was near and then suddenly Eva plopped down beside her, smiling happily. Lily looked at her and Eva immediately threw her arms around Lily, squeezing tightly.

"I'm so glad to see you," she said breathlessly, kissing Lily soundly on the cheek for emphasis. "I may even forgive you for not telephoning when you got home," she added with a mock-petulant frown. "I had to telephone this morning to learn that you are home," she added.

Lily realized that she must have been out walking when the call came. She also noted that her mother had not told her of Eva's call. The estrangement worked both ways, she thought, but Eva was pouring words into the afternoon shade.

"I asked your mother when you were coming home," Eva was saying, "and she said that you had arrived Saturday evening. If you had telephoned, I would have put off Frank yesterday afternoon and come right over."

She paused, looking into Lily's face, and her voice trailed off. "Something has happened," she said in a hushed voice, clasping Lily's hands in hers.

Lily didn't respond, but let her eyes show her despair.

"It's not because you can't go back to Vassar," Eva declared. She shook her head several times. "It's her, isn't it?"

Lily swallowed but didn't respond.

"What did she do? Tell me," Eva commanded.

Lily's eyes began to swim. It was as impossible for her to hide her state of mind from Eva as it was for Eva to hide from Lily. She shook her head in reply, unable to find any words.

Eva grasped Lily's arms, her face transformed by sympathy and anger. "She's broken your heart, hasn't she?" she demanded.

Tears slowly made their way down Lily's cheeks until they were diverted into her grimace. Eva gasped and enveloped Lily in her arms. When Lily could no longer weep silently, she pulled Eva close and muffled her sobs in Eva's shoulder.

They sat like that for some time, Eva stroking Lily's back without speaking. Then Lily sat up, needing to blow her nose. Eva pulled a handkerchief from her little waist bag and gave it to Lily with a small smile.

"I hope you're impressed that, for once, it was I who had the fresh handkerchief," she said impishly.

Lily wiped her eyes and responded with a trembling smile, nodding. They leaned back against the tree. Slowly, Lily's composure returned.

Eva asked, "Will you tell me what happened?"

Lily shrugged. "Nothing to tell. Everything is finished. I have nothing to look forward to."

"Well," Eva replied slowly, "you have me."

Lily turned her head tiredly and saw Eva looking hopeful.

"You'll always have me," Eva repeated, "even when I'm Mrs. Frank Marshall. We're sisters. Remember when you said that?"

Lily half-smiled and nodded. Taking Eva's hand, she said, "Yes, we are."

Eva squeezed Lily's hand. "And I'm going to need your help in getting ready for my wedding. You have that to look forward to."

Lily smiled, shaking her head. Eva began enumerating the various tasks that needed to be done, warming to her subject. Lily's mind drifted away as it had so often done since she returned home. She was thinking about how much she valued Eva's sympathy. Even though her friend's internal compass needle always returned to herself, Eva was the only person in Buffalo who understood that Lily was grieving the loss of Helen in her life.

And suddenly, in her mind's eye, she saw Helen, traveling home to Glens Falls just as she had two years earlier after Julia Fremont abandoned her. And she felt immensely sorry for Helen for the first time. Of all people in the world, Lily could have comforted her. The irony of such heartbreaks was that the person who could most comfort one was also the source of the pain. Lily had Eva, but who would comfort Helen? Helen, who thought being in love was the equivalent of lying down in the street and waiting to get run over. Helen, who insisted that she was not a strong person.

Lily wanted to rush to the Exchange Street train station and go to Helen, to tell her to have faith, to be patient. And, as those words formed in her mind, she realized in herself something not quite bold enough to be called hope. It was resolve.

Eva was speaking to her. "I don't mind that you weren't listening to me, but look what you've done to my handkerchief!"

Lily looked down and saw that her hand was clenched. Opening it, she had to agree that Eva's pretty lace handkerchief had been crushed into a soggy nugget.

"I don't have another with me," Eva commented, "so I hope you do."

Lily shook her head, looking at a point far off. "I won't need another. I'm not going to cry anymore."

CHAPTER 29

The summer of 1904 was the season of weddings in Buffalo. Lily's brother Will married in June and Eva married in August. In between, she attended the wedding of two classmates from Central High, including Art Lacy and Lulie Hartung, an event which surprised only because it had been delayed for a year.

Will and Mae's wedding occurred two weeks after Lily's return from Vassar and she observed much of the celebration preparation as if through a scrim as a result of her grief. Even the fact that she needed to give up to the newlyweds her spacious bedroom with its window seat didn't fully register until she went to bed in Will's old small room for the first time.

It was possible that Mama Kepler tried to restrain herself from making her disapproval of the wedding known, but no one in the family or among her friends was left to wonder how she felt. Her comments came in short bursts, like the noise little strings of firecrackers make when lit on the Fourth of July.

The wedding day was very warm, which was unfortunate because it had also rained quite steadily the day before. Wedding clothes clung damply to hot skin and wrinkled deeply at the slightest exertion. Even the brims of leghorn straw hats seemed to swoon at the edges.

Lily's only role was to be in attendance at the wedding, held at St. Stephen's Catholic church on Elk Street in the First Ward, the heart of the South Buffalo Irish neighborhood. Her mother's mouth alternated between grim determination to bear the unbearable and a flickering sneer as their carriage passed some pedestrians. These were not people that mattered to Elda Kepler, these dockworkers, scoopers, factory girls, in her exact phrase, "drunkard Irish papists," that her son was marrying into.

The sun came out for the day when the wedding guests were assembled in the church. It streamed through the stained-glass windows and Lily watched Mae's family and friends smile in response, nodding at the light as if to say, "You see, this is a sign they'll have good luck." The groom's side of the large sanctuary was sparsely populated with just the Keplers and a handful of relatives that attended such events. A couple of them were looking curiously across the aisle at the bride's family as if close observation might reveal the ways in which the ethnicities were different and unequal.

Lily came into full awareness when the organ began the processional music and she saw Mae come down the aisle in her wedding dress. She wore a white organdy dress in a style that she could wear again after the wedding. She looked beautiful just the same, not the least because of her joyful smile.

The small wedding party took up very little room at the altar. Only one of Mae's sisters served as maid of honor; Will had a very grave Albert as his best man. The Keplers stood when the others stood, but they did not kneel during the unfamiliar wedding mass. The priest smiled kindly on them as he followed the newlyweds down the aisle at the end of the service.

"Did you get a good look at them?" Mama muttered as she settled in the carriage afterward. "They have nothing but children, swarms of little things squirming all through the service."

No one replied to that comment. Lily looked over at her father and Alfred, perspiring in their suits and vests. Gertrude did not attend the day's event because she was too far along in her pregnancy to be seen in public. Lily hoped at least Gertrude might be cooler than the rest of them.

The wedding reception was to be a modest affair, as the wedding had been. No invitations had been sent, just an announcement in the papers two weeks before, as was the custom among those with less real or imagined social position. Mae's family did not have sufficient room or yard to host the reception, and so it was held at a cousin's newer home in South Buffalo.

The party was lively when the Keplers arrived. Friends had already tapped kegs and uncorked whiskey bottles, tasting to verify the quality of the beverages. Tables were arranged on the spongy lawn and covered with cloths that gently rippled in Lake Erie's blessed summer breeze. Lily saw women setting out a generous spread of ham and cold chicken, salads, slaws and baked pies. On one table stood a three-layer cake, iced in white with piped rosettes and garlands.

Will and Mae stood by a table that contained a punch bowl, laughing and greeting guests. Fiddlers materialized as if from the air and began to play. Lily looked at the happy scene and had to push back the urge to sob. She had declared two weeks earlier that she was through with weeping, but understood that was a naive attitude now that so much gaiety and loving happiness surrounded her.

Later she found herself sitting beside her mother on straight-back chairs that had been arranged around the perimeter of the lawn. She had been introduced to

Mae's sisters and brothers, parents, grandparents, and some of the cousins, and was exhausted from the effort to be cheerful. Her father was having a fine time with Mae's male relatives, laughing and slapping backs. Poor Alfred, never too social on any occasion among strangers, stood nearby, glass in hand, smiling automatically whenever someone spoke to him.

Mama Kepler had been introduced by Mae to her family, after which Mama had decided that her job was done and she took a seat, sending out a very small smile that, after a few hours, faded to a blank look.

"How happy they all are," Mama said quietly, not turning to address Lily. "One of them has married *up*. And in their own church. More papists."

Lily slowly rose from her seat and walked away. Mae caught her arm and grinned so broadly that Lily smiled back.

"I am so happy that we will be sisters!" Mae said warmly. Then she embraced Lily tightly.

"I am, too," Lily replied, still smiling. "Will could not have done better in all the world."

Mae laughed, then leaned close and said, "Now, if only we can thaw out your Mama."

They both chuckled knowingly.

"Don't worry about Mama," Lily cracked, "she's outnumbered in the Kepler family!"

Little squares of the wedding fruit cake were handed out, then Will and Mae prepared to leave for their honeymoon. The fiddlers began to play, "Auld Lang Syne" and everyone stood and raised a glass to the newlyweds, some singing sentimentally, others more boisterously. Lily joined in the singing until her throat closed as she felt the sadness of the song vibrate within her. "Should old acquaintance be forgot, and never brought to mind?"

And then the couple waved goodbye amid shouts and ribald laughter, and they were gone. The party was in full swing, but the departure of the Wilhelm Keplers was the signal for Mama to stand and catch her husband's eye. They left South Buffalo for the familiar neighborhood of Humboldt Parkway directly.

LILY stopped in front of Ulbrich's store on Main Street. She shifted the packages she was carrying for Eva and looked into the big display windows of the book and stationery store.

"Lily!" Eva came up beside her. "I turned and you were gone. Why did you stop?"

Without shifting her gaze from the windows, she replied, "I'm going to get a job. I think I would like to work here if they're hiring."

Eva sighed and shifted her own parcels. "Why on earth would you want to do that?" she said, impatient to be going. "Besides, your mother would never allow it. Come on, now. My feet are tired."

Lily turned to follow Eva as they continued their way back to the Bond house. They had just finished what Lily hoped was the last shopping trip before Eva's wedding in three days on August 24. This trip was one of several last-minute excursions they had made.

"I will get a job in any case," Lily said quietly. "It certainly will be a better use of my time than going to china-painting classes with Mama."

"But she said how much she enjoyed doing it together, so you will hurt her feelings, you know," Eva said, having apparently chosen her sympathies.

"Well, then, you may take my place, since you are nearly a daughter these days."

When they reached Eva's house, they piled up the parcels in the hallway. Eva was delighted to see that the big box containing her wedding dress had been delivered from the seamstress. Lily had attended the final fitting two days earlier.

They had lemonade in the parlor, lounging with bare feet. Eva was running through the schedule for the wedding festivities, with the rehearsal at Calvary Presbyterian Church on Delaware, the ceremony, and the reception supper at the exclusive Iroquois Hotel on Main Street.

"I've never been to the Iroquois," Lily commented.

"It's where Frank's family will be staying," Eva said. "Frank told me that his family is accustomed to the best, so he made arrangements there. My father will be staying there, too, you know." She paused and sipped her lemonade. "I hope they approve of me," she added with uncharacteristic doubt.

Lily put her hand on Eva's arm. "But you met them and they welcomed you! No worries there!"

"Lily," Eva began, hesitantly, "will you stay the night before the wedding?"

She turned to see Lily's face now and her own face fell. Lily had withdrawn her hand.

Lily understood what Eva was asking and felt pained at having to refuse her. "I can't, Evie," she said softly.

Eva pursed her lips and turned her head away. "She's ruined you!" she spat.

Lily said nothing in response, which served to encourage Eva in her tantrum.

"She's always there between us, I see it in your eyes! And how can you still care about her after the way she treated you?"

Lily put down her lemonade. "Eva," she began, touching Eva's arm again.

But Eva jumped up, shaking off Lily's hand. "She's *ruined* you!" Eva repeated, almost taunting.

Lily stood up and grasped Eva's arms tightly. "She has *not* ruined me," she replied, voice tight with intensity.

They stood like that, glaring at one another, until Eva's lip began to tremble.

"You're hurting my arms," she pleaded.

Lily released her and sat down again wearily. Eva began to cry quietly. Lily called her back to the sofa.

"One last night, that's all I asked," Eva sniffled. "To be together the way we were since we were small."

Lily didn't respond except to offer her handkerchief.

Eva grimaced. "Who's going to have a ready handkerchief after I'm married?"

"Frank will, even though you may have to make sure there's a clean one in his pockets."

Eva looked at the cloth in her hands. "I wish I was marrying you this week instead of Frank."

"Are you having doubts about marrying Frank?" Lily frowned. She had been having her own doubts about that. "Because you don't have to go through with it. It's not too late to change your mind."

Eva shrugged. "No, I will marry Frank Marshall in three days. He needs me. And, well, what better thing do I have to do?"

EVA's wedding day was a perfect August day in Buffalo. With moderate temperatures, no one cared that the leaves on the elms along Delaware Avenue were dusty, or that the only flowers still perky were the gaudy little marigolds.

Lily had arrived at the Bond house early in the morning with her maid of honor dress and accoutrements. She and Eva had their hair done by Mr. Foster and tried to remain serene in the midst of people coming and going in the house downstairs. Eva's father had arrived the day before; he was also in the parlor. The girls went down in their dressing gowns and nibbled at the platters of cold cuts and cakes Aunt Martha had thoughtfully laid out. With the wedding at 4 p.m., residents and visitors alike needed something to tide them over until the supper at the Iroquois.

Two hours before the ceremony, Lily and Aunt Martha began the long process of dressing Eva. It was as painstaking and laborious as if Eva were being prepared to be crowned a queen. All the new underthings, the fine underwear and chemise, each had to be smoothed against her skin and the satin ribbons snugged just so. Then her white stockings went on; this was the last step Eva could assist with because the next layer was her corset. after which she would be less mobile. This was also new and worn when she had her dress fittings. After her corset came the corset cover, this one of very fine cotton that became nearly invisible.

The petticoats were each pulled on by helping hands and tied. And then the dress, the fabulous Venetian lace confection that her father had given her *carte blanche* to have made by a seamstress. Lily and Aunt Martha lifted it over Eva's head carefully and rested it on the bride's waist. To her credit, Eva had remained as calm as a statue thus far.

Lily lifted one arm of the dress and Eva slipped her hand into the sleeve. Aunt Martha did the same with the other arm. Lily adjusted the front panels while Aunt Martha fastened the many buttons on the back. The sleeves were very wide and puffed from the shoulders to the elbow, where the material became snug on Eva's arms. The front, fitted closely to breasts whose voluptuousness was restrained by the corset but not erased, featured a neckline that showed a bit more *décolletage* than her Buffalo peers. As had been her life habit, Eva had given directions to the seamstress that no one countermanded.

When they finished buttoning buttons and adjusting the skirt, both stood back to look at Eva, who had begun to smile her delighted smile. She could see herself reflected in the mirror of her dresser. Tiers of imported ivory lace cascaded down the skirt and flowed away behind her in a long train. The dress was an embarrassment of riches, Lily knew. Because of its design, it would never be worn again after this day. How different from Mae's!

Lily turned her attention to her maid of honor dress, whose design Eva had also directed. They had disagreed on the color, a minor dispute in which Lily had prevailed, and so the dress she stepped into was a pale blue silk with ivory lace panels of the same lace as Eva's dress. She was uncertain if she would ever wear it again after this day, but she found the dress comforting when she saw herself reflected in a mirror. With her thick auburn hair piled high and frozen into place by pomade, she stared at the young woman in the mirror. She, who thought of herself as a bookworm, now saw an attractive woman who had her face. She allowed herself to be pleased for a moment.

Eva had given her a wedding token that brides gave to their attendants. It was a simple but lovely pearl necklace and earring set to wear with her dress. Aunt Martha helped Lily put them on because Lily's hands had begun to tremble. The solemnity of the event had finally struck home with her and she felt as if she were the one being attached to a man for life. She looked over at Eva, her lacy veil fastened to her dark hair, pulling on her gloves now, and realized that their friendship would be forever altered in an hour. And now she wasn't certain that she wanted that to happen. Eva, a married woman? What would that mean for Lily?

They rode up Delaware Avenue to the church, passing people going about their ordinary business. Eva calmly held in her lap a long bouquet of deep red American Beauty roses; Lily's smaller bouquet was comprised of pink Bridesmaid roses. When Eva decided on them, Lily had kept to herself that the Bridesmaid rose was the class flower of the Vassar class of 1907, the class that was to have been hers. Today, she embraced the connection sentimentally, as a secret compensation.

Calvary Presbyterian was a large church as befitted its large congregation. The distance to the altar appeared oceanic, the rows of pews like waves punctuated only by Gothic arches that accentuated the sanctuary's length.

Eva strode with slow majesty to the altar with her father on one arm and her uncle Walter on the other. Lily had never seen her so self-possessed. She looked over at Frank, who was gazing at the petite, beautifully attired woman coming up the aisle to stand beside him. He seemed to look at his bride with love. He also seemed to have flushed cheeks.

The ceremony was simple, as Protestant ceremonies are, and much shorter than Will and Mae's Catholic mass had been two months previous. The church's pipe organ boomed congratulations as the newlyweds hastened down the aisle and to their waiting carriage. Lily followed on the arm of one of Frank's brothers, both complete strangers to each other who were acting out their roles.

Despite her sophisticated appearance, Lily felt self-conscious in the splendor of the Iroquois Hotel. She followed the wedding party upstairs to a private dining room with thick carpets, brocade drapes, and dark wood paneling whose finish gleamed. Eva and Frank were greeting guests and Lily was relieved to see her family enter.

"Go over to the door," her mother hissed. "You should be in the reception line with the others!"

Lily did she was told, pausing only to receive compliments from Mae.

The dinner was more elaborate than any Lily had ever attended. A soup course came first, then swiftly following was trout with cucumbers and boiled potatoes, and after that roast beef with string beans. Wine glasses were filled, then taken away and new glasses filled with another wine. Lily followed the habit of others around her in taking only a few bites of each course and a sip of each wine. By the time the sorbet was served, she realized that it was the only way to survive such a meal. When she asked the nature of the bubbly wine served with the sorbet and learned it was Mumm's champagne, she smiled for the first time all day. The memory was familiar, and not painful. She was heartened by that and thoroughly enjoyed the effervescence.

After dinner, the guests relaxed and began to socialize in little groups, the Marshall side among themselves and the Bond side among themselves. Lily had the chance to chat with her family and to hear Mae rave about her dress and how beautiful she looked. Lily returned the compliment sincerely; she thought Mae had a quiet confidence today in addition to looking radiantly happy. Her smiles matched her husband's and Lily was glad to be related to them.

She spoke with Aunt Martha and Uncle Walter who cheerfully said, "Now it's your turn, Lily! Be sure to invite us to your wedding!" It was not the first such comment she had received; she replied with her practiced modest blush, prompting a guffaw.

A small musical trio had been hired to provide occasional music which began to compete with the party's conversations which were already competing with each other to be heard. Amid the din, Lily wandered out of the room and strolled down the wide hallway and through the ladies' lobby. She briefly sat in one of the white upholstered chairs that encircled the pillars and thought about the St. Denis Hotel. It was obvious now that the St. Denis was a more ordinary hostelry than the Iroquois. But it had been heaven to her.

On her way back to the private dining room, Lily paused beside a window that overlooked Main Street. While lost in her thoughts of happy days and nights in New York City, she jumped at the sound of a man's voice close in her ear.

"I'm glad to find you," Frank Marshall slurred. "Something I want to make clear."

Lily stepped back and turned to look at him. His face was moist, a forelock of his handsome black hair fell over his forehead. He was plainly intoxicated.

"In this little competition we have, you and I," he said, pointing in her general direction, "I'm here to tell you that I won."

Lily had no idea what he was talking about, but did not reply to the drunken man. Frank seemed to sense her disapproval because he gripped her arm very tightly and leaned so close she could smell the sharp, sour brandy on his breath.

"She's mine now," he said with some menace. "Mine. Not yours any more. So you keep your filthy hands off my *wife*."

It was Lily's turn to be angry. "Remove your hand from my arm," she said slowly and clearly, her voice arctic cold. "*Frank*."

After a beat, Frank let go and backed away, smirking as if victorious. He moved toward the dining room with heavy steps and as he did, Lily saw her brother Alfred. He was staring at her, mouth open.

Lily massaged her arm where Frank had gripped it and Alfred approached.

"Did he hurt you?" her brother asked, his brow wrinkled.

"I'm all right, brother," she said.

"I only just came up at the end and noticed that he seemed to behave very improperly. I was about to intervene when he released you."

Alfred seemed at loose ends. "I think I should speak to him," he said, seeming to seize upon the right course of action. "Tell him a thing or two about how men in our city are expected to treat women."

Lily tugged his sleeve. "You don't need to. And, in any case, he's too drunk to comprehend what you would say."

Alfred looked in the direction of the dining room. "A groom at his own wedding, drunk. And in the Iroquois, of all places."

"Yes."

He looked at Lily thoughtfully. "Does Eva know what she's getting into? I mean, I've heard things about him and you know how seldom I'm in town and at the club. So, if *I've* heard things..." he left the rest unspoken.

Lily slipped her arm through his and turned them toward the dining room. "I don't know what will happen, Alfred," she said honestly.

Two days later, Gertrude had her baby, a boy. They named him after Lily's father, but Henry instead of Heinrich. Lily approved of this modern gesture by her conservative brother and sister-in-law. Mama Kepler, not needed for the first week because Gertrude's family tended to her, fretted, clucked, and baked for the day when she would be invited to Alden so she could fuss over her first grandchild.

CHAPTER 30

Lily slipped away from the annual Kepler's Labor Day picnic as she did every year and wandered over to the amusement park section of Lein's Park. She was alone this year for first time in memory. Eva had accompanied her since they were children.

She found a bench by evergreens that shaded the September sun. It was not as warm as it had been at last year's company picnic, but there was no breeze. Sounds from the ball field and the attractions seemed suspended in the air like dust motes. Or perhaps, Lily pondered, she was just feeling disconnected, out of place. *Perhaps I'm the one suspended*, she thought, glancing around, *and everyone else is in motion.*

Eva and Frank had just completed their honeymoon trip around the Great Lakes by boat and were on their way to Connecticut to visit Frank's family. Lily had received a postcard from Mackinac Island with a few lines about the fun they were having. Things were already different now between them, she thought. Married women had their own circles, talking about their husbands, socializing in couples. Two children raced past Lily, brushing her skirt, and she imagined Eva with children, something else that they would not have in common.

One year ago, her world had been entirely different. Will and Eva were single with no sweethearts in sight. Alfred and Gertrude were not going to have a baby. She was going to Vassar College. Now she was only beginning to digest all of these changes, but one thing had become clearer to her. She was going to act now, to do something to occupy her time in a meaningful way. And she was going to get a paying job because she had to acquire funds. Money was power and she was determined to stop being powerless. But how?

"Well, here you are!"

Mae's voice, full of warm good cheer, startled Lily into the present. She smiled in greeting.

"I saw you sneaking away and decided you must have a really good spot over here where you don't have to chit chat with strangers all afternoon."

"You have found me out," Lily admitted. "Eva and I used to escape and have ice cream floats over here every year."

"I was afraid I was disturbing you," Mae commented, still standing, "because you looked so deep in thought."

Lily smiled, somewhat embarrassed at how she must have appeared. "I would be delighted to have you join me," she said, shifting over on the bench. "My own thoughts are not that interesting or amusing. In fact, I'm beginning to bore myself silly."

Mae laughed kindly and sat down beside Lily.

"You must have come to last year's picnic, yes?" Lily queried.

Mae nodded. "I did. Had a fine time, mostly sitting in the shelter with other girls from the office."

"Had you noticed my brother yet?"

"I knew who he was, of course, the boss's son," she shrugged. "But he seemed a boy who liked only his sports and teasing girls. So, I didn't pay him much mind. I was new at my job and working hard to advance so I could make better wages."

Lily considered that. "What did you think you would do with the money you made?"

"Oh, well, there's no end of wishes!" Mae laughed. "I've been giving some to the folks, of course, to help them out. But I take out a bit for myself and then save the rest. I didn't have any specific thing in mind, just the enjoyment of having money in the bank. I don't think my family thinks I saved any. And I don't tell."

They sat quietly, each with her own thoughts about the subject.

"Why do you ask?" Mae wondered.

"I don't have any money of my own," Lily replied, "and I think it's time I got a job and made some money."

"In my family, that would be considered a sensible idea. But what will your Mama and Papa think of that?"

Lily answered with quiet firmness. "It's something I have to do, regardless."

Mae didn't respond.

"Women are completely helpless without money," Lily said, finding words for what had been diffuse feelings. "Without money, we are totally at the mercy of family or some man!"

She looked at Mae to see how she reacted to such a passionate outburst. Mae was smiling beneath her raised eyebrows. Lily chuckled to see the expression. "Well, where did that come from, I wonder?"

"What you say is true, of course. There can't be a woman living now who doesn't know it," Mae said. "But women find all kinds of ways to cover up the truth by telling girls how important it is to attract a good man, meaning one who doesn't drink up his wages."

Lily looked at her thoughtfully. Mae was speaking with understanding.

"But," Mae said brightly, changing the subject, "I came to find you to tell you some good news. You might be getting your bedroom back before the end of October."

"You have found a flat then?" Lily was excited for Mae because it was clear she and Will wanted to be on their own and away from the often-cool atmosphere with Mama on Humboldt Parkway.

"Better," Mae said with some excitement. "Will has been talking with a man building doubles over on Winslow, and he thinks one might be finished up by then. We could have our pick of upstairs or downstairs."

"A new flat," Lily said admiringly. "Everything new."

Mae squeezed Lily's arm. "I know!"

They smiled and nodded happily at the thought. Though Lily liked having Will and Mae in the house to make a crowd and diffuse attention from her, it would be very nice to have her spacious room back and especially the window seat.

"And," Mae added, drawing out the word, "it will be good to get settled in our first place before—you become an aunt again."

Lily met Mae's look with growing understanding. "You're?"

Mae nodded. "I come from a long line of fertile women," she laughed.

Lily had to catch her breath at this news. "As my roommate used to say, 'Bully!'" she said heartily.

Mae laughed. "We haven't told anyone yet, not even my Ma. But we'll have to pretty soon because it will become more plain by the day what we've been up to!"

Mae was so happy that Lily couldn't help but smile all over. Now she understood why Mae had looked so radiant at Eva's wedding.

"I'll work as long as I can persuade my husband to let me," Mae was saying. "The money will be nice to have for furnishings, you know. Things besides those that Kepler's sells!'

Lily chuckled. "A Kepler's connection is handy to have. We furnished our room at Vassar with things Papa sent from the store."

The mention of college tamped down the excitement of Mae's news.

"I'll bet you are thinking about college these days," Mae offered sympathetically.

Lily nodded, saying nothing.

"How is your friend Helen?" Mae was asking kindly. "I liked her very much when we met last spring."

Lily paused, wondering what to say. Then she decided to be honest because she had come to trust Mae's integrity and goodness.

"We're not in touch," she said tentatively. "She was upset with me because I couldn't persuade Mama and Papa to let me return this fall." There it was, succinctly.

"Oh, Lily," Mae said sorrowfully, "surely she didn't blame you. Don't you think she was only distressed to be without your company this year?"

Lily sighed, then sighed deeply again, surprising herself at finding the pain still so close at hand. She couldn't reply.

Mae seemed to understand and clasped Lily's hand. "Why don't you write her? She'll see that you bear no grudge about the way you parted and then you can correspond."

Lily pursed her lips together and tried to smile. It's not that she hadn't thought about writing, but that she had no idea what to say to the woman who had returned the ruby ring.

"You were so happy last spring when the four of us played cards and had tea!" Mae squeezed her hand. "Write to her, Lily. She hasn't forgotten you, I'm sure of that."

WHEN Eva and Frank returned from their honeymoon trip, they moved into a furnished townhouse not far from her aunt and uncle.

Eva visited the Kepler's almost before she had unpacked, breathless with news of the lake voyage, the grandiose hotel, its amenities, the views, the rich people. Mama Kepler listened enthusiastically, Lily more quietly. She thought Eva seemed the same but different, more attuned to doing what might be expected of a married woman. Eva made several comments directed at Mama Kepler about learning from the other guests at the hotel some small detail of carrying oneself or addressing the servants. Mama nodded sagely, as if these were important to know. The moment Mama left them alone, Eva instantly turned to Lily.

"Let's go up to your room," she whispered. "I have a present for you!"

"I am staying in Will's old room," Lily replied. "You don't want to go up there."

They went out to the bench around the tree in the backyard. Once ensconced in almost the same spot they had sat in June when Lily first came home from Vassar, Eva brought out a handkerchief.

"Here," she said, presenting it. "I bought this for you." When Lily hesitated, she added, "It's *inside* the handkerchief!"

Lily unwrapped the handkerchief to reveal a pin. It was a stylized small sprig of a flower made up of small irregular freshwater pearls attached to a gold leafy branch.

"Do you know what it is?" Eva was supplying the enthusiasm for both of them.
"Tell me."

"It's Lily of the Valley, see all the little flowers and the wide leaves coming from the stem?"

Lily nodded. "I do see. It's very pretty and looks quite expensive."

Eva dismissed that. "Oh, everything's very dear up there. Rich people stay there for weeks in the summer. This is a trinket to them. But I bought it with my own money that Aunt Martha and Uncle George gave me for the trip. And that's what I told Frank when he complained about the price."

Lily raised her eyebrows in response, but Eva ignored that.

"Do you know what Lily of the Valley means?"

"No," Lily answered, her tone a question.

"Well, the lady who sold it to me clinched the sale when she told me that it means 'a return of happiness.'"

They sat for a few moments, both gazing at the pin in Lily's hands. Lily felt sure the flower had something to do with weddings because she had seen them in the bouquets of brides the past summer, but she kept it to herself.

"My wish for you," Eva said more quietly than she had spoken since her arrival, "is that you will be happy again."

Lily looked idly at the lawn before them. A few scattered gold leaves heralded the coming autumn. A year ago, she was preparing to go to Vassar.

"You shouldn't be thinking of me on your honeymoon," she replied quietly. "That time is for becoming acquainted with your new life as a married woman."

"Well," Eva replied lasciviously, "I certainly did that!"

Lily touched her arm warningly. "You're not going to share details, are you," she said declaratively.

Eva giggled. "Of course not, but I will say how much I enjoy what old people call 'the marital act.' Every morning we lounged in bed for hours, missing the breakfast hours entirely."

"Details, Eva."

"I'm sorry, dear," Eva sighed. "I can only say that Frank was the perfect husband, deferring to me at every turn. In the evenings, he stepped out just for a few hours to mingle with the other gentlemen for cards and brandy. But otherwise, he was at my side, strolling or riding around the island in the afternoons."

Lily didn't respond to that, thinking about Frank and his brandy.

"But now," Eva cheerfully continued, "I have to learn to cook. We are taking our meals at Aunt Martha and Uncle Walter's while she is teaching me to prepare simple foods. It's not as easy as it looks, you know."

Lily smiled. Eva had blissfully avoided any domestic instruction while growing up, skills Lily's mother made sure her only daughter acquired.

"I have such trouble getting the townhouse stove to draw. The whole place smells like smoke most of the time. I want you to come visit but not until I've fixed it up a little nicer. The furniture is quite worn and needs covers."

They spent the rest of their visit on Eva's plans for entertaining one day when her cooking was up to par and decorating with money her father had given them as a wedding present. Eva readily confessed to having turned over responsibility for their money to Frank who was, after all, in the banking business and could keep track of such numerical things.

CHAPTER 31

Lily entered the headquarters of the Women's Educational and Industrial Union, pausing inside the newest building on Niagara Square. She had never been here before but knew of the organization, of course. Her mother was indifferent to membership in the Union, open to any woman of any circumstance, perhaps especially because the organization didn't discriminate between social classes. Elda Kepler wanted to rub shoulders with those with high social standing, not shop girls or immigrant women.

Lily understood the organization's mission, that women would help each other to advance in economic opportunity, and she wanted to find a way to constructively fill her many unscheduled hours. It didn't hurt that she was tweaking her mother's nose by seeking engagement with the Union.

She walked quietly through the main hallway, reading signs on the doors and looking for some administrative office. While peering through a glass door, she was startled by a voice behind her.

"Were you looking for someone?" The voice was friendly and quiet, and Lily could tell that the woman speaking was smiling.

She turned to face Harriet Townsend, president of the Women's Union since its inception twenty years earlier. She was a living legend in Buffalo, whose photos Lily had seen in the Express more than once. Being so close to her in the flesh made Lily stammer.

"I—" Lily gestured foolishly, "I was hoping to speak to someone about offering my assistance."

The woman instantly replied with a radiant smile. "Well, any time I can begin a Wednesday with such an offer is a good omen!" she said. "Follow me."

The woman was short, which surprised Lily, having imagined the woman who had accomplished so much in Buffalo would be taller, more substantial, perhaps like those mythical Valkyries. But Mrs. Townsend might be anyone's kindly grandmother with her white hair wound into a bun on top of her head. She led the way to an office located off the hall near the entrance and into an inner office where she gestured for Lily to sit while she herself rounded a big desk and sat down.

"Would you care for a glass of water?" she asked hospitably.

"No, thank you, Mrs. Townsend," Lily replied respectfully.

Smiling, the woman replied, "Please call me Hattie. And you are?"

"Lily Kepler."

Hattie Townsend wrinkled her brow. "Any relation to Kepler's Furniture?"

"Yes," Lily replied nodding, "it's the family business."

"Oh, yes?" Hattie said, nodding once. "Well, then, what did you have in mind?"

That was the question of the hour. Lily hadn't been able to formulate the answer over the last couple of days when she had made up her mind to do something and get out of the house and away from her mother's suggestions, requests, and pointed comments about her sulky attitude.

Lily forced a small smile. "I'm not quite sure. I want to be useful. I attended Vassar College last year and wonder if that might qualify me to assist with the kindergarten classes you offer. Or perhaps I could teach English."

"I see," Mrs. Townsend replied. "How many years did you attend Vassar in all?"

Lily suddenly felt quite stupid. "Just the one."

The woman nodded slightly. "Why are you not returning this year?"

Lily looked at her hands, trying to think of how to put it. "My parents felt that it would be better for me to be at home, that one year was enough," she paused and then finished it, "to indulge my dream of a college education."

Too late she heard the bitter tone of her last phrase, and regretted it. It would not make a good impression.

"I see," the woman replied. Then she sighed. "Do you speak Italian?"

"I'm afraid not," Lily answered. "Just German, a little French and Latin."

Mrs. Townsend nodded. "What we need are women who can speak Italian because so many of our members who wish to learn English are newly arrived Italians or Sicilians."

Lily thought of the irony that her German was needed at the College Settlement in New York City which had a surplus of Italian speakers among the college women workers.

"And the kindergarten classes are taught by qualified teachers," the woman added.

Lily nodded, understanding that she was not qualified to do anything. "Thank you for speaking with me," Lily said apologetically, preparing to leave.

"Are you interested in teaching as a profession?"

"I'm not sure," Lily answered honestly.

Mrs. Townsend was looking at her thoughtfully. "Why don't you see Dr. Bender in City Hall and tell her of your desire to be useful? She's Superintendent of Primary Grades for all the schools."

"I hadn't thought of that. Thank you, I will."

"You never know what might come of it. She's very inspiring," the president of the Women's Union added, nodding.

Lily rose and turned to go. As she reached the door, Hattie Townsend had one more thing to say to the young woman.

"Keep this in mind, Miss Kepler: adversity can be a good teacher. I wish you well."

Once she was outside the building, Lily exhaled deeply and gazed around the rundown Niagara Square. A streetcar screeched around the bend in front of the Central High School and she looked at her alma mater across the square. How easy everything had been for her there. How easy everything except Greek had been at Vassar. She belonged to high school and college once and now she didn't belong anywhere. *I can never be happy here*, she declared firmly.

And then, instead of crossing the square to catch the Genesee Street cars that would return her to the Kepler home, Lily walked up Court Street and turned onto Main, heading for Ulbrich's Bookseller and Stationer.

"I have a job," Lily announced during a lull at the dinner table that night. Instead of looking at either of her parents, she sought the faces of Will and Mae across the table. Mae looked back, her eyebrows raised.

"It's at Ulbrich's, and right now all they need me for is Thursday, Friday and Saturday," she continued, aware that she was hurrying to get all the facts out at once. "I start tomorrow."

"Don't talk foolish," her mother said matter-of-factly. "You're not going to work in a shop."

Prepared for this response, Lily replied in what she hoped was a mature tone. "I've already been hired. I start tomorrow."

"Well, tell them your family doesn't allow it," Mama said in a clipped tone. "My only daughter will not be a common shopgirl."

Lily looked at her plate without seeing it. "I'm nineteen now, Mama, and I choose to go to work. I would rather be attending classes in college now, but since that is not possible, I will work in a paying job."

"I will call Mrs. Ulbrich tomorrow and tell her you will not be employed," Mama said, raising her voice and the stakes in this fencing duel.

Lily had no countering parry. She raised her head and looked down the table to her father, who had been mildly observing the scene. He did not seem to acknowledge her appeal, but must have seen her face and her lips quivering with helpless frustration.

"Mama," he said calmly, "we are shopkeepers. How is it not right that she wants to go to work?"

Lily, Will and Mae turned their heads in unison from Papa to the other end of the table where Mama sat.

"Because I want better for her than that!" she replied defensively.

Papa shook his head calmly. "The Ulbrich's are good people, with an honest business and a good reputation. It's a nice, clean job."

Mama gaped at him. He simply added, "Leave it alone, now."

Lily, filled with relief, felt as if she would cry, but she didn't. Instead, she looked at Mae who was trying not to grin.

The week after she started her job at Ulbrich's, Lily walked into City Hall early in the morning to keep an appointment she had made with Dr. Ida Bender, Superintendent of Primary Grades. She had no idea what she expected from the meeting but, having reviewed her performance with Mrs. Townsend, she was determined not to seem as foolish or arrogant as she had that day. The value of her one year at Vassar was now firmly in perspective.

What she could not have prepared for was Ida Bender, M.D., who rose from behind a table piled with books, folders, folios with strings untied and stepped around it to greet Lily by shaking hands. Her smile was both warm and bemused. She invited Lily to sit.

"I hope you haven't had to wait long," she said apologetically.

Lily avowed that she had not. She was immediately charmed by the middle-aged Superintendent, her reddish-colored hair streaked with white and her large and very dark brown eyes.

"I spend most of my time visiting the schools, and I try to set aside at least two mornings a week to set my office in some order," she said, chuckling as she gestured at the table, "but people seem to think these hours are good times to share their crises."

She laughed and Lily had the strong impression that Dr. Bender enjoyed her job and the crises.

"Now, the secretary noted that you were referred to me by Hattie Townsend."

"Yes," Lily said.

Dr. Bender cocked her head, puzzled. "That's very curious. Do you know why?"

Lily took a breath. "Well, I offered my services to the Women's Union and learned that I have no qualifications for assisting with the kindergarten or teaching English to immigrants. But, because I had expressed my desire to be useful, she suggested that I speak with you."

Dr. Bender nodded once, taking that in. "What qualifications do you have?"

Lily bowed her head, chagrined. "I'm uncertain if I have anything to offer. I did attend one year of college last year."

"And where was that?"

"Vassar."

"Good for you, Miss Kepler!" The woman said heartily and sincerely.

Lily was heartened and smiled just a little in response.

"And you are not returning, why?"

There was something about Ida Bender that persuaded Lily to be honest. "Because my mother—mostly—decided that I cared more for my friends than about finding a suitable husband," she said without malice or sarcasm.

The woman smiled into Lily's eyes and Lily felt long-held tensions loosen. "And was your mother correct?"

Lily smiled. "Yes, she was."

They laughed. Then Ida Bender's expression shifted to one of sympathy.

"This must be a difficult time for you, when your friends are packing their trunks to return to school."

Lily nodded. "It's why I want to be useful somehow. I have a job at Ulbrich's but it's only Thursday, Friday and Saturday each week."

"But working in a shop isn't a career goal for someone like you," the woman said, as if she knew. "What are your plans? Do you want to be a teacher?"

Lily exhaled. "I don't know. I only know how to be a student."

Ida Bender liked that answer, it was in her smile. "Would you be interested in visiting a classroom and observing the teacher and pupils?"

"Is that possible?" Lily hadn't thought of that.

Dr. Bender chuckled. "Of course, it's possible. I'm the queen of all I survey!"

They both laughed at that.

"I'll tell you what," she said in a more serious vein, "on Monday, you report to School 16 at 8 a.m. That's on Delaware near Bryant. Can you do that?"

"Yes," Lily said, nodding.

"When you get there, go to the office and ask for Miss Lapey. She's the assistant principal there."

"What shall I tell her?"

Ida Bender smiled broadly. "She'll be expecting you."

She stood up and Lily did, as well, recognizing that their meeting was over. Lily hated to leave this woman's presence. She felt almost happy for the first time in ages.

Lily climbed the steps to one of Buffalo's newest school buildings, School 16, also called the Delaware Avenue School, just before eight a.m. the next Monday. She was not alone, but merely the tallest person in the crowd also entering the building in a seething mass of childhood. Stopping in the hallway, she was nearly pushed over by the children who apparently did not expect their progress to be impeded.

She looked around for the office and spied a bemused woman standing across the hallway. She motioned for Lily to come to her. Excusing herself several times, in increasing tones, Lily reached the woman. Before she could ask the location of the office, the woman spoke.

"Miss Kepler, I presume?" the woman asked, chuckling.

"Oh," Lily replied, surprised. "Are you Miss Lapey?"

The woman nodded. "I've been on the lookout for you." She looked around, taking in the students, now filling the halls with chatter. "I thought you might be somewhat overwhelmed with the morning rush."

"It's—" Lily began and then said simply, "There are such a lot of children!"

Miss Lapey lightly took Lily by the elbow. "Let's go to my classroom."

Lily followed, perplexed. "Dr. Bender said you were Assistant Principal. You also have a class?"

"Oh, yes," the latter assured her, "our ever-growing student population requires the exalted Assistants to teach, as well."

Lily was introduced to Miss Lapey's third grade classroom. From an empty seat at the rear of the classroom, she observed the teacher as she asserted control of her charges, which Lily counted at 41 pupils this day. The woman was compact, shorter than Lily, dressed simply in a white shirtwaist and fawn brown skirt. Her hair, medium brown but partly steel gray, was pulled back into a bun. It was practical and probably had been stylish when Miss Lapey was young, but she was not young any more. Still, it was her face that was her best feature. Lively eyes kept surveying the classroom as she took attendance and spoke to a student individually here and there. Now and then she would address a child by name and look directly into his or her eyes with raised eyebrows. That was sufficient to tame the child in question. Lily felt the woman's authority and decided that Miss Lapey was a very experienced teacher.

A few weeks later, Lily wandered slowly along Humboldt Parkway after her day at school. The October day was one of those perfect Buffalo days when the season was suspended windlessly under a fading, but still warm sun. Perhaps it was the quality of the light, perhaps the caress of the sun on her cheek, but Lily was in no hurry to reach home because in her mind's eye she was strolling along a familiar path at college on just this kind of day last year. She was almost a month into her Greek tutoring with Helen and had not yet found words to describe the depth of her feelings for her tutor. But she smiled now to recall how happy she had been then, just at the beginning of the journey they took last year. Today was the first time she had set free all those memories. And she found they did not make her sad, perhaps because she didn't see them as part of any past tense.

Instead of finding only Gert at home, Lily opened the door to voices coming from the family parlor. It was Eva and her mother talking up a storm. She stood in the doorway and they stopped to recognize her.

"I'm glad you're finally home," Mama announced. "I was telling Eva that I have to get to my committee meeting."

She rose and turned to Eva. "Now dear, remember about the crackers. I can't tell you how long I lived on crackers, but it passes. I will pay you a call next week to see if you have more questions."

Mama left the room and Lily turned a curious eye to her friend.

"Crackers?"

Eva sent Lily her trademark expression that said she had a secret. "Your mama suggested that crackers would not make me sick like everything else has."

Lily was blinking uncomprehendingly.

"They call it morning sickness," Eva added, eyebrows raised.

Lily shook her head slowly. "Why?"

Eva laughed. "Are you really so ignorant of these things? I'm going to have a baby, silly!"

Lily's jaw dropped as she dropped into a chair. "Oh," she said. "Oh!"

Eva laughed gaily. "That's what Frank said, too."

Lily was still dazed. "You're going to be a mother."

Eva nodded. "Next May."

As they talked, Lily worked on imagining Eva ceding the spotlight to a baby. Eva was describing how relieved she was that Mama Kepler wanted to help her because Aunt Martha had never had children and was no help at all with her questions. And she confessed to having so many questions.

"Are you happy for me?" Eva asked.

Lily smiled. "I am. This will be your greatest adventure." And then she wondered. "How did Frank take the news?"

"Oh, he's happy," she replied, too quickly Lily thought.

"How is he really?" Lily pressed.

Eva looked off in the distance and then said, "I think he might be a little overwhelmed. Of course, I am too, sometimes. But I think he imagined that we might have children someday, just not now."

Lily sent her a look.

Eva chuckled. "I know, it was quite a honeymoon of debauchery! What did he expect?"

"A honeymoon with consequences," Lily observed.

CHAPTER 32

Will and Mae had moved into their new flat, and Lily had her room back. And with it came flooding over her thoughts of Helen, thoughts she had tried to suppress by work. She had sent a newsy letter to Belle, feeling fraudulent in doing so because she secretly hoped Belle would share it with her roommate Helen or send news of her. Belle had sent back a cheerful note with superficial news about campus and no word about Helen. At night, sitting on her window seat, she held the letter in her hands, trying to imagine how close the paper had been to her beloved. It was too hard and brought an upwelling of the old leaden sadness and longing.

Lily suspected that her mother had contacted Mrs. Ulbrich to ask that Lily be kept out of the public eye. She had been relegated to the upstairs rooms where the mail order part of the business was conducted, far from the shop floor where she had imagined she would be surrounded by piles of new books and customers looking for advice. Instead, she was surrounded by brown paper, string and paste for the labels, regularly acquiring paper cuts. And instead of customers, she worked with girls mostly her own age who seemed to live for gossip. Lily snobbishly doubted to herself that they had ever read any of the books in the store.

And then one blustery day, she was greeted by Clara, Mrs. Ulbrich's daughter who managed the store, and was assigned to the floor of the store to help arrange several shipments of new books. Lily felt as if she had been paroled from Devil's Island. When her shift was complete, she intimated to Clara that she enjoyed working in the bookstore and would be glad of the opportunity to assist there again. The woman's response was a puzzled look, but the next week Lily began working in the store, assisting customers and learning how to write up a purchase and take customer orders for books. It helped her state of mind greatly to be surrounded by books and people who liked them. One of the other girls on the floor told her that they borrowed new books to read but made sure not to open the book completely so as to save the spine. Lily learned to do this and began to catch up on her reading.

The first snow of the year was falling when Lily was stacking Frank Baum's newest book, *The Marvelous Land of Oz*, near the front windows of the store. Behind her she heard a man's voice.

"Miss Kepler?"

She turned to see a vaguely familiar face, with a full mustache and sad brown eyes. "Mr. Hudson?"

"I am very surprised to see you here," he said as he removed his hat. "I would have thought you were back at your Vassar home."

Lily pushed a stray hair back from her face. "I didn't return this year. My family thought it best."

Roger Hudson's face immediately clouded. "I'm sorry, I didn't mean to pry."

"Oh, no, you weren't," Lily assured him.

"I would like to start over," he said, "and say how delighted I am to see you, Miss Kepler."

"And I, you, sir."

They smiled.

The Keplers were unused to having their telephone ring during the dinner hour; Mama and Papa looked at each other, then at Lily, who rose and followed the ringing to the hall. When she returned, she took her seat, put her napkin back on her lap and said, offhandedly, "It was for me."

The call had been from Roger Hudson who invited Lily to attend the performance of *Higgeldy Piggeldy* at the Star Theater on Saturday evening. He promised that it would be a memorably hilarious performance because it starred Marie Dressler. Lily, caught entirely off guard, had agreed to attend as his guest.

When she responded to inquiries from her mother at the table, she communicated these things, which caused her mother to quite literally draw back in her seat in surprise. Lily answered the innumerable questions that followed. Her father said that he had met the elder Hudson once. Her mother thought Lily should buy a new dress, this being the first time Lily had ever agreed to be seen on the arm of a male person, let alone an established professional who would be taking her to the theater and dinner afterwards at the Iroquois.

Lily found it all uncomfortable, and not just the family interrogation. She wondered why she had automatically agreed to the date, which she grudgingly admitted to herself was the nature of the engagement. It was a date. Later, alone on her window seat, quilt pulled close around her against the cold evening, she recalled talking with Roger in Uncle Walter's library last Christmas. He had stood out among her peers for his calm demeanor, his good manners, and his kind but sad eyes. And she had been glad to see him in Ulbrich's, too.

Before she went to sleep, Lily had made an inventory of all the people she encountered regularly and concluded that her life lacked a friend. Eva was rapidly entering the alien world of motherhood. She admired Miss Lapey but she was much older. Assisting the students in Miss Lapey's class helped Lily realize that teaching was not what she wanted for herself. After the previous school year of continuous chatter at Vassar, she was parched for ideas, arguments about books, jokes, gossip. Why not Roger Hudson? she thought.

THE black and white marble tiles of the Star Theater lobby were barely visible beneath the feet of the theatergoers in their evening best, men in their silk hats and tails, women in their furs, beads glinting from their gowns. Buffalo's finest theater always drew first rate traveling productions and tonight's crowd ignored the life-size portraits of Richard Mansfield and Julia Marlowe on the walls as they greeted acquaintances, creating stationary clots in the procession toward the short stairs leading to the theater floor.

Roger, impeccably dressed, his starched shirtfront a blaze of white, led the way for Lily, careful to make sure he didn't get separated from her. As she eased her way through the crowd behind him, Lily was glad she had assented to her mother's authoritative recommendation that she buy an evening dress. She had attended performances at the Star when she was in high school, but always matinees with classmates where schoolgirl dress was the norm. This was quite formal and she felt relieved to blend in with the rest. She was especially grateful for her mother's loan of an opera cape that Lily did not recall ever seeing her mother wear. It made her feel quite mature.

Higgedly Piggeldy was everything Roger had said it would be. She had never heard of Marie Dressler but fell under her spell from the moment the tall, stocky woman bounded onto the stage singing, "A Great Big Girl Like Me," a tremendous pin in the shape of a pickle encrusted in diamonds on her expansive breast. She and Roger exchanged glances and laughed out loud with the rest of the audience. Lily laughed more that evening than she had in almost six months.

The night was chilly autumn, the dampness carrying a faint whiff of the lake. But the weather was clear so Roger offered his arm and they walked the block to Main Street and the Iroquois Hotel. They entered through the lady's entrance and were enveloped by the warmth of the hallway. Lily remembered Eva's wedding reception last summer, so short and yet so long a time ago; they had been upstairs. But she had never been in the main dining room, where they paused inside the double doors. Roger was immediately approached by the *maitre d'* and welcomed by name. When they were seated, Lily commented on this.

"I dine here once or twice a week," Roger replied casually. "My alternative is leftovers my housekeeper leaves in the icebox."

Lily took in the room, a high-ceilinged room done in crimson and gold which gleamed under the chandeliers. A small orchestra played pleasantly but quietly on a balcony above them. They had glided to their table over the thickest deep red carpet. Each damask-covered table had an electric lamp covered with a shade, giving the impression of intimacy for the respective diners. Though she observed quite a number of other diners, their conversations were just a murmur in the big room. She had never been to a restaurant this elegant and felt somewhat intimidated.

Roger may have noticed this because he made things easy for her when it came to ordering. He explained that after the theater, people usually had lighter fare, such as club sandwiches or chafing dish entrees.

Lily smiled at that. "Last year, I discovered a wide variety of foods that may be prepared with just a chafing dish. Even fudge!"

Roger laughed quietly. "I don't suppose Vassar awarded credits for that skill!"

She chose chicken croquettes. Roger ordered a bottle of Riesling for them, after asking Lily if she would care for some wine. He was suave in his manners, and confident without being arrogant. As he chatted amiably, Lily looked at him and realized how perfectly groomed he was, not a hair out of place, the fit of his evening dress the handiwork of an excellent tailor. He could have been a magazine advertisement.

They talked over the play, laughing again at many of the lines and marveling at Marie Dressler's hysterical facial expressions. Their dinner appeared out of the shadows as if by magic, placed precisely before them with almost a flourish by white-gloved waiters. Their wine glasses were refilled and they talked on and on as if they were old friends. Lily found that she could freely answer Roger's questions about life at Vassar.

"You must miss it very much," he said, sympathetically. "I remember the way you described it at Miss Bond's holiday party."

She looked into his brown eyes, and saw that he must understand.

He gently fingered the stem of his wine glass. "I had my own sudden separation from Harvard."

When he didn't continue right away, Lily said, "Yes?"

Roger paused, then glanced at her, and began. "It was my last year in law school. I was having a grand time. I had the best rooms, which I shared with my very best friend. Elliot."

He paused as if saying the name had broken the flow of the story. He smiled a grimace and continued.

"Elliot and I were making plans to spend several months in Europe after graduation. You know, to see everything before settling down to careers."

He looked over at Lily, who nodded that she understood. Then he looked away.

"We were talking about opening a law firm together. He insisted that it be ordered alphabetically: Crandall and Hudson, Attorneys at Law."

Lily was getting a feeling about Roger and Elliot, but dismissed it.

Roger grimaced. "And then, the telegram arrived."

He looked at Lily and she could see despair in his eyes. "My father had suffered an attack of apoplexy. Of course, I had to travel home at once." He sighed. "I don't know what I expected would happen. I was in shock, my mother needed me to be here. I was their only child."

He stopped and gazed into the distance, as if looking for something he had lost.

"My father was bedridden, unable to speak or move his arm," he resumed, patting his own left arm. "I went to his office and tried to be of some assistance with his work. His partner was some help but he was much older than my father and handled very little of the work on any day.

"Meanwhile the spring term was ticking away. I wrote Elliot that I didn't know when I could return. Then my father had another attack. And died. The crocuses in the front of the house were coming up. I think of that every spring when I see them. It's odd what one remembers."

He looked directly into Lily's eyes. "And then I realized that I wasn't going to be able to return to school, that I wasn't going to spend the autumn in Europe with Elliot. What I was going to do was pick up my father's work, in his office, at his desk. And live in the old-fashioned family home and support my widowed mother."

Lily then understood why, when they had first met, she had noticed how sad his eyes were. She couldn't think of a thing to say to him.

"That Christmas, I received a note from Elliot. I hadn't been able to write him for quite a while. What was there to say? He said that he was being married the day after New Year's. And that he would always remember me."

Roger finished his wine. "So. Now you know that I do understand something of your longing for your Vassar home."

"Yes, you do," Lily replied quietly. "Thank you."

He shook his head as if banishing the mood. "This is no way to end an evening with Marie Dressler!" And he laughed.

On the way home, Lily and Roger were quiet in the confines of the cab, thinking their own thoughts, gently jogged by the rhythm of the horse's clip-clopping. Then, as they turned onto Humboldt Parkway, Lily felt a sudden compulsion to seize the moment, to risk as he had.

"Her name is Helen," she said into the dark stillness, and then turned to look at him. She hadn't spoken the name aloud since June.

He was looking at her, questioning, perhaps hopeful.

"My Elliot," she added. "Her name is Helen."

Slowly, Roger's mustache turned up at the edges and he smiled, nodding. "I thought that might be the case," he said, happily.

As if finally freed to speak about Helen, Lily poured a stream of half-sentences and phrases which sketched the emotional bond they had and how it had gone wrong when she learned she was not going to return. She didn't realize that they were clasping hands hard until the cab pulled up at her home.

"Well," Roger said, giving her hands a squeeze as he let go.

Lily was ashamed. "I'm sorry to have unloaded all of that on you!"

"No, no," he assured her. "I'm glad to know it. I had a feeling last Christmas that we were alike. It's awfully nice to be able to share our feelings with a friend who understands."

Lily suddenly felt like weeping, and could only nod in agreement, her lips pursed.

"I have two things in mind to say before I leave you at your door," he was saying. "First, would you join me in another evening at the theater next week?"

Lily smiled gratefully. "Yes, I certainly will, my friend!"

He nodded firmly. "Good, then. Second, you may not want advice, but I regret very much not communicating my state of mind, my feelings, to Elliot, after I was called home. I don't know that it would have made a difference in the last analysis but, surely, he must have been pained to have been entirely abandoned. I thought only of my own grief. So, if I were you, I would write to her, and be honest and explain yourself and avoid being too protective of your feelings."

Lily surrendered now to tears that silently coursed down her cheeks.

"I didn't mean for you to—" he broke off and pulled from his jacket a crisp and perfectly ironed handkerchief, offering it to her.

After she blotted her cheeks, Lily shook her head. "You didn't, and please don't be worried. It's just that talking about Helen has been such a relief. And I know I should write to her, and just haven't found the words to say. Your advice is good, and needed."

ONCE again, Lily sat in the plush red seats of the Star Theater beside Roger. This was their fourth Saturday evening in a row at the theater. After their frank conversation that first night at the Iroquois, their friendship flowered in an atmosphere of ease, free of concerns over courtship or the possibility of marriage. Lily's mother had her hopes up, and no one could blame her; Lily had never spent any time voluntarily in the company of a young man. But Lily pretended to ignore her mother's probings.

This evening at the theater, however, was fraught with emotion for Lily. Two weeks previous, Roger had enthused about Maude Adams, who was stopping at Buffalo during a tour reprising her first big hit, *The Little Minister*. As he described her captivating acting abilities, Lily felt panic rising at the thought of watching that play again with its passionate memories of Helen in her brother's dress suit. Roger, ever observant, queried her about her distress. Lily mentioned that a dramatic club at Vassar had performed the play a year ago. Roger gave her a questioning face.

Lily sighed. "Helen played the *little minister.*"

Roger replied with a long, "Ooooh," and nodded. "I hope you'll give Maude Adams a chance to charm you," he said encouragingly.

Maude Adams did charm Lily, along with everyone else in the theater. The play had immersed Lily deeply into her state of mind a year ago, when she was yet unaware of her growing love for Helen. She saw scenes of their interactions as if from an unseen perch. Perhaps it was Maude Adams' spell, but emotions she had pushed out of her consciousness filled her now and overflowed by the end of the play. Her tears mingled with the thundering applause.

That night, alone in the sleeping house, she sat in the pool of light from her student lamp at the table in her room and began a letter to Helen. The salutation nearly stopped her. She tried "Dearest Helen," then crossed it out and wrote, "Dear Helen," and then simply, "Helen." None was what she wanted. She took out a fresh sheet of stationery and began again.

"Good Evening Helen,

"I have just returned from the theater where I saw Miss Maude Adams play Lady Babbie in *The Little Minister*. She was quite wonderful in her role but not quite as good to my mind as Belle was just a short year ago. You may tell her I said so.

"I thought of you as Mr. Dishart, so exquisite in Harry's dress suit. You took my breath away, dear. Afterward, I watched you and Belle thronged with adoring girls and could not join them. I wanted to be more to you than one of the crowd.

"You are in my thoughts daily, Helen. My dream is for us to be reunited so that we may talk again of a shared future. My feelings have not changed.

"Will you reply and tell me that you think of me, too?

"Ever your—"

"Lily"

She saw that it was just what she intended. As Roger had urged, she did not try to be too protective of her feelings. Quickly, before she could have second thoughts, she enveloped and addressed the letter. Now she would be sure to mail it. She rose to go to bed and placed her hand over the envelope. She was thinking, *Please answer, my beloved.*

Thanksgiving was approaching and with it came a swirl of emotions. Mama Kepler asked Lily to invite Roger to the Kepler Thanksgiving dinner, an invitation not made out of sympathy for a man she assumed to be bereft of other offers. Lily knew that her mother was casting a line to him in hopes of drawing him into the family, with more meaningful interweavings to come. She communicated the invitation and was relieved when he chuckled in response. They had both discussed her mother's hopes for Lily's future matrimony and he was expecting such an overture. Still, he had accepted an invitation from another family who regularly asked him to dinners as an "extra man." Lily warned him that Christmas was next on the calendar and he would be invited again.

And Thanksgiving dinner found her gazing at the cranberry jelly on the table while the family, now expanded by Albert and Gertrude's infant son and Mae, now visibly pregnant, chattered noisily amid the passing of aromatic dishes. She was transported to the dish of cranberry jelly on the McIntyre's Thanksgiving table a year ago and with that came the treasure house of memories of her time with Helen at Glens Falls.

She had not yet received a reply to her note from Helen and she repeatedly forced the silence out of her mind. Perhaps as a compensation, she found something to concentrate upon. Her days in Miss Lapey's classroom exposed her to the reading materials the third-grade children used. She thought them dull and repetitious and she could see that the children did, too. Ulbrich's had very little in the way of children's books and that inspired her to try a children's story.

In what would become, *The Frog Who Wore Red Suspenders*, Lily began to tell the tale of a young frog of unusual personality who decided one day to break with standard dress in his village on the shore of a large pond. Instead of the usual gray or green suspenders that all the other boy frogs wore, he chose bright red suspenders which made him visible from a long way off. It made him very happy. It also made him the object of disapproval and even ridicule, which was the villagers' way of trying to change his behavior so that he conformed to the way everyone else dressed. One or two villagers dared to speak up on his behalf and that led to strife among the ordinarily placid village.

Eventually, the frog realized that he had to leave the village, that there was no place for him there anymore. As he hopped away across the mud flats in his red suspenders, he had faith that another village on the pond might find his appearance pleasing. He was hopeful and whistled a happy tune.

Lily worked on the story until she had struck what seemed to her an entertaining and suspenseful tone, one that would catch the attention of the students. Then she mentioned to Miss Lapey one day after school that she would be happy to read a story to the class if permitted. After reading it, the teacher assented. The class enjoyed it and pleaded with Lily to tell what the frog found in the next village, if others were as mean to him as his own village, and that sent Lily back to the desk in her bedroom where she penned another chapter. And then another. The students were more than her audience, they tutored her in the kinds of plot and details that they longed for. Class lessons were created that allowed the students to sketch characters from the story and write new characters and plot twists. Their imaginations were stimulated and they willingly put pencil to paper. Miss Lapey said one day, shaking her head in pleased amazement, "Look what you have started!"

CHAPTER 33

There was snow for Christmas, wet, heavy lake snow that turned the streets slushy and dirtied the bottoms of ladies' skirts. The December days sped by for Lily, who divided her time between Ulbrich's which fortuitously increased her hours, her assistance for Louise Lapey at School 16, and the late-night writing of her story chapters.

Still, two days before Christmas she could no longer occupy her thoughts and the lack of response from Helen brought waves of sorrow and longing to the forefront. That night, she tucked herself onto her window seat and wound her Vassar muffler around her neck. She might have wished it a talisman that would transport her mind to a year ago when she received it from Helen. Instead, it served to muffle her sobs.

The next day was Christmas Eve. Lily worked at Ulbrich's until past supper time and her feet hurt as she climbed the steps to the Kepler home in the dark, resigned to a sharp comment by her mother. The days she worked late meant her parents ate alone in their dining room and her dinner had to be kept warm.

But then she saw it on the hall table and forgot her feet and the coming criticism. There was a postcard addressed to her. The handwriting was Helen's. There was no written message, only Lily's address. But the postcard communicated worlds as Helen must have known it would. The illustration was of a young boy, wearing ice skates. On his head was a knit skating cap with strings extending from the earflaps that ended in little fuzzy balls. His expression was one of delighted joy. To accentuate the season, glitter was glued to the card over its snowy background.

She became aware that her mother was speaking to her from the kitchen door. She looked up to hear that a plate was in the oven for her and that she would need to be ready to go to church by 8:30. Lily smiled at her mother's reproachful tone and thanked her. She felt bullet-proof.

At St. Peter's services that night, Lily held her little drawstring purse in her hands. It contained the postcard. Afterward, she pored over it at her desk, lightly running a finger over Helen's handwriting. No longer did she have to rely solely on her memories for sustenance. Here was proof that Helen was present in her life. *You are there.* She tucked it under her pillow when she went to bed. *You are there. My love.*

SHE awoke early Christmas morning and worked over in her mind how she might go to Glens Falls, where she knew Helen was this morning. The obstacles loomed. How to explain why she was going away? Mama Kepler would know that Lily had received no communication that might resemble an invitation. She considered leaving without her parents' permission, but instantly realized that her entire savings, after Christmas purchases, had dwindled to $3.63, not enough for even a one-way ticket to Albany. And, if by some miracle, she could leave with her parents' permission to visit Helen, what then? What would she say when the McIntyre door opened? What if she had misinterpreted the postcard's message and Helen had not meant to encourage her? Then, if she presented herself, might not Helen rebuff her? The prospect was so humiliating that she pulled the covers over her head.

The Keplers planned a midday holiday dinner to accommodate their married childrens' plans with their spouses' families. This was in keeping with their past traditions but Alfred and Will would be leaving soon after the meal, which pained Lily's mother. Alfred and Gertude's son, Henry, was four months old and Mama Kepler mentioned often that she did not see enough of the baby.

Roger was also invited and accepted the invitation with a charming note to Lily's parents. Lily had warned him of the hints and hopes that her mother had been making regards Roger, but he had smiled and reassured her that he was practiced in the ways of conspiring mothers of marriageable daughters. Part of the reason her savings were so depleted was that Lily had purchased Roger a handsome pair of cufflinks, gold vermeil with the stamped face of a woman done in the latest artistic style. She had searched a number of stores looking for something to match his sophisticated tastes and knew right away when she saw these that they were just the thing.

Mama, Papa, and Lily opened their gifts after breakfast; Lily thought it was a subdued exchange and realized how much liveliness Will had taken away with him when he married. She gazed at the tree, which she and Mama had decorated alone the day before, and remembered when Alfred was at home and there were five in the family on Christmas morning. And she had another thought, also, that she might not be at home a year from now. How quiet would it be for her parents then?

Will and Mae arrived first, bringing laughter and gifts. They were followed by

Alfred and Gertrude, who handed Henry to his grateful grandmother. While the group was busy greeting one another, the bell rang and it was Roger. Lily let him in; they greeted each other and Lily gave him a mock-grimace with a nod to the front room. He laughed and they joined the greater Kepler family. Introductions were exchanged all around. He made a fuss over Mama Kepler and the baby in her arms. She could hardly have smiled more broadly, whether because of little Henry or Roger was not apparent.

It was a happy dinner hour; Roger conversed easily with Lily's father and Alfred. Every time Mae caught Lily's eye across the table, she grinned broadly, eyebrows raised. Lily knew that Mae was also thinking of Roger as potential husband material for Lily. After dinner Mae took Lily's arm and pulled her aside.

"He is such a lovely man, and a gentleman, too!" she enthused.

"He is both," Lily replied nodding. "And my dearest *friend*."

Mae gave her a sly look. "And maybe something more to come."

Lily sighed and decided to be honest with Mae, as she had always been. "We will never be other than friends, Mae," she said quietly, leaning in. "Both of us agreed on that when we first became acquainted."

Mae wrinkled her brow. Lily knew that nowhere in Mae's universe lived people like Lily and Roger. But then Mae surprised her.

"People marry for friendship all the time," she said mildly. "It makes things easier."

Will came into to the room then, leaving Lily to wonder if she meant what she seemed to say.

After the cake and pies, Lily and Roger left the table and sat in the front parlor with the tree. Lily plucked a small wrapped box from within the branches and turned to see Roger pull a package from a small table. In the clamor of the crowd earlier, she had not noticed that he had placed it there. He was delighted with the cufflinks and thought them just right, and much needed, too, he avowed. Lily opened her package to find three volumes of Emily Dickinson's poetry, each beautifully bound with a gold-embossed sketch of the Indian Pipe plant on the cover. She was speechless for a minute; he had come to know her so well and was truly her comfort and compatriot in this city.

Roger waited and then asked, concerned, "Do you already have these?"

"Oh, no," she quickly replied. "I don't. They are so beautiful," she added, running her fingers over the Indian Pipe.

Then she gave him a sidelong look and said with suspicion, "You didn't order these from Ulbrich's, did you?"

He laughed and agreed that he had not patronized her workplace, but only to keep the secret. They had a good laugh.

In the private moment they shared, Lily brought out the postcard from Helen that she earlier secreted to show him. She was happy to say that this was Helen's response to her letter and explained the meaning of the skating and the hat, so like the one she had made for Helen last Christmas. Roger was happy but gently asked if Helen had not included a note in addition. Lily agreed that a note would have been ideal but that this was a meaningful message, and Roger agreed.

Then he had news to share that would be momentous in more lives than his.

"After the new year, I am taking on a valet," he said. "That is, I have become acquainted with a young man whom I will be able to assist by providing employment for him," he added, sounding very stilted and unlike his usual self.

Lily leaned to get his attention and, when his eyes met hers, he was blushing, a smile growing under his mustache. "Roger," she said declaratively.

He laughed shyly. "Well, you have guessed there is more to my news!"

"What is his name?" she inquired.

"Well, he wants to be called *Mike*. He doesn't tell people his Sicilian name, wants to be American."

Lily teased the story from Roger that he had met Mike at his club where Mike was working as a masseuse. It was clear by Roger's almost-boyish enthusiasm that he was smitten with Mike. Soon other family members joined them but not until Roger had invited Lily to dinner at his home after the new year to meet Mike.

THE week between Christmas and the New Year was crowded with engagements for Lily. She visited Eva with a warm shawl, a present suggested by her mother. Lily had not been visiting Eva with much regularity in the past couple of months. Her life had become filled with theater evenings with Roger, working at Ulbrich's, writing her little stories and assisting Louise Lapey at School 16. She felt guilty to share these with Eva who was becoming more confined to her furnished townhouse by her pregnancy and an apparent lack of money. And Lily was coming to understand that being married to Frank Marshall was no bed of roses for Eva. She spent much of her time nearby with her Aunt during the day and stayed for dinner when she knew Frank would be at his club until late.

Eva received Lily with desperate joy, clutching her tightly in the dim hallway of the townhouse. They repaired to the drawing room where Eva had laid out a modest spread for tea, with a sweet date bread and bread-and-butter sandwiches.

Lily knew right away why her mother had suggested that she purchase a warm shawl for Eva. The place was chilly, and Eva wore a thick cardigan and fingerless gloves. She remarked on the temperature in what she hoped was an offhand way.

"Oh, yes, it is positively frigid," Eva agreed, "but my father sent me money for Christmas and I have paid the coal man with part of it, so tomorrow there will be a delivery."

Lily was speechless, which Eva noticed.

"You're going to worry, I can see that, and you mustn't," she said with some forced cheerfulness. "Frank doesn't bring much money home, and so we are a little behind in our bills. I, we, eat so often at Aunt and Uncle's that our food bill is low. But the coal man wouldn't extend more credit and so I've had to economize on heat and use most of what we have for the kitchen stove. But all will be well tomorrow!"

Lily did not question further about Frank and the money. She wondered how often she ate at her aunt and uncle's by herself. Her mother had commented that she thought Eva was alone much of the time and that her husband was at fault in this and other things.

Eva patted her stomach and said she was feeling very well and talking with a few of their classmates who had already given birth and shared their experiences. Lily felt separated from Eva and her fellow mothers; she had nothing to contribute.

"Mama Kepler says you and Roger Hudson are thick as thieves," Eva commented suggestively. "I think it's wonderful, don't you?"

Lily tried to dissuade Eva from thinking she was headed for the altar, but it was no use. She let Eva warm to the topic and only spoke up when Eva suggested that she and Frank and Lily and Roger go out on the town together. She replied that it would not likely happen. Lily knew from Roger's sparse references to "your friend Eva's husband" that he had no use for Frank Marshall. He had not provided details as to why.

Another engagement Lily had during that week was an invitation to tea at Louise Lapey's home. She went to an old brick house on Ellicott Street and was greeted warmly by Louise who ushered her into a small parlor with old-fashioned upholstered rosewood chairs. As they sat and made small talk, a tall woman entered with a large tea tray that was handsomely laid with matching china and an array of sweets and sandwiches.

"Thank you, Emma," Louise said kindly to the woman, who gave Lily a small smile and withdrew.

As she poured tea, Louise commented, "Emma is not a servant, but Ida's sister. She's a better cook than we are and we gratefully rely on her in that regard."

Lily accepted the cup of tea, wondering who Ida might be. She needn't have wondered long, because Louise called, "We're having tea right now, dear. Will you be joining us?"

From an adjoining room came, "Coming," and that was followed by the entrance of Ida Bender, Superintendent of Primary Grades. Lily felt the urge to stand but suppressed it.

Ida came directly to Lily's chair and held out her hand. "Thank you for coming, Lily!" she said heartily.

Lily said the invitation was most kind and then could think of nothing else to say. The germ of an understanding about this household was trying to develop and she had to push it aside in order to focus on the conversation.

They ate and conversed on a number of subjects which Lily enjoyed very much. And then Louise introduced the topic of Lily's stories about the frog who wore red suspenders.

"I am hoping that you will retroactively approve what I did with your stories," she began contritely. "When you lent them to me for approval, I shared them with Ida."

"Who liked them immensely!" Ida added.

"Oh," Lily could only reply. "I don't mind, but I wouldn't have thought they were worth the attention of anyone not ten years old."

"As it happens, stories written for ten-year-olds are exactly what I am looking for," Ida said. "I am writing a textbook for new readers. It will be a primer. I have planned it out with the assistance of Lou here and other teachers. And now I must insert simple stories from which reading lessons in vocabulary and grammar can be extracted."

"I see," Lily said, beginning to understand where Ida was headed.

"Yes, I think you do," the latter replied. "I need at least ten very small stories about topics that appeal to children. Each story will require use of certain vocabularies which I can supply. I will pay $2 for each story I can use. Do you think you would be interested in this?"

Lily's hand flew to her mouth involuntarily. Someone would pay her for stories, which shocked her senseless. And the money; ten stories would be $20, money that would go a long way towards her secret plan to travel to Helen.

"Yes," Lily gasped.

Ida retrieved a small sheaf of papers from what was apparently her office and went over them with Lily. She gave Lily a page with the vocabulary she wished to have used in one story. They agreed that Lily would prepare a draft and they would review and revise it as a template for her to refer to in the subsequent stories.

When Lily left, her feet didn't touch the ground, she would later say. She found two women who shared a home and she was brimming with the joy of discovery. The piece of paper she carried was undeniable proof that her writing was good enough to be useful. She felt more confident than she had in a year.

The Hudson home was almost the last house used as a residence on the lower end of Delaware Avenue. Homes on either side and across the street had been converted to rooming houses, renovated for business uses or demolished and replaced by modern business structures. It was what Lily's generation called *old-fashioned*, with a mansard roof and slender pillars supporting a front porch that no one would want to use these days. Close to its neighbors on the narrow city lot, and close to the street as homes were fifty years ago, Lily knew it would be dim inside. The house was also close to Frank and Eva's townhouse around the corner on West Mohawk.

She put these fleeting observations aside as she rang the bell. The door was opened by Roger's housekeeper, Mrs. Haley. Short and stout, she was hearty in her greeting and expecting Roger's dinner guest. Lily, who had cut her morning short at School 16 in order to be on time, found herself early. She followed Mrs. Haley into her kitchen and was quickly engaged in easy conversation by the maternal woman. Lily suspected that Roger rarely had guests to dinner. Mrs. Haley had a number of pots going at once and it seemed there was to be a full spread. While they waited, she chatted about the thirty-four years she had been housekeeper for the Hudson family. Now she worked mornings because there was only the bachelor to look after.

Roger blew in a few minutes later and soon appeared a young man dressed in a white shirt with collar and tie. This was Mike, whose smile could have lit any dark room. His English was heavily accented and his words were often punctuated with a grin, or a nod of his head, or short laugh. He was handsome, of medium height and muscular, with very dark hair, brown eyes, and the longest eyelashes Lily had ever seen.

As they sat before Mrs. Haley's roast beef, mashed potatoes and gravy, Lily lost track of the other accompaniments because she was observing the nonverbal interactions between her dearest friend and his new lover. Mike was beamish when he looked at Roger; Roger was almost giddy with happiness. She had never seen him like this and smiled throughout the meal watching their infectious joy.

Roger explained that Mike was taking classes in English and would be attending the Central High School when his English improved. Mike was also continuing to work at the Club as a masseuse, in addition to earning a salary as Roger's valet because his family was relying on his wages. He added that he was tutoring Mike evenings.

For his part of the conversation, Mike told Lily that she was beautiful and her hair was also beautiful, causing both Roger and Lily to burst into laughter which served to confound Mike who had to be reassured that he had not misspoken. Lily thought him the sweetest, most naïve seventeen-year-old young man she had ever met.

And, when she observed them openly gaze into each other's eyes, either trusting Lily to be accepting of this show of affection or oblivious to her presence, she knew that her relationship with Roger would be changing

Later that night, on her window seat wrapped in her quilt, she felt sorrowful that she would undoubtedly be seeing her friend less often, and guilty for those feelings because Roger deserved to enjoy the kind of happiness that she had known with

Helen. She only wished that she could have her own happiness back. If she could not have Helen in the present, she had been solaced by being able to share anecdotes from their time together with Roger. Now, with Roger spending evenings with Mike, she would once again be silent, and longing to be where Helen was.

THE third week in January was the most bitter weather the city had experienced that winter. A frigid wind blew off the lake through the streets, driving everyone indoors. When the phone rang Sunday morning at the Kepler house before the family left for church, it carried tragic news.

Uncle Walter had died suddenly in the night. Eva was nearly hysterical on the phone and it took some time for Mama Kepler to discern who had died. She gave the phone to Lily, who eventually understood that she should go to Eva.

When she arrived, Eva fell into her arms, loosing whatever restraints she might have had on her grief. Lily ascertained that Frank was asleep, apparently oblivious to his wife's sobs. She sat with Eva for a time, then went to the kitchen and built a fire in the new stove that Uncle Walter had insisted the landlord provide. She found some bread and jam and made tea. Eva seemed calmer with Lily's presence and had something to eat.

Eva explained that she had gone over to the Bond house when news came of her uncle, but Aunt Martha had eventually sent her home because Eva's agitation was too much to deal with in addition to her own shock. Lily sighed and put an arm around Eva in sympathy. The young woman who, a short year ago, had been queen of everyone was now almost unwanted by those she had depended on. Lily knew that part of Eva's heartbreak was because she had lost a stalwart supporter in Uncle Walter who had helped Eva stay steady in the face of Frank's increasing unreliability.

Eva's father arrived before sundown that day. He assisted his still-stunned sister-in-law with funeral arrangements. Calvary Presbyterian, the scene of Eva's festive wedding just five months ago, now was decorated with crepe for a funeral. Walter Bond had been respected and the attendance at his funeral was appropriately large. The Keplers attended. Frank also attended but looked blank and inattentive to his wife or anyone else.

Later, Eva took Lily aside as the latter prepared to leave the funeral buffet and told her that her father had given her an open invitation to move to Canandaigua if things became too difficult at home. She added that he had given her money with a warning not to share it with her husband. Lily saw that Eva's father, an outsider, had evaluated the situation with a clarity those close to Eva had not.

As daily routines returned, a second and larger blow struck Eva's life. Aunt Martha announced that she was moving to Cleveland to live with her sister, also a widow. She was gone before the end of February, sending Eva into a trough of despair. Lily and her mother, in rare agreement, determined that they needed to help the young wife who would give birth in four short months. Eva related that her aunt's parting words reminded her that it was her duty to live as a wife to Frank "for better or worse."

Lily alternated with her mother in bringing food to Frank and Eva; the latter was now confined most of the time to the townhouse because the sidewalks were icy and a danger to her. Lily sat with her and listened mostly. Where her mother's role was more supervisory, making sure Eva was managing household tasks, Lily was the shoulder to cry on, less officious and judgmental.

"Last year, when we were courting," Eva whined once, "Frank was so fine. He couldn't be nice enough or thoughtful enough."

Lily doubted that memory was entirely accurate when compared to her own, but she replied, "New relationships are always perfect, dear. It's what comes after that tests us, I think." She hadn't realized that until she said it. Maybe she was being tested, as well.

Chapter 34

Lily's busy schedule at Ulbrich's, School 16, and attending Eva left her little time to brood about Helen. She also worked late into the evening on the little stories for Ida Bender. That had proved to be much more challenging than she had anticipated because Ida was a severe critic and knew what she wanted for the textbook. After many early revisions, Lily caught on to the formula and was making good progress with the remaining stories. She was also relieved to find that she and Roger still had time together. Almost weekly, she had midday dinner at his house, usually without Mike present. Mrs. Haley was obviously fond of Lily and enjoyed making what she called "real meals" for her bachelor and his lady friend.

And then the focus turned to babies. Mae gave birth the first week in April just as winter began to show signs of waning. She and Will named their first child Mary Louise; "Louisa" was Mama Kepler's middle name. That gesture, along with Mae's invitation to visit in those first weeks, began to slowly change Mama Kepler's heart about Will's wife. Mae gave Lily a sly smile as they watched Grandma Kepler coo over the baby she held in her arms.

Eva's body had taken on proportions that at times made Lily cringe. She was nearly as wide around as she was tall. It gave Lily worries about how such a small woman could give birth to what surely must be an enormous infant and still live. Vivid memories of Daisy at just this stage in her pregnancy, her luminous personality with its touch of deviltry, rose up whenever she watched Eva struggle to get up from a chair.

Late one evening as the Kepler house was preparing to sleep, the phone rang. Lily started, paused two heartbeats and then flew down the stairs to stop its jangling. As she picked up the receiver, she caught a glimpse of her mother at the top of the stairs looking down at her.

It was Roger, in a strained voice she had never heard from him. He was saying that Eva was in their front hall in her nightdress, hysterical. Frank apparently had struck her and, terrified of further violence, she had run around the corner to his house. Would Lily come to help?

She instantly said that she would and Roger said he would send a cab. As she ascended the stairs, she told her mother what had transpired.

"That does not surprise me in the least," Mama Kepler spat. "He's a drunkard and a failure as a husband!"

They agreed on that and Lily went to dress hastily. As she put on her coat and gloves, her mother called down, "Bring her here." Lily nodded.

The scene at Roger's house was relatively calm. Eva sat clutching a blanket to warm her and hide her nightdress, everyone attending to modesty. Mike stood nervously, Roger patiently; he was visibly relieved to see Lily. Eva had a bright red mark on one side of her face where she said Frank struck her.

Lily announced that she would take Eva to the Kepler home after they stopped first at her townhouse to retrieve a coat and proper shoes to replace the slippers she was wearing. Roger insisted on accompanying them for their safety. Leaving Mike behind, the three of them crowded into the cab and rode around the corner to the Marshall home. While Lily and Eva went upstairs to collect a few things, Roger sought out Frank who was in the parlor. Lily had never heard Roger raise his voice nor imagined a situation that would provoke him to do so, but when they both heard the loud voices from downstairs, Lily stopped Eva from packing and urged her downstairs and out of the house.

They waited in the cab until Roger emerged. He was still fuming and related in short bursts that he had severely upbraided Frank and nearly knocked him down for his violence against his wife, but had restrained himself. Lily clasped his arm and thanked him warmly. They all parted in the clammy darkness, Roger to his house and the cab out to Humboldt Parkway.

With an arm around Eva who, despite her belly, seemed so small that night, Lily felt a relief that surprised her. Her visits to Eva had been fraught with worry about how Eva would manage the last days of her pregnancy and then childbirth. She didn't even have a telephone to call for help. And now she would be safe in the care of Mama Kepler and have her baby in peace surrounded by medical attendants. Sharing her bedroom with Eva seemed the most natural thing and Lily didn't mind that idea a bit. All would be well now.

Two days later, Lily learned how wrong she had been when the phone rang again, this time at 6:30 in the morning. Mama Kepler, an early riser, answered it and went up to Lily's room.

"There's a Mrs. Healy or some such for you," she said quietly so as not to wake Eva.

Lily sprang out of bed and hurried downstairs without stopping to put on slippers or robe. She knew there was no good reason for Mrs. Haley to telephone at this hour.

"Miss Kepler, oh Miss Kepler," she began in a strangled voice, "something terrible has happened. Mike killed a man who broke in with a pistol. There's blood all over the front hall rug. It was a shock to the heart when I came in this morning."

Lily interrupted her. "Who was the man, Mrs. Haley?" she demanded.

"Young Mr. Hudson," as she always called Roger, "has gone to the police headquarters so I can't ask him to repeat it. It's not a name I've heard before."

But Lily had an idea of the identity of the man with the pistol. She closed her eyes. "Was it possibly *Frank Marshall*?"

"That's the name," Mrs. Haley said immediately. "I don't understand why he would –"

Lily cut her off again. "And you are certain that he's dead?"

"Oh, yes, that's what young Mr. Hudson told me. He said the man pointed the pistol at him and Mike leaped at the man and stabbed him in the neck. He was dead right away." She paused. "Can you imagine it? Right here in this respectable old home, where young Mr. Hudson's parents entertained the best people in the old days."

Lily wasn't listening. She was dividing her concentration between Eva and Roger. She needed to help both. She ascertained that Roger was expected back home in a while and told Mrs. Haley that she would be coming over directly.

Mama Kepler had been standing a few feet away. Her hand was over her mouth and it was clear that she had assembled the story from listening to Lily's end of the conversation. They stared at each other for a minute, letting the news register.

"Frank is *dead*?" Mama Kepler asked quietly.

Lily nodded. "He went to Roger's with a pistol and Roger's valet killed him." She added, "We have to tell her," intending that it be both of them together. Lily was fearful of breaking that news to Eva.

They both looked toward the stairs and then ascended to Lily's room where they found Eva sitting up, as if waiting for them.

Reading their faces, she said without emotion, "It's Frank, isn't it?"

Lily nodded.

"He's dead, isn't he?" she said matter-of-factly, nodding. "I've been thinking all winter that he would be killed somehow out on the streets in the night, drunk. Wander onto trolley tracks, or miss a step and fall down stairs onto a sidewalk."

She looked at the two messengers who said nothing. "So? What was it?"

Lily swallowed and said in a sympathetic tone, "He went to Roger's with a pistol. Roger's valet killed him."

They were silent. Then Eva said, "Frank was looking for me, was that it?"

There was no reply.

"What a stupid man! Why would he think I would still be there?" Then she nodded. "If he was sober, he would know I'm with you."

Lily slowly moved to assemble her clothing preparatory to going to Roger's home. That seemed to break a spell that had been over all of them.

"My baby is fatherless," Eva whimpered, resting her hands on her belly. Her lip began to tremble. "No father at all."

And then she began to cry. Mama Kepler sat beside her on the bed and took the new widow in her arms. Lily slipped away to dress.

MRS. Haley had indeed been correct about the front hall rug. An enormous brown stain, still reeking damply of iron, covered the rug and a bit of the floor around it. Lily felt queasy tiptoeing around it. She had never experienced any scene of violence or death. The fact that she knew the person whose blood darkened Roger's hall made it more sickening.

Mrs. Haley, who had already adjusted to it, guided Lily to the kitchen and sat her down at the table.

"Now," she said, speaking as a woman who believed mundane details were the antidote to the unbearable, "have you had your breakfast? No, of course you haven't. So, here's a cup of coffee. Young Mr. Hudson always has coffee in the morning. And I've got biscuits coming in a tick. You'll have some of those."

Lily didn't think she could eat anything, but dutifully had some coffee.

"Mike has been arrested then?" She had carried the question all the way across town.

"Oh, yes, he's in the lockup," Mrs. Haley assured her. "The police were called right after it happened."

"Poor Mike," Lily said quietly, recalling his open friendliness. "Poor *Roger*," she added, certain of the distress he would be feeling.

"It's a bad business, for certain," Mrs. Haley agreed, taking a seat at the table with her own cup of coffee. She worried about the carpet, getting it clean, wanting to remove the visible signs of the tragedy.

Lily said, "There's no cleaning it. I'll help you roll it up and throw it out. My family's store will send another rug today."

"Oh," was the reply. They rolled up the carpet together and carried it out to the trash can. Lily felt useful and in control until she saw the reddish smudges on the palms of her hands. Holding her hands in front of her, she went to the kitchen sink and scrubbed her hands again and again with soap.

Mrs. Haley's biscuits came out of the oven when Roger returned. Lily went into the hall and met his exhausted look with her own empathetic face. She stepped to him and clasped him by the arms without speaking. They embraced for the first time since they had known one another. She felt his tension.

"I'm so worried about him," he said. She nodded.

They sat at the kitchen table instead of the dining room, as if the situation required everyone to huddle close in a warm, bright room. Roger had coffee and ate two biscuits, perhaps without being aware of it. He described to Lily what had transpired around midnight the night before.

He had gone up to bed and was awakened by the bell and banging on the door, accompanied by shouts. He and Mike had gone down and realized that Frank Marshall was at the door. Frank would not be dissuaded from going away and loudly threatened to break all the windows and doors in the house if he were not admitted. So, Mike opened the door and Frank lurched into the hall. It was only then they realized that he had a pistol in his hand.

Frank started demanding that Roger produce his wife, something Roger insisted that he could not do because she was not there. Frank then demanded to know where she was, which Roger would not say. At that point Frank raised the pistol toward Roger and demanded to know where his wife was.

Lily listened, rapt. Roger started shaking his head in wonderment. "I was staring into the barrel of the pistol and suddenly Mike was flying – I mean, flying in the air – across the hall and onto Frank. They both fell to the floor."

He hesitated. "I must have thought we would take the pistol away from Frank and send him on his way. And then I saw the blood coming out of Frank's neck. So much blood. Mike was covered with it when he got up. That's when I saw the small knife in his hand. I didn't know he owned a knife. While we waited for the police to come, I asked him about it and he said everybody in his neighborhood has a knife. 'Because you never know.' That's the way he said it. 'Because you never know.'" His voice was almost a whisper now.

Lily broke Roger's trance. "The police will understand that Mike acted in self-defense, won't they?"

Roger looked at her as if he saw her for the first time that morning. He blinked. "Self-defense. Yes. It should be a straightforward case. But," he said gathering energy, "I need to contact a colleague who is a criminal attorney. I can't defend Mike myself. Real estate is my area."

Then he stood. "What time is it? I have to locate a judge who will grant bail to Mike so I can bring him home. It's Saturday and normally there are no hearings until Monday."

He looked at Lily with eyes that were more anxious than she had ever seen in anyone. "He cannot remain in the city jail until Monday. *Cannot*, Lily! He is too young, too cocky, he's a foreigner. You have no idea," and excused himself without finishing the sentence.

Later, before she left Roger's, she phoned the store and spoke to Will. He was very surprised to get her request for a rug but took the dimensions she specified and agreed to make sure it was delivered before the afternoon, when Mrs. Haley would leave for the day. Then she walked most of the way home, letting the events of the morning sink in.

During church services the next day Lily became increasingly worried about Mike being in jail and the things Roger hinted about the conditions there. After Sunday dinner, she telephoned his house. There was no answer. Mrs. Haley would not be there, of course, but that Roger did not answer only increased her sense of foreboding. She phoned once more later in the afternoon, with the same result.

That night she was oblivious to Eva's snoring because she was awake much of the night. She wanted to make sure to rise when she knew Mrs. Haley would be at the Hudson house so that she could find out if her anxiety was unfounded. She checked the clock repeatedly until she decided in the early morning to tiptoe downstairs in her nightgown and call.

Mrs. Haley sounded as worried as Lily felt. Roger had stopped at the house minutes ago only to change his clothes, she said. Mike was in the General hospital since Sunday morning when the guards had discovered him beaten unconscious. Lily listened through tears as Mrs. Haley said that Mike's condition was very serious and the doctors didn't know if he would come to.

Realizing that she was silently sobbing into the phone, Lily managed to implore Mrs. Haley to phone her if there was any change or if Roger came home while she was there. The housekeeper, whose sorrowful voice hinted that she had endured such things in her life, gave her words of encouragement, implored her to pray to the Holy Mother for Mike, and promised to call with news.

Lily didn't know what she could do to help. She sat on the floor beside the phone and cried as quietly as she was able. Roger had not been able to get Mike out on bail. Mike had suffered at the hands of criminals he was locked up with. He was so handsome, almost beautiful. She could see his smile, so easy and open to all the wonders of his America. She realized that she was helpless to make any difference right now.

After her shift at Ulbrich's, she walked down to Franklin Street and rang the bell at the Hudson house. There was no one at home; Mrs. Haley had left hours before.

After they went to bed, Eva nagged Lily to tell her what was bothering her. Lily left nothing out in telling about Roger and Mike, needing Eva to understand the pain Roger was surely feeling this evening. To her credit, Eva raised her eyebrows and said, "Oh," reflecting only modest surprise. Then she lay her head on Lily's shoulder and patted her arm to comfort her. Lily wept again and eventually fell into an exhausted sleep.

Mrs. Haley called around noon the next day, just before Lily was to leave for Ulbrich's. Lily knew from the voice on the other end of the line that what would come next was going to be the worst. Mike had died early in the morning, never having regained consciousness. Lily pressed her hand over her mouth to keep from crying out. Finally, she asked if Roger was at home. He was and wouldn't take any food, Mrs. Haley emphasized.

Lily telephoned Ulbrich's to say she would not be in and went directly to Roger's house. She had no idea if he wanted to see anyone but she understood that no one else knew the magnitude of his loss and she had to be there.

Odd things attracted her attention that day. She observed that the crocuses were blooming beside the front steps of the Hudson house as they had when Roger's father died. The replacement carpet she had ordered for the front hall was large enough to cover the blood stain on the floor, but she had the fleeting thought that the colors in the pattern were brighter than she would have chosen. Mrs. Haley was still there, shocking Lily with an embrace when she entered the home. All was silent, even talkative Mrs. Haley. The housekeeper motioned to a room on the left and Lily understood that she would find her friend there.

It was the home's library, not a large room, dimly lit without the lamp on. Roger sat behind a large desk piled with folios tied with string. She stopped two steps into the room which was as silent as the rest of the house. What could she possibly say to the unshaven man slumped in a chair that at this moment made him look small? His collarless shirt was unbuttoned at the neck. It seemed an eternity before he raised his eyes to look at Lily.

The pain that emanated from them bored into her and tears streamed down her face.

"Roger," she finally said in a faint voice.

"Thank you for coming," he replied hoarsely.

Encouraged, she asked, "How may I help?"

Roger pursed his lips and shook his head. "No one can help."

He looked down at the book before him, wiping his hand across the cover. Lily saw that it was a school book about American history. He must have used it for Mike's evening tutoring lessons.

And then he looked up, focused. "There is something you could do for me. It is a great favor to ask."

"Anything, my friend!" Lily replied instantly.

Roger held up an envelope. "I have some cash for the family, Mike's wages and money to help with the funeral expenses. I want to get it to them."

"I would be happy to deliver it," Lily emphasized, grateful to be able to do something.

He shook his head. "I never met his family, you see. But I know that they attend St. Antony of Padua church on Court Street. Mike mentioned a Father Casassa who speaks English. He could see that the family receives this."

Lily didn't hesitate. "I'll take it there right away."

Roger nodded vaguely. "That would be so – kind – of you."

She stepped closer to the desk to accept the envelope. The family name and the priest's name were written on the outside.

"Would you like me to come back and sit with you?" she asked softly.

Roger frowned and shook his head slowly and firmly.

"No." And then he added with effort, "Thank you."

LILY took the streetcar to Niagara Square and walked the short distance to St. Anthony's church which rose behind the old Wilkeson mansion on the square. It seemed a fairly new church, a stolid brick and stone building with a steeple much shorter than her own St. Peter's. It may have been unassuming from the outside, but she caught her breath as she stepped inside. It was vibrant with decoration, gold trim, saints standing in sky-blue niches. She was reminded of Mike, whose full name, Miceli Tuttolomondo, was written on the envelope. His ebullient personality would have been right at home in this church.

There were only a few worshippers in the pews at this time of day, but she was fortunate to locate a man in priestly attire. He asked Lily to wait while he brought Father Casassa. Presently, a priest approached her with a firm step. He greeted her kindly but for the first time since she entered the Catholic church, Lily felt that she was a stranger. Perhaps it was his quizzical expression at seeing a young woman with an uncovered head in his church.

Lily explained the purpose of her visit and presented the envelope from Roger. The priest frowned in sorrow and related the hopes, now dashed forever, that Mike's family had invested in him. As she fought back tears, she accepted his thanks for the gift and his promise to visit the family at once to deliver it.

And then she was outdoors again, on a morning that showed bits of blue sky through the clouds, the same shade of blue as decorated the niches in the church. She decided not to walk to Ulbrich's and work part of her shift, and instead took the streetcar to Front Park. There she sat on a bench overlooking the Niagara River, now carrying ice floes from Lake Erie which in a couple of hours would tumble over Niagara Falls. The priest had asked if she knew the meaning of the family's name, *Tuttolomondo*. When she shook her head, he translated it as "all the world." Lily sat on the bench a long while, grieving for a young man who believed that he could achieve anything, *all the world*.

CHAPTER 35

There was no mourning to speak of at the Kepler home for Mike or Frank Marshall. Telegraphs were dispatched and soon Eva's father arrived from Canandaigua; one of Frank's brothers arrived to take charge of his brother's body. No one suggested that Frank be buried in Buffalo's Forest Lawn, or likely even thought of it; he would be returned home to Connecticut for burial in the family crypt. Frank had remained an outsider since the day he arrived and had left few lasting good impressions among those who were acquainted with him.

What Frank did leave were debts, of which Eva's father rapidly began making an account. Eva knew about the household bills but not about the ones at his club for membership fees and his bar tab. And once news of Frank's death appeared in the papers, several liquor stores and tailors promptly sent their bills. In all, Frank owed a considerable sum around town. Mr. Bond communicated this to the Marshall brother and the two had a long discussion about Frank's estate. Within two days, an agreement had been reached. The Marshall family would pay Frank's debts, carry his body home to Connecticut, and make no claims on the unborn child, aside from setting up a trust for it.

Eva readily approved the arrangement. Her father spent an afternoon alone with her in the Kepler parlor and invited her to come to Canandaigua to live with him. For the first time, he spoke at length about her mother and smiled when he said how much Eva resembled her. He agreed to her request that she stay in Buffalo until after she gave birth and was able to travel with the baby. She needed the Keplers now even more than she needed the protection of her father.

LILY was asleep when Eva cried out and clutched Lily's arm painfully. Eva's water had broken, which terrified her. Lily sprinted to get her mother who calmly took charge. Eva's baby was coming.

Twelve hours later, it was still coming. Eva refused to let Lily leave her side except for minutes at a time and Lily was exhausted and feeling not one bit well herself. The doctor had been summoned hours earlier but he left and suggested that the Keplers could have a nurse in to watch the mother if they wished. Mama Kepler immediately agreed, earning Lily's gratitude because the nurse had a calming effect on her, never mind her effect on the mother in labor.

At length, for Lily later could not say how many hours had passed, the critical hour arrived and the doctor returned. Eva was crying out in pain so close to Lily's ear that she felt it in her teeth. Lily's hand, which Eva had in a death grip, lost feeling entirely. But the worst for Lily was the fear that Eva would die in childbirth, as had Eva's mother and Daisy. The doctor didn't seem to be anxious enough or even concentrating hard enough on his task, as far as she could tell. She tried not to think only of herself, but the entire experience was the worst of her life.

The blood was the last straw. When the baby was entering this world, Lily saw red everywhere; at the same instant she saw Frank Marshall's blood spread over Roger's foyer and on her hands. She fainted away, off her chair and onto the floor. She barely heard the doctor curse in her direction.

Eva named her baby girl Sarah because she liked the nickname, "Sadie." The baby was perfectly formed with large brown eyes and dark hair. Eva came through the experience without complication. Tired as she was, Lily stayed in their room, sleeping on the window seat, to make sure that Eva was all right. Mama Kepler bustled about, more cheerful than Lily had seen her in a long time; so much to be done, bed linens to change, diapers to be sent out, advice to give Eva who hung on every word. After a few days, Lily's bedroom began to smell a bit like sour milk with Eva producing a lot of milk and leaking when Sadie was not hungry. And Eva was bouncing back to her old self, wholly absorbed in the tiny living thing she had birthed. Lily took the opportunity to turn back to her life and work, and plans.

LILY was in bed in Will's old room, once again hers for the duration. She was away from the new mother's schedule of round-the-clock feedings which had kept them both bleary-eyed. Eva was managing surprisingly well, with a cheerfulness enhanced by Mama Kepler's doting and encouragement. No one thought it unreasonable when Lily said she would withdraw to Will's room.

She was lying on her side, gazing at an envelope on the bedside table. It contained twenty dollars, payment from Ida Bender for the stories Lily had written for the reading primer. She had managed to save another twenty-four dollars from her work at Ulbrich's after gifts for Eva's baby had been subtracted. The train tickets to Glens Falls would amount to around five dollars.

Her plan was simple. She would write to Helen before graduation which was now two weeks away and ask if she might visit Helen upon her return home. If Helen agreed, she would make the trip without a moment's hesitation.

This had always been in the back of her mind, but she had been stymied about how to leave home. She knew her parents, her mother actually, would object to revisiting the Vassar friend scenario, and she had never been able to think of a persuasive reason to make the trip.

But Eva, the cause of so much of Lily's joy and sorrow regarding Vassar, had provided the reason. In a month, Eva would be able to travel to Canandaigua to live with her father. It was only reasonable that Lily accompany her, something Eva herself would surely wish, and stay with her for some time to see that she was settled.

Lily would accompany Eva to Canandaigua and continue to Glens Falls instead. She had no qualms about deceiving her parents, something she might have felt a year ago. But that was then, and Lily was a much different person now.

She wrote to Helen.

HELEN did not write back. Vassar graduation, the event in which Lily was to have carried the traditional daisy chain in the procession, came and went without a word. Belle had hastily scrawled a note to say that she sent her love and was leaving for Paris to stay with her parents, "possibly forever," as she put it. But no word about Helen, and no word from Helen.

Lily forced herself to wait ten days before writing again to Helen's home address in Glens Falls. It was now just two weeks before Eva would be traveling to Canandaigua. There was already an understanding that Lily would travel with Eva and stay awhile. She had carefully put it to Eva that it was not her intention to stay with Eva but to continue to Glens Falls to see Helen. Lily hesitated to bring it up, but Eva did not upbraid her or pout as she would have a year ago. She looked at Lily for a minute and said, "I am not surprised."

Every day brought no mail for Lily, and she began contemplating simply turning up at Helen's home. Each time she imagined it, she ended up embarrassed. What to say to the McIntyres' about her presence? What would Helen say, she who had not answered Lily's letters? If she coldly refused to speak to Lily, what then?

It was too awful to think about, and Lily tried to concentrate on other things. The school year had ended and she was free to work as many hours as Ulbrich's would schedule her. All she could think about was money because it was the only thing in her control.

Then a week before she and Eva were scheduled to leave for Canandaigua, Lily came home from a long day at the store and there was a postcard on the little table by the door. She instantly recognized a photo of Cooper's Cave in Glen's Falls and her heart leapt. Flipping it over, she did a double-take. In what was certainly Mrs. McIntyre's handwriting, was an address. "Helen McIntyre, College Settlement, 95 Rivington Street, New York, New York."

That night, ensconced in her little room, she held the post card and thought about how it came to be sent. Mrs. McIntyre wanted her to know where Helen was staying. Why? Was it a simple courtesy? She could have forwarded Lily's letter to Helen in New York without notifying Lily. Had she forwarded the letter to Helen and also notified Lily? She could not shake the feeling that there was a message from Helen's mother for her. She recalled how kind Mrs. McIntyre had been to her, that she had especially mentioned at Thanksgiving how improved Helen's spirits were, how she hoped that Lily and Helen would remain friends, and hoped Lily would visit again.

Regardless of what Mrs. McIntyre had meant, Lily knew where Helen was. They had visited the Rivington Street Settlement when they went to New York. She knew how to get there from the St. Denis Hotel. She knew how to get to the St. Denis from the New York Central Station. She had nearly fifty dollars, more than enough for the trip and a stay at the hotel.

She lay awake long into the night, working over a momentous decision that was forming in her mind.

LILY told Eva first because her complicity would be necessary. She chose a time when Sadie was asleep, Eva was rested, and Mama Kepler was out of the house. Eva was dumbstruck at Lily's declaration, blinking and then slowly shook her head.

"You can't do that," she said.

"But I can, you see," Lily said calmly. "I have money saved and I will get a job in New York after I arrive."

"What about your mother and father? They won't let you move away, certainly not to New York."

Lily took a breath. "I'm not going to tell them, Eva. It's not their decision any more. They decided I could attend Vassar and then they decided I could no longer attend Vassar. *I'm* deciding now."

Eva had to think about that for a minute. "Your parents will be brokenhearted," she said with surprising sensitivity.

Lily looked at her hands. "My father won't understand. But my mother will decide that I have ruined her plans to see me well married so that I might be a credit to her. She tried very hard with Roger, dropping heavy hints every time he was here, browbeating me to be nicer to him so he would find me a desirable potential wife. You of all people understand why none of her ideas could ever come to fruition."

Eva looked glum, then perked up. "At least I'm going away, so you're not leaving me."

Lily rolled her eyes. "The silver lining is yours, my dear!"

Then she became serious. "I only need two things from you, both vitally important. Are you listening?"

Eva was glancing over at her sleeping daughter. She nodded and gave Lily her attention.

"First, I want to ship my trunk with yours to Canandaigua. Hold my trunk until I tell you where to send it. It would certainly look odd if it were known that I am packing a trunk for a visit of a couple of weeks. So, we need to pack my trunk as if you needed to borrow it to move all of your things."

Eva tilted her head. "Well, I could use some of your trunk space. I have a lot of things."

"I'll help you pack your trunk so all of your things will fit," Lily replied firmly.

"What else?" Eva sighed.

"I need you to keep absolutely silent about my plan. Absolutely, Eva."

Eva nodded. "My lips are sealed."

TIME was short and Lily's list of good-byes awaited. She first called Louise Lapey and made arrangements to pay a visit.

School was out and Louise greeted her in a dress that looked so comfortable and loose that Lily suspected she was not wearing a corset. It made her smile. They sat at the rear of the house with the windows open, bringing in city air that was not fresh but a breeze just the same. Ida joined them and they made small talk until Lily made her announcement.

Louise and Ida glanced at one another.

"I guess this means I failed to persuade you to be a teacher," Louise said in jest.

"But you did encourage me to be a storyteller, and for that I thank you – and your students," Lily replied.

"Will you find work in New York?" Louise asked.

"Yes, of course. I will visit the employment agencies when I arrive and see about permanent residence in one of the women's hotels."

Louise looked at Ida, and both seemed to have the same idea.

"My publisher, American Book Company, is located in New York," Ida said. "Would you be interested in a reference from me on your behalf?"

"Would I!" Lily exclaimed to their mutual amusement.

Ida left the room to prepare the letter immediately. Louise lightly fanned herself and pushed a strand of gray hair back from her forehead. She was looking at Lily thoughtfully.

"Why New York? Not enough excitement in our Buffalo?"

Lily had to think of how much to say to these women who were clearly a couple just as she wished to be part of a couple.

"It's not that Buffalo lacks excitement," she began, "but what I want is to be happy. And I think I have a better chance of that in New York," she finished, looking frankly into Louise's eyes.

The woman smiled broadly, as if to telegraph that she understood. "And so, you must go."

Lily nodded. "I must."

Ida returned with an envelope. "Here you are, my strongly worded recommendation that my editor James Baldwin find you a position and avoid regret that he missed a prime opportunity in you."

They chuckled and Lily felt abashed at such kindness. Louise asked if she would continue to write about the frog who wore red suspenders and Lily agreed that her students had provided more story lines than she had been able to flesh out for them. She assured them she would continue.

As she left their home, Lily felt genuine regret that she would likely not ever see them again. How much they might have been able to share about their lives together and years of devotion, if women of their generation shared such information.

Two days later, after the trunks had been sent off to the train station for shipment to Canandaigua, Lily made a somber journey to Roger's office on Erie Street. She had not seen him since that day when he gave her the envelope for Mike's family. She had called and left messages with Mrs. Haley and sent him a note, without reply. Now she had to say good-bye to a friend with whom she had enjoyed an easy and warm friendship, she who understood his grief as probably no one else did.

The young male secretary stepped into Roger's office and returned shortly, holding the door open for her. The room, its walls lined with towering shelves of thick tomes, gave off a whiff of mustiness as if it were an attic. Leather chairs had indentations that might have been made by old Mr. Hudson's clients forty years or more in the past. It made her very sad to observe her friend, a man still young, captured within his father's sphere and likely destined to spend his working years this way.

Roger had risen from his seat behind a large desk, dark like the wall panels, and was coming around to greet her.

"What a very nice surprise," he was saying warmly, taking her hand and giving her a smile that was less than his past cheerfulness.

She gave him her best smile. "I am so glad to see you, but I hope I have not interrupted your work."

He assured her that she had not and invited her to sit. He took the chair beside her and turned it so they could talk companionably.

She took the bold step first. "How have you been, dear?"

Roger exhaled and looked off into the distance. "I am doing as well as expected." His thin smile was more a grimace. "This," he gestured with a nod at the office, "gives my days a routine, a discipline if you will. I put one foot in front of another and time passes."

She nodded and they sat for a minute in silence, the kind of comfortable silence that friends have.

"I am making some changes, however," he said, brightening. "I've taken on a lawyer, one much younger than my present septuagenarian partner, and plan to lighten my load. I should have done that long ago.

"And I've sold the old house," he continued to Lily's audible surprise. "Yes, I've been urged for years to sell it so it can be knocked down and a business building put up. The agents have been persistent and last week I bargained for the best price, which is quite generous for what will become a vacant lot."

"Where will you live?" Lily inquired, glad to see him engaged in changes.

"I've taken rooms at the Lenox," he replied archly. "It's very fashionable, you know, and I have a number of acquaintances who rave about it. I expect to move up there in a week or so."

"And Mrs. Haley?"

Roger smiled warmly. "She could have retired years ago, she's nearly 75. So, I've retired her, with a pension, and she has first choice of any of the furnishings she can cart away." He shook his head. "All that old Victorian stuff that my mother liked, I have no use for it. I'm going to be very up-to-date at the Lenox. And I hear the food is good, which I made sure to tell our Mrs. Haley so she won't worry about my withering away."

They chuckled over Mrs. Haley. And then Roger frowned and ran his finger around the decorative brass nails on the arm of his chair.

"I've, uh, set up a scholarship over at the Canisius High School," he said haltingly. "It's to pay the tuition of a promising young man whose family is new to this country."

Lily felt her eyes well up and pressed her lips to stop from breaking down.

After a minute, he said gruffly, "Well, what am I going to do with my money?"

She smiled in admiration and love for this good man.

"Well," she began, "I have news, as well." And she told him of her plan to move to New York permanently. She told him about the letter of reference that Ida Bender had written to smooth the way for her to find a position quickly.

He listened, smiling and nodding. He told her that this was the right thing for her to do. And then he looked closely into her face and asked, "Might this have anything to do with your friend Helen?"

She closed her eyes and heard him laugh. "Helen is in New York, working at a settlement house," she confessed. "She doesn't know that I am coming. And I don't know if she will be glad to see me or even see me at all. So."

"So," Roger echoed. He gazed at her, then nodded once. "You are a brave girl, Lily. I am proud to call you friend."

As they prepared to part, they embraced for the second time since they had met. He asked if she would write and she immediately said that she would. Who better would understand her journey?

CHAPTER 36

The next morning, a day before Lily and Eva and Sadie were to leave for Canandaigua, a messenger arrived with a letter for Lily. It was from Roger's law office. Lily tore open the envelope and saw at a glance some of the contents and immediately put it in her pocket. She needed to be alone and the house was a hubbub of packing and final preparations and the only place she could think of was the bench surrounding the big tree in the backyard. As she had done during the days of grief when she returned from Vassar more than a year ago, she secreted herself on the far side of the tree, unseen by anyone in the house.

Her quick peek into the envelope had revealed that it contained cash, and now she pulled out all of the contents. Roger had sent her fifty dollars and a note. With trembling hands, she opened the folded paper. There were three lines in the message:

"New York is expensive.

"Try to be very happy.

"Remember me.

"R"

Pressing the envelope to her breast, Lily sobbed. She wept because the money meant that she had time now, able to stay longer at the familiar St. Denis while she found a job and somewhere to live. It was a luxury.

She wept because Roger was consigning his lost dreams of happiness to her, and she grieved for him anew.

And she was inconsolable because she was leaving him and everyone she knew, including her family, for a future with perhaps only strangers. That last had been buried beneath her resolve to find Helen but with tomorrow approaching, could no longer be denied. What was she thinking? How could she imagine that she was strong enough to go into such a future alone? Was she courageous as others said, or only impetuous?

That evening, after dinner, she wandered the house to memorize every detail and then found herself on the front porch where her father sat smoking his cigar. She sat down beside him on the swing and they silently observed the summer evening. Other awning-covered porches were populated with residents basking in the evening warmth, their murmured conversations drifting along like wavelets on a shore. Children playing called out and their soprano laughter echoed along the street. Lily thought the evening perfect and took it all in.

Her father made the same conversation that he had initiated the night before she left for Vassar, inquiring about preparations. She assured him that all was in readiness.

"It's good that you are traveling with Eva and her baby," he said, nodding.

Lily felt like a traitor. "Yes," was all she said. Then she saw the pure goodness in her father's heart as she had never understood before. She recalled his reply to her desperate letter imploring him to say she could return to Vassar for a second year, how gently he had phrased the refusal. It surely had been hard for him, but she could see now that he had no choice given his wife's adamant refusal to permit it.

"You know, Papa," she said haltingly, "it was all right that I didn't go back to Vassar." She hadn't known that she would say it but she needed him to know that she did not blame him, that things turned out as they should have.

He patted her knee, his old affectionate gesture. "You're a good girl," was his reassuring reply.

That night, Lily chose to sleep in her old room with Eva and Sadie, aware that she wouldn't be able to sleep much regardless of Sadie's hungry cries. She wanted to sit on her window seat one last time. She felt detached, as if she had already left and was observing herself in her old room with a dispassionate gaze. There was the table where she had done her homework and written her stories, and there was the bookshelf now empty except for a couple of very old texts. There was the bed that she and Eva had shared on countless nights from the time they were children, giggling in the dark, innocent and carefree. Here was the window seat on which she had dreamed dreams of attending college, the same cushioned seat where she and Helen had made love during their spring vacation visit.

All the memories were here, but also stored in Lily's mind, available to her whether she was here or in New York. She understood with some certainty that it was time for her to leave this place.

"Do you think my father will think me fat?"

Eva's plaintive query brought Lily's attention back from her absent gazing out of the train window.

"No, of course not," she automatically reassured. "Mama told you that your figure will come back in time."

Lily recalled their farewells on the Kepler porch that morning. Her mother had reluctantly and tearfully handed the basket containing the tiny sleeping Sadie to Eva. Lily had realized a truth about her mother that she had not previously looked for: her mother loved being a mother. Beneath her social-climbing dreams and drive to see her only daughter married, Elda Kepler wholly embraced her maternal role. Where Gertrude had rationed visits to Mama's first grandchild, Mae had cheerfully shared Mary Louise with her mother-in-law. It had been a balm for Mama Kepler. And then the gift of the refugee Eva into the family home transformed her into her best self, useful at last.

But Lily also recalled her mother's farewell to her. When she kissed her mother and said that she would write, she sensed a wariness in her mother that was unfamiliar. Did her mother know that Lily would not be returning from Canandaigua? Had she discovered that Lily's trunk was missing? Or had she detected something in Lily's demeanor, her happy anticipation, that led her mother to suspect deception?

She hadn't leisure to contemplate more because Eva was talkative, her excitement bubbling over.

"Here, you hold her for a while," Eva was saying. Lily accepted the basket and smiled at the sleeping infant's repose.

"It will be so nice to have a housekeeper," she sighed. "With all the lessons Aunt Martha and Mama Kepler gave me, I still will never be a very good cook, I think."

Lily nodded. "You have other talents."

"Oh, do you think so? Like what?"

Lily thought quickly. "Well, you are very sociable and outgoing. You will be able to make friends quickly in Canandaigua."

Eva sighed again, relieved to hear it. Then she turned to Lily and asked in a confidential tone, "Will you miss me?"

Lily chuckled. "Of course I will!"

"Well, I will miss you."

Lily smiled. "You will have so many new and exciting experiences with your father and Sadie and the social whirl in Canandaigua that you won't have time to miss me."

"But *you* understand me," Eva said meekly.

They became quiet after that. Sadie slept, heedless of the gentle rocking of the train or perhaps aided by it. Lily gazed at her face and her tiny hands with the same wonderment as she had all the weeks since she was born. What would she become in twenty years? Would she run away from home? She looked away to dispel those thoughts.

In a while Eva gestured for Lily to give her the basket. Then she turned to Lily with a worried look.

"What if she won't see you after you get there?"

Lily had naturally turned that thought over and over in her mind but they had not spoken of Helen.

She shrugged. "I won't know until I go to the settlement house."

"But what if she tells you to go away?" Eva's voice sounded genuinely worried.

"Then she does," Lily replied with a short nod.

"Will you go home then?"

Lily turned to look at Eva in surprise. "No! I thought you understood that I have left all that behind. I have a reference letter for a job in New York and I will make my life there."

Eva sounded chastened. "I was thinking about your mother and father."

"Who wouldn't have let me go if I had told them."

They fell silent again. It occurred to Lily that in the past Eva would by now have leaned close to her or taken her hand. But now Eva's focus was on her baby, her arms firmly around the basket. Where a year ago, Eva had been frivolous and impulsive, she now had a purpose that she took with all the gravity that having another's life in one's hands required. Lily was rather proud of her.

When the train stopped at the handsome Canandaigua train station, Eva spotted her father first on the platform. He came into the car, his face bright with pleasure, looking about to see what he could carry. Lily took charge, pointing to Eva's heavy suitcase overhead and her large satchel of baby things. Amidst the shuffle of disembarking passengers, father, daughter and granddaughter made their way to the steps. Lily watched them go, feeling suddenly left behind. Then Eva stopped in the doorway and wheeled around.

"Kiss me goodbye!" she called. And Lily stepped to her, embracing what she could around Sadie's basket, and kissed Eva on the cheek. Eva, ever with her heart on her sleeve, was smiling through tears. "Write to me, dear!" she called and then turned toward the steps where her father was waiting to receive her and Sadie.

Lily was entirely alone and felt it during the remainder of the first leg of her journey from Canandaigua to Albany. She began to wonder, *Who's adventurous now?* She would need to be vigilant every minute now, careful of her belongings and observant of strangers. Her chest felt tight and she took deep breaths, cognizant now of both being alone and in the midst of a crowded train of others with their attendant perfumes and odors. The rhythm of the train, regular now that it was up to speed, the same rhythm that had rocked Sadie in her sleep, was a prod to her mind.

Clack-clack

Lily closed her eyes at the thought of what her action would do to her father.

She knew he had persuaded her mother to let her enroll at Vassar. When she announced that she had secured a job at Ulbrich's, it was her father who had overridden her mother's objections. Was it only yesterday that he had patted her knee and said, "You're a good girl"? He was such a good man. What would he think? Had she broken his heart?

Clack-clack

It wasn't too late to turn back, to retrace her route and get off at Canandaigua, join Eva.

Clack-clack

Yes, it was. Sentimental though she might be for her parents and siblings and wonderful Mae, she was done with Buffalo and the sadness it held for her. Even if Helen was not interested in seeing her, Buffalo was the past and New York was the future, whatever it held.

Clack-clack

Helen. I must stand before you, face to face, and – what? Know. Know what? I will read your face as I always could, and I –

Clack-clack

Lily forced herself to focus on calming herself, on slowing her breathing. She reminded herself that she was no longer a child, no longer a dreamy-eyed freshman with mind and heart open to any experience that might present itself. She had never imagined that Helen would be part of that, that her feelings for Helen would wash over her like a November storm surge overtopped the breakwalls on Lake Erie. She closed her eyes again at the memory of falling in love with Helen.

Clack-clack

But, she thought firmly, *but I am not that girl anymore. I have grieved, worked for pay, written stories thoroughly criticized and edited. I have seen the blood soaked into Roger's front hall of a man who was alive hours before. And I have seen the blood that accompanies the birth of that man's child. These things I have done, and they changed me.*

Clack-clack

And if you won't love me, well then, I will make my way. I will.

This resolve carried her to Albany, where she disembarked for her train to New York city. Suddenly, the familiarity of the station, where she and Helen had departed for Glens Falls, and then for New York City, where they boarded the train to Buffalo, all of the joyful memories flooded back. Her fears evaporated into the vaulted ceiling. Her way forward was clear and familiar.

The final two hours seemed like a bookend to a journey that had begun on that June day a little over a year ago when Lily left Vassar in shock and grief. She wondered if the intervening months had been a test; she chose to think that they had.

Where Eva had needed Sadie and the consequences of marrying hastily to come into her own, Lily had needed some means of discovering her own inner strengths.

She recalled what Belle had said when she visited Lily in the infirmary after Helen had broken with her. She had said, "I want you to be the brave girl I know you to be." She wondered if Belle had imagined that Lily might charge into the College Settlement house to seek a restoration of her relationship with Helen. Or might Belle have related the story of her rape to show Lily that she could survive losing Helen forever?

The train drew closer to New York and Lily with it. She was going to learn the answer to that question soon.

CHAPTER 37

It was so familiar that Lily grinned as she stepped down from the train at the Grand Central Station. She felt at home and didn't hear the clamor of the crowds or the chuffing of a train leaving or a blast of steam released from air brakes. She paused, looking around, and right on cue a redcap appeared with an offer to take her suitcase. He was much older than the young man who had assisted last year when Lily visited with Helen, more gracious than enthusiastic. She smiled at him as if to an uncle she hadn't seen in years and surrendered her bag.

The ride through the congested city streets was just as she recalled it so many times since that wondrous week in the city with her beloved. When she passed through the doors of the St. Denis, she felt at ease. The clerk at the desk might have been the same as before, but he disappointed her when she requested the same room in which Lily and Helen had enjoyed so many passionate hours. That room was taken but, he was eager to add, the room directly above it was available, and identical in every way. It was also, he added encouragingly, quieter than the one she had hoped to secure.

And the room was just the same as the one below except for the bedspread, she was certain of that detail. The view from the fourth floor was better, she thought, but she couldn't be certain of that. She smiled to recall that they had spent little time looking out of their window.

She opened her suitcase and laid out her silver-gray suit and pink shirtwaist to wear tomorrow when she visited the College Settlement. It had received little wear back in Buffalo, there being no one aside from Roger that she wished to impress sartorially. She wondered if Helen would remember when they bought the suit in Glens Falls. *Of course, she will*, Lily dismissed that doubt.

After a plate special dinner in the English Grille, she ran a bath and took her time in the white tiled bathroom. Memories rose up of that magical week when they could forget about every schedule, obligation, family opinion, of everything but each other. She no longer had to push them away because they were reminders of what she had lost, because she would meet Helen tomorrow. She was free now.

At 3 a.m., Lily abruptly awoke. This was the hour when gauzy memories, un-formed hopes, lofty but vague plans had evaporated. The darkness now brought only anxiety. Eva's queries about Lily's leaving her family without informing them and worries about Lily's prospects for a job in New York loomed before her. *Will my family ever forgive me?*

She had the letter recommending her to Ida Bender's publisher, but what if he wouldn't hire her? The money she had with Roger's largesse would keep her for some weeks, but what if she couldn't get a job to support herself before it ran out? It was too horrible to imagine that she would have to return to Buffalo and her family.

But there was Helen. Or was there? Helen had not answered her letter last fall except with a Christmas postcard that recalled their skating evening. Even Roger had asked if there was no letter included. And her two letters in the last month had gone unanswered. What was waiting for Lily tomorrow at the College Settlement? Would she find that Helen had no interest in resuming even a friendship, never mind something more? What if Helen was at the Settlement with a new sweet-heart? The thoughts made her shiver with a cold sweat on the warm July night.

Lily got up and paced the room, then opened the window wide and leaned against the sill. The city was not quiet, only less clamorous than the day. As she breathed in its various odors, she saw herself as a stranger in a city where people knew where they were going and how things were done. Had she so dreadful-ly miscalculated her ability to navigate here, alone and possibly friendless? *What have I done to think that I was brave enough for this?*

And then another memory arose. She saw the Gate Lodge at Vassar and the long drive to vine-covered Main at its end. Nearly two years ago, Lily had stood at that gate, suitcase in hand. She had been alone, without friends. But she had not hesitated to walk that drive and open the door to her future. She nodded, lips pursed. *You can do this.*

Rivington Street at midday was very warm, teeming with people and hand carts that offered everything from fresh vegetables to clothing. When a horse-drawn vehicle appeared, it had to haltingly make its way, waiting for the crowd to part temporarily. The opening it made closed immediately behind it. Lily followed the others on the street because the sidewalks were impassable. She marveled over the change in the street scene since she had walked Rivington with Helen a year ago. Where that day had been the Jewish Sabbath, today was Friday, and everyone seemed to be hustling to complete their work before the day ended.

She searched for the red door that would indicate the College Settlement and passed by it until she realized that the door was standing open. This was it, the end of thirteen months of pushing away hope. Seeing Helen was no longer a dream. Lily consciously took a breath to steady her nerves, and stepped over the threshold.

Standing in the hall, she had little recollection of being here last year. Miss Williams had taken charge of them and the memory was a blur. This had been a handsome home a half-century ago, she could tell from its dark woodwork and elaborate newel post in the long stairway. She heard voices but they seemed distant and so she tentatively stepped into a room. It was furnished as a parlor, empty now. As she stepped back into the hall, a young woman spotted her and halted her step on the staircase.

"Hello!" she brightly greeted Lily. "Do you require assistance?"

Lily forgot her rehearsed lines. "Hello, yes, thank you," she stammered. "I think a friend is staying here and wonder if I might speak to her."

The young woman stepped closer. "Of course, what is her name?"

It was time. Lily sighed. "Helen McIntyre."

The other beamed. "Oh, yes! Helen is here and," she paused, looking along a hallway, "I think she is on the playground with the little ones. Let me send her in to you."

And she hustled along the hallway, disappearing through a door. Lily felt her heart thumping and stepped into that empty parlor to calm herself. It seemed an eternity before she heard footsteps coming down the hallway. She turned to face the doorway but didn't step back into the hall. She didn't want Helen to see her first.

Helen paused in the hall within view and Lily could see that she was thinner than at Vassar and the planes of her face had become sharper. And then, as if she knew she was being observed, Helen slowly turned to see Lily standing in the parlor clutching her little purse.

They stood for a long moment as if in a *tableau*, and Lily tried to interpret Helen's eyes. Was it panic, or pain, or shock that they telegraphed?

"Hello," Lily finally said quietly with a tentative half-smile. She stepped out of the parlor, closing half the distance between them.

Helen seemed to exhale. She took a step toward Lily. "How did you know where I was?" she asked in quiet wonder.

Lily knew what to do with that. She pulled the postcard, now curled and creased, from her purse where she had carried it from Buffalo.

"Your mother, I believe," she said as she handed the card to Lily.

Helen looked at her mother's handwriting, pursing her lips. Then she handed it back to Lily.

"Why are you here?" Helen said in an uncertain voice.

Lily had known this would be Helen's query, had gone over the scenario a hundred times, trying to find the words. She wanted to say, *I'm here as I promised, to be with you always.* But saying this to the woman who had not answered her letters was not possible at this moment.

Lily tried to sound bright and casual. "Well, specifically, I've come to invite you to a plate special at the St. Denis. I'm staying there for the time being. It's dinner time and I wonder if you could get away."

Helen stared at her blankly. Then she stammered, "You mean, now?"

Lily nodded. "If you are able to leave your duties."

Helen thought for a moment, blinking. "I have to check. Will you wait?"

"Of course," Lily said immediately. As she watched Helen retreat through that door at the end of the hall, she thought, *I've been waiting for a year. A few minutes is nothing.*

Shortly, Helen returned. "Yes," she said in a stronger voice, "I am free for dinner." She pulled at her skirt. "But I must change first or take the dust of the playground with me."

Lily nodded, and Helen gestured for her to come upstairs while she changed. They both seemed to relax a little. Helen's room had three beds. Helen explained that she was alone for the time being with others not scheduled to arrive until the autumn. She opened her trunk and pulled out another waist and skirt and began to change.

"Do you like the work?" Lily asked as Helen pulled off her damp waist.

"I only just started a few weeks ago, but I think I will like it. The girls who are here now are just grand, but the cook Miss Williams touted a year ago is long gone." She shook her head. "Sometimes I long for VC grub, to be honest."

Lily smiled. "I thought you seemed to have lost weight." She immediately wondered if she should have said that.

Helen didn't respond to that. "How long are you staying?" she asked in a quiet and very neutral voice.

"I've moved to the city," she replied, closely watching Helen who was still turned away as she finished buttoning her waist. "I have a reference for a job in a publishing house and will stay at the St. Denis until I find more permanent lodgings."

Helen stopped what she was doing. Lily watched her breathe in and out and suddenly seized upon the notion that Helen had a sweetheart and that made Lily's reappearance unwelcome. Then she turned away to dispel that thought for the time being and spotted something familiar in Helen's open trunk.

"Is this the Huyler's tin we bought when we were here?" she asked too brightly, desperate for a diversion.

Helen glanced over as she began to pull on her skirt. She confirmed that it was. While opening the tin, Lily started to ask if there was still any chocolate left. She stopped mid-sentence when she saw the contents. Helen had observed her, too. Near the top in plain view were the photos Helen and Lily had taken and Lily's letters. Lily closed the box and stepped back from the trunk.

Quickly, Helen indicated that she was ready. They weaved around the throng on Rivington Street and made their way back to the St. Denis. Chatting was impossible on the journey which left Lily alternately thrilled and anxious about the next hours with Helen. So much about her future would be revealed and she had a moment when she wished the time had not yet arrived when she would know. Hoping for the best had been the fuel that had sustained her for so long.

When they reached the hotel, Lily retrieved her key from the desk and asked Helen to come upstairs before they had dinner. Once on the fourth floor, Lily opened the door and held it open for Helen to enter.

Helen stared around open mouthed. "Is this the room?" she breathed, not needing to complete the question.

Lily smiled for the first time and explained that their room was one floor below but the same except for the bedspread. She went to the window and was expounding on the improved view when she turned back to see Helen sitting on the edge of the bed, one hand gripping the iron footboard.

Helen looked up at her in anguish. "How can you even speak to me? How can you even want to see me?"

"I don't understand what you mean," Lily said, frozen in place.

Helen's lips began to tremble. "I was so horrible to you, even Belle said so. I hate myself for causing you pain that I can only imagine," she trailed off, shaking now with weeping.

Lily was dumbfounded. This was nothing like the scenarios she had rehearsed for this hour. Helen was weeping uncontrollably now. Lily sat beside her on the bed and put her arms around the woman she loved more than anyone in the world. Her only thought at this moment was to comfort Helen.

Helen clung to her and the feeling of those arms brought Lily tears of relief. The iron bands around her chest loosened. Whatever the future held for them, it would be all right now. She was home.

EPILOGUE

Endings, if fortune shines bright, are also beginnings. Lily and Helen would rarely be separated for more than a few days at a time in their nearly fifty years together. Lily secured a position opening mail at the American Book Company, thanks to Ida Bender's recommendation. Within a few years she became an editor, all the while working on her stories about the frog who wore red suspenders. Another company eventually published the first collection of *The Adventures of the Frog Who Wore Red Suspenders*, illustrated beautifully by colored lithographs contributed by a friend of the couple. It was a great success and, with the critical commentary of Mae and Will's children, she added to the frog's adventures with volumes that saw him travel to Africa and China and the Amazon. She made a comfortable living from the little amphibian who wanted to find others who would accept him as he was.

Helen left the College Settlement at the end of the year. Her grateful parents willingly paid for her courses at the New York School of Philanthropy. She found the new field of social work, both theory and practice, exciting and challenging and secured a position on the faculty after her advanced degree. Within a few years, she edited a textbook on social work instruction that was used by colleges across the northeast for many years until the 1930s brought the shift in social services from private to governmental agencies.

They moved to Greenwich Village, then becoming a Bohemian neighborhood that welcomed New Women like Lily and Helen. When the suffrage fight in New York intensified after 1910, they marched in annual parades and volunteered at the national suffrage headquarters on Fifth Avenue. And they celebrated in the streets with their fellow suffragists in November 1917 when the vote was won in New York State.

Lily's parents did not attempt to force her to return to Buffalo after she communicated to them her whereabouts and plans. Although she wrote them once a month, she never received a reply. Her good fortune was that Mae, who always had seemed to understand Lily, was a willing and supportive correspondent, sending along information about the Kepler family. It was Mae who sent the telegram three years later telling Lily that her father had died suddenly of a heart attack. And so, Lily visited Buffalo for the first time since she left and attended his funeral. Her sorrow was compounded when her mother refused to permit her to stay at the family home on Humboldt Parkway; Will and Mae sheltered her. After the funeral, she never saw her mother again in life. She admitted that she had willingly paid the price of estrangement from her family, but Lily carried a homesickness always.

Will and Mae would have five children in all, two girls and three boys. Theirs was a boisterous home and Mae didn't regret trading her career in bookkeeping for housekeeping. Lily and Helen visited them over the years, enjoying the chance to spoil their relatives large and small. When the time came for college, firstborn Mary Louise, a thoroughly modern girl who styled herself Mary Lou, chose Cornell over Vassar because she liked boys and the school colors. The Will Keplers prospered with the family store and, despite severe reductions during the Depression, the business continued into the early 1960s when descendants closed it and moved to the suburbs. The Kepler family home on Humboldt Parkway was a casualty of the construction of the Kensington Expressway in the early 1960s.

Lily saw Roger during those periodic visits to Buffalo and he and Helen became acquainted. He seemed content enough and had a wide circle of friends. But he gave no indication that he had anyone special to share his life. The scholarship he established anonymously at the Canisius High School paid for a total of thirty-one immigrant young men to have an excellent Jesuit education; some became lawyers and doctors. The Depression depleted the funds and it is forgotten today.

Eva found her happy ending several times over in Canandaigua, first with her father who said he had a new lease on life because of her. Little Sadie became a demanding, spoiled girl very much like her mother who had a great deal to learn about being a parent. As Lily predicted, Eva was welcomed into Canandaigua society, small though it was, and felt entirely at home. Her letters to Lily eventually slowed to a monthly update. She met a widower only a few years older than she who brought his two children into her life. She married him with the stipulation that her father spend the rest of his days under their roof. As usual, she got her way.

The McIntyres welcomed Lily as a permanent member of the family. Mrs. McIntyre understood much about her daughter and had decided during that first Thanksgiving visit that Lily was an ideal friend for Helen. The women traveled up the Hudson to Glens Falls numerous times a year to spend holidays with them and with Harry and his family.

Belle resided in France with her parents. True to her prediction, she fell in love with a poor but handsome and cultured man from an old noble family. And true to her prediction, she gave birth to a boy and girl and declared her progeny-producing job complete. When war broke out in 1914, her husband was called to fight. An officer, he was near the front but not on the fighting line until the 1916 battle of the Somme where 200,000 French soldiers were killed, wounded, or missing and the fighting was desperate. He was gassed and sent home by stretcher to the family estate and Belle's care. He never fully recovered and died from the after effects in 1919.

Belle took charge of the estate vineyards and cattle herds, hiring war veterans to do the work and made a success of it to ensure her children's future. The worldwide Depression wiped out much of her family's wealth but no loss could compare to what came when the Nazis invaded France in 1939. She determined that her children would not become casualties of another war and the extended family fled to Spain and then Portugal. From there, they sailed to New York where Helen and Lily helped them settle in for the duration.

Lily's books on the frog who wore red suspenders were eventually supplanted by the modern and colorful Little Golden Books in the 1940s. Today, one may find on eBay or the occasional flea market table plastic sheathed pages of the color lithographic illustrations torn from her books.

Lily Kepler is barely remembered by her relations, even though she lived until 1967. The few present day great nieces and nephews who care about genealogy can locate photos of her with another woman in the shoebox of old family photos left by great-grandmother Mae. On the back of one studio photograph is written in pencil, "Lily and Helen, Vassar, 1904."

Susan Eck is a native Western New Yorker. After a career in teaching, she was an administrator at the University at Buffalo. Her third career has been as a student of local history. With *Remember This*, she has written the novel she always wanted to read.

www.ingramcontent.com/pod-product-compliance
Lightning Source LLC
Chambersburg PA
CBHW051227260626
47162CB00002B/301